The Aviator's Lady

GABRIELLE MEYER

BELLE MAY PRESS

Contents

Dedication 1

1. Prologue 2
2. Chapter One 20
3. Chapter Two 31
4. Chapter Three 42
5. Chapter Four 52
6. Chapter Five 66
7. Chapter Six 78
8. Chapter Seven 89
9. Chapter Eight 95
10. Chapter Nine 106
11. Chapter Ten 116
12. Chapter Eleven 127
13. Chapter Twelve 140
14. Chapter Thirteen 145

15. Chapter Fourteen 151
16. Chapter Fifteen 161
17. Chapter Sixteen 174
18. Chapter Seventeen 190
19. Chapter Eighteen 202
20. Chapter Nineteen 214
21. Chapter Twenty 227
22. Chapter Twenty-One 238
23. Chapter Twenty-Two 252
24. Chapter Twenty-Three 263
25. Chapter Twenty-Four 279
26. Chapter Twenty-Five 287
27. Chapter Twenty-Six 299
28. Chapter Twenty-Seven 311
29. Chapter Twenty-Eight 320
30. Chapter Twenty-Nine 329
31. Chapter Thirty 340
32. Chapter Thirty-One 345
33. Chapter Thirty-Two 357
34. Chapter Thirty-Three 369
35. Epilogue 372
Historical Note 376
Also by Gabrielle Meyer 380

About the author 381

For my dad, George VanRisseghem.

Because this is his favorite story.

Prologue

APRIL 4, 1903

EMMA

Emma Merrick waited long after the rocking chair stopped creaking before she lifted her head off the pillow to look across the nursery. Nanny Marie sat in her favorite chair, her knitting needles resting in her lap, her chin dipped low on her chest. Her soft snores were the guarantee Emma needed to tap her friend Rebecca.

"Wake up," Emma whispered.

Rebecca had promised she would stay awake to help Emma, but it had taken Nanny Marie so long to fall asleep, Rebecca had dozed off.

Emma tried again. "Wake up."

Rebecca swatted at Emma's hand and then her hazel eyes opened. She pushed aside her brown hair to peer at Emma.

"You fell asleep, silly."

Rebecca offered a drowsy smile and then her eyes became fully alert. "Your mother's party!"

"Shh." Emma put her finger to her lips and then pushed aside the covers to climb out of her bed.

Rebecca tossed a glance at Nanny Marie and then slipped out next to Emma. She took Emma's hand and together they tiptoed across the room, hiding their giggles behind their free hands. Rebecca always slept with Emma when Mother had a party. Rebecca's mama, Martha, was the head cook, and she had to stay at the main house until the early morning hours.

Excitement bubbled in Emma's tummy. Nanny Marie kept her clothes perfectly organized in the large armoire, and Emma knew exactly where her favorite party dress was hanging. She had just worn it to her seventh birthday party, and Mother had said how fine and pretty she looked. Her father had also come to the party for a few minutes, though he stood near the door and left as soon as she had blown out her candles—but for just a moment her parents were in the same room, and they were both looking at her.

Rebecca opened the armoire, and Emma lifted the blue dress from the hook. She nuzzled it to her chest, unable to stop smiling.

"It's so pretty," Rebecca breathed. "You're a lucky girl, Emmie."

Emma didn't feel like a lucky girl—but tonight nothing mattered. She was going to her mother's party—and she must look her best, because Mother's parties were always filled with pretty ladies. Sometimes Emma and Rebecca snuck out of the nursery and sat on the staircase to watch the people from behind the banister. The guests danced and laughed and ate lovely food—and Mother was always happy when she was having a party. She talked to everyone who came, and she paid attention to what they said.

Rebecca unbuttoned Emma's nightgown and helped her shimmy it off her body, then they pulled her party dress over her shoulders. Her arms became stuck, and she had to do a little jig to get the dress to fall just right. She glanced at Nanny Marie, her heart pounding—but the gentle old lady was still asleep.

It wasn't easy to dress without a grownup's help, but they did their best. Rebecca slowly buttoned the long row of buttons and then tried to tie the sash. "I can't get it even," Rebecca whispered.

Emma didn't care. "I don't think Mother will mind."

Rebecca found the matching blue bow Emma had worn in her hair and wrapped it around Emma's curls. When Nanny dressed her, she had made the bow stick out wide on either side of her head, but Rebecca's attempt left it limp and hanging lopsided.

Next Emma put on her stockings and her little black shoes, and then she put on white gloves—because Mother always wore white gloves to her parties.

Emma smiled at her reflection in the mirror and Rebecca stood back and admired her.

"Your Mother will think you look so pretty."

Emma hoped so.

"What will you wear?" Emma asked Rebecca.

Rebecca shook her head. "My mama would be angry if I went to the party."

Emma took her best friend's hand. "You'll be my guest."

Rebecca offered Emma a smile, her missing front teeth making a hole in her mouth, causing a lisp. "I'll watch you from the stairway."

They slowly crossed the nursery and quietly opened the door. Emma cringed when the door creaked, but Nanny kept sleeping.

The music drifted up the stairway as they descended to the second floor. The nursery was on the third floor of the mansion—high above so Emma wouldn't bother Mother when she slept during the day.

The music became louder with each step they took. Would someone ask her to dance? Would she have punch and sandwiches?

But, more importantly, would Mother talk to her and laugh—and listen? She had so much she wanted to tell Mother, things Mother didn't want to be bothered with during the day.

Emma squeezed Rebecca's hand so tight, Rebecca wiggled her fingers. "You're hurting me."

"I'm sorry." Emma loosened her grip and then started to descend the second set of stairs, but her nerves suddenly took her by surprise, and she felt sick to her tummy. Her legs wobbled and she sat on the carpeted stairs and pulled Rebecca down with her.

"Go on," Rebecca urged Emma with a gentle smile.

Emma glanced at the party and easily spotted Mother in the large foyer wearing a beautiful green gown which shimmered under the lights. She was standing with a man Emma didn't know, leaning close and giggling over something he said. She held a tall crystal glass in her hand, and she tipped the bubbly liquid into her mouth. She was so pretty. People said Emma looked just like her. It made Emma proud.

She took a deep breath and stood once again—but this time Rebecca stayed where she was.

"Have fun and remember I'm watching," Rebecca said.

Emma placed her hand on the railing and straightened her back—just like Mother did. She descended the stairs like she imagined a queen would do.

People didn't seem to notice her arrival as they laughed and talked and drank from the pretty crystal glasses. Emma pushed her way through the crowd, feeling warm and uncomfortable. The music was so loud, she wondered how they could hear one another talk.

Just as Emma was about to approach her mother, she and the man moved off toward the hallway leading to the family's private rooms.

Emma glanced up and found Rebecca's hazel eyes between the spindles. She offered an encouraging smile.

Emma followed Mother and the strange man down the shadowed hallway. Mother giggled and spoke in low tones as they went deeper into the heart of the house. Emma stayed behind, not sure if she should follow—but wanting Mother to see her party dress and hear the poems she could recite and the sums she could do on her slate.

Mother opened the library door, and they disappeared inside.

Emma stood outside the closed door. Should she bother her mother?

Her father's office door opened just down the hall. Emma turned and pressed herself against the library door, biting her lip.

Father stepped out of his office in his evening clothes. His hair was almost all silver and he had a silver goatee on his chin. Emma had always thought he was handsome, and she heard other people call him distinguished, so she thought he was that, too. When people talked about Major Matthew Merrick, there was always awe in their voice. But he was much older than all the other fathers she knew and she wondered why.

He walked down the hall with the same purpose he always had—his bright green eyes looking straight ahead.

The hall was shadowed, and the threshold of the door was deep. Emma stood perfectly still, and for the first time in her life, she hoped he would not see her. If he did, he would ask her why she was there, and she would have to tell him she had followed Mother and the strange man.

He passed by without noticing her. She watched him retreat down the hall and then she turned back to the library door and opened it slowly.

Mother and the man were on the sofa, and Mother was pressed against him, allowing him to kiss her face and neck.

Emma made a surprised noise, and Mother's eyes opened wide. She stood, shock and anger racing across her face. "Emma!"

The man stood next to Mother, readjusting his tie. He was much taller than Mother with dark hair and eyes. He barely glanced at Emma and then said, "Who is she?"

"My daughter." She said the words as if the truth was a great burden to bear.

"You don't come across as the motherly sort," the man said with a strange chuckle.

Mother's face became hard. "She was a mistake."

"Maybe I should leave."

Mother placed her hand on the man's chest. "Don't go anywhere, Edward. I'll deal with this inconvenience. It won't take but a moment to get rid of her."

"Alright—but only a moment." He put his lips to her hand. "Then I want your undivided attention."

Mother made a funny moaning noise and then swept across the room and took Emma's elbow. She hauled her into the hallway and pulled her toward the back of the house and the servant's wing.

"You're hurting me, Mother," Emma cried.

"What were you thinking?" Mother hissed. "You should be in the nursery."

"I wanted to come to your party." Emma's voice sounded small and weak to her own ears. "I wanted to wear my pretty dress again."

"Who dressed you?" Mother demanded. "You look ridiculous."

Tears filled Emma's eyes as she looked up at her mother. Her face was no longer beautiful but contorted in anger. She yanked Emma down the hall at a rapid pace.

They reached the kitchen and Mother pushed open the door. The room was aflutter with last-minute preparations for the midnight buffet. The head cook, Martha, stood in the midst of it all directing the maids and kitchen staff.

Sam, the chauffeur, stood from his place at the table in the corner of the room. He clutched his napkin in his hand, his face revealing his shock at seeing the mistress of the house.

Everyone else stilled in their work, staring at Mother and Emma.

Mother marched Emma over to Sam and shoved her toward him.

Tears streamed down Emma's cheeks, and she felt every eye upon her. What must they think of her in her ugly dress with her ridiculous bow in her hair?

"Take her back to her nursery and tell Nanny Marie she is no longer employed."

Sam put his hand on Emma's shoulder. "As you wish."

Mother turned from the room without a glance at Emma and walked through the door.

Martha ordered her staff to continue their work and then came to the corner where Sam and Emma stood. Kitchen noises soon filled the room once again.

Sam knelt and took a clean kerchief from his pocket. He smiled at Emma with sad brown eyes and dabbed at her cheeks. "There now, lass. Everything will be better soon." His rich Irish accent wrapped around her like a warm blanket. "And look at that pretty dress you're wearing." He held her at arm's length, admiring her outfit. "You look like a princess at a ball."

Martha ran her hand down Emma's curls. "And your hair bow matches your dress perfectly, Miss Emma. I'd say you're as pretty as a queen."

Emma shook her head, her arm hurting from where her mother had yanked her. "I don't look like a princess—or a queen. I look like an ugly little girl."

Sam's eyes looked sadder than ever. "I've never seen a prettier girl. You look just like your mam."

Emma's tears started all over again. "I don't want to look like her. I don't want to be anything like her."

Sam and Martha shared a look and then Sam stood and took Emma's hand. "Come, lass. I'll take you to your room."

He held her hand as they walked up the back stairs. "Now, why did you go to your mam's party without an invitation? If it was punch you were needing, I would have gladly brought you some."

"I wasn't going for the punch."

"Ah, then the pickled cucumbers? I know you have a fondness for those. Martha has a jar in the pantry just for you."

Her tears stopped and she shook her head. "Not for the pickles, either."

He put his hand to his chin, as if thinking deeply. "Was it for those little sandwiches Martha makes?" His eyes grew large, and he rubbed his tummy. "I'd sneak into a party for those sandwiches."

She smiled—just a little. "Not for the sandwiches."

His face was animated as he leaned toward her. "If not for the food, was it for the gossip?"

"The what?" Emma asked, her face tilted in curiosity.

He looked surprised. "You don't know what gossip is then?"

She shook her head, climbing the stairs with him. "Is it good?"

He laughed. "Sometimes—unless it's about you."

Emma looked at Sam and Sam looked at her. He smiled, and his whole face lit with something foreign and yet something her heart recognized and craved.

Love and acceptance.

"You have a happy face, Sam."

He winked at her. "You make me happy, Miss Emma."

She made *him* happy? "I wish I made my mother and father happy." She dropped her head until her chin rested on her chest. "But they're never happy when they're with me. They don't even see me."

They reached the second floor and Sam knelt again. He still held her hand as he looked her in the eyes. "You make them happy—it's other things that make them sad." He studied her face and smiled. "You make everyone in this house happy, lass. Don't feel hopeless about your mother and father. When you grow up, they'll finally give you the attention you deserve."

It seemed a long time before she was grown up.

Rebecca appeared at the top of the main stairway in her nightgown, her eyes enormous at the sight of Sam.

He laughed and motioned Rebecca to join them. "Were you in on this, too?"

Rebecca smiled at Sam and took his other hand. She glanced around Sam, her eyes excited. "Did you have fun, Emmie?"

Emma hated to disappoint her friend, so she put a smile on her face, though her heart continued to mourn.

CADE

November 14, 1903

Jacob Kincade Bailey stood on a weeping branch of the willow tree and hugged the trunk, watching the shiny black carriage pull away. The Mississippi flowed beneath the overhanging branch, and he swayed slightly with the force of the water.

The man in the carriage had scared him—almost as much as Grandfather scared him. Their angry words had hurt Cade's ears, and though he and Grandfather were not done chopping down the tree they'd come to harvest, he had run away when they weren't looking.

He always came to the river when he was frightened or needed to be alone. He often thought of the grand adventures awaiting him down the Mississippi. His favorite story was *Huckleberry Finn*, but when he tried to build a raft to float down the river, his mother made him tear it apart.

"Cade!" Grandfather's angry voice drifted to Cade on the willow branch. He didn't want to reply, but his mother and father expected him to be obedient—even to his grandfather.

"You better make yourself known, boy!" Grandfather walked close to the river, his white beard catching Cade's eye. "I'll take a switch to your backside when I find you."

Cade touched his head where it still hurt from his grandfather's powerful hand. He recalled the look of mortification on the strange man's face when Grandfather had struck him—that had probably hurt the most, to have a stranger witness his grandfather's behavior.

He didn't hurt Cade in front of his parents—but only when they were alone. When Cade told his father, he only looked sad and said Cade must always obey.

Grandfather hollered again, but this time he stumbled a bit. His face was bright red and sweat glistened off his brow—but still, Cade did not answer. He hoped his grandfather wouldn't look up and see him—if he did, he would be furious and there was no telling what he might do.

"Cade!" The word came out slurred and Grandfather's knees buckled. He fell to the ground.

Cade's eyes grew wide, and he quickly climbed down the tree trunk and knelt by his grandfather. "I'm here, Grandfather."

Grandfather's brown eyes found Cade's face. His voice sounded funny. "Why didn't you come when I called you?" He breathed heavily. "Look what you've done to me."

Cade couldn't move. *He* had done this to his grandfather?

The left side of Grandfather's body looked limp, but his right hand came up to Cade's chest and he gripped the front of Cade's shirt. "Get your father—and hurry." He pushed Cade away.

Cade lost his balance and sprawled out in the dirt.

"Go!"

Cade scrambled to his feet, his heart pumping and his stomach tight with fear. He ran toward the house like a bear was on his trail.

His father was working in the house on Mama's sink, so he rushed into the kitchen. The backdoor slammed behind him and his mother looked up with a startled expression. His father's legs were sticking out from under the sink.

"Cade, what's wrong?" His mother came to his side and placed her hand on his shoulder to steady him.

Cade's nine-year-old brother, Henry, was on the floor next to Papa helping him with the plumbing.

It took a minute for Cade to catch his breath. "Grandfather."

Papa moved away from the sink, his dark hair mussed. "What about Grandfather?"

"He's hurt—by the river."

His parents shared a wide-eyed glance and then his father raced out of the house. "Come with me, Cade, in case I need help."

Cade ran behind his father, his eleven-year-old legs unable to keep up.

They sprinted down the hill toward the water and Papa made it to Grandfather's side first.

"Father?" he called, shaking Grandfather's shoulder. "It's me, Nathan."

Grandfather moaned and opened his eyes. Cade stood nearby, panting as he tried to catch his breath.

"Don't let him take the farm, Nathan."

Papa frowned and leaned closer to his father. "Don't let who take the farm?"

"Merrick. He'll try to get it as soon as I'm dead."

"Don't say such things." Papa shook his head. "Let's get you up to the house."

"Bury me next to your mother," Grandfather said. "I want to be with Elizabeth."

"Father—you'll be fine."

"I'm dying." His words were so weak and garbled, Cade barely heard. "Promise me you won't sell to Matthew Merrick."

"Just rest."

"Promise me!"

"I promise." Papa glanced up at Cade, questions in his eyes.

"He's always wanted this land." The left side of Grandfather's face looked like it was sagging and drool pooled out of his mouth. "I only kept it, because he wanted it. I would have sold out years ago and been as successful as him..."

"Father, you must try to rest." Papa's voice sounded strange to Cade's ears—as if he might be crying.

"He had everything," Grandfather said. "But I had Elizabeth—or so I thought. In the end, he had her, too."

"You're not making any sense." Papa wiped his cheek and lifted his father's head into his lap.

Grandfather stared at Papa and then his eyes wandered to Cade. "You must promise, too. If this farm ever falls into your hands, you must keep it away from Matthew Merrick at all costs."

Cade looked between his grandfather and his father, confused and afraid.

"Promise!" Grandfather demanded.

"I promise," Cade said quickly.

Grandfather's eyes closed and his head went limp.

"Cade!" Papa lifted his father's shoulder. "Take his feet. We'll need to get him to the house."

Cade raced to his father's side and did as he instructed. Together, they carried him up the hill and toward the house. Cade's arms and legs burned from the effort, but he couldn't fail his father and grandfather now—not when all of this had been his fault.

Mama met them on the drive and took Cade's position at his feet.

Cade opened the kitchen door, and his parents carried Grandfather over the threshold and laid him in his bedroom at the back of the house.

"He's still breathing but just barely." Papa wiped his brow. "I'll go for the doctor."

Papa raced out of the house while Mama took off Grandfather's boots and pulled a cover over his still body.

Henry came to Cade's side.

Mama turned and saw them standing in the doorway. "What happened?"

Cade was quiet, remembering the last moments before Grandfather fell. If Cade had obeyed, his grandfather would not be sick.

His stomach felt funny, and his eyes smarted with tears. What would Mama say when she discovered Cade had caused this? They had told him to obey, but he was always disobeying—always making mistakes. Sometimes, he just couldn't help it.

"A man came in a black carriage. He looked very wealthy with a dark suit and a trim hat—he asked Grandfather if he could buy the farm, but Grandfather became very angry."

"Major Merrick." Mama crossed her arms the way she did when she was worried. "Then what happened?"

"They yelled for a while, and I ran to the willow tree to hide." Cade swallowed the emotions rising from his stomach. "Then the man in the carriage left and Grandfather started talking funny and he fell." He dropped his gaze, hoping she wouldn't ask for more.

"Then you came for help?"

"Yes, ma'am." Cade nodded.

Mama sighed and her eyes looked very sad. "Major Merrick has been nothing but trouble for your grandfather."

Henry pointed to Cade's head and spoke quietly. "Did he hit you again, Cade?"

Cade touched his forehead. It felt tender and was probably bruised. He smoothed his hair over the spot hoping his mama wouldn't see it.

She would be sad if she knew Grandfather hurt him.

The doctor had come and told them Grandfather suffered an attack of apoplexy. There was no way to know how long, or how much, he would recover.

The desire to run came over Cade, just as it always did when faced with trouble. If he left home no one would care. His mother may be sad for a while, but at least she wouldn't have to worry over him like she so often did. He could set out on his own, maybe go to California where it was never cold and where he could find work. He didn't know how far California was, but it shouldn't take him too long to walk.

Cade snuck up the stairs through the parlor and quietly put his clothing into a large handkerchief. Tears blurred his vision as he tied the little sack closed. He would miss Henry, but surely his brother would be better off without him, too. Henry often followed Cade around and got into trouble, just because he wanted to be like him.

When he came downstairs, he could hear his parents talking in low tones in the kitchen, and his brother was helping get supper on the table. No one would notice him slip out the front door.

He took his red-and-black-checkered coat off the hook by the front door and put his black hat over his head. His bruise was tender where Grandfather hit him. He tilted up the hat so it didn't rest on the bump and stepped out the door into the darkening world.

The wind hit his wet cheeks as he walked down the drive toward the road. He lowered his head against the cold air and wished he had thought to grab a pair of mittens and a scarf. The temperature had dropped since the afternoon, and soon his hands and feet felt numb.

He followed the road toward the south, thinking he would walk as far as Little Falls and then stowaway on a train car headed for the west coast. He'd have to beg for food until he could find a job to support himself.

The night became darker, and the air became colder. Cade buried his chin into his coat collar and his hands into his sleeves. Snowflakes began to fall from the ominous sky overhead, slowly at first and then faster and thicker. Soon, the snow was gathering on the ground, and the wind picked up in its ferocity. Cade couldn't feel his feet and he stumbled to the ground. He began to cry and looked behind him to see how far he had come. There was nothing but darkness, snow, and wind.

He tried to stand, but his feet wouldn't support him. A bush sat at the edge of the woods, and he crawled on his hands and knees until he got to the little bit of shelter. He burrowed under the branches and wrapped himself into a tight ball. He had dropped his bundle of clothes, but he wouldn't go back to get them. Right now, he wanted nothing more than to fall asleep...

"Cade!"

Cade opened his heavy lids. The snow had almost buried him under the bush.

"Cade! Where are you?"

Was Papa calling for him?

Cade blinked several times and tried to stretch his legs. He was so cold, it hurt to move.

"Papa!" He yelled back, but his hoarse voice was lost in the wind and swirling snow.

"Cade!" Papa called again, and this time his voice was farther away.

Cade's heart pounded. He would die if he didn't get to his papa. He pushed himself up from the ground. The snow fell from the branches and landed on his face.

He was too cold to care.

He pulled himself out from under the bush. "Papa!" He cried with all his might. "I'm here."

"Cade?" Papa's voice was still far away.

"Papa!" Cade yelled. "Here!"

Papa suddenly appeared out of the swirling snow. He ran to Cade's side and lifted him into his powerful arms. "Cade!" He held him close, and Cade could hear tears in his voice. "Thank God you're safe."

The snow blew in a vicious storm around them, blinding Cade. He couldn't see the road or even the bush he had been under.

"Let's get you home, son." Papa held Cade's bundle of clothes and trudged through the snow toward their house.

The wind blew and the snow hit them with a dizzying force, but Papa continued to carry Cade.

The farther they went, the slower his father moved until he stumbled, and they both went sprawling to the ground.

Papa reached over and drew Cade to himself. His movements were slow. "Are you hurt?"

"No." But he couldn't tell. His body was so numb and cold.

Papa stood and lifted Cade again. "We have to be close."

Papa kept walking. They were going up a hill now, but still Cade could see nothing.

Finally, a light flashed in and out of the blinding snow.

"Home." Papa's relief was strong.

He walked toward the light, and soon they were at the kitchen door. Papa opened it, and he stepped over the threshold into the warm house.

"Thank God!" Mama cried as she raced across the kitchen and pulled Cade into her arms. He was tall now—almost as tall as her—but she held him like he was a baby again, tears falling down her face.

"Get him some warm blankets," Mama ordered Henry. She put Cade down on the ground next to the potbelly stove and began to take off his outerwear. "Cade, what were you thinking? You know better than to be outside at night."

A fierce thud sounded near the door and they both looked up at the same moment.

Papa had collapsed on the kitchen floor.

Chapter One

San Francisco
September 1917

Cade

Cade Bailey opened his eyes and stared at the small drops of blood soaking into the dirt beneath him. He didn't notice the whir of the propeller until it ceased and then silence echoed in his ears. He licked his dusty lips and tasted the blood. Gravel fell from his hair and face, raining down onto the patches of brown grass.

He hung suspended from the cockpit of his airplane in a sort of daze. For a moment, he couldn't recall where he was, or how he had ended up in this peculiar situation. On instinct, he reached toward his chest and unlatched the belt holding him into the aircraft. With a thud, he fell to the ground and sprawled out in the dirt, looking up at his crumpled biplane. A yellow and white striped tent hung off one of the wings, fluttering in the warm breeze.

He stared at that bright canvas for a long time, slipping in and out of a dark fog.

Voices drew near, calling his name.

He tried to lift his head and speak, but he had no energy to move.

A familiar man appeared at the side of the plane, his eyes wild with fear. "Cade!"

It took a moment for Cade to find his name. "Jimmy." Cade tried to sit up, but the world spun, and he fell to the ground again.

Jimmy knelt beside him and laid a hand on Cade's shoulder. "Don't move. We're getting an ambulance here immediately."

"What happened?" Cade blinked, trying to conjure up a memory from the past few minutes. The sun shined in his eyes, and he lifted his limp arm and put it over his face. "Where am I?"

"You're at Bay Meadows airfield, performing a stunt show." Jimmy swallowed and his Adam's apple bobbed. "I thought you were dead."

More people gathered around Cade, their faces lined with worry—but Cade felt surprisingly calm.

"I want to sit up," he said.

"Are you sure?"

Cade nodded and Jimmy's arm slipped under his shoulders.

Memories began to return to Cade in little snippets...

He had dipped his airplane low over the cheering crowd, loving the feel of the sun on his shoulders and the power within his grasp. He zoomed past them, close enough to see their round eyes. The wind from his airplane had torn off their hats and whipped at their dresses. Thousands of spectators had stood below, their eager faces tilted toward the sky and his red Curtiss JN-4. The more daring he became, the more they had cheered.

He had one more trick and then he'd land his plane and take on passengers.

The airfield had been crowded—too crowded. People had stood on any available surface they could find. Automobiles, buildings, and roads were covered. Everyone wanted to see Daredevil Kincade, the stunt pilot in Bennett Studios latest film, *Flying High*. He performed all the tricks from the movie and added in a few he had perfected while touring the United States last summer.

The time had come for his final trick—the nosedive. Jimmy, Cade's manager, had told him not to do the trick. He said it was too dangerous—but it was the stunt the crowd had been waiting for. Cade could almost see Jimmy standing on the airfield, shaking his head in frustration as Cade tilted the control stick back.

But what could he do to Cade from down there? He smiled. Up here in the air, Cade was the boss, and no one could tell him what to perform.

The plane ascended into the heavens. A handful of white clouds drifted in an endless sky of blue. Sunshine sparkled off the bay and touched the hills around San Francisco with a golden glow. His heart rate increased the higher he climbed.

He had leveled the airplane at five thousand feet and then took a deep breath. He tilted the control stick forward and the plane went into a nosedive. The engine screamed in protest as it raced toward the earth. Wind blew against Cade's face and over his goggles and leather flying cap. He braced his feet on the floor and reveled in the rush of adrenaline that coursed through his veins. He couldn't hear the crowd, but he knew they would be going crazy with excitement.

Faster and faster he sped. The buildings and people had come into focus as the ground grew closer. At the very last moment, he had pulled up on the control stick and leveled out the airplane, zooming past the crowd.

They had gone wild.

He would do one final loop and turn the airplane around to come in for his final landing...

But then what? Cade searched his memory as he ripped off his goggles. His airplane sat next to him in a mess of struts and splintered wood. What had happened after his final loop? Something had gone wrong—terribly wrong. He closed his eyes and tried to think.

As the memories came into focus, sweat began to pool on his forehead and his heart pounded with terror.

He snapped his head up and looked across the airfield. A great mass of people had gathered near the airplane hangar as two ambulances rushed to the scene.

Cade swallowed the dread as the last few moments came back in vivid, horrifying detail...

While he was in the middle of his final loop, upside down, a gust of wind had pushed against his plane, and for a moment, the aircraft wobbled. He had struggled to gain control. He was able to turn the plane right side up, but he had been going too fast and had still not gained control as he sped past a yellow and white striped tent. The right wing clipped the tent and pulled it out of the ground. It clung to the wing, making the movements of the airplane more unsteady. An airplane hangar sat just behind the tent and a handful of people stood on top watching the airshow. Cade tried desperately to avoid the hangar, but his wing grazed the top, sweeping four people off the building.

Mortified, he veered to the left, toward the empty field. He would crash the plane, but it was far better than barreling into the crowd. With one final yank on the control stick, he landed on one wheel, and then felt the entire airplane spin out of control. It flipped two or three times before it finally stopped.

And then there had been nothing...

Until now.

A cry tore from his chest as he tried to stand. He had to get to the hangar and see if those people had survived. Jimmy held him in place, but Cade jerked away. He found his footing and then stumbled. The ground rolled and swayed as he stood again and tried to race across the empty airfield. People called out for him to stop, but he had to see.

"Oh, God!" Even as he uttered the prayer, he knew God wouldn't answer his cry for help. Cade's many sins taunted him as he tripped and fell to his knees, his chest rising and falling. "It's not for me," he pleaded to God, "it's for those people."

He stood and hobbled across the airfield. His head spun and his ankle throbbed. Sweat dripped from his temples and down his cheeks.

The crowd saw him coming and made a path. Already, medical workers were beside the four people who lay on the ground. Two naval officers and two young women. One of the women was crying.

Jimmy reached his side and grabbed Cade's arm, restraining him from going farther.

Pitiful glances were sent in Cade's direction, and hushed voices whispered behind hands.

The two men and one of the women were put on stretchers and taken away in the ambulances, but the other girl was left on the ground. The remaining medical aid quietly slipped a blanket over her still body.

Cade's legs wobbled and gave out, but Jimmy held him firmly on his feet and whispered in his ear, "Keep it together, Cade. People are watching. You're a legend in their eyes—don't show them you're only human."

Gasps and moans arose from the crowd. Women clung to each other and men dipped the brims of their hats to cover their eyes. Slowly, they began to disperse.

"The police have arrived." The airfield manager approached, his whiskered face grim. "They want a full report. They're getting some eyewitness accounts now. It's clear it was an accident, but they want to talk to you."

It felt like Cade was in a nightmare. How could this have happened? He'd flown for years, in countless airshows, performing hundreds of tricks, and not once had there been an accident. He was too skilled to make such a foolish mistake.

If only he had listened to Jimmy and not done the stunt.

He couldn't take his eyes off the form of the young woman. Who was she? Who would tell her family what happened? What would they think of him?

"Come on, Cade." Jimmy tugged on Cade's shoulder. "Don't let it get to you. Everyone will eventually forget. But next time, listen to me."

There wouldn't be a next time.

The old, familiar desire to run settled over Cade like a blanket of panic, smothering him with an intensity he knew all too well.

He had to leave.

Emma

Minnesota

October 1917

Emma Merrick lifted her hand and pounded on the door for the second time. Weeds grew around the foundation of the little house and white paint peeled on the clapboard siding. The sound of a toddler's muffled cry seeped through the door. The pitiful wails tugged at Emma's heart and made her lift her hand to knock harder.

The autumn afternoon was full of surprising warmth. The sky overhead was a brilliant blue and the sun shone down on the colorful countryside. A flock of crows settled in a cornfield just beyond the house as she waited for someone to answer the door.

She hated to walk into the house unannounced, but what choice did she have? The Minnesota headquarters of the American Red Cross had requested that a Town and Country Nurse visit Mrs. Girvan and her child. The husband, Lieutenant Girvan, was at Kelly Airfield in Texas and he was worried about his pregnant wife. She was close to her due date and had no one in the area to help.

The child's wails increased. With one hand clutching her emergency kit, and the other turning the doorknob, Emma pushed open the door just a crack. She was instantly met with the smell of a dirty diaper—and something else she couldn't identify. The toddler, who looked about eighteen months old, stood next to the potbelly stove, her blond curls matted and her full diaper sagging to her knees. How long had the child been like this—and where was Mrs. Girvan?

Emma pushed the door open all the way and stepped over the threshold into the chilly house. "Hello," she said over the cries of the child. "I'm Nurse Merrick with the American Red Cross. Lieutenant Girvan asked us to come for a visit."

The toddler continued to wail, and Mrs. Girvan didn't answer. Emma reached into her bag for a sack of cookies she had brought from home. She withdrew a molasses cookie and placed it into the child's hand.

Immediately, the little girl opened her big blue eyes and looked at the cookie. It went toward her mouth, and the crying stopped. Emma placed a second cookie in her other hand and touched the girl's head. "I'll come see about you in a moment. Right now, I need to find your mama."

She crossed the room and opened the door at the back. *Please, Lord. I hope I'm not too late.* "Mrs. Girvan, I'm Nurse Merrick from the American Red Cross."

Mrs. Girvan lay on the bed, her legs entwined in dirty sheets, with a naked infant beside her. The baby nuzzled its mother, a weak cry coming from its lips. It couldn't be more than a few hours old.

"Mrs. Girvan." Emma spoke softly, but firmly, not wanting to startle her.

The woman lay with her eyes closed. Sweat dripped from her pale face and her hair was a mess of blond curls.

Emma put her hand on the lady's shoulder and then noticed the blood soaking the bed. Her pulse thudded as she spoke louder. "Mrs. Girvan."

The woman moaned but didn't open her eyes.

A quick assessment confirmed Emma's fear. The woman was bleeding more than usual after a birth. Emma had knowledge in assisting births and caring for infants, but she had no experience with this type of bleeding.

She raced into the main room and looked for a telephone.

Nothing.

They were across the river from the old village site of Crow Wing, over twenty-five miles from the hospital, and Emma hadn't noticed any neighbors within shouting distance.

She would have to get Mrs. Girvan into to her automobile and bring her to St. Gabriel's hospital on her own.

Emma worked quickly. She changed the toddler's diaper and gave her more cookies to eat. Then she bundled up the baby and put him and the little girl in the backseat of her Model T. Carefully, she wrapped a thick blanket around Mrs. Girvan's shoulders and managed to get her to the car, wishing, once again, that she was taller and stronger.

Emma was sweating by the time she cranked the car and sped off toward the hospital.

"Thank you," Mrs. Girvan murmured as she lay with her head bobbing. Her voice was so weak, Emma could barely hear her. "We wouldn't...have made it...without you."

Emma reached over and patted her arm. "Everything will be fine." But would it? The young mother had lost so much blood.

Why had Mr. Girvan enlisted in the army when he had a wife and children to look after? As a farmer, he would have been exempt under the current conscription law. It was such a senseless decision on his part.

But everything seemed so senseless to Emma. The war. Her parents. The endless social obligations demanded of her. Everything seemed pointless but her work as a Town and Country Nurse with the Red Cross.

For the first time in her life, she was doing something she was proud of.

Emma turned onto the dirt road leading to town, her eyes on the three delicate lives inside her vehicle. The little girl sat devouring her cookies and the baby lay in a tight bundle. *Please, God, do not let these children lose their mother.*

Emma drove as fast as she could down the rutted road. Farmland spread out on either side of the vehicle, interspersed with colorful wooded groves and gently sloping hills.

Mrs. Girvan's head lolled forward.

"Mrs. Girvan?" Emma shook her shoulder, but the woman didn't respond. Blood had pooled underneath her. Emma pushed the pedal as hard as she could. The Model T reached twenty-five miles an hour, but it would take them at least an hour to get to St. Gabriel's Hospital.

Did they have that much time?

The baby began to whimper from the backseat and soon the toddler joined in.

"Hold on, little ones," Emma said to the children. "We're going as fast as we can."

"Mama." The toddler stood on the seat and tried to get to her mother. The Model T bounced and rumbled over the uneven roads and the child fell on her bottom, but she stood once again.

Emma held the girl back with one hand, hating to keep her from the one person who might bring her comfort in this scary time.

How many years had Emma tried to get to her own mother, only to be held back? She wished she could allow the girl to climb into her mother's lap—but Mrs. Girvan was too frail.

"Let her come," Mrs. Girvan whispered. "I want my daughter."

Emma removed her hand and the little girl climbed over the seat. She snuggled into a little ball on her mother's lap and closed her eyes. Emma could see it took a great deal of effort for Mrs. Girvan, but she put her arm around her daughter and held her, peace settling over her countenance.

The girl's face became serene as she nestled into place—unaware that her mother's life was slipping away.

Emma's heart tugged at the love between mother and daughter. Never once had she been allowed to climb into her mother's lap or been welcomed to draw close—not even now, no matter how hard she tried.

Suddenly, just above the treetops, an airplane appeared ahead of them. Emma's mouth slipped open as she stared at the modern wonder. The biplane had two parallel wings, one on top of the other. It looked sleek as it flew over the Model T. It was painted a shiny red and had one bright blue dot under each bottom wing. It looked just like the airplane in *Flying High*...

Her eyes grew wide.

Cade Bailey?

The plane zoomed by, flying toward the Bailey farm.

If only she could fly an airplane, they would reach the hospital so much faster—

She put her foot to the brake, an idea taking root.

Chapter Two

Cade

It had been a month since the accident, but Cade's hands still shook as he held the control stick of his biplane. He couldn't close his eyes without seeing the form of the young lady outlined under the blanket.

Cold wind numbed his cheeks as he glanced out the side of the cockpit, toward the fields and hills of central Minnesota. Over the years, he had traveled thousands of miles, flying over all forty-eight states, but he had never seen his childhood home from the air.

The Mississippi River ran like a sparkling ribbon through the woods and fields. The oaks and maples were at their autumn peak, painting the landscape in reds, yellows, oranges, and purples. Pine trees added splashes of green, and the white bark of the birch trees stood in stark contrast.

Cade dipped the wing, banking left, and headed toward the north field on his grandfather's farm. They would have already harvested the wheat there and it would make a good, level landing pad.

A sudden rush of nerves overtook him. Seven years had been too long to be away—yet not long enough. Memories, both good and bad, began to crowd his thoughts.

He had never intended to return home, but he owed his parents a final goodbye. He had been exempt from the draft because he was a licensed pilot, pursuing his vocation, but not anymore. Tomorrow, he would go to the local draft board and enlist in the war. They would expect him to fly, no doubt, but he hoped to become a trainer at one of the airfields—and not a combat flyer. He had already taken one too many lives.

He lowered his plane to the field. It bounced a few times and then it slowly came to a stop. He cut the engine and looked at the old place.

Sunlight filtered through the lazy clouds, dancing over the white clapboard house and red barn. Nothing had changed since he went away, though the bright red paint had dulled over time. The Mississippi meandered through the edge of their property, within sight of the house.

Three people appeared on the outskirts of the field, and Cade had to swallow the anxiety rising in his throat.

He could make out his mother, clutching her hands to her chest, and Henry next to her—not so young any more. They both stood still, as if anticipating Cade's first move.

With a deep breath, he pulled himself out of the back cockpit of his biplane and jumped to the ground. The Curtiss JN-4 he had crashed at Bay Meadows was now in a dump in San Francisco. This second plane had been the one he used in *Flying High*.

He removed his leather flying cap and goggles, tossing them into the cockpit, and then turned to his family.

From behind Mama and Henry, his little sister Gracie appeared and raced toward Cade and the airplane. She ran like a colt, all arms and legs, excitement on her face. She probably wouldn't remember him since she had only been three when he left. He tousled her hair as she ran past him toward his airplane.

Mama and Henry followed, a bit more reserved—until something overcame Mama and she raced the last few yards into Cade's arms, her sobs flooding his heart with regret.

He wished he could erase the past seven years and offer her an explanation for his departure. She deserved so much more than he had ever given her.

She was much thinner than he remembered, and her hair had more gray, but she still smelled of fresh baked bread and the climbing roses she tended in her garden.

She pulled back, her hands on his shoulders. "Let me look at you." Her blue eyes shimmered with tears, yet a smile lifted her wrinkled cheeks. "This is a day to give thanks to God."

Cade swallowed the familiar discomfort at the mention of God—though a part of him had craved her steadfast faith. "Hello, Mama."

"Won't your father be pleased." She wiped her cheeks with a handkerchief.

"Is he in the barn?"

A shadow passed over her face and she touched her handkerchief to her mouth.

Cade's chest tightened as he glanced at Henry for an explanation.

Henry put his arm around her shoulder and turned on Cade, hostility in his eyes. "Dad hasn't been out of the house for the past six months." He glanced over Cade's shoulder. Though Henry was only a year younger than Cade, he looked at least ten years older. "Gracie! Get away from that thing."

Grace was running her hands over the shiny red paint. She jumped at the sound of his voice and backed away.

Disappointment welled up in Cade. He tried to smile, but sadness outweighed his humor. "You used to be just as curious and carefree as her."

"I grew up, Cade. Someone had to."

The barb stuck in Cade's raw heart, ripping another piece of tender flesh away. When had Henry become so bitter?

Mama laid a hand on Henry's chest. "Not now, please."

"Where is Dad?" Cade asked, looking at his mother.

"He's in bed."

"In bed?"

"It's his heart." Henry's eyes were full of steel. "Doc Roberts doesn't think he'll make it through the winter."

His heart? Cade looked at his mother. "Is that true?"

She dropped her gaze and nodded.

"He was never the same after he rescued you from that snowstorm—and the past seven years of your silence has taken its toll." Henry's displeasure with Cade was obvious in the set of his jaw.

"I need to see him." Cade rushed by his mother and brother and ran toward the little white farmhouse.

Chickens scattered about his feet as he raced across the yard and up the front steps into the house. The living room was neat and tidy with the rag rugs Mama had woven and the worn rockers by the fireplace where they had sat and read the Bible to the children. Cade almost expected to see his grandfather sitting in his chair near the window, close to his beloved books—but it had been empty now for the past five years while Cade had been making a name for himself as an aviator. He crossed the room and opened his parents' bedroom door, clutching the doorknob for support.

Lying in the bed was a man who barely resembled his father. His gaunt cheeks were pale, and he had lost a great deal of weight. The room felt stuffy and heavy with the smell of sickness.

Cade ran his hands down his face, wishing he could wipe away the reality. Why hadn't anyone told him what was happening back at home?

Dad must have heard Cade, because his eyes opened and he offered Cade a feeble smile. "My son." He lifted his hand, beckoning Cade to his side. "I knew you would return before I went home."

More memories flashed into Cade's mind—horrible memories of the time he had run away into the snowstorm and the sickness that had robbed his father of health afterward.

The desire to flee overwhelmed him. It would be much easier to get into his plane and fly toward the horizon, never looking back. He'd done that seven years ago, at the age of eighteen, when he had gone to see Glenn Curtiss fly an airplane at the state fairgrounds. It was the first time Cade had seen an airplane, and he had been entranced. He'd found a job with Mr. Curtiss and had left without telling his folks.

But how much more pain and heartache would it cost his family if he left again?

"Come to me," Dad said.

Cade forced his feet to move toward the bed. He knelt beside his father and cleared his throat, the sound echoing off the faded wallpaper and time-worn photographs on the walls. "Hello, Dad."

Peace settled over his father's gentle face.

Cade fought the old anger rising inside him. His father had no reason to feel peaceful. He was lying on his deathbed, accepting his fate like he always had. Dad had never been a fighter, in life and now in death.

He lifted a bony hand and rested it on Cade's shoulder. "I wish I was well enough to throw you a party. You've done very well out in the world, son."

An image of the young lady who died flashed before Cade's eyes, and he wanted to deny his father's statement. "None of it matters." Especially now, seeing what it had done to his family.

"It does matter—" A coughing fit overcame Dad, and he took a moment to catch his breath.

He opened his mouth to speak, but Cade stopped him. "You don't need to say anything."

"I do—a great many things." Dad's eyes filled with tender hope. "I asked God to spare my life until I could speak to you—and He's answered my prayer, Cade. He's brought you home."

Cade put up his hand to stop his father.

"No, let me continue." Dad studied him with intensity. "I know now that it was my fault you left. I should have stood up to my father and guarded you from his harsh treatment. I thought I was doing him good—"

"It wasn't your fault." Cade shook his head. How could his father blame himself? "I shouldn't have run away."

"Cade, I need to speak to you." Henry's harsh voice interrupted their conversation from the doorway.

Cade looked at his brother. "Now?"

Dad laid his hand on Cade's shoulder. "We'll have plenty of time to talk, son." He offered a light squeeze. "Now that God brought you back, He won't take me until I've said what I need to say."

Henry turned from the room, a scowl on his face.

Cade stood and walked out of the room, regret pulsing inside his chest. He found Henry alone in the kitchen seated at the old wooden table. His hands were placed on the scarred surface, his eyes staring down at his calloused fists. Henry was exempt from fighting the war because of his work on the farm, just like thousands of other young men across the country. "What do you want from us, Cade?"

Cade stood at the door, his shoulders slumped. "I don't want anything."

Henry's eyes were so full of resentment it hurt to look at him. "You know we're about to lose the farm, don't you?"

Cade took a seat, his legs unsteady beneath him. "How's that possible?"

"Three years of miserable crops left nothing in the bank, so we took out a mortgage to pay Dad's medical bills."

Cade leaned forward. "How much do you owe?"

"Five hundred dollars."

"Surely it should be easy enough to come up with five hundred dollars—"

"You know how hard it is to raise that kind of money—especially during the war. This land has never been good for anything. Everything we make needs to be put back into the farm."

"What about other work?"

Henry shook his head. "You don't get it, do you? I'm the only one running this farm. When would I have time to find other work?"

"The only thing I have is my airplane—nothing else." Cade had given every penny to the family of the woman who had died—and even that hadn't eased his guilt. It took all his willpower to speak his next words. "I could sell the plane, but with the war on, I'd only get a couple hundred dollars."

Henry's eyes became dull, and he looked older than his twenty-five years. "Why did you even bother to come back?"

Cade wished he had come back sooner—much sooner, but what was done was done. "I'm enlisting in the army. I felt the folks needed to know."

Henry stood so fast, his chair crashed to the floor. He didn't look back as he stormed out of the kitchen, slamming the door behind him.

Emma

Emma scanned the farm, hoping she had found the right place. A tidy clapboard house and barn sat at the top of a little hill. A windbreak of pine trees guarded the west side of the house and to the east the green grass sloped to the Mississippi.

The baby cried in the backseat, his hungry wails filling the Model T, while the toddler slept on her mother's lap. Mrs. Girvan's white face had begun to change to a sickly gray, filling Emma with panic.

She pulled to a stop at the farmhouse and glimpsed Cade Bailey's biplane in a field just beyond the house. Her relief at finding the right farm was short-lived when the toddler woke and began to cry.

A man came to the farmhouse door, just as Emma stepped out of the car.

"Are you Cade Bailey?" she asked.

His curious gaze swept over her, taking in her Red Cross uniform, a frown marring his handsome face. "I am."

"I need you to fly my patient to the hospital in Little Falls. She'll die if I don't get her there in time."

His curiosity turned to concern as he stepped out of the house and let the door slam behind him. "What patient?"

Emma opened her door further and the children's cries tumbled out into the yard. "Mrs. Girvan just gave birth and she's in need of a doctor, with all haste. I'll follow behind in my car with the children. You can land in the field just south of St. Gabriel's hospital and someone will surely see your arrival. They'll help you get her inside."

Mr. Bailey moved to the opposite side of the vehicle and opened the door. His face betrayed his surprise at seeing the blood and the frail state of the woman. He didn't hesitate but scooped her into his arms and raced toward his airplane. Emma ran behind, holding onto her hat to keep it from flying off her head. "How long will it take you to get her there?"

"Twenty minutes, if the wind is at my tail."

Emma prayed for wind. Together they lifted Mrs. Girvan into the front cockpit. The whole time, Emma told him all she knew of the birth and what she thought might be wrong. He looked distracted as she spoke, but she hoped he would tell Dr. McCall everything she had said. After Mrs. Girvan was situated, Emma twisted the propeller at his command. The engine whirred to life, and the airplane began to move over the uneven field. Emma raced back to her car without waiting to watch them take off.

Just as she sat down behind the wheel of the Ford, the airplane flew overhead, pointing south. Within moments, it disappeared over the horizon and Emma was left with the children.

All the way to the hospital, she soothed the children and prayed for a miracle.

The sun hung low in the sky when she pulled up to the yellow brick hospital an hour later. Mr. Bailey's airplane stood off to the south, near a barn the sisters of St. Gabriel's used to house their horses and dairy cows.

Both children had been lulled back to sleep, but as soon as the engine stalled, they woke with a start. Emma took the infant in one arm and the crying little girl in the other as she raced into the front doors.

Mr. Bailey sat in the waiting room, his leather flying cap and goggles tangled in his large hands. Upon her entry, he jumped out of his chair.

Emma didn't stop to talk to him. Instead, she went to the nurse's desk where Sister Mary Rose sat making notes on a patient's chart. Her black and white habit covered all but her youthful face. "Sister, how is Mrs. Girvan?"

Sister Mary Rose looked up at Emma's question, her calm expression like a balm. "Dr. McCall is with her now." Her gentle gaze rested on the children as she stood. "Sister Agatha is here waiting to take the children to the orphanage for now. We'll see that they're properly cared for until other arrangements can be made." She offered Emma a warm smile. "You've done a good thing today, asking Mr. Bailey for assistance. It might have saved Mrs. Girvan's life."

Sister Agatha approached to take the children.

Emma looked down at the girl, wishing she knew the child's name. Her big blue eyes ran over with tears, and her blond curls were a mess on her head. Emma bent and placed a kiss on the child's cheek and then hugged the baby tight before relinquishing them to Sister Agatha.

Sister Mary Rose laid her hand on Emma's arm. "Why don't you go home and rest?"

There would be no rest at home. "I think I'll wait to speak to Dr. McCall."

Sister Mary Rose nodded, as if she knew Emma would say as much, and then she turned back to her chart.

Emma finally looked at Mr. Bailey and found him watching her. Her hand slipped up to her disheveled curls and her lopsided hat. She must look like a fright with sweat, blood, and tears staining her Red Cross uniform.

She quickly moved to stand before him, hoping he understood the depth of her appreciation. “I can’t thank you enough, Mr. Bailey.”

“Do you think she’ll—” he paused and cleared his throat. “Do you think she’ll survive?”

Emma clasped her hands, a silent prayer racing heavenward. “I hope so. I’ll wait to speak to Dr. McCall. I can send word to you once I know more.”

“Do you mind if I wait with you?” His eyes looked so troubled, she suddenly realized what an ordeal she must have put him through. She had placed the life of a woman in his hands—and so soon after his accident in California.

“Of course not.” She took a seat and indicated the one next to her. “Please, wait with me. I’m terribly sorry for the trouble I just put you through.”

“I’m happy I could help.”

She was struck by the color of his eyes. They were pure green, like her father’s. So rare and unique.

She had watched Cade in the movies and read about his exploits in the *Little Falls Daily Transcript*. The locals were all proud of their native son’s accomplishments and mourned with him when they heard about his accident in San Francisco. His handsome features were more attractive in person, even with his face unshaven and his hair mussed from the flying cap.

A glimmer of interest lit his gaze, and Emma sensed he was seeing her for the first time, as well.

Chapter Three

Cade

Cade's heart hadn't stopped its erratic beating since he saw Mrs. Girvan lying unconscious in the Ford—but now it beat for a different reason. The nurse sitting next to him wore a blue dress with white cuffs and a Red Cross pin attached to her white collar. The dress was plain, but the young lady wearing it was not. Auburn curls slipped out of her bun and lay against her smooth cheeks, while dark brown eyes blinked from behind long eyelashes.

Hospital personnel scurried around the front hall. Patients and guests sat in the spacious waiting room, some playing chess, others visiting or reading books—but the only person he really noticed was the nurse beside him.

"You were able to get her here in less than half the time it took me." Her eyes revealed her wonder. "Just think of all the possibilities air travel could offer."

The military was in the process of testing those possibilities, even now. Airplanes would change the face of warfare—and he planned to help them.

"Lives could be saved," she continued. "Town and Country Nurses could cover a much greater distance, visiting patients in remote locations."

"Are you a Town and Country Nurse?" he asked.

She fingered her Red Cross pin, a tint of pride coloring her cheeks. "I'm the first Town and Country Nurse in Minnesota."

There was something contradictory about this woman that fascinated him. She had been tender with Mrs. Girvan and the children, yet tough in the face of a life-threatening emergency. She had been brave to show up at a stranger's home the way she had—yet she seemed almost apologetic about her actions now. Her eyes revealed innocence—but in an intense sort of way. She couldn't be more than twenty, or twenty-one, yet the wisdom in her eyes said she had lived a lifetime in those short years.

"Will you allow me to hire you?" she asked.

He blinked several times, knowing he missed something. "Pardon me?

She sat up straighter. "I would like to hire you and your airplane. There are remote parts of the state I can't reach by automobile—but if I had your airplane, I could go anywhere."

Hope shined from her face, making him wish he could help her. "I'm sorry, but I'm enlisting in the military tomorrow. I won't be here to help."

The momentary hope vanished, and lines edged the corners of her eyes and mouth. She looked down at her hands and spoke softly. "This war seems to be taking everyone away."

A man in a white jacket stepped out of a room down the hall and they both rose to their feet. She spoke first. "Dr. McCall, how is Mrs. Girvan?"

The doctor drew near, his face shadowed with fatigue. "She will survive—but it will be many months before she's fully recovered. She lost a great deal of blood today." He turned to Cade. "Thank you for your service, Mr. Bailey. It saved Mrs. Girvan's life."

Cade pressed his lips together and nodded, the magnitude of the moment overpowering his emotions. A month ago, his airplane had taken a life. Today it saved one. And he had the nurse to thank for it. He wished, with all his heart, he could stay and do what she had asked of him. Maybe then he could attempt to redeem the life he took. "It was my pleasure."

The doctor turned to the young woman. "And thank you for your quick thinking, Nurse Merrick. You two made a good team."

Cade looked at the woman standing next to him, a funny sensation prickling the back of his neck. "Nurse Merrick?"

Relief shined from her brown eyes as she nodded. "Yes. Emma Merrick."

"Matthew Merrick's daughter?"

Something changed in her demeanor at the sound of the name. The skin around her mouth tightened and her eyes lost a bit of shine. "Do you know my father?"

Cade's disappointment was swift and complete. He couldn't hide the hard edge that tinged his voice. "I'm afraid I do."

She studied him for a moment and then smiled, though the gesture didn't quite reach her eyes. "It was a pleasure meeting you, Mr. Bailey."

Cade nodded and then left the hospital without another word.

Just hearing Major Merrick's name brought back memories from the day Grandfather fell ill. From what Cade had gathered, Major Merrick had brought nothing but heartache to their family. He had no wish to get involved with anyone named Merrick. It was the one thing he and his grandfather had agreed on.

Emma

Starlight pinpricked the evening sky as Emma stopped the Model T outside the carriage house. She turned off the engine and sat in the stillness, the weight of the day lying heavy upon her mind and heart. The quiet echoed in her ears as she dropped her head and gave way to the frustration and fear that had threatened to engulf her all day.

She was weak and vulnerable. She couldn't separate herself from her patients. Their pain was her pain. Their fear, her fear. What made her think she was strong enough to be a nurse? Every time she closed her eyes she thought of Mrs. Girvan's children and how close they had come to losing their mother.

A light tap at the window brought Emma's head up. Samuel Turner, their chauffeur, stood outside her vehicle, his eyes filled with compassion. He opened the door and offered her his hand.

"There, there, lass." His Irish brogue was still as strong as it had been when Emma was a child. "What's the matter?"

She stepped out of the Ford and tried to smile. "I'm fine."

He returned her smile and opened his arms. "I can see when something's wrong."

She entered his warm embrace. He smelled faintly of axle grease and pipe tobacco.

"I almost lost a patient today."

His heart beat against her cheek and his chest rose and fell in a steady rhythm. He patted her back. "But you didn't."

She stepped away from his hug. "It was a miracle she didn't die. I realized how limited my abilities are. On my own, I was powerless to prevent her death."

"Only the good Lord can prevent a death—you're just a human, doing what you can."

She sighed. "I wish I could do more."

"Like what?"

"I want to fly, Sam."

His brows rose. "Fly? What would ever give you that idea?"

"Cade Bailey returned home, and I had him fly my patient to the hospital. It saved her life. Just think of all I could do if I had my pilot's license."

Sam touched her head, as if checking for a fever. "Are you ill?"

Emma smiled and swatted at his hand.

He grinned. "I do not want to tell you this, but the guests have started to arrive, and your mother has been looking for you."

Emma groaned as she glanced at the stone house, dreading all that awaited her. The Merrick Mansion had been built to impress—and it did a splendid job.

The only person it failed to impress was Emma.

"You better go inside and get fixed up. Tomorrow you can tell me all about flying."

Emma stood on tiptoe and kissed his cheek. "Thank you, Sam."

She walked across the cobblestone drive, trying to prepare herself for the party. All her life she had longed to be included in her mother's world—hoping to finally be accepted—but now she had become a pawn, being strategically placed about for her mother's benefit.

Emma passed through the shadows of the servant's entrance.

"Child, your mother is furious," Martha said when Emma entered the bustling kitchen. Maids and footmen scurried about the room, preparing the midnight buffet.

Martha stood in the center of it all, her gray hair tucked away under a white mobcap. A stiff white apron covered her thick middle as she directed the chaos. "If I was you, I'd hurry on up to your room and get ready—" she stopped midsentence when Emma reached around her and stole a pickled cucumber from a relish tray.

"Stop that!" Martha swatted at her hand and Emma giggled. "Take the letter from my apron pocket."

Emma lifted the letter and looked at the handwriting. "It's from Rebecca."

Martha grinned and years melted away from her face. "She's going to have a baby, in the spring. I'm going to be a grandma!"

"A baby?" Emma clasped Martha's shoulders, a squeal of delight slipping past her lips. "Truly?"

Martha nodded. "I'll go and stay with her after the baby is bor—ach! My pudding!" Martha raced away from Emma to stir the bubbling concoction.

Emma held Rebecca's letter as she went up the servant's stairs to the second floor. Rebecca had been married in July and was now living in northern Minnesota, near the Canadian border—hours away from the nearest town and days away from a railroad station. Emma longed to go to her friend, but it would be impossible to take that much time away from work.

She thought again of Cade Bailey's airplane. If she only knew how to fly, she could make the trip in just a few hours.

Emma nibbled on the pickle. Maybe Cade knew where she could learn. If she went to him in the morning, before he left to enlist, he could tell her.

With a renewed purpose in her step, she walked through the servant's quarters to her room.

The back of the house was reserved for the staff, with white painted trim and simple furnishings, but as soon as Emma stepped out of the servant's hall and into the front of the house, it felt like she entered a different world—and, in many ways she did.

Emma lived in one world by day and one by night—always passing through the servant's hall from one to the next. At night, parties, balls, and endless obligations ruled her every move. Her conscience crawled, and guilt assailed her. But during the day, she helped to birth babies, care for the sick, and serve those in need, eagerly doing her part to fight the war.

She despised the one and loved the other.

Thirty minutes later, Emma descended the grand staircase wearing her elaborate formal gown. It draped to the ground in yards of burgundy silk and satin—so different than her Red Cross uniform.

With a deep breath, she plastered on her prettiest smile and made her entrance into the party.

The lavishly decorated two-story foyer was filled with glittering, laughing people.

Emma swallowed, hoping once again that tonight would make a difference. Maybe tonight her parents would see her—ask about her work, take an interest in the things that mattered to her.

"There you are, my dear." Mother lifted her bejeweled hand toward Emma as the crystal chandeliers glistened off the gemstones sewn into her gown.

She looked as exquisite as her home.

Emma joined her mother at the bottom of the stairs, her gaze floating over the guests.

"Your father hasn't made his appearance, if that's what you're looking for," Mother said for her ears alone. "He's hiding in his office, as usual." She made a pretense of telling Emma a delectable secret as she leaned into her ear. "If you breathe one word of the war or your work with the Red Cross, so help me, Emma, I'll revoke my permission and you'll quit your job tomorrow." She offered a dazzling smile as she spoke through her teeth. "I won't have you muddy my party with your devotion to the cause."

Emma's heart ached. "Your secret is safe with me—I won't tell anyone we're at war, lest they run away from your party in terror."

Mother patted her hand. "That's a good girl." Her flawless skin glowed with the excitement of the party. At the age of forty-five, she was still beautiful, and she knew it. She lived to host balls and parties—and attract the attention of younger men. "Now, I have someone I want you to meet..."

The party droned on as Emma danced with the endless line of suitors her mother presented, wishing this night was over and she could speak to Cade Bailey about something that truly mattered. The only bright spot was the buzz traveling around the room about Cade's arrival in Minnesota. Everywhere she turned, someone was talking about his movies, or his stunt flying, or the death of the woman in San Francisco.

Just before midnight, Father materialized in the north parlor. Emma watched him circle the room, his white hair and goatee easy to pick out of the crowd. He strode with an air of confidence born of great wealth and power, though she knew he would prefer to be inside his office, buried in his work.

It wasn't until she was old enough to attend her mother's parties that she could get these rare glimpses of a man who was a great mystery in her life. At the age of seventy-seven, he was surprisingly healthy and agile—to her mother's dismay. While many of his counterparts had slowed in business and recreation, he was still very active. He stopped by Mother for their customary appearance together, and Emma knew what the entire room was thinking.

Major Matthew Merrick had married a woman thirty-two years younger than him. They didn't touch as they stood side by side and barely glanced at one another. In Emma's lifetime, she had only seen them together during obligatory times. Her birthday parties, holidays, and at elaborate parties like this one.

Never once had she seen them share an intimate smile or a playful word—with each other or with her.

If it hadn't been for the family Emma had created with the servants, she would have no one. Where her mother and father lacked love and affection, Sam, Martha, and Rebecca had made up for it tenfold.

Finally, Father stepped away and continued around the room. He drew closer to Emma, nodding a greeting to those he passed. When he stood in front of her, his eyes registered her presence, but no warmth filled his greeting. He nodded at her, like he had the others.

Her heart thudded and she studied him, hoping to see something like acceptance, or even approval, in his eyes.

"Sir." She had never called him Father—and he had never asked her to.

He continued until he reached the exit and disappeared once again.

Emma wanted to disappear into the kitchen and receive a warm embrace from Martha or a reassuring word from Sam to remind her that she was loved. Instead, she stayed at the party with a fake smile and disappointment in her heart.

What had caused this man she called Father to be so cold and distant? She took a deep breath, trying to accept that she might never know.

Chapter Four

MAY 1863

MATTHEW

Matthew stopped on the Woods Trail and tugged his lapels, affecting an air of authority he didn't feel. He cleared his throat and mustered all the confidence he possessed. "Major Matthew Merrick," he said into the quiet afternoon air. The title felt like a new pair of shoes, pinching in all the wrong places. He put his hands behind his back and rocked on his heels trying to look older. More important. This time he inhaled a deep breath, allowing his chest to puff out. "Major Merrick."

"Major Merrick, what?" came a grumpy old voice.

The air rushed out of Matthew's lungs as he spun around and found an old man stepping onto the trail. He had to be at least sixty, with white hair and a beard that rested on his chest. Though he was old, there was a spark of life in his eyes that belied his age. The man wore buckskin pants, a white shirt, and a leather sack secured to his back. He walked toward Matthew with a tall stick in his right hand. "Well?"

"Well, what?"

"Who's this Major Merrick, and why do you keep saying his name?"

"I'm Major Merrick."

"Were you trying to remind yourself just now? Or are you talking to invisible friends?" The spark turned to a sparkle and he chuckled. "I heard there was a new agent at Crow Wing. I didn't think you'd be so young—or odd."

Matthew grinned and extended his hand. His fiancée's father, Mr. Baker, was the new Superintendent of Indian Affairs and he'd convinced Governor Hibbing to give Matthew this important job at Crow Wing.

The man's handshake was strong and secure. "I'm Thaddeus Tucker, but most people just call me Tuck. Where you headed, Major?"

Green vegetation crowded the trail and mosquitoes swarmed around their heads. Matthew swatted at one attached to his neck. "I'm on my way to Chief White Thunder's home. I met the chief last week when I first arrived in Crow Wing and he asked..." Matthew hesitated, hating to admit what he was about to do. His first meeting with the chief had gone well—better than Matthew expected—but it had not ended pleasantly, at least not to Matthew's way of thinking.

"What did he ask you?" Tuck demanded.

"He asked me to teach his daughter how to properly conduct herself in the white man's society."

Tuck's eyes crinkled at the corners as he squinted against the sun. "What self-respecting man teaches a woman how to be a woman?"

Matthew groaned. "That's what I've been asking myself every day since the chief made his request."

Elizabeth, as she had been named by her forward-thinking father, was in Crow Wing village for the summer with her family. Chief White

Thunder wanted her to attend the fort dance next month and had called on the new agent to prepare her.

"Why didn't the chief ask one of the ladies at Crow Wing to teach her?" Tuck asked as he started to walk down the trail.

Matthew followed along. "He said he didn't trust any of those back-biting women."

"Wise man."

Matthew smiled to himself as they walked in silence for a few minutes. Finally, he asked Tuck, "Is your home in Crow Wing?"

Tuck looked out at the river, but his eyes didn't settle on the rushing water or the swaying trees along the banks. He looked beyond it all. "My home is in heaven, Major. I've been trying to get there most of my life, but God seems to think I have work left to do here on earth."

Matthew was struck by the man's odd words. He had encountered a few religious people in his life and when he did, he always felt unsettled in their presence. He had never taken the time to learn about God.

Maybe someday.

"What about you, Major? Is there a mansion with your name on it in heaven?"

A mansion? In heaven? What was the old man talking about?

"I don't know about any mansions in heaven—but if I do my job well, I'll have a mansion right here in Minnesota one day."

Tuck winked at Matthew as if he knew something Matthew didn't. "'Lay not up for yourselves treasures upon earth, where moth and rust doth corrupt, and where thieves break through and steal: But lay up for yourselves treasures in heaven, where neither moth nor rust doth corrupt, and where thieves do not break through nor steal: For where your treasure is, there will your heart be also.'"

Matthew didn't know what to say, so he remained quiet as they continued to walk.

When Crow Wing's outlying buildings came within sight, Matthew felt both relief and dread. Tuck was a funny little fellow, and Matthew was eager to be rid of him, but he wasn't keen to teach a seventeen-year-old girl how to dance and flirt with soldiers.

People bustled along the main thoroughfare through the village, their feet shuffling on the wooden boardwalk lining the banks of the river.

Matthew stopped, ready to turn east toward the chief's home. "It was nice to meet you, Tuck."

Tuck studied Matthew intently with his bright blue eyes. "I'm happy our paths crossed, Major Merrick. It's not often I encounter a man about to embark on a new journey. Just remember this: 'Enter ye in at the strait gate: for wide is the gate, and broad is the way, that leadeth to destruction, and many there be which go in there at: Because strait is the gate, and narrow is the way, which leadeth unto life, and few there be that find it." He grinned and his teeth were surprisingly clean and even. "That just means to stay far away from the wide, easy path that leads to destruction." He put his hand on Matthew's shoulder. "I'll be praying for you, son."

Matthew stared after the man as he continued down the trail and disappeared into the crowd, trying to shake off the sense of foreboding in Tuck's words.

With a deep inhale, Matthew continued down the path and entered the heart of the village.

The Mississippi and Crow Wing rivers converged near the settlement, making it a perfect location for loggers, fur traders, and entrepreneurs. Over two hundred people called Crow Wing home, though it was a transient location with people coming and going every day. Chief White

Thunder had two summer homes in the village, one for each of his wives. Matthew had been told to go to the house near the east end of the valley where the chief's oldest daughter would be waiting.

He tipped his hat in greeting as he passed people along the way but received contemptuous glares and outright hostility in return. Matthew would have a tough job convincing people that he would be a better agent than the last one who had caused nothing but trouble.

First, though, he must impress Chief White Thunder, and then the others might follow.

Matthew climbed the hill and walked between the hotel and trading post overlooking the confluence of rivers and then descended into the valley toward the chief's cabin. It looked as simple as all the others with a door in the center of the front wall and a glass window on either side. A handful of children played in the dusty yard, while a dog barked at a squirrel in a nearby tree. When the children saw Matthew approach they ran into the cabin yelling in a language he was trying hard to learn.

A woman came to the door, squinting against the bright afternoon sunshine. Her dark skin and black hair spoke of her native heritage, but she wore a red gingham dress with a wide skirt. She looked him over with probing black eyes and spoke in broken English. "You come to teach my daughter?"

Matthew removed his hat, conscious of his need to appear the gentleman while maintaining his authority. "Yes. I'm Major Merrick. I've come to teach Miss Elizabeth."

Again, the woman sized him up. He felt like squirming under her appraisal, but he held his chin high—maybe too high. He dropped it a notch not wanting to appear aloof.

The woman stepped back into her cabin but left the door open.

Matthew turned and looked out over the valley toward the Mississippi. Helen, his fiancée, had been wise to remain in St. Paul away from this wilderness. She would wilt like a plucked flower without water in this place.

Movement at the door brought Matthew's attention around. Children peeked out from behind the mother, their eyes eagerly searching his face. The woman crossed her arms over her chest. "Elizabeth not learn today."

Matthew leaned forward. "Pardon me?"

"Elizabeth not to learn today," she repeated.

He had walked six miles from the agency to the village, giving up his entire afternoon. More importantly, the chief wanted him to do this. He could not take no for an answer. "Is she not at home?"

"She is home. She not want to learn today."

Concern and frustration welled up in his chest. "Chief White Thunder asked me to come. I cannot leave without teaching Miss Elizabeth."

The lady tightened her arms across her chest and shook her head. "Not today."

He began to cross his arms, too, but put them back at his side. "Yes, today. I won't be back in the village until next week. Chief White Thunder wants Miss Elizabeth to attend the military dance at the end of the month. I don't want to make the chief angry." It was an understatement. Everything relied on the chief's good feelings toward Matthew. He only had a few months to convince the chief to support a massive land treaty. As a chief among the Chippewa Indians, White Thunder's support would guarantee that the others would follow.

If Matthew succeeded, he would be promoted as the governor's Chief Legal Counsel at the capital and Helen would set a date to marry him. If he failed, his political career in Minnesota would be ruined and he was certain Helen would call off their engagement.

He couldn't fail. His mother and sister's health and well-being depended on it.

The woman's arms loosened, just a bit, and she glanced over her shoulder into the cabin. "You come. But Elizabeth not happy."

That made two of them.

She shooed the little ones outside and stepped into the cabin, Matthew following. It took a moment for his eyes to adjust to the dimly lit room, but when they did, he saw the buffalo hides scattered on the floor and a fireplace against one wall. The mother went to the fire and squatted in her gingham dress, tossing glances over her shoulder while she stirred the food in the copper kettle. The aroma of simmering venison filled the cabin and made his stomach growl.

He sensed another person in the room, and he turned to find the young lady in question. She stood in the corner, looking much like her mother with her feet planted and her arms pinned across her chest. But unlike her mother, she was stunningly beautiful. Matthew had heard rumors of her beauty, but he had only believed them to be the romanticized imagination of lonely men. She wore a simple gown much like those he saw in St. Paul, but unlike the socialites he knew, this woman's long hair was unbound, falling straight down to her waist in a curtain of ebony silk. Though her beauty caught his eye, it was her snapping black gaze that captured his attention.

She quirked her eyebrow. "*You're* the new agent?" Her English was flawless, with only a hint of an accent.

Matthew looked down at his black sack coat and wrinkled trousers, and realized he was gripping his hat with white knuckles. He loosened his hold and met her challenge with one of his own. "*You're* the chief's daughter?"

A hint of humor sparkled in her eyes for a moment and then died away, replaced with contempt. "You are young."

"Twenty-three."

"Too young to teach me anything." She tossed her hair over her shoulder and turned from him, as if brushing him aside.

"I am old enough for the governor to appoint me to the position of Indian Agent."

She didn't bother to look at him and he didn't bother to tell her he'd only been appointed at the insistence of his soon-to-be father-in-law. "I don't want you here."

He almost laughed. "I don't want to be here."

His response seemed to surprise her. She turned back, accusation in her eyes. "You wouldn't be here if you didn't want to be."

"We do things we don't want to do all the time."

She scrutinized him for a moment. "What *do* you want?"

He rarely met a person he could be candid with. As a lawyer, he had learned to skirt around the truth trying to plead his case or sway his opponent. This woman was different. Surprisingly, he *wanted* to tell her the truth.

The look in her eyes demanded it.

"I want your father to trust me and agree to sign the treaty this fall. If he does, the governor will promote me to Chief Legal Counsel. Your father holds a great deal of power over my future."

Elizabeth continued to examine him. Her eyes were wide and expressive, entrancing him with their depth of intelligence. "You think if you teach me how to dance and flirt with the white men, my father will think you are a great leader, and he will trust you?"

Hearing it spoken in such a frank manner made it sound absurd. But it was true. "Yes."

Her dark eyes filled with victory. "Then it is *I* who hold power over your future."

Elizabeth

June 1863

Elizabeth sat beside Matthew on the high buggy seat trying to keep her eyes on the trail—and not on the man beside her. The road to Fort Ripley was filled with ruts, and she worked hard to remain seated while they bounced over the uneven terrain.

Her mind whirled with all the things Matthew had taught her these past four weeks as she prepared herself for the dance at the fort. Father had not told her why it was so important that she attend the dance, but it was easy to assume he was using her to convince everyone that all was well between him and the soldiers.

She felt lightheaded and short of breath, but whether that was from the man sitting next to her or the new corset she wore, she couldn't be sure. In the fading light of day, she examined her cream-colored gown in layers of silk and satin, and her delicate lace gloves covering her brown hands. Her hair was styled exactly like the picture Matthew had shown her of his twin sister in Washington, DC. She had caught the glimpse of approval in his eyes when he first saw her.

Was she prepared for this entry into the white man's world?

"You surprised me," Matthew said quietly, not taking his eyes from the trail.

Her thoughts stopped tumbling and all else faded away as she looked at her companion. She admired the strong lines of his handsome face and the way his brown hair curled at the nape of his neck. When he smiled, his green eyes shined, and his cheeks creased with dimples. He was a fine-looking man—one of the finest Elizabeth had ever seen.

"You surprised me, too," she said. "You are a good man, Major Merrick." She paused and added, "A good, but stubborn man."

A smile lifted Matthew's cheeks, and she could see he tried to hide the pleasure her words stirred in him.

They rode alone in the buggy along the Woods Trail to Fort Ripley, seven miles below Crow Wing village on the Mississippi River. He had asked for a chaperone to accompany them, but Father trusted Matthew—which pleased Elizabeth.

"How did I surprise you?" she asked, her voice softer than she intended.

He studied her and his eyes pooled with an emotion that made her pulse skitter. He swallowed and looked back at the road. "You knew much more than I anticipated when I arrived at your cabin the first day."

She glanced out across the Mississippi River, her eyes sweeping the thick brush and tall grasses. "I know more than most people think from my years at the Belle Prairie Mission School with Mr. and Mrs. Greenfield." She had only returned to live with her mother two years ago.

Silence dipped between them. The horses' steady hoof beats, and the chorus of frogs, were the only sounds along the trail.

"Why did you agree to the lessons?" he asked.

She looked at him, appreciating his clean-shaven face and strong cheekbones. He looked nothing like the burly fur traders lining the riverbanks, or the young braves in her band. What would he think when she told him the truth? "Because I thought you were handsome, and I wanted to get to know you."

Her words seemed to startle him. He clicked the reins a bit too hard, setting the horses at a gallop.

Elizabeth clutched the side of the buggy and offered him a sideways glance. The man puzzled her to no end. They had spent hours together over the past four weeks, and in that time, he had both endeared her—and infuriated her. His moods rolled like the wind over the prairie, rising and falling unpredictably. One moment she thought he liked her—and the next he became surly and cross.

"I have a clerk coming to Crow Wing this week." His abrupt change in topics surprised her. "It is past time I had help with my duties. The Superintendent of Indian Affairs is coming with him. We will meet with your father to talk about the treaty."

The treaty. It was the subject he spoke of often.

The buggy slowed once again, and Elizabeth said in a low voice, "Will your clerk take over all your...duties?"

"Such as?"

She lifted a bare shoulder and toyed with a pleat of her skirt, suddenly unsure of herself.

He must have sensed her mood, because he said, "I much prefer the straightforward Elizabeth to this simpering coquette."

Simpering coquette? She crossed her arms and narrowed her eyes. If he wanted her to be straightforward, she would be. "Will you come to see me again, or will your clerk be sent to deal with me?"

He paused, and for a moment she held her breath. Finally, he spoke. "It's best if I don't see you again."

"Why?"

The fort appeared just ahead, and a ferry sat tied to the eastern shore, ready to take them across the river. Matthew jumped down from the buggy and walked the horses onto the large raft, never looking her way.

As the raft ferried them across the river, he discussed mundane affairs with the ferry driver and then walked the horses onto dry land when they stopped. He paid the driver, and they were on their way.

She wouldn't allow him to ignore her. "Why won't you come to see me again?"

The fort's gates were wide open, and buggies and wagons passed through the stockade, evidence of peaceful times. Matthew pulled into the fort and handed the reins over to a private waiting to take the horses to the large barn for the duration of the evening. Matthew walked around the buggy and offered a hand to Elizabeth.

She paused before laying her small hand inside his. As always, his touch stirred deep feelings inside her. She exited the buggy in the cumbersome gown and stood inches away from him, the skirt falling into place around her in a silent cascade of fabric.

He took a step toward the officer's barracks, but she didn't move. "Why, Matthew?"

Through the hues of emotion in his eyes, she saw a battle waging within him. She didn't care what he would say—as long as he told her the truth. "Is it because I'm an Indian?"

He frowned. "No, of course not."

"Then why?"

He watched her carefully. "I have a fiancée in St. Paul."

The truth felt like a blow to her stomach. Another woman claimed his heart—why had he not told her? "A fiancée?"

"Helen."

Elizabeth imagined Helen to be beautiful and charming. She must be magnificent to catch Matthew's attention. Elizabeth had to pretend his revelation didn't hurt. "Why isn't she here with you?"

"She would not come with me to this wilderness. Helen is too genteel for this place. She's waiting for me in St. Paul."

Elizabeth nodded as if she understood—but did she? Why would a woman allow Matthew Merrick to leave her side? Didn't she long to be with him, to warm him on cold nights, and sit with him at the end of the day? To listen to his worries and ease his burdens?

"Do you love...her?" She couldn't bring herself to say Helen's name.

He still held Elizabeth's hand, and he looked down at it now. "No." When he lifted his gaze, his eyes told her the truth, even before the words shuddered across his lips. "I don't love Helen. Not like I should. And I don't believe she loves me, either."

Hope flickered in her heart like the first hint of dawn spreading over a dark world.

People milled about the parade grounds, and lively music spilled from the officer's barracks on the opposite side of the fort. The buggy had been pulled away, but the two of them did not move.

"Why are you marrying her if you do not love her?" She craved his honesty—and had from the moment he walked into her father's cabin. In a world of men who lied and cheated to get ahead, she valued Matthew's desire to tell her the truth no matter the cost.

"I am marrying Helen for the same reason she is marrying me."

"Because you will gain something from the marriage."

He swallowed, and she saw shame in his eyes. "Yes."

"And what does Helen possess that only she can provide for you?" What she wanted to ask was what Helen possessed that Elizabeth lacked.

He didn't waver. "Connections."

"Because you want more than this life." She lifted her free hand and indicated the fort and the wilderness beyond. "You want power and wealth in the white man's world and Helen knows people who can help you achieve it?"

Pain filled his countenance, and he seemed to struggle with whatever battle was waging in his heart. "I want more than power and wealth. I want to find my father one day and prove to him that I'm not a mistake. I want him to know who I am and be ashamed of what he did to my mother, my sister, and me."

She dropped her gaze and studied their clasped hands. She didn't know what his father had done, but it must be bad if he was willing to have a loveless marriage to prove something to him.

"I know I have disappointed you, but I can't change who I am or what I want. My mother and sister deserve to live in a fine home and have everything they desire—everything my father denied them." His voice pleaded with her to understand. "I have worked my whole life to gain status and wealth—and I don't believe it's wrong for me to want either when I can use it for the people I love." He paused and she lifted her gaze, surprised at the vulnerability in his eyes. "I won't allow you to sway me, Elizabeth. I know what I want, and I know what I must do to get it."

She pulled her hand from his and took a moment to gather her composure.

He was warning her not to press him for more than he could give her. But could she heed his warning?

Chapter Five

JULY 1863

Matthew

Matthew paced along Crow Wing's riverside boardwalk weaving in and out of fur traders, Indians, and shop owners. The smell of the musty river mingled with the odor of dirty bodies and warm flesh. He shoved his hands in his pockets and turned toward the south watching for the stagecoach bearing Mr. Baker and the new clerk.

Chief White Thunder waited for them at his home—no doubt frustrated by the delay.

Matthew looked over the heads of the milling crowd toward the end of the eastern valley. Would Elizabeth be present for the meeting? It had been a month since the dance—but not one day had passed without his thoughts straying to the dark-haired young woman. He tried to put her out of his mind, to think of Helen and the impending nuptials, but when his mind was left to wonder on its own—as it so often did in an evening—it always found Elizabeth. Thoughts of her kept him company on dark, lonely nights.

"Ho, the stagecoach!" shouted a fur trader, his thick beard matted from months of uncleanliness.

Matthew shoved aside thoughts of Elizabeth and focused on his fiancée's father, Mr. Baker, who was about to arrive. As the newly appointed Superintendent of Indian Affairs for the Northern Superintendency, and former territorial legislator, Mr. Baker had amassed a great fortune in land holdings, business ventures, and political negotiations.

And he had been the one to introduce Matthew to Governor Hibbing.

The coach rounded the bend, its gleaming red surface shining under the afternoon sun, and came to a stop next to the saloon. Mr. Baker exited the conveyance first. His white beard came to a point just beneath his chin, and his matching white hair gleamed under his black derby. People sent cursory glances in his direction, but if anyone knew who he was they didn't give him much notice as they went about their business.

"Merrick," Mr. Baker called, waving him over.

Matthew hurried to Mr. Baker's side and extended his hand. "It's good to see you again, sir."

Mr. Baker squeezed Matthew's hand. "And you, Major Merrick."

Matthew swallowed and asked what he knew was expected. "How is Helen?"

Mr. Baker grinned and pulled a letter from his pocket. "She wanted to deliver this in person, but I wouldn't dream of letting her travel all the way here just for one night." He handed Matthew the letter. "I believe the letter contains all the wedding details."

Matthew took the letter and placed it in his pocket for later, trying to find a spark of enthusiasm for his future plans.

Mr. Baker nodded toward a gentleman exiting the stagecoach. "Major Merrick, may I present Jacob Bailey, your new clerk."

Matthew offered his hand and was pleased with the strength of Mr. Bailey's grip. He was not much older than Matthew and stood with a great deal of confidence. His cheerful brown eyes assessed Matthew and the little village in one grand sweep. A black derby covered his dark red hair, and his matching beard was neatly trimmed. His grin was quick and infectious. "It's a pleasure to meet you, Major."

"And you, Mr. Bailey."

"Please, call me Jacob."

"Pleasantries will need to wait," Mr. Baker said. "I'm eager to speak to Chief White Thunder. Shall we make haste?"

Matthew helped them with their luggage, leaving Jacob's trunk at the hotel for safe keeping until they could transfer it to the Indian Agency later that day.

"How have relations been between you and the chief?" Mr. Baker asked, his shrewd gaze scrutinizing Matthew's face as the men made their way up the hill and then descended into the valley toward the chief's home.

Matthew licked his lips and tried to muster a bit of the same confidence that Jacob displayed so effortlessly. "Things have gone well."

"Have you spent much time with him?"

"I've had many meetings with the chief, and I've attended two council meetings with the Mississippi and Red River bands."

Mr. Baker appeared pleased, but his voice remained grave. "I will watch the chief closely today, examining how he responds to you. This matter is very serious, and I need to make sure I have the right man in place to move our treaty negotiations forward."

Matthew rubbed his sweating palms against his pant legs. He could not disappoint his boss or the governor.

The cabin was strangely quiet as the men approached. Matthew was accustomed to seeing a passel of children playing in the yard. If the children had been taken away for this meeting, then surely Elizabeth was gone, as well.

A stab of disappointment was quickly followed by relief. Matthew couldn't risk Mr. Baker seeing his attraction to the young lady.

He forced himself to return his thoughts to the important meeting about to unfold.

The door opened before the men arrived, and Elizabeth's mother, Straw Weaver, greeted them with a grave nod. Today she wore a bright purple gown with wide hoops. Matthew made introductions and then she motioned them inside while the men took off their hats.

Smoke from the fireplace filled the room and made Matthew's eyes water. The chief sat on a buffalo robe on the ground wearing a black sack coat much like Matthew's, the ends of his long braids touching the fur beneath him. He was a youthful looking man, in his early forties. Well respected with his people and those in Washington, DC.

Matthew's gaze immediately found Elizabeth. She knelt, tending the fire, but when they entered, she rose and stood perfectly still. She wore a pink gown with full skirts and mutton sleeves, and her shiny hair was pulled back into a knitted snood. She was breathtaking.

Matthew introduced Mr. Baker and Jacob to Chief White Thunder and then turned to Elizabeth. Her brown eyes studied him as if she were feasting on his appearance after a long famine. The look made him stumble over his thoughts, but he spoke evenly, hoping to hide his reaction. "May I present Chief White Thunder's eldest daughter, Elizabeth?"

Mr. Baker crossed the room and took Elizabeth's hand in his. He bowed, a smile on his face. "It's a pleasure to meet you, Miss Elizabeth. Your beauty is spoken of all the way to St. Paul. I wish my own daughter, Helen, was here to meet you. She longs to meet a real Indian princess."

Elizabeth curtsied just as Matthew had shown her and offered the superintendent a gentle smile. "I'm honored to have you in my father's home." She didn't look at Matthew, but he knew she was conscious of him. "And I hope to meet your Helen one day."

"This is Mr. Jacob Bailey, my new clerk," Matthew said quickly.

Jacob followed Mr. Baker's lead and bowed over Elizabeth's hand. His brown eyes reflected his attraction to her, and he grinned at her like a man self-assured. "I'm pleased to meet you, Miss Elizabeth. I'm also taken with your beauty."

Elizabeth blushed at his praise, and her eyes shined. Her reaction surprised Matthew—given her hostility toward Matthew the first time he had entered this cabin two months ago.

The meeting proceeded and Chief White Thunder began by speaking highly of Matthew's work among the Chippewa. Mr. Baker nodded but pressed on to discuss the treaty. He made it known that Chief White Thunder would be greatly compensated with six hundred acres of prime land, as well as his annual annuity money if he could persuade the other band chiefs to sign the treaty.

Matthew listened intently, but he was conscious of Elizabeth's every move. As the afternoon wore on into evening, and the conversation began to go in circles, Matthew couldn't stop himself from stealing glances at her. She worked silently as she prepared the evening meal. He admired her graceful movements, and from time to time, she looked his way, offering him a smile.

Jacob watched Elizabeth, as well, and more than once he caught Matthew—a knowing look lighting his eyes.

Matthew wanted to linger over the delicious stew Elizabeth served, but he sensed Mr. Baker was finished with the meeting and it was time to take their leave.

The chief nodded at Matthew, his eyes solemn. "I would speak to you alone."

Mr. Baker was near the door, a bit frustrated at the lack of a promise from the chief, and he nodded at Matthew. "You've done well, Merrick. See that you take care of the chief's needs. We'll wait for you at the hotel."

Mr. Baker and Jacob said their goodbyes and left, but not before Jacob smiled one last time at Elizabeth.

As soon as the two men departed, the chief sat on his buffalo robe once again, and Matthew sat cross-legged next to him. Matthew wished he felt more at ease in this home so far removed from the realities of his early life—and the life he had started to build in St. Paul.

"You have done well with Elizabeth's schooling." Chief White Thunder nodded at his daughter who cleared the dishes from the table. "I am pleased."

Matthew felt a flush of pleasure come over him, and he caught Elizabeth's eye, but he controlled his face to prevent the chief from seeing his true feelings.

"Lieutenant Grey at Fort Ripley said Elizabeth acted like a lady at the dance." The chief's stoic face revealed no emotions.

"Elizabeth was every bit a lady at the dance," Matthew said, unable to temper the admiration in his voice. "She is a wonderful student."

"Good." The chief nodded. "I want her to have more lessons."

Elizabeth turned her back on them just then, and Matthew couldn't discern her feelings on the matter. Did *she* want more lessons?

"I can arrange more lessons with my clerk—"

"With you." Chief White Thunder pointed at Matthew's chest. "You will teach Elizabeth."

Elizabeth stilled in her work, but she didn't turn to look at him.

Matthew wanted to protest—he couldn't teach Elizabeth. She was too much of a distraction to him. He could hardly keep his mind focused when he was away from her—but to see her on a regular basis would be almost impossible.

"Mr. Bailey would make an excellent teach—"

"You." The chief crossed his arms.

Matthew glanced once again at Elizabeth, and this time she turned her head and looked at him, her beautiful eyes catching the light from the fire.

Chief White Thunder watched him closely, and Matthew worked hard to conceal his thoughts, keeping his face a mask of indifference.

"I trust you, Major Merrick," the chief said. "I know you are a good man, and Elizabeth is safe with you."

Matthew wanted to protest the chief's statement—Elizabeth was not safe with him when he was so attracted to her.

But she would have to be.

"I will come next Monday," Matthew said. "And we will continue our lessons."

The chief nodded, as if pleased with the arrangement.

Matthew wished he felt the same.

Matthew pushed open the door to the Indian Agency and took one handle of Jacob's trunk. Together, they hauled the heavy piece of luggage into the dark building, scraping its sides on the doorframe. They had left Mr. Baker at the hotel in Crow Wing and brought Jacob's belongings on a borrowed cart.

"My sister doesn't travel with nearly as much stuff as you," Matthew jested. "What's inside this trunk? Rocks?"

Jacob's laughter was quick and hearty. "I don't go anywhere without my books—especially to places with little entertainment to pass the time."

Matthew struck a match and put it to the wick of a lantern. Light filled the front room, revealing the sparse furnishings of the agent's house. A round table sat in one corner with two straight-backed chairs nestled beside it and a checkerboard on the top. A black cook stove sat in the other corner beside a cabinet filled with food staples and a handful of dishes. There were no rugs on the plank flooring, or curtains at the glass windows, or even pictures on the walls—nothing feminine to brighten the place.

Jacob glanced around the room but didn't comment.

Matthew pushed the trunk the rest of the way and closed the door. "We don't want the mosquitoes coming in after us. It would make for a miserable night of sleep." He pointed to the door on the right, next to the cook stove. "Your bedroom is in there—mine is next to it. Tomorrow, I'll show you around the agency. Through that door," he pointed to the third door in the room, "is the office. And out back are the warehouse and stable."

"Looks comfortable enough."

"It's been tolerable these past two months." Matthew lit a second lantern and then held up the cold coffee pot. "Feel like some coffee and a game of checkers before bed?"

Jacob's gaze turned competitive. "I'll offer a fair warning. It isn't often I lose something once I set my mind to win."

Matthew would enjoy some friendly competition after two months of solitude. "That makes two of us then." He started a fire in the stove and put the coffee pot on to warm. "Make yourself at home."

The chair scraped the floor and Jacob took a seat, stretching his long legs under the table. He was a good inch or two taller than Matthew and carried more muscle on his frame. Matthew grabbed two empty mugs from the cabinet and brought them to the table. "Tell me about those books in your trunk."

"My father taught me to read at the age of four and encouraged my love of literature. Each book I own is connected to a memory I have with him. Now that he's passed on, I can't seem to part with the books."

The only book Matthew had brought with him was the Bible his mother had given him before he came to Minnesota—though he had never opened it. Since meeting Tuck on the trail that first day, he had considered searching the Bible for the strange verses the old man had quoted—but Matthew had struggled with reading his whole life. The letters on the page were often jumbled and hard to understand. He had been ridiculed by his schoolmaster as a child and made to feel like an idiot. He finally began to make sense of the words when his sister Margaret took pity on him and taught him what she knew. Every word he had ever read had been a challenge—but he had fought hard for his education, determined to prove to his father he was worth something.

"I'm sorry to hear about your father," Matthew managed to say.

"He's been gone two years now." Jacob looked down at his folded hands, appearing to gather his emotions. "He was a good man. I miss him."

Matthew didn't want to continue this conversation—he couldn't risk Jacob asking about his family. He couldn't tell Jacob that his father was a congressman from Massachusetts who'd had an affair with his mother and left the moment she was pregnant. Eight months later, she had given birth to twins, a boy and a girl, and had lived a life of poverty and shame, while his father had gone on with his prosperous life.

"My father was a United States Senator," Jacob continued. "He was friends with Governor Hibbing. When the governor asked me to come to Minnesota to take on this position, it sounded like an adventure I couldn't resist." He grinned, and it was the smile of a privileged young man who had very few cares in the world.

Matthew's gut twisted with jealousy. Both men were fathered by politicians—but one was legitimate and the other was not. Neither man had been given a choice, but Jacob had been the lucky one. While Matthew had scrimped and saved to go to college, Jacob had probably spent lavishly to entertain himself. While Matthew had worked his way to Minnesota and slowly gained the trust and admiration of the governor, Jacob had probably dined and danced at politicians' homes. While Matthew had poured his life savings into charming Helen Baker, Jacob had probably poured his father's fortunes into numerous debutantes for fun. But now here they were, two men from two very different backgrounds doing the same work.

The only difference was that Matthew was the agent and Jacob the clerk—though it could change at the whim of the governor.

Matthew positioned the checkerboard between them and motioned for Jacob to make the first move.

"I heard that women are pretty scarce in these parts." Jacob changed the subject as he moved a black checker.

"It's true. As soon as a girl is old enough, she's usually married off. A week after I arrived, the hotel proprietor married a thirteen-year-old girl."

Jacob looked up quickly. "That's indecent."

Matthew shrugged and moved his red checker. "It's not something you hear of often back home—but out here there are few rules to govern society."

Jacob was silent as he made his next move. When he finished, he looked up, a hint of mischief in his gaze. "The chief's daughter appears to be of age, if my eyes don't deceive me."

Matthew masked his emotions at the mention of Elizabeth and moved his checker. "She is seventeen."

"Close enough." Jacob's voice dipped low. "There are no rules to govern a dalliance with a native girl, either, I'd wager."

Matthew barely controlled his temper as he met Jacob's gaze. "You're to stay away from Elizabeth, do you hear me? We can't risk the chief's ire."

"Or yours, apparently."

"We have a job to do—and we'll do it well. The governor and Mr. Baker hope the treaty will be signed in October by Chief White Thunder. If you make trouble with his daughter, it could ruin everything."

Jacob put up his hands. "Easy there, Matt. There's no need to worry."

"I won't worry as long as you keep your eyes and hands to yourself."

Jacob lifted his brow, accusation crowding the humor in his gaze. "I saw you in the chief's cabin. You couldn't keep your eyes off the girl—"

"Don't concern yourself with me."

"You may look but I cannot?"

Matthew sensed he needed to establish his authority here and now. "As your boss I am commanding you to stay away from Elizabeth."

Jacob lightly punched Matthew on the shoulder. His lips smiled, but there was a challenge in his eyes. "So you can keep her for yourself, Matt, old boy?"

Matthew stood, looking down at Jacob. "You will call me Major—and I will not tolerate insubordination. Do as I say or I will report you to the superintendent."

"Ah, yes, your soon-to-be father-in-law."

Matthew stared at him but didn't bother to answer. Right now, it didn't matter who the superintendent was.

Jacob was silent as he stared back at Matthew. Finally, he spoke. "No need to get upset. I'll do as you say. I was just having some fun."

The coffee began to boil, and Matthew walked across the room to take it off the heat. "You can have all the fun you want but stay away from Elizabeth and we'll get along just fine."

Chapter Six

OCTOBER 1917

CADE

The sun peeked over the horizon, sending rays of light dancing on the frost-kissed earth. Cade leaned against the open barn door and inhaled a lungful of air. Two pails of fresh milk sat on the ground next to him, their steam rising into the cold October morning.

His eyes roamed the old familiar farm. Without Grandfather's presence, the place had a different feel. What would it have been like to grow up here without his cruelty and anger hovering over everything? Would Cade have loved this place like his father did? Or would he still have needed to get away? He picked up the milk pails and followed the hard-packed trail from the barn to the house, not wanting to contemplate things that could never be undone.

He wasn't ready to tell his parents he was enlisting, but he needed to get it over with so he could make the early afternoon train to St. Paul. He exhaled into the cool air and watched it funnel out of his mouth in a cloud. His chest felt tight as he glanced at his biplane. He would leave it for Henry to sell—and hopefully it would be enough to help save the farm.

The back door of the farmhouse creaked open, and his mother stepped outside. She didn't wear her shawl, and something about her stance made Cade's heart thud a little faster.

"Is it Dad?"

Tears glistened in her eyes. "It's Henry—he's left." She pulled a letter from her apron pocket. "I just found this in his room."

Cade set down the pails and took the missive from her shaking hands. He quickly read the two brief sentences.

I've gone to enlist in the army. It's Cade's turn to stay home.

He gripped the edges of the paper, feeling the weight of the message pinning him to this place.

Mama's chin dropped. "Not Henry."

"I'll go get him." Desperation tightened Cade's voice as he put his arms around his mother. Henry couldn't go to war. What if he didn't come back? It was Cade who should go. It was his turn to sacrifice for the family. "He couldn't have gone far."

"I haven't seen him since supper last night, and his bed was untouched. He's probably already at Fort Snelling."

"No." Cade pulled away from his mother and ran his hands through his hair. "I was supposed to go—not Henry. He should be here, safe on the farm."

"It's too late." Mama's eyes were red and swollen from her tears. "Who will run the farm?"

Cade's heart filled with panic at the thought of staying. He couldn't stay—he wasn't capable of staying. When things became tough, he would run. He always had. What would happen to his mother and sister then?

He put his arms around his mother again. "Don't worry. Henry will be fine." He choked on his next words, saying them only because they needed to be said and not because he wanted to say them. But what choice did he have? "I'll stay until he comes back."

A glimmer of relief crossed Mama's face, even as grief creased her gentle eyes and mouth.

He walked her back into the house and poured her a cup of coffee, then he went outside and crossed the field toward his airplane. Anger at Henry welled up in his chest and he clenched his fists. His brother had no business going to war. It was selfish and inconsiderate of him to leave.

Cade stopped short, realizing it was exactly what he had done seven years ago. Had Henry felt this way then?

He needed to get away—to release the anger burning like hot coal in his stomach. He turned the propeller and jumped into the cockpit, quickly starting the engine. With shaking hands, he put on his leather helmet and goggles and then he took off toward the east.

He flew aimlessly over the land of his childhood. The sun rose higher in the sky, shifting the shadows over the hills and fields. He stayed within a ten-mile radius of the farmhouse, circling around and around, as if his plane was tethered to the farm and could only go so far.

He soared over the lakes and rivers where he had spent hours fishing and over the woods where he had hunted deer. He crossed familiar fields, already harvested, and the one-room schoolhouse where he had learned about the immense earth he inhabited.

But it was the spot near the road, where his father had found him nearly frozen to death, which resurrected the strongest memories. Matthew Merrick had visited that day and Cade had run away when the men had become angry. Shortly afterward, Grandfather became ill and then Cade had run away again, which prompted his father to come looking for him. Father had become sick and nearly died. He had never regained his strength and the farm had suffered because of it.

The whir of the engine blocked out all noise, but could never drown out his thoughts.

If he was a praying man, he would ask God to give him the strength to stay—but he wasn't a praying man. He believed a man made his own destiny, fighting for what he wanted. His father, on the other hand, believed a man needed to be still and wait on the Lord.

Cade had no time for a God who asked a man to be weak.

The sun had fully risen by the time he landed his plane in the north field. He sat in the cockpit for a long time, running his hand over the instrument panel, fighting the emotions welling up inside. It felt like he was pouring salt into a wound at the thought of selling his airplane, but it was the only way they could make a dent in the mortgage payment.

It was his last connection to freedom, and it was slipping away like everything else.

His legs felt heavy as he jumped out of his airplane and strode across the field toward his bleak future.

He would pay off the mortgage and get the farm back in shape—and as soon as Henry returned, he would leave.

EMMA

The early morning sunshine kissed the autumn colors and made them vibrant against the blue sky. Emma took a deep breath to still her nerves. She gripped the wheel of her Ford until her hands ached. The drive out to the Bailey farm took over an hour—no small trip, especially if Cade had already left or if he didn't have any advice for her.

She pulled into the Bailey's drive and stopped near the barn. She wasn't surprised when Cade stepped out of the building. He wore denim trousers and a white shirt, buttoned down the front and rolled at the sleeves. His handsome face needed a shave, and his hair looked tousled. He carried himself with an intriguing mixture of confidence and defeat—stirring Emma's curiosity.

She stalled the engine and stepped out of the Ford. The back door of the farmhouse opened, and an older woman poked her head out into the chilly October morning.

"It's all right, Mama," Cade said.

Mrs. Bailey studied Emma for a moment and then went back inside, closing the door gently behind her.

"It's a bit early to make a house call, isn't it?" Cade asked, leaning against the doorframe, his arms crossed over his chest.

Emma closed the car door and walked around the Ford to stand in front of him. She wore her Red Cross uniform under a heavy wool coat. "I'm not here to make a house call."

He openly studied her but didn't speak.

"I'm here to ask a question."

Still, he didn't speak.

She sensed he didn't like her—but she couldn't understand why. Had she done something to make him upset?

Emma cleared her throat. "I'd like to learn how to fly."

He continued to watch her, but she couldn't discern his thoughts. His gaze was disconcerting, and she suddenly felt less confident with her idea. Did he think it was foolish?

"What do you want from me?" he asked.

"I'd like to know where I could learn."

"I can't help you."

"Why?"

"You're a Merrick."

A frown etched her brow. "But that's ridiculous."

"Your father betrayed my grandfather a long time ago and it's caused our family a lot of trouble."

A cold wind snaked around her ankles as anger squeezed her chest. "I am nothing like my father. Whatever he did has nothing to do with me." Emma hardly knew her father. He had lived a lifetime before she was even born—and that life was a mystery to her. Other than carrying his name, she had nothing to do with him. "I simply need the name of a flying teacher."

"I don't know anyone who could teach you." He turned toward the barn—but she wouldn't take no for an answer. She raced around him and barred his entry into the barn.

"Please," she said.

He stood close to her—too close. His eyes flickered with surprise and awareness. A bit of bluster dropped from his countenance.

"Just a name," she said, "and then I won't bother you again. You're going to enlist—"

"Not anymore."

She paused. "You're not leaving?"

He looked away and his jaw became tight. "No."

If he wasn't leaving, then..."Could you teach me?"

His gaze returned to her face. "No." He squeezed past her and entered the barn.

Emma followed him into the warm space. The unmistakable smell of animals greeted her nose, but it wasn't unpleasant. A tabby cat walked up to Emma and rubbed against her leg. "I can pay you."

Cade didn't bother to look over his shoulder as he sat on the stool next to a black and white Holstein and started to milk her.

"Whatever you ask, I'll pay," she said.

"I won't take Merrick money."

Emma ground her teeth and crossed her arms. "There's nothing wrong with my money."

He grunted.

She walked over to him and stood by his side. "I'm offering you a job—one that won't take you away from the farm. I just need enough lessons to pass a licensing test—and then I won't ever offer you Merrick money again."

"I'm planning to sell the airplane."

"Why?"

His eyes became hard. "We need the money."

"But why would you sell the plane when it could make you money?"

He looked at her, this time he appeared to consider her offer. After a moment, he nodded. "Fine. Wait for me to finish here and I'll take you up on your first flight."

Emma clutched the lapels of her coat, surprised by the suddenness of his offer. "Now?"

"Why not?"

She looked down. "Is this the right thing to wear?"

His eyes followed the length of her body before looking away quickly. "That's fine."

She stood by and watched as he finished his chores and then he put on his wool coat and walked out of the barn, toward the field.

Emma practically ran to keep up with him, her heart thudding against her ribcage, half in trepidation and half in excitement. She had only seen one other airplane, when she was fifteen. A pilot had flown into Little Falls and done an exhibition at the county fair. That airplane had been a simple machine—nothing like the sleek biplane in front of her.

"You'll sit in the front cockpit," Cade said, not bothering to glance back to see if she was close enough to hear him. "The airplane has dual controls, but I don't want you to touch anything this first time up."

"I won't fly toda—?"

"No."

They arrived at the airplane and Cade reached inside and pulled out two leather caps and flying goggles. "Put these on." He handed her one of each and then moved around to the front of the plane.

Emma's hands trembled as she took off her Panama hat and set it on the ground. She put the cap over her curls, tucking them in where they escaped, and then put on the goggles.

Cade was busy inspecting the airplane, but she caught him glancing in her direction, and the look sent a skittering sensation through her midsection.

She wasn't prepared to analyze the reason.

"Go ahead and get into the cockpit," he said.

She picked up her hat and looked at the airplane carefully. The front cockpit was high off the ground, wedged between the bottom and top wings, requiring her to climb—and Cade was near the propeller. Was he testing her to see if she was independent and determined enough to fly?

She squared her shoulders and approached the airplane, ready to meet every challenge he threw at her head on. She tossed her hat into the cockpit and grabbed a wire with her right hand and the back cockpit with her left, stepping onto the bottom wing. It slanted under her feet, making her thankful for her sensible boots. She was also thankful for the years of ballet lessons her mother had insisted on and the strength and agility it had given her. With little effort, she climbed the wing and pulled herself into the front cockpit.

She glanced up—feeling a bit triumphant—and saw that Cade had been watching. He didn't say anything as he looked away, but she saw the admiration in his face.

An instrument panel was directly in front of her on a wooden board. The whicker seat was pleasant, though not entirely comfortable, with the top wing directly above her head. A thrill ran up her spine as she waited for Cade.

Finally, he jumped into the cockpit behind her and the engine roared to life. The propeller spun so quickly, it looked like a solid blur. After a moment, the airplane began to roll across the uneven field. Emma gripped the side of the cockpit as the airplane picked up speed, pushing cold wind against Emma's face. She snuggled deeper into her jacket, thankful for the warmth it provided.

Emma knew the moment the wheels left the ground. A strange, weightless feeling came upon her, and she looked over the side of the airplane at the fading field. The higher the airplane climbed, the wider Emma's smile became. An extraordinary sensation overcame her—one she had never felt before.

Freedom.

The sky was a brilliant shade of blue, and the autumn colors filled the earth below like a canvas painted by the Master's hand. The river and lakes sparkled in the early morning sunshine, and the farmhouses became tiny specks. Emma looked out as far as she could see for miles and miles. Hills and valleys gave way to forests and patchwork fields. The river looked like a long ribbon, weaving through a magnificent tapestry.

Emma turned and met Cade's eyes. She couldn't help but smile—and finally he offered her a smile in return. How could he not? Something magical bonded them together—this view of the world. How was a person ever the same once they beheld the earth from this perspective?

She settled back into her seat and watched the landscape roll and level out below her.

Cade flew above the earth for about twenty minutes, dipping and banking the airplane, allowing her to feel the different movements of the aircraft.

All too soon, he directed the plane toward the farm and landed in the field.

Emma was breathless. Was it possible she could one day pilot an airplane?

Cade jumped out of the cockpit behind her.

She took off her flying cap and goggles and threw her head back with a laugh, feeling the sunshine on her face. "That was incredible!"

He stood on the ground and watched her.

She climbed out of the cockpit and stepped onto the lower wing, a grin on her face. "I'll never be the same."

He lifted his arms to help her from the wing. She bent over and put her hands on his shoulders. His hands grasped her waist and he lowered her to the ground.

They stood facing one another.

"Thank you," she said, unable to voice all the feelings mixed up inside of her.

He swallowed and took a step back, his voice gruff. "You can pay me next time you come."

He walked back toward the farmhouse and Emma's smile fell.

Chapter Seven

Emma

Emma stifled a yawn as she descended the stairs in her evening gown. Her head felt heavy, and her feet ached from standing too long at the hospital. After her flying lesson, she had gone to work and stayed much later than she should have. Mother had a dinner party planned and she would be upset with Emma once again.

The front parlor was aglow with light as Emma entered. A dozen guests mingled, their tinkling laughter filling the room with an atmosphere of gaiety that grated on Emma's nerves. For once, she'd like simply to come home from a long day of work and relax.

Mother stood near the ornate fireplace. She wore a lovely lavender gown with a diamond tiara in her auburn curls.

Emma began to walk across the room to join her mother but stopped short when she saw her father standing on the opposite side of the room. He so rarely attended Mother's soirées she had not anticipated his presence.

He glanced up at her arrival and his green eyes swept over her appearance. Just as quickly, he looked back to the gentleman who faced him. He said something to the man and then nodded in Emma's direction.

The gentleman turned and Emma was immediately taken with his appearance. He was tall with dark curls and stunning blue eyes. When he smiled, she found herself smiling in return.

Father led him to Emma and her stomach tightened with unexpected nerves. Very few people had that effect on her.

"Thomas, may I present my daughter, Emma Merrick." Father looked at Emma. "This is Thomas Overton, my new business manager."

Emma extended her gloved hand toward Mr. Overton.

He took her hand and bowed over it. "It's a pleasure to finally meet you, Miss Merrick. Your father has told me much about you."

He had? Emma looked at her father, never more surprised. She wished she knew what he had said. He hardly knew her well enough to share more than her birthday and her name.

Belatedly, she remembered her manners and smiled at Mr. Overton. "It's a pleasure to meet you, as well."

Mother joined them and stood next to her father. "I can see your father introduced you." Mother smiled at Father and Emma began to feel uncomfortable.

"Mr. Overton, I've taken the liberty to place you next to Emma at supper tonight." Mother turned her smile toward their guest, her dark brown eyes flirting with practiced subtly. "Will you escort her into the dining room?"

"It will be my honor."

"Splendid!" Mother glanced at Emma, her gaze roaming over her appearance. She offered Emma the slightest chastisement with her eyes but then turned away without another word.

Father cleared his throat and stepped away, muttering, "If you'll excuse me."

Emma looked at Mr. Overton. "I'm sorry for their abrupt departure."

He laughed and Emma found herself liking him instantly. He had a calm, confident demeanor that put her at ease. "Please don't worry." He leaned close, as if sharing a secret. "I'm happy they left. I'd much prefer to talk to you."

Her cheeks warmed at his flirting.

"I've been hoping to meet you," he said. "You're even lovelier than your father claimed."

Father had said she was lovely? She was speechless.

"You look a great deal like your mother," he continued.

Emma glanced at her mother and couldn't disagree. They shared the same brown eyes and auburn curls and were precisely the same size. Her mother was stunning—but in a cool sort of way.

"Where do you hale from, Mr. Overton?"

"Please, call me Thomas—or Tommy, if you prefer."

She smiled, happy to be done with pretenses. "Thomas suits you."

"And may I call you Emma?"

"Please do."

"I'm from Minneapolis. I worked for your father at his mill. When he offered me the job here, I couldn't refuse."

"Will you be managing Elk City, or his lumber business?"

"His lumber business—but here, here, I don't want to talk about myself. I want to learn about you and your work. Is it true you're the first Town and Country Nurse in Minnesota?"

She stared at him. "How did you know?"

His smile came effortlessly. "Whenever I tell people I work for Major Merrick, inevitably your name arises. People have told me wonderful things about you."

The heat in Emma's cheeks traveled to her neck and she couldn't meet his eyes. "That's quite a compliment."

He laughed. "I appreciate your humility. Most young ladies who are as beautiful as you, with wealth and status, have far too much pride in themselves."

His frank assessment left her speechless again.

"I'm sorry. I can see I've made you uncomfortable." His voice quieted and he tilted his head to get her to look at him. "I really do want to hear about your job. I'm fascinated with the American Red Cross and the work they're doing to mobilize the country's war efforts."

Just then, Mr. Stearns, the elderly butler, walked into the room and bowed. "Dinner is served."

Father offered his arm to one of Mother's friends and they left the parlor first, followed by all the other couples. Mother would be the last to leave the room, a young, handsome gentleman on her arm.

The dining room was decorated in rich mahogany wood with a long dining table loaded with piles of fruit in silver bowls. Three tall candelabras sat in the middle of the table with a long white tablecloth beneath.

Emma and Thomas found their place cards and he held the chair for her to sit. He took the seat next to her and hardly looked at anyone else at the table.

"Do you like your work, Emma?"

She took her gloves off and laid them in her lap, glancing at her mother, sitting too far away to hear. "I knew I wanted to be a nurse when I was a young girl—but I never dreamed I would have the opportunity."

"And how did you come by the opportunity?"

Was he truly curious? Or was he just passing the time? Her mother was watching her now. "I don't know if this is the right time to talk about my work."

"I wish you would." He glanced at Mother and then back at Emma. "I'm enjoying myself immensely."

She took a sip of her water. What would it hurt to talk about the Red Cross? It was a refreshing change of conversation around this table. "When I graduated high school, I enrolled in St. Raphael's Training School for Nurses in St. Cloud." She didn't add that she had fought her mother for an entire year before her enrollment. When her mother realized she would have no choice, she only gave her consent after Emma promised her studies would not interfere with her social obligations. "I graduated in May with the class of 1917 and went to work at St. Gabriel's Hospital here in town. When I heard the Red Cross was looking for Town and Country nurses, I immediately contacted the headquarters in Minneapolis and volunteered."

His handsome brow dipped and he moved aside to allow the footman to place his bowl of creamed soup in front of him. "I'm curious why a young woman from a family like this would choose to pursue a profession."

There was no censure in his voice, but Emma couldn't help but feel chastised. He was not the first to ask her this question, though he asked it much kinder than others had.

The footman placed her bowl before her, and she looked at the steam rising in a curl of tantalizing scents. "It may surprise you—but I do not care for this lifestyle. I'm thankful—but—"

"But it doesn't fulfill you."

She turned to him and nodded. "Exactly."

"I admire you, Emma." He offered her one of his easy smiles and she felt herself relax in his company. "I hope you have great success in all your endeavors."

She almost told him about her flying lessons—but she could not risk her mother overhearing.

Mother would never allow her to continue if she found out.

Emma lifted her spoon and dipped it into her soup.

"Would you allow me to call on you sometime—when there are less people around?"

Emma stopped her soup midway to her mouth and turned to look at Thomas.

While going to school and pursuing her work, she'd had little time for suitors—and had never met any she'd like to make time for. Until now.

Emma's gaze fell on her father at the head of the table. He sat watched her closely for the first time in her life.

Chapter Eight

NOVEMBER 1917

Cade

Cade sat at the kitchen table, the family ledger open before him. He stared at the paltry sum in the right column and ran his hands through his hair. They were still fifty dollars short of the first mortgage payment due in December. He only had four weeks to come up with the money. Already the crops were all harvested and sold, and Cade had paid the notes at the grocer's and the feed store. Mama made a few dollars selling eggs and butter—but there was no other income coming from the farm. There wasn't anything much to sell, either.

Emma Merrick had paid him for the first flying lesson, but that was nothing compared to what they needed. She was due to come for another lesson—but with the approaching winter, they would cease soon. He had considered selling his plane again, but the thought of using his plane to make money was more appealing—and, in all truth, he couldn't get what he needed for it anyway. With the war, very few people were spending money frivolously.

Somehow, Cade would need to find work, though he could hardly find time to keep up with the farm.

"Cade." Mama touched him on the shoulder.

He had been so lost in thought he hadn't heard her approach. He glanced up at her now and saw the worry lines around her mouth. "Is Gracie feeling any better?"

She shook her head. "She's running a fever now, and her abdomen has become too tender to touch. I fear it's her appendix. I think it best if we bring her to the hospital. I know it will cost more money, bu—"

"It doesn't matter how much it costs." Cade closed the ledger. "I'll bring her in the plane—the Ford will take too much time and it's a bumpy ride."

"Should I come?" Mama asked. "I want to be with Gracie, but I also need to stay and take care of your dad and the farm."

He stood and put the ledger on the shelf. "I'll take care of her—and try not to worry."

Ten minutes later, Cade carried Gracie out to the biplane, Mama trailing behind with a bag of her things.

Gracie was an exact replica of their mother, with blonde hair and big blue eyes. She was also paper-thin, and it took no effort for Cade to carry her.

"I'm happy you're home," Gracie whispered through her tears.

Cade held her closer and was careful, lest he cause her more pain.

Mama kissed Gracie and said a prayer for her, then Cade set the little girl in the front cockpit and tucked blankets in around her. "There's no reason to be scared." He smiled, hoping to reassure her. "It will be bumpy for a couple of minutes, and then we'll be in the air and to the hospital as soon as I can get us there."

Tears trailed down her cheeks, but she nodded.

Cade climbed into the back cockpit and Mama twisted the propeller. He started the engine, and the plane moved over the ground, each bump making him cringe.

Gracie was so small he couldn't see her head in the cockpit in front of him. He could only hope she was okay.

He flew directly toward Little Falls. It was the largest city nearby with two hospitals. One was run by Dr. Hall and the other by the Franciscan Sisters. The latter hospital was bigger and would be more prepared to handle an emergency. It was on the outskirts of town and offered a field to land in nearby.

It was also the hospital where Emma Merrick worked.

The Mississippi ran through Little Falls, dissecting the growing town in half. The western banks of the river were crowded with industries, all vying for power from the dam—and the eastern side was populated with shops, businesses, and homes.

Cade flew over the town toward the southern border and landed in the field near the sisters' barn. He pulled himself from the back cockpit and climbed the wings to get to Grace.

She had fallen asleep on the way, her head leaning against the side of the cockpit.

He gently lifted her, and she cried out in pain. He hated to move her, but there was nothing to be done about it.

A nurse exited the hospital—Emma. She raced across the field and Cade met her half way, holding his sister in his arms.

"We think it's her appendix," he said to Emma. "She's running a fever and has terrible pain."

Emma's brown eyes filled with concern as she glanced at Grace. "Follow me."

Cade followed her into St. Gabriel's, past the waiting area where he had sat with Emma two weeks ago, and to an examination room down a hall.

"We'll take care of her from here," Emma said. "You can wait in the front."

Grace's face was pale, and her eyes were glazed with pain. Cade bent over and placed a kiss on her forehead and then left the room.

He took a seat in the waiting area, clutching his cap and goggles in his hands. He hated to think about how much all of this would cost—and where would they get the money? His gut twisted with dread, and he bent over to put his elbows on his knees. He hated feeling like a failure—and he hated even more thinking about failing his family. Grandfather had held on to the farm through thick and thin for almost fifty years—would Cade be the one to lose everything?

The door opened to the exam room and Emma stepped out, closing the door softly behind her.

Cade stood at her approach.

Her cheeks were flushed, and a wayward curl peeked out from beneath her white nurse's cap. Her face was serious. "Dr. McCall is with her right now. He needs to perform an emergency appendectomy."

Cade nodded, not surprised.

"After the surgery, she will need to stay in the hospital to recover. It may be a few weeks, depending on how advanced her appendicitis is."

He despised himself for thinking about the price—but how much would a two-week stay cost? "Do whatever is necessary."

Her eyes became gentle. "She's in good hands, Cade. Dr. McCall is the best surgeon in town. I'll update you on the progress."

Cade watched her walk back down the hall toward his sister's room. She glanced at him and offered the smallest smile, then pushed the door open and disappeared.

Cade couldn't sit, so he stood in the waiting room and paced across the wood floor.

Nurses, patients, and visitors came and went—and still he waited.

The afternoon sun slipped below the horizon and soon the hospital lights were turned on. If he didn't fly home soon, he would be stuck in town for the night.

He eyed the hard, wooden benches, hoping they wouldn't be his bed for the evening.

A door creaked open, and Emma appeared once again. She removed a mask she wore over her face, and the first thing he noticed was her beautiful smile. "She did splendidly."

Cade let out a sigh of relief. "Is the surgery over?"

"Yes. She's resting now. Dr. McCall would like her to stay here for at least two weeks."

"Two weeks?" Cade didn't want to do the financial math in his head.

"Yes. Tonight is critical. The appendix was very inflamed, and the doctor wants us to monitor her to see if the infection was isolated or if it has affected her whole body."

Cade glanced outside. Night had fallen, and it was now too late for him to fly home.

She must have read his thoughts. "We don't have visitor sleeping quarters, I'm afraid, and visiting hours will end at eight o'clock." Emma nibbled on her bottom lip. "There are cots set up for the nurses who work here overnight—maybe I can get one for you, and we can find a quiet corner to put you in."

"Anything will be better than these chairs."

She smiled, and he was struck by the look of compassion on her face. "I'll see what I can do. Why don't you go in and see Grace?"

He did as she suggested. Grace was asleep in her bed, looking serene for the first time in days. He laid his hand on her forehead, thinking of all the years he had missed with her.

After a little while, the door opened, and Emma stood in the hallway. She motioned for him to join her.

He couldn't stop himself, even if he tried.

Their footsteps echoed off the bare stairwell as Cade followed Emma to the basement of the hospital. He just wanted to find a quiet place to sleep. He was exhausted and tomorrow would be another busy day at the farm. He needed all the rest he could find.

Emma's white hat shined bright, despite the shadowed stairway, and he had the opportunity to study her as they descended. He admired the way she carried herself with a mixture of grace and determination. It was clear she had a heart to serve others, but where did that heart come from? As Major Merrick's daughter, she could have everything she desired. They were the wealthiest family in the county—perhaps the state. Very few people with that much money lowered themselves to serve the way she did.

"I set up a cot for you in the dining room," she said quietly. "It isn't much, I'm afraid, but no one will bother you down here until morning when the kitchen staff comes in to prepare breakfast."

She pushed open the door and he followed her into the kitchen. He was met with the familiar smells of pot roast and chocolate cake lingering in the room. She reached over and switched on the lights and then turned abruptly.

He wasn't prepared for her sudden closeness.

She took a step back, her cheeks filling with color. "Pardon me. I-I was just going to ask if you'd like something to eat. You've been here for hours."

"You've done more than enough. I don't want you to go to the trouble of preparing something for me."

"I'm simply doing my job."

He studied her, surprised at her humility. "You've done more than the others would."

She lowered her eyes until her eyelashes brushed her high cheekbones. "How about coffee?" She stepped over to the stove and took a match from the dispenser.

"I'm fine, really."

She struck the match and turned the stove's knob, opening the gas. "You might be fine, but I need some coffee." The gas caught fire and she shook out the match.

The hospital kitchen was modern with two large windows at the top of the room looking out at ground level, revealing the starry sky.

Emma took a coffeepot and filled it with water and then she set the brew basket inside and filled it with the coffee grounds. The wonderful aroma met Cade's nose and made him almost groan.

"On second thought." He took a seat at a table in the corner. "I think I will have some coffee." He used the opportunity to watch her work. His mother had always said she could tell a lot about a woman by how she handled herself in the kitchen.

Emma located a loaf of bread and a jar of jam and brought them to the table. She went back for a knife and coffee mugs, and on her third trip she found the sugar and cream.

"I'm surprised you know your way around the kitchen," he said.

She tilted a brow and took a seat, her eyes sparkling with a challenge. "If you took time to know me, you'd find many things that surprise you."

When he first met her, he thought he had her all figured out. She had been raised with all that money could buy, and she could do anything her heart desired. She seemed to have a natural ability as a nurse, but he assumed it was a passing hobby until she made an advantageous match.

Now he wasn't so sure.

He picked up the knife and cut a couple slices of bread, handing one to her, then he took a scoop of jam out of the jar. "What might I learn that would surprise me?"

She studied him, her eyes very serious. "Once you said you wouldn't help me because I'm a Merrick."

He remembered quite well.

"And I tried to tell you I have nothing to do with my father—but what I should have said is that he has nothing to do with me."

He set down his bread. "What do you mean?"

"I was born when he was well into his fifties." She rearranged the items on the table, not looking at him. "He's never liked me. Maybe, if we had a conversation, he'd find I'm a likable person." She smiled at him, but there was a great deal of sadness behind her words.

He stared at her, truly surprised at her revelation. "Haven't you ever had a conversation?"

She shook her head. "He's never gone out of his way to spend time with me. I think—" she paused and looked unsure if she should continue.

"You think what?"

"I think I was a mistake."

"How could you be a mistake?"

"I don't know. I've just always felt like I was an inconvenience to my parents. I feel like every time my father looks at me, he sees someone—or something else—that makes him upset. I can't explain it."

He knew exactly what she meant. "My grandfather said I reminded him of someone he despised."

It was her turn to study him, her brown eyes sad. "That's awful."

He didn't like the direction the conversation was going. He hadn't intended to divulge something he'd never revealed to anyone else.

Emma must have sensed his discomfort. She scooped jam out of the jar and spread it on her bread. "What is it like to be famous?"

He smiled ruefully at the question. "Now that I'm back, it almost feels like I dreamed that part of my life."

"Do you think you'll ever fly like that again?"

Thoughts of the girl lying under the sheet at Bay Meadows filled his mind. He stood and walked to the stove to check the coffee. "It looks like it's starting to boil."

She approached him. "I'm sorry, Cade."

He loved the sound of his name on her lips.

"I shouldn't—"

"Right now all I need to do is worry about saving our farm," he said. "I can't think about flying."

"Saving your farm?" She frowned. "I didn't know it was in danger."

Why had he told her? It wasn't anyone's business, least of all Matthew Merrick's daughter. He still recalled Matthew visiting the day his grandfather suffered from apoplexy, and later, his grandfather making both him and his father promise to never sell to Merrick. What would happen if Merrick found out they were about to lose the farm? Would he swoop in and try to take it?

He leaned against the sink. He needed to say something. "We have a mortgage payment due in a little over a month—and another one due in June. I'll find a way to make the money."

"Have you thought of doing an aerial show? I've heard they can bring in a great deal of money."

He wouldn't discuss it. He pushed away from the sink and walked back to the table. "Why did you become a nurse?"

She reached for two spoons and brought them to the table. "No one has ever asked why I wanted to be a nurse. They usually want to know why a privileged young woman would get her hands dirty when she doesn't need to."

She took off her white cap and laid it on the table with a gentleness he was coming to admire in her. "It's the one thing I do that makes me feel like I have value—that I'm not a mistake and there is a purpose for my life."

Once again, she took him by surprise. It wasn't a passing hobby, but her purpose in life.

"Why did you become a pilot?" she asked.

She had been honest with him, and he owed her the same courtesy. "It was my only escape from my grandfather."

"Did you truly escape?" she asked.

Had he? "Not really, I suppose."

"That's because true freedom only comes from one source."

"What is that?"

"Jesus."

He studied her. "I didn't know you were a Christian."

Her face filled with a sadness he couldn't explain. "Then shame on me," she said. "I had hoped everyone could see."

The aroma of freshly brewed coffee filled the air, and she stood to take the pot off the burner. As she walked away, he was struck by how obvious her faith was now that he knew. He recognized the same selfless love and patience in Emma that he saw in his parents—but where he saw his parent's faith as weakness, in Emma Merrick, it was a strength.

The difference puzzled him.

She came back with the steaming coffeepot and poured some amber liquid into his mug.

"Why do you want to fly?" he asked.

She poured her own coffee and then set the pot on a trivet on the table.

"I want to get to every person I possibly can to offer them care and hope." She sat across from him and hugged her mug between her slender hands. "It takes me hours to travel by automobile. When I have a pilot's license, I could go almost anywhere in a fraction of the time. Just think how quickly I could arrive after a disaster or in an emergency."

His reasons for flying seemed selfish compared to hers. The least he could do was help her. "I'm at your disposal, should the need arise, until you can fly on your own."

A beautiful smile filled her face.

If offering to help her made such a smile possible, he would do it again and again.

Chapter Nine

MATTHEW

Matthew sat in his office staring out his windows at the starry night. Any moment, Mr. Stearns would announce Emma's arrival home from the hospital, and when he did, Matthew would tell Emma what he expected her to do.

He had long since come to terms with the fact that he would have no male heir. After Jacob's passing five years ago, he had wanted to tell Nathan the truth—but he realized what a scandal it would cause. He was in no position to admit he had a son with an Indian woman. Not only would his business suffer, he wouldn't put it past Edith to divorce him and take half of his fortune. She would use any excuse she could find.

Besides, it wasn't fair to tell Nathan after all these years. It would only upset him—which was the last thing Matthew wanted.

In the ensuing years, his thoughts had often turned to Emma and what she meant to his estate and legacy. She so closely resembled Edith, he had been convinced she was a wolf in sheep's clothing, just as Edith had been before they were married. He had waited for the day she would reveal her true nature.

As the years had passed, he often inquired after the girl from Sam, who had a pulse on everyone's activities at Elk Manor. What he found surprised him. Despite Emma's upbringing, she appeared to be a sensible young woman with a heart to serve others.

It made Matthew's decision easier to make.

A knock at the door sent Matthew's pulse racing. "Come in."

"Miss Emma has returned home, sir." Mr. Stearns was so old and bent over, he could hardly walk straight, but Matthew couldn't see a way to let him go after so many years when the man still wanted to work. "I told her you wanted to see her."

"Send her in."

"Yes, sir."

Mr. Stearns slowly backed out of the room and Emma appeared at the door.

Every time he looked at the young woman, he was struck by her shocking resemblance to Edith. She gazed at him with the same brown eyes, and her auburn hair curled in the exact same way. It was like looking at Edith for the first time at Helen's funeral, and his resentment mounted.

She walked into the room slowly, as if she were walking into the lion's den. "You asked to see me?"

He motioned to a chair on the other side of his desk. "Have a seat."

She looked a bit pale as she sat in the chair he indicated. They were now eye to eye, and she watched him carefully.

He was surprised by how nervous he felt to talk to her. He must look at this as a business meeting and nothing more. "I asked you in here to discuss the future."

She didn't say anything.

"I have put off the conversation much too long, and I'm not getting any younger."

Suddenly, he felt the need to pace. He stood and walked to the fireplace and back. "I've made a decision regarding my business and estate. Since you're my heir, I imagine you've wondered what will happen to everything when I die."

She looked a bit surprised. "No, I hadn't wondered. I imagined you had everything decided long before now."

"Well, I hadn't."

"What is there to decide?"

"I need an heir—a male heir."

Pain flashed across her face. "Am I not a good choice as an heir?"

Why did he feel the tug at his heart when she looked at him that way? "I would like to leave my business in the hands of a capable man."

Her brows rose. "Am I not capable?"

Thunderation! Why was she making this so difficult? "Most women don't prefer to deal with business matters—but would rather entertain and socialize."

"You're speaking for my mother—not me."

"I'd prefer to shelter you from the business world." There, he'd said exactly what he meant, finally. "I need a man who is tough and tenacious. That's why I hired Thomas Overton. I've been watching him for years, and he's what my business needs."

"So, you plan to appoint Mr. Overton as your heir?"

"That's why I wanted to see you." This conversation had gone so much better in his mind. He had anticipated her quiet acquiescence—not all these questions—and he definitely didn't anticipate her steering the conversation. "I do not plan to appoint Thomas as my heir.

I plan to leave everything in your name—however, I would like to see Thomas take over for me when I can no longer run my business."

"I don't understand. You want me to promise to keep him on as a general manager once I inherit everything?"

"No." This was the part of the plan that would depend on her—but he would give her little choice. "I want you to marry Thomas and then the business will automatically transfer to him."

Her brows rose on her pretty face, just as he expected. "Marry Mr. Overton? I've just met him."

"You looked as if you got along fine."

"But—"

"My decision is in your best interest." He sat at his desk, his face serious. "Thomas is a capable, hard-working man and he would make you a fine husband."

"I like Mr. Overton—but it's much too early to know if I could marry him."

"Then find out." His voice rose with impatience. "I've told him my hopes in regards to a match, and he's amenable to the idea."

Her cheeks filled with color. "You told him?"

He sighed. "I will give you time to get to know him, but I fully expect your cooperation in this matter."

"And if I don't cooperate?"

He hated to say what must be said. He hardened his heart so it would not sting. "I mean to see Thomas Overton in charge of my affairs. If you don't cooperate, you'll be cut off from everything." It was for her good—she must see that.

"And what if I want to marry someone else?"

"Then let him support you."

Emma stared at Matthew, and he met her gaze with a detached sense of justification. She wasn't his—what did it matter if she walked away from his legacy?

"Will that be all?" she asked coolly.

"For now."

She stood and walked out of the room, her head held high.

Matthew was alone once again.

Emma

Emma crossed the cobblestone drive wearing her warmest clothing. The late October morning held a chill, but it would be even colder high in the airplane. Thinking of the upcoming flying lesson made her spine tingle with excitement and helped her forget, for just a moment, the conversation she'd had with her father two nights before.

But the memory soon returned, and she was left with the same nagging uncertainty. She liked Thomas—but she wasn't prepared to marry him. Would her father truly cut her off from his will if she refused? She despised her parents' lifestyle, but if she was honest with herself, she knew no other way of life. Could she survive on her own—and more importantly, could she accept being rejected from her father once and for all?

"Where're you off to on this fine morning?" Sam appeared at the carriage house door, wiping his hands on a handkerchief, a smile on his face. "Will you be needing a ride, lass?"

"Not today." She returned his smile, happy to see him this morning. "I'll take the Ford on my own."

He looked at her with a raised brow. "Today's your day off. Usually I drive you to the Red Cross workroom. Are you not going there today?"

Sam knew she had wanted to fly, but she hadn't told him she was taking lessons. He and Martha had always been so protective she was afraid he'd tell her it wasn't a good idea—or worse, go to her mother and have her make Emma stop.

"I thought I would go see a friend." It was true. After their evening in the hospital kitchen, she had come to think of Cade as a friend. "I'll spend some time there and then I'm going to the workroom at the library to make my quota of bandages for the week. I wouldn't want you to have to wait around for me all day."

"What friend will you be seeing?"

She'd been raised close to Elk Manor, never attending public school or doing the things most young women her age had done. Her friendships had been with the staff's children, like Rebecca, and her mother's friend's children—though those relationships had tended to be very formal. Her coworkers at St. Gabriel's had become friends, and she'd made a few friends at the little church she attended with Sam and Martha in Little Falls. What could she tell him that wouldn't make him suspicious?

"It's a new friend I made while doing my work for the Red Cross." Again, another half-truth. She stood on tiptoe and kissed his cheek. "I won't stay long. I'm anxious to get to the workroom. We're behind quota and the state headquarters are asking every woman in town to step up her production time. Will you get the Ford for me, please?"

He gave her a suspicious look but didn't press for more information.

Minutes later, she rumbled down the road toward the Bailey farm, thoughts of Cade keeping her company. She relived their conversation in the hospital kitchen once again, feeling cozy at the memory. She had assumed he was cold and hard—yet she had seen a side of him that made her realize he was also warm and empathetic.

She couldn't deny her attraction to him—but was it mutual? There had been few young men who so captured her imagination and attention. Was it simply because he was a pilot and lived a fascinating life? Or was it more?

And what of Thomas? Her mind spun, like it had the past two days. She wanted to spend more time with him, as well. He did appear interested in her—but was it simply to please her father?

The ride out to the farm took an hour, and she couldn't stop the incessant questions from tumbling through her mind. By the time she arrived, her stomach was uneasy, and her head hurt.

Today, Cade stepped out of the barn wearing a dark brown wool coat. He waited for her to park her car and then stepped over to the Ford and opened the door.

"Hello," he said.

She took her gloves from the seat beside her and stepped out of the vehicle, suddenly feeling a bit shy. What would he think if he knew all the silly questions floating through her mind? "Hello."

"How is Gracie?" he asked. "My mother went in to see her this morning, but she hasn't come home yet. I thought maybe you had seen her."

"I saw her last night. She's sitting up and eating a bit." Emma smiled. "She's doing very well."

Relief filled his eyes. "I'm happy to hear it."

They stood for a moment in silence, so she filled the void. "I'm ready for my next lesson."

"I just need to check on my father before we leave."

"Is he not well?"

"It's his heart." Cade swallowed and looked away. "The doctor doesn't think he'll make it through the winter."

"I'm so sorry."

"Would you like to meet him?"

"I would."

They walked toward the house, side by side. Gone was the irritation she'd felt from Cade before—and in its place was a gentleness that made her feel her presence was...welcomed.

He opened the back door, and she walked ahead of him into the kitchen. It was a cozy, old-fashioned room, with a large cast-iron stove, a long dining table, and a pump at the sink. "My father's room is this way." He led her through a well-used parlor, toward a door at the back of the room.

"Dad, I have someone here to meet you," Cade said as he opened the door.

The bedroom faced west, toward a large corn field, now filled with stubs of cornstalks. The beautiful blue sky rested against a rim of trees on the horizon. A man lay in the bed. He had a very striking appearance—almost native—with high cheekbones, black hair, and a wide mouth.

He opened his eyes and looked at his son, pure joy on his face.

It made Emma smile. What would it be like to have her parents look at her with the same pleasure?

"Dad, this is—" Cade paused and looked at Emma with a bit of uncertainty. "This is Emma."

Mr. Bailey glanced at Emma for the first time and smiled. "This is already starting out to be a good day. What's her last name, son?"

Cade hesitated. "Merrick."

"Merrick?" Mr. Bailey's dark brown eyes glimmered with even more interest. "I never thought a Merrick would step inside this house."

Emma only smiled, though her curiosity continued to mount. What had happened to make this family respond to her father's name with such intensity? What did they know that she didn't?

"It's a pleasure to meet you," Emma said.

Cade helped his father sit up and then he readjusted the pillows. "I'm teaching Miss Merrick how to fly."

Mr. Bailey's eyebrows rose. "Now that sounds like fun."

"It is," Emma conceded. "Your son is a splendid pilot."

"So I've heard." Pride rang in Mr. Bailey's voice as Cade helped him settle back. "Cade has always been good at everything he's done."

"We'll be up in the air for the next half an hour or so," Cade said quickly. "Is there anything you need before we go? I brought you fresh water a little earlier when you were sleeping."

Mr. Bailey looked between Cade and Emma and shook his head, wonder in his gaze. "I still can't believe a Merrick and a Bailey are working side by side. This is good."

She couldn't look at Cade, fearing her cheeks would blush.

They left his father and walked outside, toward the airplane. She couldn't help but contemplate Mr. Bailey's words, though she didn't want to discuss it with Cade, afraid she might open a sore subject when they were just starting to become friends.

"The weather is changing," Cade said, his hands in his pockets. "I don't know how much longer we can continue the lessons before winter sets in."

"You'll teach me again in the spring, won't you?"

They arrived at the airplane, and he reached in and grabbed her cap and goggles. "I hope to."

She took the cap and goggles and removed her hat.

"Today I'll let you fly in the air for a few minutes, to get a feel for the control stick and rudders."

She couldn't stop herself from grinning. Her new dream to be a pilot was within reach—if only winter would not come to postpone her lessons—and keep her from seeing Cade Bailey.

Chapter Ten

JULY 1863

ELIZABETH

Elizabeth tossed the dishwater around the corner of the cabin and then straightened to look out over the valley, a smile turning up her mouth.

Matthew strolled along the ridge of the hill, walking past the trading post and hotel. His long, even strides would have him at her door in just a few minutes.

She hurried inside the house and set the pan on the table. Her mother sent her a curious look as Elizabeth tore off her apron and rearranged her mutton sleeves. She went to the mirror by the cabinet and tucked a few stray hairs into the snood at the back of her head. She had bought the black hair net at the mercantile before the fort dance and wore it every day now.

Hopefully Matthew liked her new cotton muslin dress. She had sewn it herself. Since he had admired the cream color of the gown she had worn to the fort, she had chosen this fabric because it was a similar color.

Within moments, there was a knock. Elizabeth shooed away her mother and opened the door. Sunlight streamed into the dark interior, silhouetting Matthew's body.

His eyes revealed more than his words ever would. He liked the way she looked. She could see it in the flicker of pleasure in his gaze and the smile that lifted his lips.

"Hello, Matthew."

They hadn't seen each other since the meeting with Mr. Baker—Helen's father—and hadn't really spoken since the dance. Today she would cherish every moment she had with him.

"Hello, Elizabeth." He took off his hat. "Are you ready for your lesson?"

She had been counting down the hours.

"*Giga-waabaminnaagaj, Nimaamaa.*" She took her bonnet off the hook by the door with one hand as she called goodbye to her mother. With her other hand, she grabbed Matthew's arm and pulled him away from the cabin. "Let's go deep into the woods today—far away from the village."

Matthew looked surprised at first, and then he smiled and put his hat back on, allowing her to lead him away.

The afternoon sun shined down on Elizabeth's shoulders and warmed her skin. Her bonnet hung over her arm by the ribbons, swinging with each step she took. A gentle breeze ruffled the trees along the path and lazy white clouds drifted overhead. She would allow nothing to rush them today.

They walked for a long time in silence. Elizabeth's hand was now hooked around his elbow, and she allowed her body to press against his on the narrow path.

A little creek bubbled past them on its way down the hill toward the Mississippi and on to places Elizabeth had only read about. At the moment, she didn't care if she ever saw another place outside Crow Wing village, though she would go anywhere with Matthew if he asked.

"I brought a book with me today," Matthew finally said. "I thought you would like to read a popular story. It might be good for conversations."

She finally noticed the book in his other hand. It had a brown cover and gold lettering on the spine. *The Scarlet Letter*.

"Is this a good story?" she asked.

Matthew continued to walk, his gaze heavy. "It's a story neither good, nor bad."

She puzzled over his words until they came to a boulder near the creek, one high enough to sit on. She took a seat, enjoying the warmth of the rock beneath her.

Matthew sat next to her and handed her the book.

"Is this your book?" she asked.

"It's Mr. Bailey's book."

She held it up for him. "Do you want to read it to me?"

He shook his head. "You need the practice."

Elizabeth had been taught to read English at the age of seven and didn't need practice, but she opened the book and read aloud to Matthew. Her heart pounded for Hester Prynne as she stepped out of the prison into the light, her baby in her arms and the intricate scarlet letter A sewn into the bodice of her gown for all to see.

"My mother wore a scarlet letter on her heart." Matthew's words interrupted Elizabeth's reading.

She looked up and found him staring into the dark woods, across the creek. "What did you say?"

He looked at her then, and his eyes were filled with pain. "My mother was an adulterer just like Hester Prynne. She suffered at the hands of a cruel society, while my father walked about a free man. He never took responsibility, leaving the care and shame upon my mother's shoulders."

Elizabeth closed the book and set it on her lap. It suddenly felt heavy with implications. "Why are you telling me this?"

He sat close to her on the rock, their legs pressed against each other. She could smell the faint scent of soap on his skin. Their faces were close enough for her to see the flecks of colors shift in his eyes.

"I've never been honest with anyone about my parentage—but I want to tell you." He swallowed. "Your honesty makes me feel safe, Elizabeth. No one has ever done that for me."

"Does...Helen know?" She looked down at the book, regretting the choice to utter his fiancée's name.

"No. When she asked if my parents would come to our wedding, I told her it wouldn't be wise to ask them to travel so far, especially while the nation is at war—she never asked about them again."

"Don't you think it wise to tell your future bride the truth?"

"If I told her the truth, she wouldn't be my future bride."

"Wouldn't she love you no matter who your parents are? No one can choose who they are born to."

Matthew reached out and took Elizabeth's hand. "You are a good friend, Elizabeth, and I trust you with the truth. I know you will not judge me." He smiled, but it was a sad smile. "Helen doesn't love me any more than I love her. She would toss me aside at the first hint of imperfection. The only reason she agreed to marry me is because her father and the governor believe I have good prospects."

Elizabeth briefly closed her eyes at the touch of his hand and willed her heart to slow its erratic beating. She couldn't trust her voice, so she said nothing.

He traced the outline of her hand with his finger. The sensation sent a thrill along her spine, and she wished he would never stop. "I wanted you to know, because I don't want to keep any secrets between us. If I can be honest with you about my parents, I believe I can tell you anything."

Her heart pounded so hard with affection, she thought it might burst. "I've missed you," she whispered. "I hoped, every day, that you would come and see me."

"I wanted to come. I could think of nothing else some days."

But there was Helen and his engagement to her. Oh, that he hadn't met Helen before coming to Crow Wing!

They sat that way for many moments, neither of them pulling away. She longed to have him say more—to tell her what her heart wanted to hear. She wanted him to do more than touch her hand—she wanted him to kiss her and hold her close, promising to never return to St. Paul and the loveless marriage waiting for him.

"My mother did her best to raise Margaret and me," he said after a while. "She wanted to be respectable and give us every opportunity she could. She worked as a seamstress and laundress my entire life. She often woke up hours before me and went to bed hours after me. She was both father and mother. Her hands were always red and chapped, and her beautiful face became wrinkled with worry and fatigue far too soon."

He brought her hand up to his lips and placed a kiss on her knuckles. He kept her hand close to his mouth. "I love my mother, Elizabeth, and

I promised her she could give up her work as soon as I could support her and Margaret."

Elizabeth swallowed the emotions rising within her and looked at her hand near his lips.

"If I fail, I will lose more than my career. I will lose hope of ever taking that scarlet letter off her soul and giving her a chance at a decent life."

"You would sacrifice your own life to give your mother and sister wealth?"

He turned to her, his face inches from hers. "What am I sacrificing? I will have everything my heart desires."

Tears pricked the backs of her eyes. "Your heart desires love, Matthew, the love that only a man and woman can share. The delicate intimacies of two souls knitted together as one for life." She rested her free hand on his cheek. "This you will sacrifice if you marry Helen."

His free hand came up to rest on hers and he stared into her eyes. His gaze was filled with sweet longing, and she knew, even if he wouldn't tell her, that he cared for her the way she cared for him.

"I have fallen in love with you, Matthew."

He rested his forehead on hers, a groan escaping his lips. "Please don't, Elizabeth. I cannot bear it."

"And I cannot bear to think of you marrying a woman you do not love."

He pulled back and studied her. "If I loved her, would that satisfy you?"

She offered a sad smile. "Yes."

He touched her chin. "I don't believe you."

"I want you to be happy. I want you to have love and joy in your life. My heart longs to give you both, but if I cannot, I would be content to know another woman offered these things to you."

"Elizabeth..." he uttered her name as he claimed her lips. She didn't hesitate but wrapped her arms around his neck and pulled him close, inviting him to kiss her and love her the way she desired to be loved. He encircled her waist with his arms, tugging her close to his body and deepening the kiss. It was exquisite joy to be in his arms.

When he pulled away, she didn't let him go, but clung to his embrace, burying her head in his chest. "Matthew—"

"Shh." He rocked her slightly, holding her in his arms. "There is nothing to say, Elizabeth. I cannot change the course of my life. I made a promise to myself, to my mother, and to Helen. It would be selfish of me to renege now." His hand ran the length of her back in a slow, steady pattern. "I will take comfort in knowing that someday you will marry for love—and will be happy enough for the both of us."

She closed her eyes and tried to remember every detail of this moment—the rustling leaves, the rushing creek, the sun on her shoulders, the smell of his soap, the feel of his coat against her cheek, and the sound of his beating heart.

Matthew

For five days it had rained, and still, the sky continued to weep.

Matthew walked down the slippery hill and into the valley toward Elizabeth's cabin. Chief White Thunder's summons had been unexpected. Matthew had been at the trading post, inquiring about a piece of land he'd heard was for sale when the summons arrived. Lumber would make a man rich if he could get in before the war ended—and *if* he had money to invest. Two hundred acres had gone up for sale about fifteen miles south of Crow Wing, between the fort and Little Falls. It was rumored to contain rich timber and was situated on ideal land for transporting logs to the river.

Matthew didn't have the money now, but after the treaty was signed, he would be ready to invest in real estate.

The door to the cabin opened before Matthew even knocked and the chief appeared in the opening, his face grave. "Come."

Matthew's pulse jumped at the sound of Chief White Thunder's voice. After sharing a kiss with Elizabeth on the rock, they had kept a respectable distance from one another. The chief couldn't know about the kiss, could he?

Elizabeth sat near the fireplace sewing, while her mother tended to a toddler. Elizabeth's head came up, a question in her eyes.

Chief White Thunder pointed to the rug near the fire. "Sit, Agent Man."

Elizabeth stood and took Matthew's coat and hat. His skin prickled at her nearness, but he managed to nod a thank you and then sat on the rug, warming himself by the fire.

The chief's eyes were solemn and his jaw hard. He sat across from Matthew, his gaze never wavering from Matthew's face.

Elizabeth stood behind her father, near the fire, hovering over them with uncertainty.

Matthew didn't speak but waited patiently for the chief to start, his unease increasing by the moment.

"I am unhappy," Chief White Thunder finally spoke.

Matthew swallowed and looked over the chief's shoulder at Elizabeth. After their kiss on the rock, they had kept a respectable distance from one another, though he sensed her desire for more. The chief couldn't know about the kiss, could he?

"Your clerk has come to me about Elizabeth."

Jacob.

Matthew's heart thudded against his chest.

"He has asked to see her—to court, is what he said."

Matthew looked at Elizabeth again and she dropped her gaze. Did she know Jacob had asked her father? Had she encouraged him? It seemed hard to believe.

"This is not good." Chief White Thunder shook his head. "Elizabeth must not make Chief Little Moose angry."

Chief Little Moose? Matthew frowned. Chief Little Moose was the leader of the Red River band of Chippewa. Hopefully he would sign the treaty in October along with Chief White Thunder and four other band chiefs.

"I don't understand," Matthew said.

"You have worked hard to convince me to sign the land treaty in October, promising me land and money." Chief White Thunder narrowed his eyes. "But we must have the other chiefs sign the treaty, as well, so I have worked hard to convince them." He pointed at Elizabeth. "In exchange for Chief Little Moose's signature, he will take Elizabeth as his wife."

Elizabeth looked up, her brown eyes filled with terror. She shook her head and then looked at Matthew, fear and pleading in her gaze.

Matthew felt as if he couldn't draw a breath. Chief Little Moose was an old man, with numerous wives. He was fierce and easily angered. Matthew had met with him many times but had never liked him, often avoiding contact when possible. How could Chief White Thunder give Elizabeth to him in marriage?

"Your clerk must stay away from Elizabeth," Chief White Thunder continued. "If you want Chief Little Moose to sign treaty you will make the clerk man understand. And you will continue lessons with Elizabeth. Chief Little Moose wants her to work with the white men for the Red River band. She must know more about the government and the laws. You will teach her."

Elizabeth's face had gone ashen, and she stared at the floor, her gaze haunted. In a space of a few moments, she looked much older than seventeen. This young woman who was passionate and beautiful—and believed in love—would have to live and die for a husband not of her choosing.

"You go now and tell the clerk man he must stay away from Elizabeth." Chief White Thunder pointed at the door. "We will sign treaty in October."

Matthew stood on weak legs. He felt as if he pulled boulders behind him as he walked to the door. He wanted to go to Elizabeth and hold her and tell her everything would be alright—but how could he?

He took his coat and slipped it over his arms, then he took his hat and placed it on his head. He felt as if he moved in slow motion while no one said a word in the cabin.

Matthew opened the door and stepped outside. Turning to close the door, he caught Elizabeth's gaze and felt as if his heart would break at the fear in her eyes.

Slowly, he closed the door and braced himself against the rain.

This treaty was much bigger than her or him. It would affect the lives of thousands of Indians and hundreds of thousands of settlers. If the Union won the rebellion in the south, the west would have a population boom, and the government must have land for the settlers. Thousands of dollars had already been invested in this treaty, countless hours of work by hundreds of politicians and government workers. It was no small undertaking and would change the course of history in Minnesota.

But how could he let it happen if it meant that the woman he loved was forced into a marriage of misery?

Chapter Eleven

Elizabeth

Elizabeth raced up the Woods Trail in the cover of darkness. Rain poured from the sky, mingling with the tears trailing down her face. Did God's heart break with hers? Was He weeping with her this night? The mission workers had taught her about God and His son Jesus—and she believed in Him. But tonight, she wondered if He orchestrated her marriage to Little Moose—and if He had, could He be trusted?

The swollen river lapped over the banks covering the trail. Mud oozed up to her ankles and splashed onto her muslin gown, but she didn't care. The moment her father had left the cabin to go to his second wife, Elizabeth had prepared to leave. Her mother cried and begged her to stay—threatening to sound the alarm—but Elizabeth knew Mother wouldn't stop her. Her mother understood what it meant to be given in marriage to a man she did not love.

Tonight, there would be no man, nor beast, to stop her. Nothing stirred but the wind as it lashed through the trees and swirled across the water.

Lightning flashed through the sky, followed closely by thunder. Elizabeth's dress was soaked through and her teeth chattered. Her feet felt like stone, numb from the cold.

Up ahead, a lone lantern sat on a windowsill at the agency.

Elizabeth wept in relief and stumbled, falling to her hands and knees. Hard rocks dug into her palms, and her muscles ached, but she was almost there.

She knew Mr. Bailey had been sent north, and it would only be Matthew at home. She hoped he would not be angry at her. She had nowhere else to turn.

Elizabeth trudged the last hundred yards to the front door of the house and pounded as hard as she could. Pain radiated from her numb hands. "Matthew!"

The door flew open, and Matthew stood in the candlelight without his jacket. He wore his white shirt unbuttoned at the throat with his sleeves rolled up at the arms. His disheveled hair and weary eyes told her he was also upset.

"Elizabeth! What are you doing out in this weather?"

She sobbed as she crossed the threshold and threw herself into his arms.

He wrapped her in a warm embrace and held her tight, whispering her name.

The wind rattled the windows, and the rain pounded the roof. A small cook stove offered heat from the corner, and the room smelled of fresh coffee—but nothing compared to being in his arms.

"I won't marry Chief Little Moose," Elizabeth vowed. "I will die before I become his wife."

"Shh." Matthew ran his hand down her back and then reached out and closed the door. "You'll catch your death in these wet clothes."

"I don't care." She sounded pitiful.

"I care. Come by the stove." With his arm around her shoulders, he led her to the heat. He set a basin of water on top to warm and handed her a towel. His tenderness made her want to weep all over again. "I'll find you something dry to wear."

He went into a room and came out a few minutes later with a large white shirt, a dark blue dressing robe, and a pair of woolen socks. "This is all I could find." He handed them to her and then pointed his thumb over his shoulder. "I'll go into my room and wait so you can change by the warm stove."

He disappeared again and gave Elizabeth privacy. First, she washed her hands and face in the warm water and dried them with the towel. Her dress was heavy with water and felt as if it weighed more than her. The beautiful creamy muslin was now stained with mud, and the hem was torn. She lifted it over her head and then unfastened her corset. She took off her shoes and her stockings and put on the warm shirt and dressing gown. She drowned in the fabric but relished the smell of Matthew's scent. After she put on the woolen socks, she removed the pins from her snood and let down her wet hair, running her fingers through it.

"Are you ready?" he called, his voice uncertain.

Robe and socks covered more of her body than her buckskin dress—but for some reason, standing in Matthew's clothes, she felt exposed. Vulnerable. "I'm ready."

He opened the door and stepped into the front room. His eyes swept over her and then he looked away. "W-will those things do?"

"Yes, thank you. I feel better now." Her body felt better, but her soul still ached with fear and disappointment.

Matthew brought the chairs over to the stove while Elizabeth laid out her dress and stockings on the drying rack. He handed her a mug of warm coffee, and they both sat near the stove, he with his back to her clothes.

The wind roared like a vicious cougar, screeching and howling around the corners of the house. Here, in this safe space, she wondered how she had braved the dark night—and how she would ever return to it.

Matthew took a sip of his coffee and then spoke softly. "Why did you come?"

She looked at him over the rim of her mug and saw the concern in his eyes. "You know why I came. I cannot marry Chief Little Moose." She shuddered at the thought of sharing a life with the cruel, old man.

Compassion mingled with trepidation in Matthew's gaze. "I don't know what I can do to help."

She knew he couldn't do anything. If Chief Little Moose didn't sign the treaty, everything Matthew had worked for would be lost. But it wasn't just Matthew. The United States government wanted the land for settlement, and her people needed the money to live. The world was changing rapidly and there was little she could do to stop it. The treaty would ensure that every family had one hundred and sixty acres to farm, education for the children, and money for provisions.

If she refused to marry Chief Little Moose, her people would suffer even more than they did now.

Matthew set his coffee mug on the cabinet near his elbow and then took the mug from her hands and put it next to his. He turned to her and took her hands, rubbing her cold fingers until they burned with life once again. "I wish things were different. I wish I could prevent you from marrying Chief Little Moose." His eyes filled with pain as he moved her wet hair away from her face. The touch was so intimate, so loving, a shiver ran through her body. "I cannot imagine you married to anyone you do not love, Elizabeth—just as you cannot imagine the same for me." His hand dropped away from her cheek. "But I am not free to stop your marriage. It is between you and your father."

She grasped his hand and put it back on her cheek. "But I want you."

He stood quickly and put space between them.

Tears gathered in her eyes once again and she stood. "Do you love me, Matthew?"

He swallowed and she saw the internal struggle in his eyes. Finally, he crossed the room and took her into his arms. "I love you as I've never loved anyone before." In the next moment, his lips found hers and he kissed her with a fervency that took her breath away. He tightened his embrace, and she wrapped her arms around his waist needing the reassurance of his strength and love.

Suddenly, he pulled away and put space between them. She almost fell over at the loss of his support.

He raked his hands through his hair and would not look at her. "I cannot do this. I have a fiancée and a mother to care for. I have a career and a future—I have a responsibility to the government to see that this treaty is signed. I cannot throw all of that away for—"

"Love?" She began to cry, the tears streaming down her face.

"Yes." He choked on the word. "Love." But even as he said the word, he drew her into his arms once again.

And this time, he did not let her go.

Matthew

Sunshine streamed into the window of Matthew's office as he carefully wrote the amount of annuities he had just given to a family of the Pillager Band of Chippewa Indians. His hand shook and his eyes were blurry from lack of sleep, but he did his duty for the government just as he promised he would do.

Since the money had arrived two days ago, Indians had been traveling to the Crow Wing Agency to be paid. Many camped around the agency, while others came and left the same day. The activity was a welcome diversion for Matthew who had neither ate, nor slept well, since Elizabeth had visited him four days before.

Thoughts of her betrothal to Chief Little Moose consumed his every moment, until he worried that he would go mad from the reality of it all. In his mind, he had already mapped out a plan where he and Elizabeth could escape to the west—but he always came back to the devastation it would bring to the United States government, the Indian tribes, his mother, and even Helen who didn't deserve the scandal.

There was no way out of this situation—and the helplessness of it all settled over him like a smoldering blanket on this hot day.

Matthew's office had become unbearably warm now that the heat of August had returned, and he reached up to open a window. The room was painted white with pine board flooring, two large oak desks, and an American flag. Maps of Minnesota lined the walls—constantly reminding Matthew of the importance of his work.

He lifted his head at the sound of a horse approaching the agency.

Jacob rode in tall and proud on the back of the agency mare. He had finally returned from Red River.

He was two days overdue, but with the recent rains, there was no way of knowing if his tardiness was in part to the rough trails—or irresponsibility.

Jacob nodded hello to the families camping near the agency and rode his horse around the corner, presumably to the stable. Fifteen minutes later, he entered the office, his face red from the sun. With a flourish of ease, he tossed his hat on the hook and took a seat, dangling his leg over the arm of the chair. "You look terrible, Major."

Matthew jabbed his quill into the ink pot and scratched out a number on the ledger.

"What happened to you?" Jacob asked.

He couldn't tell Jacob his troubles—couldn't even hint at them—so he mumbled. "It's been a long week."

"I had a great week." Jacob put his hands behind his head and chuckled. "I met a pretty little maiden at Red River who kept me warm through the cold nights."

Matthew clenched his jaw and didn't bother to respond.

"She doesn't compare to Elizabeth—"

Matthew swiveled in his chair and glared at Jacob. "Chief White Thunder said you asked to court Elizabeth."

Jacob's gaze hardened and he dropped his hands. "What's it to you?"

Matthew threw his pen down on the desk. "You will stay away from her. She's been promised to Chief Little Moose in exchange for a signature on the treaty."

Jacob lowered his leg and sat up straighter, his affable mood falling away. Shock and disbelief lingered on his face. "Chief Little Moose is brutal—and old. Elizabeth can't marry him."

"The promise has already been made—there's nothing we can do."

Jacob studied him, realization dawning on his ruddy face. "That's why you look the way you do—you're in love with her."

There was no use denying it. Matthew turned back to his ledger and picked up his pen, though he couldn't see straight enough to accomplish his work.

"What would Miss Baker—and Superintendent Baker—think of your affection for another woman?" Jacob's voice was hard and full of warning.

Matthew dipped his pen, wishing his hand would stop shaking.

Jacob must have realized he wasn't going to get an argument out of Matthew, because he stood and left the office, exiting through the interior door into the house.

Matthew stared at the ledger. He just wished October would come and go so he could get on with his life and try to forget about Elizabeth.

But how could he forget her? He closed his eyes and groaned from the memory of their last encounter. He had been a fool to let her stay. It would have been better if he had forced her to leave—or left himself and slept in the frigid rain. There was much to regret now—and much to mourn. He would never be the same—and he would never look at Helen the way he knew he should. Shame coursed through him. He wasn't a religious man—but he knew what they had done was wrong.

Wasn't it the very sin his father had committed with his mother? He despised his father, yet now he was just like him—and he despised himself.

It felt like an eternity passed as Matthew sat in the sweltering office. Another family entered, and Matthew divvied out their payment, recording it in the book.

Sometime later, the door opened, and Jacob entered the office again. Matthew glanced at him—and paused.

In Jacob's hand was Elizabeth's snood. He held it up with a mixture of outrage and disbelief. "Is this Elizabeth's?"

What was Matthew to say? If he lied, Jacob would demand a sensible answer—and if he told the truth, he would demand a reasonable explanation—of which Matthew could offer neither.

"How did it get here?" Jacob asked.

Matthew stood, feeling weak and exhausted. Fear rose in his chest, but he pushed it down and walked toward the door.

Jacob stepped into his path, his height dominating Matthew.

"How did this hair net get behind the cook stove?" His eyes were like blades. "Was someone keeping you warm this week, as well?"

"It's none of your business."

"It is if this belongs to Elizabeth."

Matthew pushed past him and entered the house, his eyes scanning the room for anything else she might have accidentally left. How had he missed the snood, and how had Jacob found it?

"There's nothing else," Jacob said. "I already checked."

Matthew walked to the cabinet and took a mug from the shelf. He dipped it into the water bucket, suddenly needing to coat his dry throat.

"Will you not tell me? Must I deduce the obvious on my own?" Jacob stood behind him.

Matthew took a swig of the water and set the mug down. He walked past Jacob and went back to the office.

Jacob followed him and balled the snood in his hands and then stuffed it into his pocket. He took a step toward the door. "I will ask Elizabeth myself."

"No!" Matthew put his arm out to stop Jacob. "Do not go to her. The chief—"

"The chief should know."

Panic clawed at Matthew's gut. "The chief must not be told anything."

Jacob stared at Matthew, shaking his head, disappointment and anger in his face, telling Matthew that Jacob had cared for Elizabeth more than he realized. "I could have offered her something real. I would not have used her and discarded her like you will do to marry Helen."

"I did not use her." The words caught in his throat. He loved Elizabeth, more than life itself.

Jacob jerked away from Matthew's side and shoved his hat on his head. "If I suspect you are still seeing Elizabeth, I will not hesitate to tell the chief."

"Where are you going?"

Jacob stepped past him, toward the exterior door.

"I demand to know where you're going." Matthew stood tall, harnessing all the courage and strength he could muster. "I am your superior and you must give me an account."

Jacob scowled at Matthew. "I am going to the trading post at Crow Wing village, if you must know. I heard a prime piece of logging property is for sale."

Incredulity choked Matthew's throat. Jacob was going after the land Matthew had heard about—the land that could make him a fortune. "Where would you get the money for that land?"

Jacob's face was red, and his jaw was hard with anger, but he answered. "My father left me a small inheritance." Jacob didn't wait for Matthew to respond but exited the building and went toward the stable.

Matthew sat at his desk, envy gnawing in his chest. He wanted the land—wanted to invest in a future that looked suddenly bleak and without meaning. Now would be the time to invest—but where would he get the money? Perhaps, if he had the land, he wouldn't need to marry

Helen. He could find a way to support his mother and sister through the lumber and let Helen marry a man who deserved her.

The ledger suddenly cleared before his eyes and Matthew's gaze rested on the large amount at the bottom of the right column. With a few easy strokes of his pen, he could borrow the money, and no one would be the wiser. He would pay it back after the treaty was signed.

But could he live with himself?

His sins began to mount like a ledger tallying his misdeeds.

What would one more iniquity matter?

The words of Tuck returned, as if the old man were sitting in the room with him. "'Enter ye in at the strait gate: for wide is the gate, and broad is the way, that leadeth to destruction...'"

But then he thought of his mother, slaving over the hot water, scrubbing dirt from other people's clothing. She deserved better.

Matthew quickly made the necessary changes in the ledger, took the money from the safe, and raced out of the office just as Jacob mounted the agency mare.

Smoke rose from the campfires of the Indian families staying around the agency.

Jacob saw Matthew and didn't look pleased.

Matthew lifted his hand. "Give me the horse. I have matters to attend to in the village and I need you to stay in the office."

Jacob's eyes filled with storm clouds. "I told you I was going to the village."

"And now you're not. You need to stay here and do as I say."

Several families stopped their work, their curious gazes lifting to the scene.

Jacob narrowed his eyes. "I'll be back in a few hours."

Matthew took a step toward the horse and put his hands on the bridle. "Get off this horse and get into the office."

"How will you stop me?"

"This horse belongs to the federal government—if you leave now without my permission, you'll be guilty of stealing federal property. Do you know what people do to horse thieves?"

Jacob clenched his jaw and dismounted. He tossed the reins at Matthew, hitting his face.

Without a backwards glance, Jacob strode to the office.

Matthew mounted the horse and galloped down the Woods Trail.

The path was full of ruts and puddles of mud. Mosquitoes and gnats were as thick as fog, swarming in large numbers. They flew into his mouth and eyes, and he was forced to keep his head down to protect his face.

The annuity money burned like a hot coal in his pocket, and the weight of Matthew's conscience bore down on him, creating a headache at the back of his eyes. He forced his thoughts to silence, because he could not let a man like Jacob get another advantage.

Matthew had been fighting against men like him his whole life. He had scrimped and saved to get an education, he had worked hard to overcome the obstacles he faced with reading, and he would be required to sacrifice the woman he loved—surely, borrowing money to buy the land was the least he deserved from a world that had been cruel and unfair to him since his illegitimate conception. He wanted to get ahead—was willing to do whatever it would take.

He turned off his thoughts and focused on getting to the village. It was the only way to survive.

When Crow Wing came within sight, Matthew slowed the horse's pace. The beast was sweating and breathing hard. Matthew reached down and patted her neck. "We're almost there."

He turned left and directed the horse up the hill to the hotel where the land owner would stay until his property sold. It sat across from the trading post, its front level with the road, it's back facing the valley and the river.

Matthew jumped down and secured the horse to the hitching post. With long, even strides he walked into the hotel, straight to the lobby counter. "I'm looking for Mr. Edgars."

The hotel clerk nodded to the corner of the lobby where a couch sat nestled between two windows overlooking the street and the river. "That's him right there."

Matthew vacillated for a moment. Once he handed over the money, the deed would be done and there would be no going back.

A woman across the street caught his eye through the window. She was young with a little boy and a little girl hanging on her skirts. She looked bedraggled and destitute, her cheeks sunken and her eyes luminous in her pale face. He didn't know who she was, but she looked so much like his mother, he had to swallow the rush of shame and desperation he recalled as a child clutching her skirt the one and only time he had met his father.

They had gone to the hotel where his father had been living during the congressional season. When his father had opened the door and saw his pitiful ex-mistress with her starving children, he had looked at them with such contempt, Matthew had winced. It was then and there Matthew swore he would gain the wealth and status his father possessed and make him regret turning them away.

Matthew crossed the lobby and stopped in front of the man who held the key to fulfilling his vow.

Chapter Twelve

AUGUST 1863

Matthew

The intense heat made the thick air hard to breathe. Matthew's clothes stuck to his sweating body, and the sun scorched the back of his neck. The valley was quiet today, with few people leaving their homes to work outside. Even Elizabeth's dog, which was usually a bundle of energy, was lying in the shade of the cabin staring at Matthew with little interest.

The door opened a crack and Straw Weaver stood on the other side, her brown eyes wary.

Matthew removed his hat, his chest tight with nerves. He had not seen Elizabeth since she visited the agency. Three weeks had passed, but he hadn't been able to face her. It was Chief White Thunder who had finally prompted Matthew's return. He had asked why the lessons had stopped, and Matthew had used his work as an excuse—but there were no more excuses. The annuity money had been distributed, and the agency had quieted once again.

"*Aaniin*," Matthew said. "Is Elizabeth at home?"

Straw Weaver turned and spoke into the cabin. Eventually she moved away from the door and Elizabeth appeared in her native clothing—her arms and legs bare. The lines around her eyes and mouth revealed the depth of her anguish—an anguish he knew all too well.

"Hello, Elizabeth."

She looked up at him with her large brown eyes, and he felt his insides twist with regret—and longing. He wanted to reach out and touch her, put his arms around her and hold her tight. "I'm here for a lesson."

"Why?" She dropped her gaze and wrapped her arms around her middle. "To prepare me to marry Chief Little Moose?"

Matthew took a step toward her and then thought better of it. He clutched his hat in his hands. "Will you come with me to the creek? I'd like to talk to you."

She didn't look at him but played with the dirt under her bare toes. "What is there to talk about?"

Matthew glanced up and looked into the house. Straw Weaver watched them from her place near the cold fireplace. Her perceptive eyes didn't miss anything, and Matthew suspected she understood their relationship. She nodded, ever so gently, for Matthew to continue.

It was the nudge he needed. "Come with me. Let's leave all our troubles here at the cabin for this one afternoon and wade in the creek."

A glimmer of life returned to Elizabeth's eyes as she looked at him once again. She lifted her buckskin skirt. "Shall I change?"

He shook his head, a smile lighting his heart.

She closed the door and they walked up the hill and into the woods. The cicadas buzzed high in the trees, and mosquitoes latched onto their sticky skin, but Matthew hardly noticed the discomfort. As soon as they were deep in the woods, away from prying eyes, he took her hand. "I'm sorry I haven't come to see you sooner—I was busy, and I didn't know what to—"

"I didn't know what to say, either."

He stopped. "I'm sorry, Elizabeth."

She shook her head, regret lining the edges of her mouth. "No, I'm sorry. It was wrong of me to come to you the way I did. I was overcome by my emotions, and I should not have made you bear them with me."

"I would gladly bear any burden you carried, if I could."

There was nothing more to say, so they remained silent.

They continued to the creek and Matthew took off his shoes and socks. He rolled up his pant legs and together, they stepped into the cool water. Trees rimmed the banks of the creek offering a little respite from the heat. In the shade, the air was much cooler, and Matthew felt as if he could breathe again.

Elizabeth sighed and closed her eyes.

Matthew watched her, relishing these stolen moments, knowing they would end all too soon.

She dipped her hands in the creek and poured the refreshing water down her arms and legs, a hint of a smile on her lips.

After a few moments, they sat on the bank, under a willow tree and let their feet dangle in the water, their backs rested against the ancient tree. Matthew grabbed a twig nearby. He dipped it into the surface of the creek, playing with the water.

"Will you tell Helen?" Elizabeth asked quietly.

Matthew let out a deep sigh—one he hadn't even realized he was holding. In the weeks since his night with Elizabeth, he had thought very little of his fiancée—though he knew she deserved better. He didn't love Helen—had never loved Helen—but it was no excuse for him to be dishonest, especially concerning something so important. What kind of a man was he if he kept this from her?

What kind of a man was he to allow it to happen in the first place?

He closed his eyes, berating himself for getting into this mess. Keeping it a secret would be the easy thing to do—telling Helen and facing the consequences would be the hard thing. Tuck's words came back to Matthew, and he swallowed the uncomfortable ache that settled in his throat. Hadn't he warned him to follow the narrow, harder path that led to goodness and life?

"I will tell her." Matthew knew he couldn't live with himself if he entered a marriage with Helen and she didn't know the truth.

A crawfish swam out from behind a rock, darting to and fro. Matthew poked his stick into the water, scaring the little crab-like urchin back into his hiding place.

"I will never tell Little Moose." Elizabeth's voice was bitter. "He deserves nothing from me." She looked at Matthew, panic in her eyes. "I would rather die than be his wife."

Matthew took her hand and then pulled her into an embrace. He held her until her tears subsided. He felt helpless. He had nothing to offer her. No solution. No words of comfort. No hope.

His mother would have offered to pray, but Matthew didn't know how—and he didn't even know if it would truly matter. Did God care about what happened to him and Elizabeth when He had better things to concern Him?

Elizabeth pulled away and Matthew stood. "We should return to the village. I'm waiting for a letter from the governor. It should arrive on the afternoon stage."

It was the final instructions for the October treaty negotiations. They would meet at the headwaters of the Mississippi River at Lake Itasca. Mr. Baker would come with a military presence. They anticipated over a thousand Chippewa in attendance, as well as dozens of representatives from St. Paul and Washington. There would be much work to do.

Elizabeth didn't move but studied him with her soulful brown eyes—the eyes he had come to love. "Must we leave?"

How he wished they could stay forever—but eventually they needed to return.

"I will come back in September when I'm able—and then..." He couldn't continue.

She rose from the bank and took his hand in hers. She placed it over her beating heart. "And then, in October, we shall go our separate ways—but our hearts will remain here." A bittersweet smile lifted the corners of her lips.

He held her hand and helped her climb up the creek bank. Without a word, he took a pocketknife from his trousers and popped open the blade. On the backside of the willow tree, he gently carved a heart and then he put the initials M and E on the inside.

"Here is where our heart shall always remain." He smiled at her. "Not two separate hearts, but one."

She entered his embrace and stood there for a long time, her quiet tears staining his shirt.

Chapter Thirteen

NOVEMBER 1917

EMMA

The workroom had been especially busy as Emma made her quota of bandages. Two dozen women had sat within the spacious workroom at the Carnegie Library knitting, stitching, and chatting about the war, the community, and their families. Emma had enjoyed herself, but now, as the sun swung toward the west, she looked forward to a quiet evening at home. Maybe she'd read a book or take a long bath. Her shift at the hospital tomorrow would come early.

She still felt exhilarated from her morning lesson with Cade. It had been a thrill to hold the control stick and test the feel of the plane. She replayed the moment when she turned and looked into his eyes and saw the pleasure he took having her in the front cockpit over in her mind. That had made her feel more exhilarated than anything.

She drove up the circular drive toward her home, not surprised to see another Ford under the ornate portico. Mother or Father probably had a caller—Emma just hoped she would not be expected to dine or entertain with someone this evening.

Sam greeted her at the carriage house door, as was his custom. "Did you have a fine day?"

"It's been a lovely day."

He lifted a brow. "And how is your new *friend*?"

"Wonderful," she said with a smile as she turned toward the house.

"Did he let you fly?"

She stopped and turned, her eyes wide.

"You've never been able to hide anything from me, lass."

"But—"

"I have me ways." He sat in the driver's seat and took the handle of the door, his face serious. "Just be careful. If I discover you're putting yourself into any danger, I'll be telling your mother." He closed the door and then pulled the car into the carriage house.

Next thing she knew, he'd demand to meet Cade and inspect the airplane himself...but at least he wasn't tattling on her right away...and he cared enough to be concerned.

Emma passed through the servant's entrance and into the kitchen. Martha stood at the center island, her white cap hiding her graying hair. There was only one maid in the room, washing her hands at the sink.

"Hello, Martha," Emma said.

Martha set a letter on the counter before she wiped her cheek and glanced at Emma. Her eyes were red, and her mouth turned down.

Emma walked over to her and put her hand on Martha's arm. "What's wrong?"

"It's Rebecca." She lifted the corner of her apron and put it to her eyes. "She's lost the baby."

Emma's good mood seeped out in one sigh. "I'm sorry." She put her arms around the woman who was more like a mother to her than her own.

Martha clung to Emma, her sobs wetting Emma's shoulder.

Tears gathered in Emma's eyes. Poor Rebecca. "How is she doing?"

"That's what's worrying me." Martha pulled away, her eyes filled with anxiety. "When she wrote this letter, it had been over a week since she started cramping and bleeding, and she was running a fever. Is that normal?"

Concern tightened Emma's chest. A fever usually indicated an infection—which was not normal after a miscarriage.

"She's so far away from a doctor—and they don't have any money." Martha's eyes pleaded. "I wish I could go to her, but it would take several days to get there—it could be too late, and even if I did go, what could I do for her?"

"I can go." Emma's mind raced with the possibility.

"You can't take that much time away from your work."

No, but if she and Cade left early in the morning with his airplane, she could see Rebecca and get home before nightfall. Traveling by automobile was almost out of the question. Rebecca was in such a remote area, the roads were unpredictable, and, in some places, unpassable if you weren't on horseback. But if Emma did go by air, it would require her to tell Martha she had been flying with Cade—and when she did, her mother might find out. But what choice did she have? Rebecca needed medical care—as soon as possible.

Emma glanced outside. The weather was growing colder which might indicate an early winter storm—so they had no time to wait. She would need to find a way to get Cade a message—but how? What if he had plans for tomorrow and couldn't take her?

She'd have to drive out to the farm this evening and tell him.

"Emma, there you are." Mother appeared at the kitchen door in a lovely blue afternoon gown. "You have a visitor."

"Me?" No one called on her.

"Yes—but look at you." Mother scanned her heavy wool coat and her winter hat. "Go upstairs and make yourself presentable and then join us in the front parlor."

But why change if she was about to leave? "Mother, I have other plans—"

"Nonsense. You have a visitor. It would be rude to turn him away—especially when I just told him I saw you pull in."

"Him?"

"Mr. Overton. He's here to see you. He's been waiting for an hour."

Thomas Overton had come to call?

"I'll continue to entertain him," Mother said, stepping out of the kitchen. "But hurry."

Emma placed her hand on Martha's arm. "Don't worry about Rebecca. I'll go to her, hopefully tomorrow, and see what I can do for her."

"Tomorrow?" Martha frowned and looked at Emma like she had lost her mind.

There was no way to avoid telling her the truth. "I will fly there."

"Fly?" Martha frowned. "What are you talking about Emma? How would you fly?"

"Have you heard that Cade Bailey has returned?"

"Of course I have," she said. "Everyone's talking about him."

Emma looked around the kitchen to make sure they were alone before whispering, "He's giving me flying lessons—and he said he could fly me in an emergency, should I have one—and this is an emergency."

"Good heavens!" Martha's hands flew to her mouth. "You can't fly in that death machine! I won't let you. What are you thinking? How—?"

Emma put her hands on Martha's arms. "Shh!" She glanced over her shoulder where her mother had just stood. "It's completely safe. Mr. Bailey is an excellent pilot."

"He just killed a woman—you can't fly with him."

"It was an accident."

"And what makes you think he won't have another accident?"

"Please, Martha. Trust me."

"No." Martha crossed her arms. "I won't let you do it—I'll tell your mother."

"I'm a grown woman—I can make my own decisions."

"Not about this." Martha started to untie her apron strings. "I'm going to tell her right now. I don't want you getting hurt—or killed."

Panic filled Emma's chest. "I must fly—I want to earn a pilot's license and treat people in remote areas—like Rebecca." Rebecca! "Martha, if I do not fly, Rebecca may become even more ill—or worse." She swallowed, hating to use Rebecca and her illness this way. "It might be too late already."

Martha's hands stilled.

"I can be to her home in less than three hours tomorrow—and I can examine her and possibly give her the medicine she needs to get better."

Martha's face revealed her uncertainty.

"I promise it's safe, Martha. I would not put myself in danger."

Martha sighed in resignation, though she didn't look happy. "Fine. Go to Rebecca—but be careful."

"You won't say anything to Mother?"

Martha shook her head, her eyes narrowed. "No—but if I discover you're in danger—"

"I know. Sam already threatened the same."

Martha pierced her lips. "You're incorrigible, Emmie."

Emma hugged Martha. "And you're a sweetheart."

"Go on and get ready to see Mr. Overton."

Mr. Overton. Emma had almost forgotten.

How would she get word to Cade now that Mr. Overton expected her to entertain him for the evening?

She would have to go to him later tonight—or hope and pray he would be willing to bring her on short notice in the morning.

Chapter Fourteen

Cade

The morning sun had not risen yet as Cade counted the money he had earned repairing the neighbor's Ford. A lantern cast a small circle of light on the kitchen table, illuminating the dollar bills. With the repair money, and the money Emma had given him for her last lesson, he was only thirty dollars short of his mortgage payment. He would need to come up with money to pay Grace's medical bills at the hospital—but hopefully they would let him make payments after December first.

He stared into the light, wondering where he could make more money. After he did his morning chores, and before he started to tackle his to-do list for the day, he would go to some of the smaller nearby towns and put advertisements in their newspapers for other mechanic work.

Mama entered the kitchen, a yawn stealing over her. "Excuse me," she said as she went to the stove and lifted a lid. "Thank you for starting the fire for me."

He tucked the money away in a little pouch. "I couldn't sleep."

Mama leaned down to kiss the top of his head as she walked to the pantry. "Your father had a restless night, as well. He's still waiting for you to have a talk with him."

Cade had avoided being alone with his father for any length of time since his return home. Part of him didn't want to know what his father had to say. It was too painful to relive the past—and the other part of him childishly believed that if he kept putting it off, his father would stay with them longer. "I haven't had time."

She rummaged around in the pantry and then came out with a container of oatmeal. "You need to make time."

Cade stood and put the pouch in a cookie jar high on the pantry shelf. "I'll try."

She went to the sink and put a kettle under the pump. "Today."

"I won't have time. I have to do the chore—"

"I'll do them for you."

"I have to go to town."

"Go tomorrow."

Mama maneuvered the pump up and down until water ran into the kettle.

For a long time, neither said a word.

Mama put the kettle on the stove and then started the coffee, her voice strained. "I wish Henry would write. We should have heard from him by now."

When Cade had run away, it had taken him months to finally write home and tell them where he was. He had never worried about how his mother felt all those months. Now he realized how selfish he had been.

Mama stood on tiptoe and looked out the kitchen window toward the road. "I see headlamps."

Cade went to the window and glanced outside. "Who would be out this early?"

"I don't know," Mama said. "But they're turning into the drive."

Cade took his coat off the hook and put on his shoes. "I'll go see what they want."

He opened the door and was met with a blast of cold air. He slipped on his coat and buttoned it high. He put his hands in his pockets as the car pulled up to the house.

Emma? His heart picked up speed as he jogged the last few yards to get to her automobile as she came to a stop. Why would she be here so early? Was something wrong with Gracie?

She barely stopped the engine before he had the door open. "What's wrong?"

She looked up at him, and he could barely make out her features in the darkness. "It's my friend, Rebecca. She's in need of medical help—it's an emergency."

He was relieved it wasn't about his sister, but he could hear how worried Emma was for her friend. "Where does she live?"

"Near Baudette, on the northern border, close to Canada." She stood and he could smell the lovely scent of floral perfume. "Are you and your airplane still available for an emergency?"

Why today of all days? He had so many things to do. If he took the day off, he'd be one more day behind. There was also the risk of getting caught in a snowstorm. He couldn't fly in snow—they could be stranded somewhere, with no way to get home.

"She's had a miscarriage, and I'm concerned she has an infection. If I don't get to her soon, it could spread and there would be no chance—" She choked on her words. "It might be too late already."

"I don't know if the weather will hold, and it will be freezing in the air."

"I'll pay you for your time and the use of your airplane."

"I'd do it for free."

"I know you have better things to do. Would thirty dollars be enough?"

Thirty dollars was exactly what he needed to pay the mortgage. A funny feeling settled in his stomach. Had God orchestrated the exact amount—or was it merely a coincidence?

"It will take us about three hours to get to Baudette—can you ride in the plane for three hours, both ways?"

"I don't care what it takes." Her voice pleaded. "I will do anything to get to Rebecca."

"I'll have my mother put some bricks in the oven for our feet."

He turned toward the house, but she reached out and put her hand on his arm to stop him.

"Thank you." She stood on tiptoe and put her arms around his neck in an embrace.

He stood motionless as she hugged him, and all too soon she pulled away. "I wore my warmest clothing."

It took him a moment to gather his thoughts. "Come into the house and warm yourself by the stove. I need to do the chores before we leave."

"May I help?"

"I'd rather you stay warm."

"You're doing me a favor—I'd like to do one for you."

"It isn't necessary."

"I know—but I want to."

How could he say no to her? "Come inside and meet my mother—and then we'll go to the barn."

They walked into the house and found Mama standing near the sink. No doubt she'd been watching them out the window. She looked at Cade with a mixture of surprise and curiosity.

He closed the door behind Emma, looking at her in the soft lantern light. Her cheeks were rosy from the cold, and her brown eyes were sleepy—but she looked beautiful.

A rush of something akin to fear—or caution—snaked through his body, taking him unaware. Cade had fallen for the charms of more than one beautiful woman before and had even thought he was in love with an actress he'd known in California. But there was something different about Emma. He wasn't simply attracted to her good looks. He was drawn to her heart and that had never happened to him before.

Yet, Emma was out of his reach. Not only was she from a different social set, but she was too good for him. He'd done things he could never admit to her, so it didn't matter how she made him feel.

"Mama, this is Emma Merrick."

Mama crossed the kitchen and extended her hand, a smile on her face as she sent Cade a curious glance. "Welcome. My husband mentioned that he met you yesterday. I was hoping I would get the pleasure, as well."

"It's nice to meet you."

"Emma needs me to fly her to Baudette this morning," Cade said before his mother could ask questions or make comments about his and Emma's relationship. "We probably won't be back until just before dark."

"You're going to fly in this weather?" Mama looked out the window, anxiety lining her face. "Is it safe?"

"I've flown in all types of weather. Could you put bricks in the oven for our feet? We'll do the chores and then leave at first light."

Mama didn't look convinced that it was a good idea, but she nodded. "Of course."

Cade and Emma milked the cows and cleaned out the stalls. Emma picked the eggs and fed the chickens, while Cade broke the ice on the top of the water troughs and fed the horses their oats. She worked with efficiency and confidence, though he doubted she had done many farm chores in her life. It was yet another thing that made him admire her.

The first blush of dawn spread over the landscape as they walked back to the house for their bricks. They said goodbye and took their bricks, wrapped in kitchen towels, and left the house.

Emma grabbed her emergency kit and her extra outerwear before they walked to the biplane, which still sat in the north field.

Without waiting to be told, Emma climbed the bottom wing and set her bag and her bricks in the front cockpit, and his bricks in the back.

Cade inspected the airplane, with one eye watching her movements. She climbed into the front cockpit and he called for her to start the engine as he spun the propeller. She did it exactly how he had taught her. He raced around the plane and climbed into his seat and then they took off from the field, heading toward Baudette.

Cade lifted first one hand off the control stick and then the other, moving them to get blood circulating to his fingertips. The roar of the engine hummed in his ears, as the sky continued to grow dark and a wall of clouds approached from the west.

Emma's head lulled to the side ahead of him. He hoped she was staying warm enough—though he doubted it. The temperature had continued to drop, and they still had twenty minutes before they reached home.

He kept one eye on the clouds and one on the back of Emma's head.

On the way to Baudette, they had stopped once to refuel and then reached Rebecca's farm just before lunch. Rebecca's husband, Hank, had been shocked to see them and had ushered Emma into the one room house where Rebecca was lying.

Cade had stood by, not knowing what to do, as Emma had embraced her friend. Both women had cried and held each other for a long time before Emma asked the men to leave the house so she could begin her examination. Hank took Cade to the barn.

After an hour, Cade sent Hank in to get Emma. They didn't have much daylight, and the storm had been approaching. Emma had emerged, her face grim. She told Cade she had done all she could, and they had returned to the airplane for their flight home. He sensed a heaviness about her that troubled him—but they had no time to talk. They raced against the setting sun and the approaching storm, both equally menacing and dangerous adversaries.

Snowflakes began to slip from the sky and Cade gripped the control stick harder, willing the airplane to fly faster.

Memories from the night he ran away in the snowstorm resurfaced. What if this storm became a blizzard and he was forced to ground the airplane?

He looked below them. They were flying over a large lake, with a forest edging three sides and a swamp on the fourth.

He had the urge to pray—though he'd never been much for prayer before. Did it really help? It hadn't helped his grandfather, though his parents had prayed for him for years. It hadn't helped the young woman who had died at Bay Meadows...though maybe it had helped the three who had survived.

Emma turned just then and her brown-eyed gaze met his. Gentleness and peace radiated from her face. He sensed she was praying and offering him a bit of her confidence.

A scripture came to mind. It was one his parents had quoted often, though he hadn't understood it until now. "*O taste and see that the Lord is good: blessed is the man that trusteth in him.*" He wanted to pray—to taste and see that the Lord was good. He wanted to trust Him to bring blessings. Could he pray—and wait—and see the Lord's goodness?

Emma turned back to the front, and Cade offered up a prayer for safety and understanding.

He couldn't explain why, but it felt good to pray and not worry about the outcome—but trust and wait on God.

The snow fell harder, and the wind began to gust. Cade held tight to the control stick, keeping the plane as steady as possible.

By the time the farm came within sight, the ground had a soft covering of snow.

He landed in the north field and taxied the airplane close to the barn.

They would not be flying anymore this year. They would have to wait until spring.

He stalled the engine and climbed from the cockpit. Emma moved slowly, but she eventually climbed onto the lower wing, and he reached up to help her down.

Putting his hands around her small waist, made thicker by her coat, he lowered her down to the ground—much closer to him than was necessary.

He couldn't help it. He wanted her close, loving the way he felt when he was with her—especially because he didn't know when he would see her again.

She stood near him—not moving away—and looked up into his face.

His heart pounded with awareness.

"Thank you—for everything." She slowly stepped back from him and removed the promised money from her pocket. "I suppose the snow means we won't fly again until spring."

He nodded and took the money, unable to find his voice.

She looked down at the medical kit she held in her hand. "Will I see you this winter?"

The way she said it gave his heart reason to hope. "Do you want to?" His voice was much lower than he intended.

Her gaze lifted to his and she studied his face. "I do."

Joy filled his chest, and reason fled his mind as he said, "Then we will—somehow."

He took her bag and they walked back to her Ford. The snow was growing in intensity, and the night was fast approaching.

She opened her car door.

"Do you think you should drive with this storm coming on?" he asked.

"I'll be fine."

He hated to let her drive back alone. What would happen if she was stalled or went off the road? "Would you like to stay until it passes?"

She glanced at the sky. "I don't think it will stop anytime soon. Maybe I can beat the worst of it. People will worry if I don't go back soon."

Cade couldn't shake the fear of letting her go. He started to move toward the barn. "I'll drive you in my Ford."

She put her hand on his chest to stop him, her eyes serious. "I'll be fine. It's barely a dusting right now. The longer you argue with me, the deeper it will get."

Her hand felt like fire on his chest, and it took all his willpower not to grasp it in his and bring it to his lips. "How will I know if you arrive home safely?"

"You'll have to trust God to get me there."

"Emma—"

"Cade."

"I'm just concerned."

She leaned forward and placed a kiss on his cold cheek and then whispered in his ear. "And I'm flattered."

She hovered there for a moment, her breath warm against his skin.

He swallowed the rush of emotions and took a step back, not trusting himself with her. "Good bye."

"Good bye."

She went to the crank, but he took it in his hands. "I've got it."

He cranked the car, and it started immediately—a surprising feat in the cold. She pulled out of the driveway, and Cade found himself praying for the second time that day.

But this time, he wasn't praying for himself. He was praying for someone he had come to care about.

It no longer mattered that she was a Merrick.

Chapter Fifteen

DECEMBER 1917

MATTHEW

Matthew stood outside the Merrick Lumber Company's main office in Elk City and wiped his feet on the doormat. His breath puffed out in a white cloud as he glanced at the Mississippi River lying frozen just beyond the large building. The logging era was coming to a close in Minnesota, and the last of the large log drives would pass through these waters in the next two years. Matthew had a fortune in logs waiting to be felled just north of Elk City around the Bailey farm, but he needed the access to the river to get them transported.

For years, he had waited to cut that property, but he was running out of time. He needed to buy back his land from the Bailey family before next winter when he planned to harvest his timber.

Sam came from behind Matthew and opened the door. "Are you feeling well today, Major?"

Matthew had felt unusually tired the past few days, often needing to take a break from his work to lie down and nap. It was a peculiar experience—this growing old. His mind was as clear and active as it had been when he was a young man. It was his body that didn't want to cooperate.

"I'm fine."

Sam studied him carefully. "I'll be waiting inside while you're visiting with Mr. Overton. It's too cold to sit in the automobile."

Matthew walked through the doorway and into a large receiving room. A secretary, Mr. Joust, sat at the front desk opening company mail. When Matthew and Sam walked in, he rose from his seat and tipped his head. "It's a pleasure to see you today, Major Merrick."

"Is Mr. Overton in?"

"He is, sir."

Matthew nodded his thanks and walked around the secretary into Thomas's office.

He needed to talk to Thomas about the Bailey land but that wasn't the only thing on his mind today.

"Major," Thomas said, rising from his desk. He extended his hand. "What brings you in on this bitter cold day?"

Matthew shook his hand and then took a seat across from Thomas. "I have two orders of business to discuss."

Thomas sat and pushed aside a stack of papers he had been working on. He folded his hands on the desk. "You have my full attention."

Matthew had come to trust Thomas like a son. The man was young, intelligent, hard-working, and fearless. All traits Matthew admired. However, he was moving too slowly with Emma. It was time they came to an agreement and then Matthew could settle his inheritance once and for all.

"I feel that we can speak candidly," Matthew began.

"Of course. It's the only way I like to communicate."

"I'm disappointed in your conduct with Emma."

Thomas's eyes grew large and he stood. "I beg your pardon, sir. I have been nothing but a gentleman."

"Sit down." Matthew waved him back to his seat. "I didn't mean to imply you've been inappropriate. I'm disappointed you haven't secured an engagement yet."

Thomas took his seat once again, his face relaxing. "I don't want to push her too fast."

"I'm not getting younger. I would like this to be settled before too long."

"These things take time."

"I don't have time." Matthew stood and walked to the window. The land was frozen—but one day it would come alive again and life would move on. He was nearly eighty years old, and though he had been in good health in recent years, he couldn't shake the feeling that his time was drawing to a close.

"What do you have in mind?" Thomas asked.

"I want you to get serious." Matthew turned and looked at his protégé. "Do whatever it takes."

"She works almost around the clock. When she's not working, she's volunteering. We've had very little time to get to know one another."

"Make time." Matthew's voice rose. "There are no more excuses. I want you at our home every day, if need be. You must convince her to marry you."

"What if she will not?"

"I will speak to her again—and reiterate her situation." He walked back to the desk and leaned on the solid oak top. It would be too complicated, and he would look like a heartless villain if he legally disowned Emma. It would be so much cleaner if she married Thomas. "I need a man who is dauntless in the face of business—and women—to take over my affairs."

Thomas sat up straighter. "I am that man."

"Good. Now prove it to me." Matthew leaned back. "I have one more thing I need you to take care of."

"Anything."

"I need you to secure a piece of property for me."

"That should be fairly simple. I'll have our solicitor draw up the papers."

"No." Matthew turned and paced across the room. "This one is not simple at all. I need you to convince this family to sell. I've been trying to secure the land for over fifty years."

"Fifty years?" Thomas's eyes grew large. "How will I succeed where you have failed?"

"That is what you must figure out." Matthew rested his hand on the back of his chair. "I have been told they have a mortgage payment due on the property in June—one they are struggling to make. They will be desperate. You have until then to get them to sell."

"Six months?"

"Yes." It seemed like a good amount of time to court Emma, as well. "You have until June first to secure the land and announce your engagement to Emma. If you do not, I will give this opportunity to someone else."

Thomas stood, anxiety on his face. "I will do my best, sir."

"Do better than your best." He walked toward the door and put his hand on the knob. "I hand-selected you for this job. Do not disappoint me, Thomas."

He stepped out into the front entrance and walked past Mr. Joust. Sam sat in a chair near the door and stood the moment he saw Matthew.

"Will you be going home now?" Sam asked, pushing the door open for Matthew.

"Yes. I need to speak to Emma. Is she home?"

"She's working at the hospital today." Sam walked ahead of Matthew and opened the back of the brand-new touring car Matthew had ordered from Detroit. The cream-colored paint and black fenders were shiny in the afternoon sun.

"When will she be home?"

"I'm not certain. She often goes to the workroom at the library or visits with friends after her shift at the hospital."

Matthew entered the car, his bones stiff. Exhaustion overcame him and he sighed as he took his seat. "As soon as she arrives home, I want to speak to her."

"Yes, sir."

"She will not be wasting her time volunteering any longer. I cannot make her quit her work—but she must be home more."

Sam offered no comment as he closed the car door and went around to the front. He started the engine, and they turned toward Elk Manor.

Matthew closed his eyes. If only he could get enough rest.

A wave of dizziness washed over him, and he gripped the door handle to steady himself. It felt as if the air was being squeezed out of his lungs, and pain began to radiate into his jaw and left arm. Panic seized him as he realized what was happening.

"Sam!" He tried to speak loudly, but his voice was weak. "Sam!"

Sam glanced behind him and alarm registered on his face. He pushed on the brakes and Matthew lost his seat. He tumbled to the floor in a heap, the pain increasing.

Sam raced around and opened the door. "What's wrong?"

"My heart." Matthew gasped as he gripped his left arm.

Sam reached down and helped Matthew back to his seat. "I'll have you to St. Gabriel's in minutes." He jumped in front, and they sped off toward the hospital in Little Falls.

Matthew gasped as the pain spread throughout his left side, stealing his breath.

"Hold on, sir!" Sam said. "We'll be there soon."

The countryside gave way to the city, but it all rushed by in a blur of pain and dizziness.

Sam pulled up to the hospital and parked by the front door. He helped Matthew inside the building.

"I have a man in need of a doctor!" Sam yelled.

A nun met them in the waiting area, her concerned face the last thing Matthew saw before his world went dark.

Matthew lifted his eyelids and was met with blinding light. A crucifix hung on the wall directly in front of him.

Had he died?

He closed his eyes again—not ready to meet his Maker.

"You gave us all a bit of a fright." A familiar Irish voice pulled him from a half-dream state.

So, he wasn't dead.

Matthew squinted and made out the silhouette of his groom-turned-chauffer. "Where am I?"

"You're in a hospital bed. You've had a heart attack, and you've lived to tell about it. Not many do. It seems that God isn't done with you yet."

A heart attack.

"How long have I been here?"

"Just a few hours. It was a minor attack. The doctor came in and examined you and said you'd be rousing soon—but not to let you get up."

Matthew looked about his sterile room. The white walls and gray linoleum floor made him feel cold, but the bright sunshine pouring into the window warmed him. Sam sat in the only chair in the room. A small table stood next to the bed, a Holy Bible on the top.

"Emma was in here, too. She said she'll come back later to check on you at the end of her shift."

When he had planned to talk to her, he didn't think he'd have to come to the hospital.

He tried to sit up, but Sam jumped from his chair and put his hand on Matthew's shoulder. "Not today. The doctor said you must rest as much as possible."

"I can't stay here. I have work to do."

"It will wait."

Matthew gave in and lay back on the pillow. He had no energy to fight Sam. "At least help me prop up the pillows."

Sam did as he was asked, and Matthew was able to rest back on the pillows in a sitting position. Just that little movement had sapped his strength.

Sam took his seat and studied Matthew, a curious smile on his face. "Did you get a glimpse of Glory?"

"A what?"

Sam's eyes lit up and he leaned forward. "Did you see Heaven?"

Matthew frowned. "No—why would I?"

"I don't know. I thought since you were so close to passing over, you might have seen something."

"I didn't see anything."

Sam lifted his hands. "It was worth asking."

Matthew felt uncomfortable and readjusted his position—but the discomfort didn't go away. He realized it wasn't a physical discomfort—but one in his soul. Had he been close to passing over? And, if he had been, where would he have gone?

Out of the cobwebs of his memory he saw Tuck walking along the old Woods Trail toward Crow Wing. How had so much time slipped away?

"What're you thinking about?" Sam asked. "You've gone far away, I'd wager."

Matthew lifted his hand and took the Bible off the table. "I did go far away—back almost fifty-five years. I met a fur trader named Tuck when I was just a young man. He gave me advice as I was setting out on my journey."

Sam's eyes filled with curiosity as he glanced at the Bible. "Did you take his advice?"

Matthew relived the past fifty-five years in a heartbeat, seeing Elizabeth, Helen, Jacob, and Nathan all in one moment. Disappointment weighed heavy on his conscience. "No—I didn't, and many people have suffered because of it."

"There now," Sam said, his voice merry. "Don't be beating yourself up over past mistakes. This here is a new day, and you've been given a second chance. It's never too late."

Matthew shook his head, sadness permeating his words. "I don't even know what I'd do with a second chance. When you're as old as me, you're set in your ways and there's little you can do to change the course of events."

"You might not be able to change the past—but you can change the future."

"I wouldn't know where to start."

Sam leaned forward and put his hand on the Bible. "I think this would be a good place—don't you? Maybe that's why you've been laid up here—to finally get time to read the book that has changed the course of history."

"I'm too far gone."

"No one is too far gone." Sam stood. "I think I'll leave you now to get acquainted with that Book. You'll never regret reading it."

Matthew barely noticed as Sam slipped out of the room. Could he be right? Was it too late for Matthew? Or could he still find redemption?

He opened the Bible to the Book of Genesis and the words spun out of control. He had to put all his effort into looking at the first word, then the first line, and the first sentence.

In the beginning God created the heaven and the earth.

He closed his eyes and leaned his head back on his pillow. Was this his second chance? And, if it was, how long did he have? It would take him weeks—months—to read through the Bible—and even if he did, would he understand any of it? How did one find salvation? How did a person have confidence they would enter Heaven when they died? He felt foolish for approaching a priest or a pastor, when he had not been affiliated with a church since Helen died. Would they wonder how a seventy-seven-year-old man had escaped the basic knowledge of Christianity?

There were far too many unanswerable questions, and the task felt daunting.

But once again, Matthew sensed his time was running short.

He opened the Bible and read the second sentence and then the third.

Soon he was deep within Genesis.

Emma

Emma approached her father's room with a bit of trepidation. Seeing him unconscious had been a shock she hadn't anticipated. Though they had never been close, still she felt a connection to him that was threatened when he was so near death. Maybe it was the fear of never getting to know him that startled her so.

But how could she change that when he had never desired a relationship? It had been plain to her that she wasn't wanted by him or her mother—but it didn't prevent her from wanting them.

She stopped at his door and peeked into his room.

He sat in bed, his back propped up with pillows, a book in his hands.

In all the years she had known him, she had never seen him read—which didn't mean much, since she rarely saw him at all—yet it was a picture of vulnerability and humanness.

He turned the page, his face serious.

She hated to interrupt him, but she was about to go off duty and would not see him again until the morning. "It's good to see you're awake."

He looked up, startled, and quickly closed the book.

It was the Bible.

Emma's brows rose. She wouldn't have been more surprised if he had been reading *Ladies Home Journal*. "I-Is there anything I can get for you?"

"No." He shook his head, appearing embarrassed for being caught reading. "I'm fine."

She had wanted to serve him, to show him some kindness, but again, he was pushing her away. She let out a resigned breath and turned from the room.

"Emma."

His voice stopped her retreat, and she looked back—hope in her heart. "Yes?"

"I'd like to talk to you." He motioned to the chair beside his bed. "Please sit."

She moved across the room and sat where he indicated. When he had been lying unconscious, a part of her had hoped if he awoke, he would be a changed man. Near-death experiences often caused people to reevaluate their lives—she had seen it countless times in her work. Would he reach out to her now?

He looked uncomfortable and didn't meet her eyes. "After this...episode, I've realized how precious life is."

She leaned forward, her heart beating wildly.

"I'd like to settle my inheritance before it's too late."

His inheritance.

"I spoke with Thomas today, and I've reiterated my desire to see a match between you."

A match.

"I know you've been avoiding Thomas—"

"I haven't been avoiding him. I've been busy." She had thrown herself into her work, hoping to pass the tedious winter months before she could start flying again. She had gone to the Bailey farm only once since the last airplane ride to check on Grace and Mr. Bailey as a Town and Country nurse—but that had been a quick visit, and she had hardly seen Cade, though their brief encounter had been sweet. Something held him back. It was as if a wall stood between them and she wasn't sure how to climb it, or if she should even try. He had given her no indication that he was attracted to her, except for that moment just after they had returned from Rebecca. The memory of it had warmed her for weeks, but Cade had made no move to contact her or see her after that, and she was left to believe he wasn't interested.

"I want you to get serious with Thomas," Father said. "He's a good man and he will be a good husband."

Emma wrapped her arms around her waist. She liked Thomas—but it was hard to think of him as a prospective husband when her thoughts were consumed with another man. Even if that other man wasn't interested in pursuing her.

"I hope you have not forgotten my warning," Father said.

"How could I?" She would be cut off if she did not marry Thomas.

"I want you to know I have put a time-limit on this warning."

She lifted a brow.

"You have until the first of June. After that, I want your full agreement to marry Thomas. If you do not announce your engagement by then..."

He didn't need to finish the sentence, because they both knew what would happen if she didn't marry Thomas.

Emma clasped her hands on her lap and stared at the floor. The first of June was only six months away. Would she be ready to become engaged to Thomas by then?

"I want you to do your best to get acquainted with Thomas in the coming months. You must spend every moment you can with him." Father's green eyes stared at her. "Do you understand?"

How could a father threaten to disown his daughter if she did not bend to his will? Emma's chest felt heavy from the weight of his displeasure. What had she done that he would despise her so? Was it that she wasn't born a male? Was it because there had been no other children after her and he felt it was somehow her fault?

She stood and put her hands in front of her waist. "If that is all, I'll leave you."

He looked upset, but she didn't worry why.

Shaking his head, he said, "Go and do as I've asked."

She walked out of his room with her head held high, yet inside, she was bending over with grief and disappointment.

Chapter Sixteen

MISSISSIPPI
HEADWATERS
OCTOBER 1863

MATTHEW

Matthew stood by the large government tent on the shores of Lake Itasca. The trees around the lake were a riotous arrangement of reds, oranges, and purples, offering a brilliant backdrop to the spectacle unfolding at the edge of camp.

Mr. Baker arrived on horseback, some three hundred troops in his wake with dozens of wagons loaded with supplies. His white beard gleamed under the brilliant blue October sky as he waved with great aplomb to the band members gathered in camp. He tipped his tall stovepipe hat at chiefs and elders as he passed. His ostentatious hat set him apart from the military troops and everyone else in camp.

Matthew clasped his hands behind his back and willed his heart to stop thumping so hard. So much of Matthew's future rode on the success of the treaty negotiations and Mr. Baker's good will—two things he couldn't ruin. Or control. Yet, he'd come to know many of the Chippewa men, women, and children who were encamped at the headwaters. They came out of their wigwams, curiosity on their faces as smoke rose from their campfires, spiraling into the cool air. The delicious aroma of roasting meat and bubbling stews wafted on the breeze.

Did they understand what was about to happen? That their entire way of life would be altered, forever?

For the better part of the week, Chippewa band members had poured into the headwaters area, constructing their wigwams and setting up their temporary camps. It could take days or weeks to come to an agreement on the treaty proposed. There was no way of knowing how long they would be in camp. Most of the band members wore their native clothing, but some wore pieces of white men's attire. Bowlers and gingham gowns were interspersed with feathers and buckskin clothes.

This thing was too big for Matthew to stop, even if he had wanted to. He hoped the government would be fair and just, but a lot of people stood to become very rich and powerful from the treaty, and he doubted they had considered anyone but themselves.

"Mr. Baker looks foolish." Jacob scowled beside Matthew.

Matthew's brows rose as he glanced at Jacob. Since Matthew had purchased the land, Jacob had only spoken to Matthew when necessary—and sometimes not even then.

A large, black carriage caught Matthew's eye. Four women sat in the carriage, their brightly colored gowns and matching parasols out of place in this wilderness. Their unexpected presence created a stir with the Chippewa—and unease in Matthew's chest.

Elizabeth stood by Straw Weaver near their bark-covered wigwam. She wore a light pink muslin gown, her dark brown hair woven into a halo of braids around her head. She and Straw Weaver whispered together, their gazes on the carriage.

Mr. Baker stopped at the government tent and dismounted, numerous other officials stopping with him.

"Hello, Major Merrick," Mr. Baker said, extending his hand.

Matthew shook his hand and swallowed the nerves rising in his throat. "Welcome to Lake Itasca. We have everything prepared for your arrival—though we don't have a tent for the ladies." Matthew nodded to the carriage pulling up behind Mr. Baker.

The ladies' faces were covered by elaborate bonnets and frilly parasols—impractical attire for camp life.

"We've brought tents for the ladies," Mr. Baker said. "No need to worry about them. They've worried enough for all of us." He cleared his throat and leaned closer to Matthew. "Their complaints have followed us all the way from St. Paul."

Just then, one of the women stood and Matthew's heart thudded harder.

Helen.

She waved at Matthew, her pristine white gloves glowing like a beacon.

Mr. Baker pounded Matthew on the back. "Go say hello to your fiancée. She was the one who insisted we let the ladies come with us."

Matthew started forward, as if on wooden legs. He put one foot in front of the other and plastered a smile on his face, but only because he knew it was expected.

Why was Helen here? She had probably never slept in a tent before in her life—what would she do to pass her time this week? Fish?

He wasn't prepared for this meeting. Had hoped to prolong it until after the treaty when he could return to St. Paul.

Out of the corner of his eye he saw Elizabeth with her mother. She stood perfectly still. He wished he could look directly at her, to see her face and read her emotions, but he dare not avert his attention from Helen.

The whole assembly watched as he approached the carriage.

Beside Helen sat her mother, Mrs. Baker. Her pinched face was red and spotted with mosquito bites. The other two women were probably the wife and daughter of an officer who had accompanied Mr. Baker.

Helen's pretty face was flushed and her blonde ringlets bounced with excitement. She extended her hand over the edge of the open carriage, wiggling it about. "Are you surprised, Matthew?"

He took her hand and finally found his voice. "More than you might know."

She giggled. "I made sure I didn't say a thing in my letters—and I made Daddy promise not to breathe a word. Are you happy to see me?"

They had an audience—one that would expect a great show of delight for this long-awaited reunion. He managed to smile—as wide as he was able. "I couldn't be happier."

Helen looked satisfied. "I knew you would be. Daddy said it wasn't prudent to come, but Daddy can't say no to me." She wrinkled her pert little nose. "He said you'll be too busy to spend time with me—but I said you'll never be too busy for me."

Matthew glanced at Mr. Baker who watched them closely.

"Your father was right. I will be very busy," he said.

Helen's bottom lip pouted. "But you'll be sure to take time to spend with me later, won't you?"

"Of course."

She nodded and took her seat. "Good. I have much to tell you about our wedding. I've set a date." She waved him away. "Now go back to Daddy. He's waiting."

Matthew was still reeling from Helen's unexpected arrival as he backed away from the carriage. His eye caught Elizabeth again, but this time he really looked at her. Though she and her family had been in camp since yesterday, they had not had a chance to speak. Now, he noticed the droop in her shoulders and the heaviness in her face.

Matthew rejoined Mr. Baker and showed him into the large, white tent set up for the treaty negotiations. Papers and maps were strewn about a large table. Here, the Chippewa would decide if they wanted to cede over ten million acres of rich prairie land and forests to the United States Government.

The coming week would require a great deal of work and concentration. He must not let his personal affairs distract him.

Elizabeth

Night had begun to fall on the camp as Elizabeth sat near the fire with her father. Mother had taken the children to bed just before he had come in from his meeting with Mr. Baker. He had not spoken more than a handful of words as he ate his wild rice and stared into the flickering firelight.

Stars sparkled like jewels in the east, while a ridge of light still glowed in the west. Loons cried from the lake, their haunting song echoing through

Elizabeth's aching chest. Tonight, after being sick in the woods once again, she had come to accept what she had denied for weeks.

She carried Matthew's child.

The truth weighed on her heart and conscience. A fit punishment she had brought upon herself. The child had been in her womb for almost two months, too long to be accepted as Chief Little Moose's child once they were married.

What would Chief Little Moose do when he found out? What would her father do?

The negotiations had not gone well, and Father had been sullen and moody.

For over a week, Elizabeth had sat near her mother's fire tending to her younger siblings and listening to the unending conversation spilling from the open flap of the large government tent nearby. An interpreter had been hired to help, but he only spoke Dakota and a strange mix of Chippewa and Métis languages. Hours and hours of endless discussions could be avoided if there was better communication between her people and the United States Government.

Elizabeth glanced away from the fire and looked toward the lake where Matthew was walking with Helen. She had her hand wrapped around his elbow and was leaning toward him. Though they were far away, Elizabeth could see Helen was speaking quickly, as she often did. She wore elaborate outfits with wide skirts and extravagant bonnets, the likes of which Elizabeth had never seen before. When Helen stood next to Matthew, it transformed him from a humble Indian Agent into an elite gentleman Elizabeth would never approach.

He stopped and moved a stick out of Helen's path. When he glanced up, he caught Elizabeth's eye, and she swallowed the rush of emotions crowding her throat.

What would Matthew do if he discovered she was expecting his child? Would he cast aside his entire future to marry her? She knew, in her heart, that he would do the right thing—but it would destroy his dreams and his hope of giving his mother a better life. She did not want to tell him the truth—but it wasn't fair to keep it from him, either.

A movement at the edge of the fire's light brought Elizabeth's musing to an end.

Chief Little Moose stood near her father, his black eyes staring at Elizabeth.

A shiver of dread raced across Elizabeth's skin. He had watched her often this week but had not approached until now. He was a tall, powerful man with a hard face and a sharp gaze that seemed to look right through her. A thick scar puckered the right side of his face—a reminder of the fierce warrior he had been at one time.

"*Aaniin*," Father said and indicated a place near the fire.

Chief Little Moose did not sit but stood over them both. "There is a council gathering at Chief Longbow's tent. It is time we come to an agreement."

Father nodded. "I will go."

Chief Little Moose looked at Elizabeth, undisguised desire radiating from his gaze. "Is your daughter ready to come to my tent?"

Elizabeth tried not to shrink back at the words. Instead, she sat up straight, her face a mask of indifference.

"No." Father stood and pulled his blanket tighter around his shoulders. "The treaty has not been signed."

"You know I will sign."

Father shook his head. "We will need to work hard to convince those who oppose this treaty. When we do, Elizabeth will be yours."

Chief Little Moose's eyes revealed his displeasure but there was nothing he could do. He looked at Elizabeth and caught her staring at him. He must have misunderstood, because his gaze filled with heat.

Her heart beat hard, and she looked toward the lake where Matthew stood watching them.

"I will return for you after the treaty is signed," Chief Little Moose said, but Elizabeth refused to acknowledge him.

Together, the men left the fire and walked toward the council meeting on the other side of the camp.

Matthew escorted Helen to her tent and kissed her hand. After she entered, he turned and paused as if trying to decide which path to take—the one toward Elizabeth—or the one that led to his own tent, near the edge of the lake. After a moment, he walked toward his tent and disappeared inside.

Elizabeth pulled a quilt around her shoulders and listened as the camp quieted. Fires flickered out and the soft sound of slumber filled the night.

Sleep would not come easy for Elizabeth. She lifted her face toward heaven and looked at the expanse of stars now blanketing the dark sky. Tonight, she felt alone with no one to guide her steps. Her thoughts wandered back to the mission where she had lived and gone to school, and to the missionaries who had taught her about the love and forgiveness of Jesus. She longed to be with them now and confess this sin that weighed down her soul.

She had proclaimed to believe in Jesus and accepted His forgiveness as a child—but did His forgiveness extend to her now? Or had she done something truly unforgivable?

Matthew's dark tent filled with lantern light. Was he struggling to find sleep, as well?

She stood and walked the uneven path to his quarters. She longed to talk to him, to tell him about the baby. It would be foolish for her to enter his tent—if anyone saw, they would both be in trouble—but this might be their last opportunity to talk. With a quick look around the quiet camp, she opened the flap and stepped from darkness into light.

Matthew sat on his cot, his head in one hand, his other holding open a thick book. He had taken off his jacket and rolled up his shirtsleeves. A small crate stood next to the cot, his lantern glowing on top.

He looked up. Surprise and then pleasure flickered in his weary gaze.

Without a word, he stood and came to her. He pulled her into his arms and held her tight. She could hear his heart beat and smell wood smoke on his clothes.

"I thought I would never hold you again," he whispered into her hair.

She closed her eyes and breathed in his scent. After a moment, she pulled away and looked toward his cot. "What are you reading?"

He followed her gaze and then let out a long sigh. "My mother's Bible."

"The Holy Bible?" Her brows rose.

He ran his hands through his hair, frustration in his stance. "At least, I'm trying to read. I have to go slow to understand, so I only read when I must."

"And this is a time you must read the Bible?"

His shoulders drooped and he picked up the book. "I'm struggling to understand what path God wants me to take. I was looking for scriptures a man shared with me last spring."

She pulled her quilt close around her shoulders to ward off the autumn chill. He was struggling to understand what God wanted, and she was struggling to understand if God forgave.

"Why are you here, Elizabeth?"

"I wanted to see you." She lowered her gaze, thinking of the baby—his baby. Was there wisdom in telling him?

"What's wrong?" He lifted her chin, his green eyes probing. "Was it Chief Little Moose? Did he say something to upset you? I saw him by your fire."

She shook her head—though Chief Little Moose had upset her, he wasn't on her mind tonight.

"Please tell me." He took her hand and led her to the cot where they both sat.

There was no use keeping it hidden. He was the father, and he deserved to know the truth. She didn't need to shoulder this burden on her own. Even if there was nothing he could do, at least she would have comfort knowing she had not kept this from him.

She swallowed and hid her shaking hands beneath her quilt. She couldn't look at him while she uttered the words. "I-I'm going to have a baby."

Matthew

Matthew stared at Elizabeth's profile. Had he heard her correctly?

"Did you say a baby?"

She finally turned to him, her large eyes vulnerable in the dancing lantern light. He was suddenly reminded of how young she truly was. Only seventeen—yet she was full of maturity and wisdom far beyond her years.

Tears welled in her eyes, and one rolled down her cheek as she nodded.

For a moment, he could only stare at her—but then he took her in his arms and held her as she cried.

A baby.

At once, joy and despair raged within his heart.

He closed his eyes and saw Helen. Just tonight, walking along the shores of the lake, she had spoken of their impending marriage and the plans she had for a grand home in St. Paul. She talked of children and the church they would attend, and all manner of mundane affairs concerning servants and social obligations.

He had listened half-heartedly, thinking instead of Elizabeth and the life he could have with her. It would look so different. He had almost told Helen about Elizabeth but had thought better of it—for now. The treaty needed to be signed before he made any confessions. There would be time enough for that later.

But now he and Elizabeth had no other choice and part of him was relieved. He refused to walk the same path his own father had taken. He would love his child and never look with contempt upon him—no matter how he was brought into this world.

"Elizabeth." He pulled away and wiped the tears from her cheeks.

She looked at him and he saw the fear of rejection in her eyes.

He offered a tremulous smile. "I love you and I will not let you walk this path alone."

Her tears stopped and she studied his face. "I don't understand."

"I want you to be my wife."

She swallowed and shook her head. Her long hair was unbound tonight, and it fell to her waist. "But what of the treaty, and your career, and your mother, and Helen?"

He put up his hand to quiet her. "We'll wait until the treaty is signed to tell your father—and then we'll leave. We'll go west. Somewhere far away where we can start over."

"But—what about your mother and your sister?"

He hesitated and couldn't meet her gaze for a moment. An image of his mother came to mind. Always, she was working over the hot laundry tubs or straining her eyes over her sewing. His last memory was leaving her at their apartment, bent over a dirty tub of water. She couldn't even take time to see him off at the train station. When he had promised to become wealthy and take her away from the work, her eyes had shined with pride. Yet, here sat Elizabeth—and his child. Surely his mother would understand—hadn't she been in the same position? "I'll find a way to support them. It might take a little longer, but it can be done."

"How? You'll have to start all over again. It could be years before you'll earn enough money."

"Let me worry about the money, Elizabeth." He kissed her gently on the forehead.

She didn't look convinced.

He moved aside a silky strand of her hair. "The minute the treaty is signed, we'll go to your father and tell him."

"What about Chief Little Moose?"

A sliver of fear raced up Matthew's spine. There was no telling what Chief Little Moose would do. "Your father had no right to promise you to him. We'll deal with Chief Little Moose when the time comes."

"He will be angry."

He would be more than angry—but they couldn't worry about that right now. For now, they must keep this a secret, lest something went wrong and the treaty remained unsigned.

"Try not to worry." He pulled her into his embrace once again, reveling in the fact that she would soon be his. Forever.

He took her hand, wishing he could protect her even when she was away from him. So many things could go wrong.

"I must go back before I'm missed." Elizabeth pulled away and stood before Matthew. She placed her hand over her abdomen. A delicate smile, like that of a tender seedling unfurling under the sun, appeared on her lips.

Matthew stood and placed his hand over hers. "This is not how I would have started our life together."

"I know."

"I love you—and our baby—" He choked on the words, overcome with an emotion he had never felt before. "More than I realized possible." He leaned down and kissed her—feeling free to do so for the first time since meeting her.

She offered him a beautiful smile and then slipped out of his tent as quietly as she had come in.

A loon called on the lake, so near, it startled him.

For a moment, he simply stood and thought of the child in Elizabeth's womb.

He had often thought of being a father—but an old familiar fear always accompanied the thought. Would he do a good job? He had no experience to rely upon. No teacher to show the way. But he would have Elizabeth, and where he lacked, she would shine.

He sat on his cot and noticed the Bible.

If he was going to be a father, then he needed to come to an understanding about God and what he believed. The best place to start would be the beginning.

The tent flap opened, and Jacob entered.

Matthew laid aside the book and rose, surprised by Jacob's presence. "What can I do for you?"

Jacob's eyes were glossy and he smelled of rum. He glared at Matthew, looking like a ferocious animal with his red hair mussed and his beard in need of a trim. Clearly, he had been drinking.

"Go to bed, Jacob."

"No." He shook his head with a bit more emphasis than necessary. "I came to tell you what the chiefs are discussing at the council meeting—but I had to wait until Elizabeth left."

Elizabeth.

Matthew took a step closer to Jacob. "You heard Elizabeth?"

Jacob sneered. "I heard every word."

Had he? Or was he bluffing?

"I also heard you." Jacob stepped close to Matthew and swayed. "So, you're going to be a father." His eyes narrowed. "How nice."

"You're drunk. Go to bed."

"Not drunk enough, apparently." He grabbed Matthew's shirt.

Matthew's pulse thrummed through his body. The last thing they needed was a fight to rouse the camp—and then Jacob to announce their news. He swallowed, fully aware that Jacob held the upper hand.

"What do you want from me?" Matthew asked.

Jacob's breath reeked of alcohol and his lips curled into a snarl. "I want that land."

The land. What good would it do Matthew once he and Elizabeth went west?

"It's yours. I'll sign the deed over to you as soon as the treaty is signed."

Jacob's snarl turned to a sick smile. "You don't think it will be that easy, do you?"

Matthew swallowed. He had nothing else to offer.

Jacob let him go and straightened his shirt, suddenly looking sober. "You stole a great deal of annuity money to buy that land. All I would need to do is tell the superintendent and you'd face imprisonment—or worse."

Panic crept up Matthew's legs, crawling toward his heart. "I said you could have the land."

"I want more than the land."

"I don't have anything else."

"You have Elizabeth."

Matthew stared at Jacob, dread mingling with the panic. "What do you mean?"

"I want the land *and* Elizabeth."

"What—?"

"As soon as the treaty is signed, you and I will go to Chief White Thunder and tell him I am the father of Elizabeth's child. He will force her to marry me."

"Are you insane?"

"And don't think of sneaking off. If you leave with Elizabeth, I'll have the troops hunt you down and haul you back here to face the superintendent—and prison."

"You *are* insane. Elizabeth would never agree to marry you."

"She won't need to. Who will the chief believe?" He took Elizabeth's snood from his pocket. "How would a man have something like this if he wasn't intimate with her?"

Matthew reached for the snood, but Jacob yanked it out of his way.

"I will never stand with you and tell her father the child is yours."

"Then you'll face imprisonment—and Elizabeth will be forced to raise the child on her own."

Just like Mother had been forced to raise Matthew and Margaret on her own.

Jacob's eyelids half-closed in victory. "Now I think you're starting to see reason."

Matthew shook his head. "I could never betray Elizabeth."

Jacob took a step toward the opening of the tent. "I came to tell you the council has reached an agreement. They will sign the treaty tomorrow—and then you and I will visit with Chief White Thunder."

"I won't."

Jacob smiled—this time his satisfaction complete. "You won't have a choice."

He stepped out of the tent and Matthew sank to his cot, panic overtaking his soul.

Chapter Seventeen

Elizabeth

Elizabeth stood on the side of Matthew's tent, her heart pounding like the beat of a war drum.

Earlier, when she had left the tent, she saw a man lurking near the lake and had quickly stepped into the tall grass beside the tent to hide until he passed by.

Instead, he had entered the tent, and Elizabeth had stood in stunned silence as she heard Mr. Bailey accuse Matthew of stealing Indian annuities—and buying land with the money.

The information was almost too astonishing to believe—but Matthew hadn't denied the claim. He had taken money from her people—from her.

He had always told her the truth—even when the truth was ugly, which is why she loved him. But to find out he had stolen money scalded her heart and her trust.

What other crimes had he committed? What other falsehoods had he told her? Hadn't he been lying to Helen all this time, too? Would he have ever told Helen the truth about his night with Elizabeth?

She pressed her hands to the sides of her head to stop the accusations and taunting.

Matthew loved her—didn't he? He wanted to marry her—or so he said. Maybe he wanted to wait until the treaty was signed for his own gain and then he would hand her over to Chief Little Moose.

Men used women as pawns to get what they wanted. She had always known this. But she had believed—had hoped—Matthew was different. He had appeared so honest the first day they met. He had told her why he was there to teach her. From the start, she believed he would always tell her the truth.

Elizabeth's stomach rolled and she ran to a stand of elm trees and relieved her pain. Tears raced down her cheeks as she wiped her mouth, almost too weak to stand upright.

The wind rustled the trees, and the moon peaked out from behind a cloud, illuminating the worn path before her. The camp was eerily silent as she stumbled to her tent. She entered as quietly as possible. Her mother was asleep with a child in her arms. The floor was littered with children, piled upon each other in slumber.

Thankfully her father had not yet returned from the council meeting, or he might have awakened and asked where she had been.

Elizabeth squeezed into the corner of the tent under a pile of furs. She pulled her cold legs up to her middle and wrapped herself in a hug—wishing she could be in Matthew's arm and despising herself for such a thought. He did not belong to her—had never belonged to her.

She lay there for over an hour, tears her only companion.

Her father entered and moved the sleeping child from Mother's arms. He began to disrobe, and Elizabeth closed her eyes and buried her head beneath her covers.

She lay awake until the first light of day seeped into the dark tent. As the sun rose, so too did her realization. No matter what Matthew had done, she still loved him—and knew, in the deepest part of her heart, that he loved her—despite the lies and the stealing. There were parts of him that had been true and decent and honorable. She had seen the look in his eyes when he learned there was a child. He would give it all up for her and the baby.

But Jacob's threat had played through her mind during the endless night, as well. If she did not marry Jacob, Matthew would face imprisonment—or worse. What would happen to his mother and sister if he was locked away? There would be no hope for any of them.

But, if Elizabeth married Jacob, Matthew could go on with his life and marry Helen and pursue the dream he had set out to achieve. She wanted to believe that somehow, someway, he could return the annuity money to her people, as well.

Marrying Matthew had never been an option—not from the moment she met him—and it had been unfair to ask him to give up everything for her. If she was honest with herself, she had to admit she was the one who had gone to him that night.

She had no one to blame but herself. Matthew shouldn't be punished for her mistake.

Before the day fully arrived, she must choose between Jacob Bailey and Chief Little Moose. She had no other option.

Both men were detestable to her—but Jacob knew about the baby and wanted her regardless. If she went with him, she would reenter the world she had known growing up at the mission, and she would not have to live in shame, bearing another man's son. If she went with Chief Little Moose—she shuddered, unable to even think about being one of his wives. She had watched her own mother living as one of multiple wives and knew it wasn't the life she wanted.

There was only one choice to make.

To save Matthew, she would marry Jacob Bailey.

It wasn't until her mother stirred and began to dress that Elizabeth realized she had not once asked Father God what choice He would have her make. But what would it matter? She had walked outside His will the night she had given herself to Matthew and she would have to face her consequences, come what may.

Matthew

Matthew stared at the stained canvas above his head, the early morning sun streaming through the thick material. People began to stir in camp. Fires started with pops and sizzles, while kettles and pans banged together and voices mingled in low, muffled tones.

He rolled onto his side, his head pounding. His eyes felt gritty, and his limbs ached from lack of sleep.

One way or another, he would have to make a choice he didn't want to make.

If he chose to leave with Elizabeth, he would be hunted down and put in prison and Elizabeth would be left to raise their child on her own, ostracized by her people and his.

If he chose to tell Chief White Thunder Elizabeth carried Jacob's child—he would betray the woman he loved and live with the guilt for the rest of his life.

Tuck's words returned to him, in clear, vivid detail.

He had taken the wide path that led to destruction—and it was too late to turn back and look for the narrow way. No matter what choice he made, Elizabeth and his child would suffer.

Matthew rolled onto his back and closed his eyes, pain and frustration knotting in his stomach. He dreaded facing the day. If Jacob was correct, the treaty would be signed today, and he would have to make his choice concerning Elizabeth.

By the time he fell asleep tonight, he would either be in chains, awaiting his trial—or he would have to watch Elizabeth marry another man.

Both would be torture.

"Major Merrick!" A young man called through the canvas walls. "Mr. Baker has called all the men to meet in the government tent immediately."

"Thank you," Matthew managed to answer.

He sat up and put his bare feet on the cold ground. The pain in his head demanded he lie back down—but he must do his job.

As quickly as possible, he dressed and left his tent. A beautiful blue sky met him the moment he stepped outside. The glass-like lake reflected the vibrant autumn colors and cloudless sky. It felt as if nature was mocking him. Displaying its brilliance when all was dark in his soul.

The camp was now alive with activity. Chiefs, band elders, and warriors somberly walked toward the government tent, while clerks and soldiers buzzed about like bees bringing nectar to the hive.

Matthew slipped inside and found Mr. Baker seated at a table with Chief White Thunder and numerous other Chippewa men. Jacob stood toward the back, his brown eyes pinned on Matthew the moment he entered.

"Major." Mr. Baker nodded to Matthew. "I'll have you act as a representative of the United States Government. You'll sign the treaty with me."

Matthew had known he would be the co-signer—yet he suddenly felt unsure about putting his name to a piece of paper that would destroy the Chippewa's way of life in one stroke of ink.

He glanced at Chief White Thunder who watched him with grave eyes. Not all the chiefs and elders were in agreement about handing over the land—but they were all tired and eager to be done with the whole affair. The fight had not started here at the headwaters. Many of them had been fighting the inevitability of this moment their whole lives.

Matthew took a seat next to Mr. Baker and watched him sign the document. He handed the quill to Matthew, who took it in his trembling hand. Without further thought, Matthew affixed his name.

One by one, the chiefs, elders, and warriors came forward to sign the document, their faces stoic and resigned.

The weight of the moment was heavy on Matthew's shoulders. These were no longer nameless, faceless people. He knew many of them, understood their culture better than he had when he'd first arrived. For centuries, the Chippewa had lived and died on these lands—and now they were ceding them over to the government to be used for white settlement. Their way of life would cease after the treaty was brought to Washington, DC, ratified by the senate, and signed by President Lincoln. Part of Matthew wanted to cry out and stop them from coming forward—but the beast was much larger than him, and he was but one voice raging against a sea of countless people clamoring for land.

Chief Little Moose moved through the group and leaned over the table to sign his name. The deep scar on his cheek glared at Matthew like a warning. This was a fierce warrior who had been in battle and survived to tell about it. Was he thinking of Elizabeth? Did he plan to take her to be his wife this very night? The thought repulsed Matthew.

After the last man came forward to sign, Jacob rolled up the document and placed it in a tube. He left the tent, no doubt to give it to the courier standing by. The treaty would be sent to the United States Senate immediately under armed guard.

As the men poured out of the tent, Mr. Baker extended his hand to Matthew, a grin on his face. "We did it, my boy. The treaty is signed, and your job is done."

Matthew shook his hand but felt no satisfaction.

"I suppose Helen will want you to shift all your attention to the wedding now. She and Mrs. Baker are ready to go at a moment's notice." He stood and Matthew followed. "The governor would like to appoint you as his Chief Legal Counsel. He will make the position official as soon as you can get back to St. Paul."

It was a job he had wanted six months ago—but now?

Chief Little Moose followed Chief White Thunder toward Straw Weaver's tent.

"If you'll excuse me." Matthew moved away from Mr. Baker.

"Of course, but I'd like for you to join us for supper tonight to celebrate." Mr. Baker nodded at Matthew. "Helen will be eager to solidify the wedding plans."

Matthew barely heard the last sentence as he maneuvered through the group of men.

He followed behind the two chiefs, his pulse pounding in his ears. Everything was about to come out into the open—but what would be the conclusion? How could any of this end well? What would Mr. Baker do? And Helen? And Chief Little Moose?

But, more importantly, what would become of Elizabeth and their child?

Up ahead, Elizabeth stood near her mother's tent. She wore a dark blue dress with a wide skirt and jet-black buttons down the front. Her hair was captured in a snood, and she wore a black shawl around her shoulders.

She looked past Chief White Thunder and Chief Little Moose to Matthew. Apprehension showed in the lines around her mouth—but it was the pain in her eyes that stopped Matthew on the path. She looked weak and vulnerable—and completely disillusioned.

It was then that Matthew saw Jacob standing just to the side of her.

Matthew looked back at Elizabeth. The depth of her disappointment could only mean one thing: she knew about the annuity. Somehow she knew. Had Jacob told her?

Chief White Thunder stopped before his daughter, but Matthew couldn't see his face. Was he surprised to see Jacob standing there?

Matthew would not stay behind and allow Elizabeth to face these men alone. He walked around the chiefs and stood on her other side.

She didn't look at him but stared straight at her father.

"Elizabeth—why are these men here?" Chief White Thunder looked at Jacob, then Matthew, and finally studied his daughter's face, his expression unreadable.

Straw Weaver exited her tent and stood motionless at the scene. Others from the camp stopped their work and gathered to watch.

Helen and her mother suddenly appeared on the path—curiosity on their faces.

Elizabeth didn't look at anyone but Chief White Thunder. "I asked Mr. Bailey here to—" She paused and swallowed. It was then Matthew saw her hand trembling by her side. "I cannot become Chief Little Moose's wife."

Chief Little Moose's eyes narrowed into slits, and he glared at Elizabeth.

"Why?" Chief White Thunder asked solemnly.

Elizabeth placed her hand over her stomach and Matthew's heartrate accelerated. He looked from Elizabeth to Jacob and then to Chief White Thunder.

"I am carrying another man's child."

Chief White Thunder's face became a mask of anger, while Chief Little Moose stepped toward Elizabeth.

At the same moment, Jacob and Matthew stepped in front of her.

"No!" Elizabeth cried.

Chief White Thunder lifted his hand and placed it on Chief Little Moose's chest. "There will be no violence." He nodded toward a group of soldiers who stood by watching. "It will not end well."

Chief Little Moose's face was set like stone. "I will not take this woman as my wife now."

"Who is the father?" Chief White Thunder asked—his fiery gaze shifting between Matthew and Jacob.

Elizabeth pushed through the men and stood in front of her father. "Jacob Bailey."

Matthew shook his head. "Elizabeth."

She quickly turned around, her eyes demanding Matthew's silence, and then she took a decided step toward Jacob.

"You have dishonored my family," Chief White Thunder said to Jacob. "You will take her and leave."

Elizabeth kept her back toward her father and her eyes downcast.

"Elizabeth," Matthew whispered.

"Say nothing," she whispered back, her voice strained.

"I will take her to the chaplain and marry her immediately." Jacob put his hand on her elbow, and she turned toward him.

Together they walked away from Straw Weaver's tent.

"Did you know?" Chief White Thunder asked Matthew, anger hardening his face, while grief softened his eyes.

"No." He had no idea Elizabeth would claim Jacob.

He could hardly breathe with the knowledge. He needed to go after them—to make sense of all that had just happened.

Chief Little Moose spat on the ground and then walked away, his head held high.

The others began to disperse. Helen stood on the path, judgment and condemnation on her face. Matthew walked in the direction Jacob and Elizabeth had walked, but he had to pass by Helen.

"Can you imagine?" Helen asked. "Did you have any idea?"

Matthew swallowed and shook his head.

"Where are you going?" Helen demanded when he did not stop.

"I—" He couldn't put two thoughts together. "I'll see you later."

Helen's lips parted and she crossed her arms—but he continued on. The chaplain's tent was on the opposite side of camp, near the birch grove, away from the others. Matthew raced down the path and saw Jacob and Elizabeth about a hundred yards from their destination.

He overtook them and threw all his weight into tackling Jacob to the ground.

Elizabeth's cry pierced the air as Matthew threw his fists against the unsuspecting man. Jacob twisted beneath him, throwing Matthew into the dirt.

Both men jumped to their feet.

"Matthew!" Elizabeth grabbed his arm before he launched himself at Jacob again.

Jacob glared at Matthew while he rubbed his jaw—but he made no move to fight.

"Why?" Matthew looked to Elizabeth for an answer. "Why would you do this?"

Tears gathered in her eyes. "For you."

"Me?" He stared at her, tears stinging the backs of his eyes. "I won't let you."

"It's the only way." Elizabeth pleaded for him to understand—but how could he? "I heard Mr. Bailey in your tent last night. I know about the annuity." She put her hands on his arms. "There's no other option, Matthew. Either way, you're lost to me. At least this way I will know you are still free to provide for your mother and sister." She looked at Jacob, anguish in her eyes. "I made Mr. Bailey promise to pay back the annuity fund for the land, so you are free. Your debt is canceled." She returned her gaze to Matthew's face. "I won't let you do something foolish for me."

Jacob took a step forward and put his hand on Elizabeth's elbow. "The chaplain is waiting." He didn't acknowledge Matthew but turned them away and prodded her down the path.

She looked over her shoulder—a final farewell in her beautiful eyes.

No matter what Matthew said—or did—she would not return to him. He knew this as well as he knew the sun would rise on the morrow and the autumn would pass into winter. It was a thing he could not control.

They entered the chaplain's tent and Matthew stumbled deeper into the woods—away from the camp and the questions and the inevitability of it all.

He dropped to the ground, his legs too weak to hold him upright—and he wept.

Chapter Eighteen

December 24, 1917

Emma

Emma lifted the basket of fruit from the passenger side and closed the door to her Ford. The afternoon sky was a mass of light gray clouds, but the roads had been clear so she had ventured out on this delivery.

The Bailey home stood like a beacon of warmth on this cold day. Her toes and fingertips were frozen from the car ride—but it would be worth it to see Cade and wish him a Merry Christmas. It had been weeks since she had seen him, and she could think of nothing else. She longed to tell him Rebecca had made a full recovery and was expecting again—but really, she wanted to satisfy her desire to see him, hoping she could then put him aside and focus her attention on getting to know Thomas—just as her father had asked.

A beautiful evergreen wreath hung on the door, and bows of evergreen and holly hung over the windows. A snowman, complete with a carrot nose and eyes made out of coal, stood proudly just to the south of the house. Emma had no doubt Gracie had created the happy winter scene.

She knocked on the kitchen door, surprised no one had heard or seen her approach.

Maybe they were not home. The thought had not crossed her mind until now—and it made her heart plummet in disappointment. She had so hoped to see Cade before Christmas and the New Year.

The door opened and Mrs. Bailey stood on the other side, surprise and delight on her face. "Miss Merrick, come in." She opened the door wide. "It's been far too long since we've seen you."

"Merry Christmas," Emma said shyly. She stepped into the warm kitchen, the smell of gingerbread and coffee tantalizing her hungry stomach.

"Merry Christmas, indeed." Mrs. Bailey closed the door. "Let me take your wraps."

"I can't stay long."

"Nonsense! You've come all this way. You must stay long enough to warm yourself and have a bit of gingerbread."

She handed the basket of fruit to Mrs. Bailey. "This is a gift for your family to enjoy over the holidays."

Mrs. Bailey took the offering, her eyes shining. "Thank you. It isn't often we have fresh fruit in the winter."

Emma took off her coat, scarf, and hat and placed them on a hook near the door. She had worn her favorite afternoon dress. The green material complimented her auburn curls—and she had been told she looked lovely in it. She hoped Cade would think so.

She glanced toward the parlor where an evergreen tree had been set in the corner awaiting its decorations. The room smelled of fresh pine and cinnamon.

Where was everyone else?

"Cade and Gracie are in the attic bringing down the boxes of decorations." Mrs. Bailey smiled at Emma, as if reading her thoughts. "They will be as pleased as I am that you're here." She put a mug of steaming coffee on the table. "Have a seat and make yourself at home." She took two plates from the cabinet and set two pieces of gingerbread onto the plates. "I think I'll join you."

The Bailey home was modest, but it was warm and cozy, and Emma found herself nestling into the chair—though her senses were perked, listening for Cade. She had spent weeks hoping he would reach out to her, to let her know he was thinking about her as much as she was thinking about him, but he had not even sent a note. Would he be upset that she'd come?

Mrs. Bailey took a seat across from Emma, her kind blue eyes resting on Emma's face. How strange it would be to have a mother who sat across from her and engaged in conversation. How strange—and wonderful.

"Are you staying busy with your work?" Mrs. Bailey asked. "I imagine you're not traveling as much."

"No, I'm working more at the hospital this winter. I hate to stay confined in the building, when I know there are so many people in need—but I have to reserve my trips for emergency situations only."

"I admire what you're doing." Mrs. Bailey took a sip of her coffee. "It's a noble profession."

Emma felt her cheeks grow warm at the compliment.

"Cade speaks very highly of you," Mrs. Bailey continued. "He's been a different man since the two of you became friends."

Emma offered a brief smile and then took a sip of her coffee, not knowing how to answer—or how to feel—at such a statement. If he felt the way Mrs. Bailey claimed, then why the silence?

Noise came from the stairway in the parlor and Mrs. Bailey's eyes lit with excitement. "They've found the decorations. Would you help us trim our tree?"

"Oh, no, I couldn't possibly intrude." Her heart beat with uncertainty, not knowing how Cade would receive her.

"It wouldn't be an intrusion. We'd love for you to join us." Mrs. Bailey stood and she nudged Emma to stand. "Come. I can't wait for Cade to see you."

Emma followed Mrs. Bailey into the parlor. The door to the upstairs was closed, but the two merry-makers coming down the steps were creating a joyful ruckus that filled the room. Their voices lifted in a Christmas carol Emma knew very well.

"*Here we come a-wassailing*
Among the leaves so green;
Here we come a-wand'ring
So fair to be seen.
Love and joy come to you,
And to you your wassail too;
And God bless you and send you a Happy New Year
And God send you a Happy New Year."

The stairway door opened and out came Grace with her cheeks rosy and her eyes shining. When she saw Emma, she raced to her side and threw her arms around her in a tight hug. "Nurse Merrick!"

Just behind Grace, Cade appeared, a large brown box in his arms. His voice was rich and melodic as he continued the carol.

When he saw Emma, he paused on the stairs and stopped singing. Pure delight appeared on his face, and he smiled at her. "Emma."

She returned the smile, her heart filled with relief and deep affection. "Merry Christmas, Cade."

He stepped into the room and set the box near the tree. He crossed the room and looked as if he might embrace her—but then he extended his hand, and she put hers inside his. Pleasure raced through her midsection at his touch and the way he was looking at her.

"Merry Christmas, Emma."

"I've asked Emma to help us trim the tree," Mrs. Bailey said.

"Oh, please do!" Grace cried. "It would be so much fun! We're going to make popcorn and hot chocolate later and listen to Mama read Henry's letter again. Then we'll sit near the fireplace and sing carols and listen to Cade read the story of Christ's birth from the Book of Luke."

Emma removed her hand from Cade's, but the sensation of his touch remained.

The invitation was tempting—though it would be foolish for her to stay when night was quickly approaching. Yet, what awaited her at home? Her mother was hosting yet another party, and she would be required to make small talk through the night. Thomas would be there—but his company did not compare to the Bailey's.

She looked at Cade—did he want her to stay?

His face was tender as he regarded her, and his eyes were filled with an invitation. "I would love if you stayed."

Emma looked around the room at the expectant faces and she couldn't say no. "For a little while."

"Yay!" Grace danced about the room, her voice soon lifting with more carols.

"I'm missing all the fun!" Mr. Bailey called from the other room.

Cade left the parlor and came back a few moments later assisting Mr. Bailey. It was the first time Emma saw him on his feet, and it did her heart good. He looked more like Cade than she had realized, though he was dreadfully thin and pale.

Mrs. Bailey and Grace arranged pillows on the sofa and Cade helped him settle into place.

"Miss Merrick, a very Merry Christmas to you," Mr. Bailey said, lifting his hand.

Emma took it in hers. "Please, call me Emma."

He smiled, and the kindness in his face made her feel even more welcomed into this tight family circle.

Mrs. Bailey opened the box of decorations and began taking them out, one by one, telling them about the history behind each ornament. Her voice was gentle, and she held the fragile decorations with a bit of awe—but then she handed one to Grace, trusting her to carry it to the tree.

As Grace placed the first ornament, Mrs. Bailey exchanged a glance with her husband. The look they shared was full of memories, love, and deep sadness.

Emma watched in fascination at the relationship between Mrs. Bailey and Grace—and Mrs. Bailey and her husband. It was truly beautiful to behold.

Cade stepped near and her attention shifted.

"I'm happy you're here, Emma." He ran his thumb over a wooden ornament in his hands as he looked down at it, his voice apologetic. "I've wanted to see you—but I wasn't sure if I would be welcomed at Major Merrick's home."

Her heart skipped a beat at the revelation, but before she could answer, Grac cried, "Look! It's starting to snow."

Emma looked outside. The window framed a picturesque scene with the Mississippi frozen in the background and the lawn rolling down to the banks covered in a white blanket of snow. Large, white snowflakes drifted from the sky, clinging to the branches of the leafless trees.

"I hope we don't get a storm," Emma said softly. "I won't be able to get home."

Cade leaned close and said for her ears alone, "I hope we do."

Cade

Cade stood at the kitchen window, looking out at the white world. The snow was falling so thick, he could not see past Emma's car parked close to the house. The snow swirled and danced in the biting wind.

"I hope you don't mind sleeping on the sofa," Mama said to Emma in the next room. "It doesn't feel right, asking a Merrick to sleep in the parlor."

"I will be fine—truly," Emma said in her sweet voice. "I'm thankful for a warm place to sleep tonight."

"I would give you Grace's bed upstairs—but—"

But Cade's room was on the other side of the wall—with no one else upstairs. It wouldn't be proper for Emma to sleep there—and it was cold. He and Grace were used to it—but Emma would freeze.

"This is perfect," Emma said in her gracious tone.

It was late. Grace and Dad had already gone to bed. Mama's voice sounded fatigued—but she had stayed up to take care of Emma.

Cade quietly stepped over to the door and stopped at the scene before him.

Mama and Emma stood with the lighted Christmas tree just behind them.

"Thank you for inviting me to join your family tonight," Emma said.

Mama smiled at Emma and put her hand on Emma's cheek. "You have been a gift to us—and to Cade."

Cade's heart squeezed at the truth of his mother's words. Not a day had passed when he hadn't thought about Emma. She was almost always the first thing on his mind in the morning when he woke and the last thing he thought about before he went to sleep. He'd wanted to go to her a dozen times, but the possibility of being turned out by Major Merrick had stopped him each time.

When Emma showed up on his doorstep, on Christmas Eve, it made him hope that she cared for him as much as he did for her. It had taken all of his willpower not to pull her into his arms.

Seeing the shine in her eyes at Mama's comment now almost undid him completely.

"Thank you," Emma said. "For everything."

Cade stepped out of the kitchen and joined his mother and Emma in the parlor. The Christmas tree had been trimmed, and the candles had been lit before Dad and Gracie went to bed. It glowed with an angelic presence, each little light radiating a soft halo of gold.

Mama yawned and then covered her mouth in embarrassment.

"Go to bed, Mama," Cade said, wanting to finally be alone with Emma. "I'll blow out the candles."

Mama looked between them, uncertainty in her eyes.

He knew exactly what she was thinking. He smiled at her. "I'll be a gentleman—and besides, you're on the other side of the wall."

Emma's cheeks filled with color, and Mama shook her head, a smile on her lips. "Good night, then. I'll see you two in the morning." She hugged Emma. "Thank you for joining us tonight. I don't remember a more joyful Christmas—even though our Henry is so far away."

"I don't remember a more joyful Christmas, either," Emma said.

Mama kissed Cade's cheek, a knowing gleam in her eye. "Don't stay up too late."

He winked at her, and she left the room.

Emma stood in the glow of the candlelight, her auburn curls soft and silky. "You are a rich man, Cade Bailey."

"Rich?"

"This family—this home—I hope you realize how blessed you are."

Blessed? He had always felt as if this farm had been a curse—but tonight he saw it in a different light.

She moved to the window and looked out at the snowy world. "I'm sure everyone at home is worried. They'll think I went off the road and am lying somewhere freezing to death."

"I don't think anyone will be out looking for you in this weather."

The night was black as the snow swirled against the windows.

Cade didn't want to go to bed yet. He had never felt more awake in his life. He motioned to the rocking chairs sitting next to the fireplace. "Would you mind if I stayed for a while?"

The look she gave him was so full of awareness and expectancy, it made his pulse climb. "I would like that."

Cade sat beside her and gently rocked his chair. The fireplace crackled behind them, and the candles shimmered on the tree.

"This is my favorite time of year," Cade said. "When I was away, I missed Christmas more than anything else."

Emma was quiet.

"What about you?" he asked. "Did you enjoy Christmas growing up?"

She rested her elbows on the arm rests and clasped her hands in front of her. She stared at the tree, but her gaze looked far away. "I didn't like Christmas—at least, not the Christmases in my home."

Cade stopped rocking. "Why not?"

"My mother has always had a Christmas Eve party, filled with dozens of people I never knew. Christmas morning, when other children jumped out of bed and ran to their presents, I was told to be quiet and let my mother sleep. I had to read or play quietly until after lunch when she would come downstairs. She often has a headache the day after a large party, and Christmas Day was no exception." Emma rocked, but it was as if she was not with him—was somewhere else entirely. "When we finally sat down to open presents, my father was called to join us, and they sat on opposite sides of the room—never sharing a word. I sat in the middle, in a pile of presents, and opened them one by one in silence. When I was finished, my father and mother would leave and I would be alone."

She turned and looked at Cade. "But it wasn't all bad." She smiled, and behind the sadness he could see a bit of joy. "The staff had a half day off on Christmas and they had a lovely party in the evening. I was always invited. It was like a great family gathering. Martha would make a wonderful meal with all my favorites, and her daughter Rebecca and I would play with the toys I had received from my parents. Sam would take me on his lap and tell me stories about Ireland and his family traditions. We would bob for apples, and sing carols, and play games—but—" She stopped and swallowed. "It never quite made up for the first half of the day."

Cade reached over and took Emma's hand.

She looked at him, her brown eyes vulnerable in the firelight.

"I misjudged you when I first met you," he said, ashamed and humbled. "I'm sorry for the way I treated you."

Her brows furrowed. "Why are you telling me this now?"

"Because." How could he explain? "Because you've had your heart broken far too often—and I couldn't live with myself if I knew I caused you more heartache."

Tears shimmered in her eyes. "Thank you."

She gently slipped her hand out of his and stood. "I have something for you." She left the parlor and went into the kitchen. A few moments later she returned with a small package wrapped in tissue paper. "I had it in my coat pocket."

She placed the package in his hand and sat down again. "Merry Christmas."

"I don't have anything for you."

"This," she motioned to the room, "the whole day has been a gift. Thank you for not throwing me out on my ear when I arrived."

He shook his head, smiling at her. "I'm happy you came, Emma."

She returned his smile as he untied the string holding the package together and then moved aside the tissue. A red box lay underneath. He lifted it out of the paper and opened the lid.

There, lying on a bed of cotton, was a pin with a pair of golden wings attached.

"Before I met you, I was confined to the earth." Her voice was low and smooth. "But you've given me wings to fly—and I'll forever cherish the freedom it has brought."

Emotion choked the back of his throat as he fingered the delicate pin. He couldn't look at her—not yet. "Thank you."

"You're welcome."

A log shifted in the fire, sending sparks flying into the air.

He finally lifted his face and found her watching him. "You've given me a far greater gift, Emma Merrick. You've given me roots. For the first time in my life, I feel as if I have found my home—I just needed to see this farm through your eyes and realize what a gift it is."

He wanted to say more—but he was afraid he might say too much. Somehow, in the past three months, he had come to care for her deeply—yet he was in no better position to offer her a future. She deserved so much better than he could provide. She wasn't meant to live on a farm—especially this farm. It had been a hard life for his mother and father—a life he didn't want her to endure.

His only other real skill was flying. He could make a decent living in the air, but he couldn't bring himself to contemplate another aerial show—and it wasn't a life he wanted when he was married, separated for months on end with the constant threat of death hovering.

He had nothing to offer Emma but himself—and he feared that would never be enough.

They rocked in silence, both gazing at the Christmas tree.

He fingered the golden wings and wished he knew her thoughts. Because, despite the obstacles in their way—he longed for her to return his affection. He knew it was selfish and would only cause them pain—but his heart had started to yearn for hers.

Chapter Nineteen

Emma

Emma walked out of the Bailey house the next morning with an armful of treats from Mrs. Bailey. A beautiful sleigh awaited her with Cade securing the bells to the harnesses. Her car would never drive on these roads, so Cade had graciously offered to take her home.

"Be careful," Mrs. Bailey called to Cade. "And if it looks like the storm will start again, be sure to stay in town. I don't want you driving in this weather."

Cade took the packages from Emma's arms and smiled at his mother. "You forget I managed to keep myself alive for the past seven years without you, Mama." His breath puffed out on a white cloud and his green eyes shone in his handsome face. He looked at Emma. "Will you be warm enough?"

"Your mother gave me hot bricks for my feet, and she lent me an extra pair of woolen socks."

Cade put Emma's packages in the bottom of the sleigh and helped her step over the runners. After he placed the bricks at her feet, he piled layers of blankets and robes over her body, tucking them in around her, until she began to giggle. "I'll be fine—if I can manage to breath with all these covers."

He smiled at her and then stepped into the sleigh on the other side.

The storm had passed, leaving the world in a frozen wonderland with icicles dripping from the trees and large drifts of snow blown across the land. Clouds in the west threatened another storm, but Emma had to get home before people went out looking for her.

"We'll bring your Ford in sometime when the roads are cleared." Cade picked up the reins and slapped them against the horses' backs to get them to move.

"Merry Christmas," Mrs. Bailey called, waving from the kitchen door. Gracie stood beside her, a grin on her face, waving so enthusiastically her whole body shook from the motion.

Emma waved back as the sleigh pulled out of the Bailey farm, the bells jingling.

The air was frosty, but it felt invigorating to be in the open sleigh, riding along beside Cade. That morning, she had helped Mrs. Bailey get breakfast on the table and had sat with the family as they laughed and teased one another. After breakfast, Mr. Bailey had been brought out to the parlor and there had been presents exchanged. Everything had been homemade with love—and Emma had been struck by the beauty of the gifts. Nothing was elaborate or expensive, but they were thoughtful and useful.

Since they had not anticipated Emma's presence, Mrs. Bailey had boxed up her favorite oatmeal cookies and gingerbread cake and sent them along as her Christmas gift.

Emma burrowed into her scarf and pulled her hat low over her head. Her feet were toasty, but the rest of her was freezing.

"You can get closer to me," Cade said, and then quickly added, "for warmth."

Emma scooted over until their legs were pressed together under the blankets. "Thank you."

They rode in silence and Emma felt comfortable not needing to fill the void with conversation. Cade's presence warmed her body and soul.

The sleigh glided over the fresh snow, almost as if they were flying—and it made Emma long for the airplane once again.

Snow began to fall in large flakes. The wind picked up and soon it was swirling around them again.

"We only have a couple more miles, but the storm isn't letting up," Cade said. "Hold tight, I'm going to encourage the horses to ride hard."

Emma pressed her feet against the floor and held on to the side of the sleigh. The snow began to fall with more intensity and soon they couldn't see much farther than a few feet ahead of them.

The stone pillars on the outside of the circular drive came within sight and Emma tugged on Cade's arm. "Here."

They couldn't make out the drive, so Cade drove straight toward the house. Thomas's Ford sat under the front portico, buried in snow at the front and the back.

Emma sighed, knowing how difficult it would be to explain her absence last night—and Cade's presence this morning. "We can go in through the servant's entrance around back. I rarely use the front door."

Cade maneuvered the horses to the back and Sam appeared at the carriage house door, his face revealing his lack of sleep. He lifted his hands to the sky—and Emma knew he was thanking God for her safe arrival.

"Emmie, where have you been?" Sam asked as the horses came to a stop outside the carriage house.

She unburied herself from the blankets and robes she was under, blinking as snowflakes gathered on her lashes. "I went to the Bailey's to bring them a gift and stayed there when the storm began."

Cade stepped out of the sleigh and Sam inspected him from head to foot.

"Sam, this is Cade Bailey," Emma said.

Cade extended his hand and Sam shook it. "It's nice to meet you," Cade said.

Sam nodded, though his eyes looked wary. "Thank you for bringing Emma home safely."

Cade offered his hand to help Emma out of the sleigh.

"I trust there were other people with you last night," Sam said to Emma, a warning in his voice.

Emma smiled at him and kissed him on the cheek. "Cade's parents and sister were there."

"Good." He took the horse's harness nearest to him. "You two go on inside and warm up. I'll see to the horses."

"That won't be necessary," Cade said.

"It's the least I can do to thank you." Sam looked at Cade and then his gaze slid to Emma. "I'll come in a bit later and get to know this young man."

Emma led Cade to the back entrance and didn't miss the look of wonder on his face as he inspected the large home.

"I'd heard rumors—but I hadn't imagined how palatial it was." Cade looked up at the stone house, his head tilted back.

Emma didn't know how she would present Cade—especially with Thomas present. She still wondered why the Bailey's had disliked her father. Was it a mutual feeling? How would Father feel when he learned a Bailey was under their roof? Would they ask how the two had met? What if they discovered she had been taking flying lessons? There were so many questions and so many possible outcomes.

They walked into the kitchen and found Martha mixing together the ingredients for a plum pudding. Other kitchen staff bustled about, and the room was filled with delicious Christmas aromas and tantalizing dishes of food.

Martha looked up and her anxious expression turned to relief. "Mercy on us! Emma! You're home." She rushed to Emma and threw her arms around her. "I didn't sleep a wink last night, fearing the worst." Martha's eyes landed on Cade, and she lifted a brow. "And who is this?"

Cade took off his stocking cap and his dark hair was tousled—and terribly attractive.

"Martha, this is Cade Bailey—the pilot."

"I know who Cade Bailey is." Martha's hand went up to her hair and she blushed. "I saw *Flying High*."

"Where is Mother?" Emma asked. "I should tell her about my arrival."

"She's in the parlor with Mr. Overton."

"How is Father?" Emma took off her hat and scarf.

"He's been resting, like he was told, but he isn't quite the same as before. He may try to join the family later."

Emma hung her coat and hat on the back hook and looked at Cade, who stood with his outer gear still on. "Will you come with me to meet my parents?" she asked.

He glanced over her shoulder, as if seeing through the walls to the front of the house. "I don't think it would be a good idea."

"Please." She was amazed by how much she wanted him to meet them—despite all the questions they would receive.

Martha moved away—as if sensing they needed some privacy.

"You need to spend Christmas with your family. I'll just be in the way."

"You won't be in the way." She took his hand and tried pulling him.

He wouldn't go. "Emma. I don't think I'll be welcomed."

She stopped and studied his serious face. "Why not?"

He glanced at Martha, who worked on her pudding—pretending not to listen. "I don't think your father will be happy to see me."

She didn't understand. "Why?"

He sighed. "There was a feud between him and my grandfather that spanned back to the 1860's, as far as I know. I don't think a Bailey would be welcome in your home."

"We can try."

"No." He shook his head. "It wouldn't go well for either of us. I think I should go."

"You can't go back in the storm."

He glanced outside. The wind blew with a ferocious whine and snow blasted the window. "Then I'll go to the carriage house and see to my horses."

She didn't want him to go—but maybe he was right. Maybe it would be easier to explain the situation without him in the room. "Please don't go home in this weather—promise me."

"Alright."

"And don't leave without saying goodbye."

"I won't."

"I'll try to return as soon as I can." She offered him a smile and then turned to face the inevitable meeting.

She walked through the kitchen and down the servant's hall toward the front of the house.

Voices drifted out of the front parlor.

"I don't know what to do," Mother said. "Should we send the servants out to look for her?"

"She's an intelligent woman," Thomas said. "I'm sure she took shelter. We should just wait out the storm."

"And what if she didn't find shelter?" Mother asked.

"Then there's nothing we can do about her now," Thomas said. "What would be the point of looking?"

Emma froze in the hall. His words were not the words of a man who cared about the woman he was pursuing. She couldn't help but think if Cade were in his shoes, he would have been out in the storm all night, if need be.

Mother sighed. "I suppose you're right."

Emma felt a pang of betrayal—was she of so little consequence? Was she not worth looking for?

She almost turned back to join the others in the kitchen—but it wouldn't be right to withhold her presence from them. She entered the room to find them sitting at a table, a deck of cards spread out before them in a game of whist. The thirteen-foot Christmas tree dominated the corner of the room, decorated by the servants a few days before Christmas.

Thomas noticed her first. He jumped to his feet, his blue eyes enormous. "Emma!"

Mother turned and anger instantly flared in her eyes. "Where have you been? We've been worried sick."

"I was visiting friends and was caught in the storm. I was invited to stay the night."

Thomas crossed the room, his arms outstretched. He wore the same evening suit he had probably worn last night to the party—and it looked much too elegant for Christmas morning. "Emma, my dear, I'm so happy to see you're well."

Was he? She allowed him to take her hands, but she didn't offer him a smile.

Cade

Cade braced himself against the stinging snow and crossed the small drive to the carriage house. He pushed open the door and was welcomed into the warm room by a glowing lantern.

Sam looked up from currying Fanny, the Bailey's mare. "There's no need to be helping, lad."

Cade's shoulder's stiffened at the thought of returning to the house. As much as he would like to be with Emma, he didn't want to be embarrassed by being thrown out by Major Merrick.

"Ah." Sam stood straight and put the brush on a shelf nearby. "You're tryin' to avoid a confrontation."

How did he know?

"I remember your grandfather." Sam patted the horse's back and walked toward Cade. "He and the major didn't see eye to eye, did they now?"

"You knew my grandfather?"

"Aye—at least, I knew who he was." He took his coat off a hook and motioned for Cade to follow him. "Let's go on up to my apartment and enjoy a bit of tea and a good conversation before the staff's Christmas party."

Cade instantly liked this man. He carried himself with confidence and wisdom. Cade wished he could be like him—and the thought took him by surprise. When had he ever cared about being wise? He had led a carefree life after leaving the farm, and had never been one to offer advice or seek counsel. Now, however, the thought of being a man of character and insight appealed to him…was he simply growing up? Or did he want to be a better man for Emma?

They exited the stable and walked up the stairs to the apartment above.

The room was a bit disorganized with stacks of books and a variety of plants set about in no apparent order.

"Make yourself at home," Sam said as he took off his coat and hung it on a hook.

Cade did the same, rubbing his hands together for warmth.

Sam went to a sink in the corner and filled a teakettle with water, then he lit the stove and placed the kettle on top.

Cade took a seat on a comfortable looking chair and studied the room.

"That's where Emmie usually sits." Sam took two mugs off a shelf and put them on a tray. He glanced over his shoulder at Cade. "She's very special to us. We're thankful you brought her home safely today."

She was very special to Cade, too.

Sam came to the chair opposite Cade and took a seat, his face serious. "I would do anything to protect her—I hope you would, too."

Cade nodded, his brows heavy.

"And I'm not just talking about her physical safety—I'm talking about her heart, too. I can see you care for her. I saw it instantly when I met you."

There was no use hiding the truth. "I do. Very much."

"I think she cares for you, too—but her life is complicated. There is no easy path ahead for her."

Cade dropped his gaze and looked at his hands. "That's why I won't tell her how I feel."

"That's a noble stance to take...but is it one you can hold?"

"I have nothing to offer her." He indicated the apartment they sat in and the property around them. "I could never compete with this."

"Aye, you couldn't—and there is a man who is trying to woo her who can."

Cade's head snapped up. "Someone else is pursuing her?"

"Aye." Sam nodded. "And he's in a position to gain everything if he wins her hand."

"Does she—does she love him?"

Sam shook his head, studying Cade. "No."

"Does he love her?"

"I couldn't say—but he'd be a fool not to marry her."

"Because of the money?"

Sam's face softened. "Because she's Emmie."

He rose to put a tea tray together, and Cade let Sam's words sink into his head—because he knew his heart wouldn't listen. There was someone else pursuing Emma, a man her father would accept and trust, not only with his fortune, but with his daughter. Cade was a fool to think he would have a chance.

When the tea kettle whistled, Sam took it off the heat. He poured the hot water over the leaves in the teapot and the room filled with a floral, earthy scent. Sam brought the tray back to Cade and placed it on the table between them.

"Emma told me you're trying to earn money to save your farm," Sam said.

"I have six months to come up with two hundred and fifty dollars."

"It's a hard time of year to be makin' that kind o' money."

It was almost impossible with winter now upon them. His plane sat idle, along with the land.

"I might have a few jobs to keep you busy." Sam poured the tea into the mugs.

Work for Major Merrick? What would his grandfather think? "What kind of work?"

"Oh, just odd jobs—the first will be on New Year's Eve." He handed Cade his tea. "Mrs. Merrick is hosting a Masquerade Ball as a charity event for the American Red Cross. I'm looking for drivers who would give people sleigh rides that night. Are you interested?"

Cade was interested in making money and seeing Emma—but the idea of working for Merrick didn't set right.

Sam took a sip of his tea. "The job will pay well."

Cade needed the money, any way he could get it. "Alright."

Sam nodded. "Good."

They passed the hour in comfortable conversation. Sam told Cade about his life in Ireland and his various positions with the Merrick family over the years. Cade told Sam of his childhood on the farm and then his work as a pilot. He was an easy man to talk to, and Cade found himself telling him more than he anticipated.

"I'm thinking it's time for our Christmas party." Sam rose from his chair and stretched. "What say you we hurry over to the main house and see what kind of Christmas cheer we can offer?"

Cade stood and nodded, eager to meet more of the people Emma considered her family, hoping to get a glimpse of her.

Together they walked to the stone house. The wind whipped harder and faster than before, blowing snow in a wild frenzy.

Sam pushed through the servant's door and Cade followed into the warm kitchen. The room was filled with delicious scents. Cinnamon, roasted goose, pumpkin pie, baked apples—his mouth watered at the thought of such a scrumptious meal.

The staff gathered together around the large kitchen table. A dozen people ran Elk Manor. Some were lifetime employees, like Sam and Martha, but others were new. Cade met Martha's husband, Cliff, the groundskeeper, and he heard more about their daughter Rebecca. He was introduced to the maids and the footmen and was invited to regale everyone with stories of his flying days.

The party wore on, yet Emma did not appear. Both Sam and Martha glanced at the door from time to time, their faces revealing their surprise.

The games commenced and Cade stood on the outside watching. They teased and goaded one another, their laughter filling the large kitchen. Cade was persuaded to finally join in the apple bobbing contest, and he came away with a wet face and no apple—but plenty of back slaps and good-natured ribbing.

Small gifts were exchanged as the party came to a close—yet Emma did not appear.

"I have a wee gift for Emmie," Sam said, looking toward the door once again. "I'm surprised she didn't join us." He couldn't hide his disappointment. "This is the first year she's missed the party."

"I imagine she's been detained by Mr. Overton," Martha offered. "An unexpected guest must be entertained. It would be awkward for all of them if Emma disappeared and joined us."

"I do hope she's had a good Christmas." Sam looked at Cade. "I'll make up a bed and you can come over to the apartment when you're ready."

Cade wasn't ready to leave—not without seeing Emma one last time. "I think I'll stay and help Martha clean up the party."

"Oh, no you won't!" Martha's cheeks blushed. "I won't let Daredevil Kincade clean up my kitchen."

"Maybe I'll have another piece of pumpkin pie," Cade said, taking a different route to stalling. "I'll be over later, Sam."

Sam nodded his understanding. "I hope Emma comes to say good-night." He put on his coat and slipped out of the house.

Martha and two of the maids cleaned up the party mess—and despite Martha's protests, Cade helped. He put all the chairs back in place and cleared the table, then he took a broom and swept the floors.

"Really," Martha said, clucking her tongue as the maids batted their eyelashes at him.

Cade only smiled and kept sweeping.

Eventually the kitchen was clean, and the maids went upstairs to bed. Martha looked around the room as her husband stood waiting near the door to take her to their cottage on the back of the property. "There's nothing left to do." She smiled at Cade. "No more stalling."

Cade had promised he wouldn't leave without saying goodbye. "Do you mind if I just sit here and wait?"

"I left some pumpkin pie under the cloth there, in case you decide to have a piece." Martha's blue eyes were filled with a bit of motherly affection. "She's lucky she found you, Daredevil."

He shook his head. "I'm the lucky one."

"Good night." Martha allowed Cliff to slip on her coat and then he wrapped her scarf about her neck. He handed her some mittens and then opened the door. "Merry Christmas," they said in unison.

"Merry Christmas."

She touched a light switch on her way out, leaving the room in semi-darkness.

Cade took a seat at the table, the silence almost deafening.

Chapter Twenty

Emma

It felt as if Thomas would never say goodnight. Emma looked at the grandfather clock in the family parlor, her heart falling a little more with each tick. Twenty minutes to midnight. Thomas droned on about the lumber company, and Emma tried to appear interested.

Mother and Father had long since retired. It had been strange to spend so much time with her parents on Christmas, but she knew if Thomas had not been there, it would have been the same as all the other years.

They had talked of many things—but mostly work. Emma had watched her father for most of the day, wondering at this man she hardly knew. Even at his advanced age he was still passionate about his business interests—yet, Emma had been forced to stifle more than one yawn—and her thoughts often returned to the party she was missing in the kitchen.

It wouldn't be Christmas without being with Sam and Martha and the others—and it seemed unfair knowing Cade was so close—yet impossible to reach. What must he think of her, abandoning him after his family had welcomed her with such open arms? Thankfully, if she knew Sam and Martha and the others, they would make him feel right at home.

Thomas finally stood and offered Emma his hand. "You look tired."

Emma rose from the sofa. "I am, indeed."

He stood close to her, the firelight dancing in his handsome blue eyes. "I can't remember a more pleasant Christmas. I appreciate your hospitality."

She had been a terrible hostess—but she had tried her best, given the circumstances.

Before she knew what he was about, Thomas leaned down and placed a kiss on her lips.

It was a brief encounter—but it shocked her out of her previous stupor. She pulled back, horrified that he would take such liberties.

She had never been kissed before.

"There," Thomas said. "A final Christmas gift from me to you." He bowed and left the room.

Emma stood in the middle of the parlor, her lips burning from the kiss and tears gathering at the back of her eyes.

She had not been given a gift—one had been stolen from her.

She put her cool fingers on her lips. Was that what it felt like to be kissed? It had been stiff and uncomfortable. Maybe she'd had unrealistic expectations—but she had anticipated something...more. There had been no tenderness, no care, no passion—nothing resembling affection or longing.

She walked out of the parlor, toward the back of the house, needing someone who loved her and desired her company simply for who she was—and not what her father offered.

But would anyone be awake at this late hour? It didn't seem likely unless one of the maids was still cleaning up the party.

A faint light leaked out from under the kitchen door. Emma pushed it open and stepped into the quiet space. Half the room was shrouded in shadows.

Cade sat at the table, his head on his folded arms. Snow continued to fall outside the large windows behind him, soft and feathery in their descent.

At her arrival, he looked up and blinked away sleep. "Emmie."

Despite the tears threatening to fall, she smiled at the pet name Sam and Martha had given her as a child. It felt good hearing it on his lips.

How long had he waited for her?

He rose from the table and crossed the room. Half way toward her, his face filled with concern. "What's wrong?"

She couldn't tell him about Thomas's kiss—it wouldn't be right. "I'm sad I missed the party. Was it great fun?"

He studied her face in the dim light. "That's not what's bothering you."

"It's not?"

"You can tell me."

No, she couldn't. "Really—I'd much rather hear about your time tonight. Did you meet everyone?"

"I did. They're wonderful. Especially Sam."

She nodded, so happy he had met her surrogate family—she just wished she could have been there to watch them interact with Cade. She longed to know if Sam had told Cade about her, but was embarrassed to admit how much she cared.

"I should go to bed," Emma said. "I just wanted to come and see if anyone was still awake."

"Why didn't you come earlier?"

"I had to entertain our guest."

"Mr. Overton?"

She nodded, unable to meet his gaze.

He spoke quietly. "Is he the man your father wants you to marry?"

She looked up at him, searching his eyes for an indication of how it made him feel. "Yes."

"Do you love him?"

"No."

"Is he the one who made you upset tonight?"

Emma didn't want to answer. She walked around him and went to the counter where Martha had left a pie under a dishcloth. She lifted the cloth and took a nibble of the crust.

Cade tenderly clasped her upper arms. "Emma—did he upset you?"

She couldn't think straight with him touching her. "What does it matter?"

He turned her to face him and kept his hands on her arms. "It matters a great deal. To me."

His touch sent shivers of pleasure up her spine, warming her from head to toe. "He—" She paused, unable to admit the truth.

"He what?"

It sounded so silly. She couldn't even look at him. "He stole a kiss," she whispered.

His hands fell aways. "And you didn't enjoy it?"

She studied the buttons lining the front of his shirt. "No. I don't—I don't think he truly cares for me the way he should to kiss me."

"Have you ever been kissed before?"

She shook her head, her cheeks warming at the question.

His hand came up to her chin, and he gently raised her face to look him in the eye. "Would you like to know what it feels like to be kissed by someone who does care?"

Her heart skittered under her breast bone and she felt breathless. All she could do was nod.

A fire kindled deep within his eyes, and he took a step closer to her. His hand slid to her cheek and he caressed the skin with his thumb. Pleasure spiraled through her body and she closed her eyes, wanting to savor every precious nuance of feeling.

His lips found hers and she almost sighed at the touch. His kiss was soft and warm, filling her with a sweetness she had never known. Within the kiss was the longing and desire she had expected—yet the exquisite intimacy was unexpected and breathtaking.

He pulled away, only far enough to look her in the eyes. His breathing was shallow as he searched her face. "Did you enjoy that kiss?"

Her lips tingled in a most delightful way as she reached up and put her hand over his, drawing him close again. "Very much," she whispered.

He kissed her again, and this time, he deepened the kiss, leaving no room for her to wonder at his feelings. His free hand went to the small of her back and he pulled her closer to him.

She fit against him perfectly as she wrapped her arms behind his neck, getting lost in his touch.

When the clock struck midnight, he pulled away a second time.

They stood for a moment, listening to the clock as it chimed twelve times and then rested in silence.

"Christmas has passed," Cade said quietly, his chest rising and falling. "One I won't ever forget."

He kissed her forehead and took a step away from her. "I should go—Sam will wonder what's keeping me." He smiled as his gaze caressed her face. "And I'm afraid if I don't go, I will try to kiss you again."

She returned his sweet smile. "Good night, Cade."

He took his coat from the hook and put it on. "Good night, Emmie."

A moment later, he opened the door and slipped out into the snowstorm, leaving Emma alone in the kitchen.

There was no mistaking Cade's feelings for her—but did he care for her enough to offer her a future away from Elk Manor? And if he did offer her a future, was she willing to accept her father's rejection once and for all?

Cade

Cade whistled as he leaned against Pauline, the Holstein Gracie had named after President Taft's White House cow. He hadn't stopped thinking about Emma's kiss since he had been at the Merrick's two days ago. His good mood could not be thwarted, no matter how much work awaited him or how tight the family budget had become.

Sleigh bells jingled on the morning breeze and Cade stood from milking the cow and moved to the window. The sun was bright in an endless blue sky and reflected off the brilliant white snow, forcing him to squint as he watched the approaching driver.

He pulled on his mittens and walked outside. The air was bitter cold, pinching at his skin.

The sleigh came to a stop beside the barn and a man lifted the robes to step out. He was tall and well dressed—much too fancy for a farmer.

"Hello," Cade called. "Come on into the barn and warm yourself."

"Sounds like a good idea."

They walked into the barn and Cade closed the door. There were no heaters on, but the animals' bodies warmed the space to a pleasant temperature.

The man extended his hand. "I'm Thomas Overton."

On instinct Cade shook his hand, but a warning bell rang in his head. What was Thomas Overton doing at his home? Had he somehow learned about his and Emma's friendship? Was that why he had come?

"I'm Cade Bailey."

"Yes, I know. The famous aviator." Overton glanced around the barn and Cade had a chance to study him a bit closer. He was a good-looking man with self-confidence to spare. "I'm here on behalf of Merrick Lumber."

Merrick—so that was why he had come.

"I believe we're both reasonable men and we can spare the small-talk," Overton said in a self-assured voice.

Cade crossed his arms and leaned against his work bench. "Go ahead."

"I am in position to offer you top dollar for your property. We can pay cash and have it in your hands within twenty-four hours."

Cade recalled the day near the river when Grandfather had made him agree to never let Major Merrick get his hands on their property. Cade had promised—but how long must he keep his promise? Grandfather was gone, Dad was too weak to work the land, and Cade had no plans to stay. Henry was the only one he couldn't ask—but Henry didn't appear willing to stake his claim, either.

"Major Merrick has been eager to purchase this property for years," Overton continued. "He will do whatever it takes to make the deal."

If they sold, Cade's parents could buy a nice house in town and have neighbors to see to their needs. It would be ideal.

But where would Cade go and what would he do with his life? For the first time, the thought of leaving the farm gave him a pang of sadness. "I would need to think about it for a while before I make a decision."

Overton nodded. "A smart thing to do—but how much time do you really have? Major Merrick told me you'll default on your mortgage next spring—so why work all winter, just to lose it later?"

How did Matthew Merrick know they were struggling to come up with a mortgage payment? He hadn't told anyone but Emma—had she said something to him? Cade had the impression that Emma wasn't close to her father, so he doubted she had told him. He didn't like the idea that Major Merrick knew so much. Something didn't feel right about the offer.

"On second thought, the property isn't for sale." Cade said, knowing in his heart that he couldn't sell the place out from under his family. "My grandfather and father worked their whole lives to turn this into a prosperous farm. It wouldn't be right to sell it now."

Overton glanced at the barn with disdain. "I wouldn't call this prospering."

Heat rose under Cade's collar. "It's honorable and provides for our family."

"Just barely—and it won't if you lose it all in June." Overton studied Cade, his jaw tight. "If you sell now, you'll get top dollar—but if you wait until spring, you'll walk away with nothing, and Merrick Lumber will purchase it for a pittance of what it's worth."

Cade couldn't fail at saving the farm. He and his father had made a promise to Grandfather, and no matter how much Cade had struggled with his grandfather, he would honor him this way. "I'm sorry, but your trip here was wasted. I won't sell." His grandfather and father had given their lives to this land. Their blood, sweat, and tears fertilized the very soil that sustained them. Even if Cade had struggled with his grandfather, he couldn't deny the legacy he'd left for his family.

Overton scoffed and his face filled with something dark. "Merrick's offer will only stand until June—after that, he will never ask again—and no one will pay you what we're offering today. Take it, or—"

"Or what?" Cade asked, pushing away from the workbench.

"Or we will get the land a different way—one that is not so beneficial to you and your family."

Cade's eyes narrowed. "Are you threatening me?"

"I'll do whatever it takes—you have my word."

"I would not sell to Major Merrick even if he offered me all the money he possessed. Some things do not have a price tag, Mr. Overton—and this land is one of them. It's my family legacy—my inheritance." Cade's voice shook, and he was overwhelmed with the depth of emotion attached to his words. When had the farm become so important to him? Was it because Emma had opened his eyes to his blessings?

"You will regret this missed opportunity." Overton moved to the door, pulling his coat collar up to his ears. "I will be back—and next time I won't be so nice."

He opened the door and Cade followed him outside.

Overton stopped and turned to Cade, pointing at Emma's car still parked near the house in a snowdrift.

"Is that Emma Merrick's car?"

Cade didn't answer.

Overton walked to the car and peered inside. "Her emergency kit is sitting on the front bench. This *is* Emma's car." He looked at Cade. "What is it doing here?"

Cade sauntered over to Overton, his arms crossed. "She left it here on Christmas Eve when she was snowed in."

"She was here, with you?" Overton looked him up and down. "Are you the one who brought her home?"

"Yes."

Overton's brows furrowed. "Why was she here?"

"That's none of your business."

"It is my business." Overton's voice rose. "She's to be my fiancée."

"Not if I can help it."

His narrowed his eyes. "Are you suggesting she would choose you—and this—this embarrassment of a farm over me and a future of comfort and prosperity?"

Cade hadn't intended to goad Overton—because as much as he cared for Emma, he knew he was not capable of offering her a future—and the realization stung. "Get off my property, Mr. Overton, and tell Major Merrick this land will never be for sale. I will make the payment in June, and I will make this farm succeed."

"I forbid you from seeing Emma again. She is off-limits."

"I believe that is for Emma to decide."

"Her father and I have an understanding."

"Yet, it's Emma who you must convince."

Overton stepped close, his breath freezing in a fog of white air. His eyes narrowed. "Do not push me, Mr. Bailey. You'll find I'm not one to mess with."

"Get off my land." Cade pointed toward the road. "You're not welcome here."

The kitchen door opened, and Gracie stuck her head outside. "Who's here, Cade?"

"Go inside." Cade held his voice steady for her benefit. "I'll be in later."

Gracie looked between Overton and Cade and then went back into the house.

Overton yanked at his gloves. "I would keep a close watch on everything—and everyone—around here. You wouldn't want any accidents happening."

He was threatening again? Cade wanted him gone. "Go. Now."

Overton walked to his sleigh and buried himself under his blankets. "This is not over, Bailey."

With that, he pulled away, leaving Cade to wonder what the man was capable of doing to get his way.

And wondering if Emma knew his true colors.

Chapter Twenty-One

DECEMBER 31, 1917

Emma

Emma stared at her reflection in her bedroom mirror. She hardly resembled the woman she was used to seeing. Tonight, she did not wear her simple Red Cross uniform—tonight she wore one of mother's elaborate debutante gowns from 1890. She had discarded her sensible corset for one of her mother's confining ones, and it gave her body a whole new shape.

She ran her hands over the decadent green silk and admired how it shimmered under the electrical lighting. The skirt was smooth in front and gathered in a series of bustles in the back, cascading down to the floor in a short train. The material slipped off her shoulders, and she wore her mother's emerald necklace with matching emerald earrings.

A maid had styled Emma's auburn curls at the crown of her head, with tendrils dipping down to caress her shoulders.

She lifted a green masquerade mask to her face and tied the black ribbon around her head to keep it secure. It matched the gown to perfection, and glittered when she turned her head.

She looked stunning—yet she found no joy in her appearance—no joy in the prospect of a masquerade ball. All of it seemed hollow without Cade's presence. More than anything, she wished he would be in attendance tonight. She longed for him to see her like this—and to hold her in his arms as they danced into the New Year.

It had been a week since Cade had been at her house for Christmas, and she didn't know when she would see him again—but the feel of his kiss still lingered on her lips. She had relived their stolen moments in the kitchen a hundred times, and each time the memory became sweeter.

Emma picked up the train of her gown and slipped out of her room. The guests would arrive any moment and she must be there to greet them. This was a benefit for the American Red Cross, which gave her a bit of enthusiasm. At least this party would have a purpose.

Father would stay in his room tonight, still weak from his heart attack. Emma had tried to care for him when he had come home from the hospital, but he had insisted they hire a nurse to see to his needs—releasing her to spend her free time with Thomas.

Emma entered the foyer and found Mother. She was dressed as an Egyptian Queen, with gold bracelets and white material draped about her body. She wore a gold mask and golden slippers on her feet.

"Emma." Mother stared at her for a long time. "I'm speechless." She turned Emma around. "That gown—it fits you perfectly."

Emma's cheeks warmed under her mother's praise.

"You will capture the interest of every man at this ball—they'll look at no one else." She stepped closer to Emma and spoke quietly so Mr. Stearns would not hear. "It's really a travesty you don't use your assets more often. You could have anything your heart desires if you just learned how to use your body."

A wall of self-defense erected itself around Emma's heart and she turned away from her mother. She would never use her body the way her mother had—and she suddenly felt uncomfortable wearing a dress that would cause her mother to make such a terrible suggestion.

Mr. Stearns opened the front door to their first guests, and Emma had no time to go upstairs and change.

Over the next hour, the house filled with guests dressed in beautiful costumes. Their masks hid their identity—though Emma could pick out a handful of familiar people.

One man in particular caught her attention. He was dressed as King Henry VIII, with a doublet sporting puffed sleeves, tight fitting breeches, and a wide, flat brimmed hat with a plume of feathers. His mask was made of gold, and his hands were bedecked in oversized rings. He bore himself with grace and elegance and could only be Thomas Overton.

His eyes caught hers just then and he offered an elaborate bow. Emma curtsied, her green fan fluttering over her face. He had stopped to see her several times since Christmas Day, and Emma had found herself entertaining him in the parlor most evenings. Though their conversations were interesting, and she enjoyed his company, she could not find it in her heart to care for him—not in the way she cared for Cade.

Thankfully, he had not tried to kiss her again, though he spoke to her of love and romance.

He came to her now, appreciation glowing on his face. "You are exquisite, Emma. The most beautiful woman in the room."

She dipped her head. "Thank you."

"There are sleigh rides outside—would you care to join me on a jaunt?"

Emma looked about the room. "I should not leave my duties as a hostess."

"Nonsense. Your mother encouraged me to ask you." He lowered his head to look her in the eyes, his gaze serious. "I will not take no for an answer."

She frowned at the command in his voice—yet this was no place to argue. "I'll get my wraps."

"Dress warm," he said.

She went to her room and found her coat and muffler and then she returned to the foyer. Other couples were coming and going through the front door, and there was a line of sleighs waiting in the circular drive. As each couple pulled away, a new sleigh drove up under the portico.

Emma and Thomas waited in line. Thankfully there was no unpleasant wind to bite at their cheeks, though it was still cold.

Thomas spoke of trivial matters, but Emma spent her time watching the other people around them laughing and having fun. The drivers appeared to be enjoying themselves, though they were so bundled up, it was hard to tell.

The couple ahead of them pulled away and it was Emma and Thomas's turn to board. The driver pulled the sleigh under the portico. He was dressed in a brown wool coat and wore a matching wool hat low over his forehead. A scarf came up to cover his mouth and nose. A footman appeared and helped Emma over the runners and into the sleigh. A warming box was at their feet, and a pile of lap robes were put over her and Thomas.

The sleigh pulled away, and the brilliant night sky filled Emma's heart with wonder. Thousands of stars sparkled in an endless canopy of black, so clear and crisp, it felt as if she could reach up and touch them.

Thomas's arm snaked around Emma's shoulders. "There," he said. "Now you'll stay even warmer."

She didn't pull away—but remained stiff beside him. Hopefully he did not try to kiss her again.

The sleigh ran along, slicing through the snow. Bells jingled from the harness and the horses snorted into the cold air. They followed the same track as the other sleighs, around a loop that circled behind the house and over near Elk Creek. Lanterns had been set out to mark the path, offering a bit of light on the snow-covered hills.

"I'm happy we have this moment alone, Emma." Thomas spoke close to her ear.

She tried to slide a little further away, but he held her tight. "We're not completely alone." She nodded at the driver, whose back was toward them.

Thomas waved aside her worry. "He's of little consequence."

The driver turned slightly at the comment, and Emma's cheeks warmed. "No one is of little consequence—"

"I have something to ask you, and tonight is the perfect time."

"Why tonight?"

"Because we're about to embark on a new year, and I'd like to start it off right."

"I wish you wouldn't—"

"I have come to care for you," he said as he ignored her. "And I think it's time to make our engagement official."

Emma glanced at the driver. He turned slightly, and she knew he was listening. She lowered her voice. "I've told you I need time."

"But why?" he asked. "If you know you're going to marry me, why wait?"

"Because I need time."

"Time for what?" Anger filled his voice. "Is this about the Bailey man?"

"Please!" She spoke to Thomas under her breath. "Keep your voice down."

"Is it?"

How did Thomas know about Cade? "I will not discuss this with a stranger present."

"As your future husband, I demand an answer."

Her future husband? "I have not made any promises to you."

"But your father and I both agree this union is best."

"I have not agreed to anything—and I have until June to decide." She held the upper hand, and he knew it. Without her consent, he would not inherit Father's wealth. "Please do not force me to give an answer now, because if I do, you will not like what I have to say."

He immediately quieted and she looked straight ahead. The driver sat up taller and lifted the reins to slap them against the horses' hides.

Emma and Thomas drove the rest of the way in silence.

Cade

Cade fulfilled his duties as a sleigh driver and went into the kitchen with the other drivers to partake of hot apple cider and warm molasses cookies. He was greeted by the kitchen staff and treated with an extra cookie from Martha.

As the other drivers sat around the table talking, Cade kept to himself and thought over the conversation he'd heard between Emma and

Overton. She had held her ground and been as kind as possible—and he admired her deeply for it. He had wanted to make his presence known when he dropped them back at the house, but she might have been embarrassed, and Overton would have been irate.

Loud music spilled from the party at the front of the house. Cade sat for a moment, feeling sorry for himself and his current state of affairs. When he lived in California, he had been the honored guest in numerous mansions. William Randolph Hearst had thrown him a party when *Flying High* had debuted—yet here he sat, a common driver while the wealthy danced and dined just a few feet away.

He couldn't handle the noise anymore, so he rose and left the kitchen in search of Sam. He would collect his paycheck and go home.

Sam was in the spacious carriage house, wiping down the Merrick's sleigh. He glanced up when Cade walked into the building, a smile on his face. "Cade, come in."

"I'm here to collect my wages."

"Did you enjoy a cup of Martha's cider?"

"I did, thank you." His words were short and curt.

"What's the trouble?" Sam leaned against the sleigh.

Cade picked up a rag and started to help, surprised at how comfortable he felt with Sam. "I drove Emma and Mr. Overton tonight."

"Did you now?" Sam smiled and continued to wipe. "And did they know it was you?"

"No." Cade rubbed hard, bringing a shine to the black paint. "Overton proposed to Emma."

Sam's hand stopped and he stood straight. "What did she say?"

"She said she needs more time." Cade stopped rubbing. "I don't like Overton. He came out to the farm and threatened my family if we don't sell our property."

"Do you not think he's a good man?"

Cade shook his head. "I'm afraid he's only after Emma for her money—and that's a terrible reason to marry."

"Do you love her, lad?"

Cade started to rub the sleigh again, surprised at how free he felt to tell the truth. "I do."

"Then go after her."

Cade stopped and looked at Sam.

"Go into that house and tell her how you feel."

"I couldn't go into the party and proclaim my love."

"And why not?"

"Look at me." He opened his arms wide. "I'm dressed like a common laborer."

Sam looked him up and down. "What if I told you I had something you could wear? Would you go then?"

Would he? What would Overton do if he showed up at the party? "Do you have a mask?"

Sam grinned. "I had me own share of fun before coming to work at the Merrick's, and masquerade balls were a very popular diversion in me day. You might not believe it by looking at me, but I was a dapper young fellow. I have a set of evening clothes I wore in the 90's—and a mask, to boot. They're yours for the evening if you have a mind to wear them." Sam set down his rag and put his hand on Cade's shoulder. "What do you have to lose?"

"I have nothing to offer her."

"Let Emma be the judge of that."

Cade had run out of excuses.

Fifteen minutes later, Cade left the carriage house wearing Sam's old evening clothes. The jacket fit a bit snug around the shoulders, but the length of the arms and legs was perfect. And true to his word, he had a black mask that Cade had tied around his head. He looked as if he had stepped out of the last century.

Instead of going through the servant's entrance, Cade walked around to the front of the house and entered through the main doors. Mr. Stearns was standing post at the front door, and he bowed at Cade when he entered.

The hall clock struck the half hour—only thirty minutes to midnight.

Cade slipped into the grand foyer, his eyes taking in the splendor of the Merrick home. Marble flooring, rich mahogany trim, crystal chandeliers, and expensive paintings decorated the main entrance. People mingled about in the foyer, their laughter and conversation ringing in his ears.

To the right, a large parlor was filled with more people, dancing along to the sound of an orchestra. To the left, the kitchen staff was busy at work laying out a scrumptious buffet. An elaborate ice sculpture dominated the center of the table, dripping into a large bowl. Every conceivable dish of food was laid around it.

Where was Emma?

His eyes scanned the foyer as he moved toward the parlor. He hugged the perimeter of the room. When he had seen her in the sleigh, she wore a long winter coat so he didn't know what color dress to look for—but he knew he'd recognize her hair.

He searched the parlor, but did not see anyone that resembled her.

She had to be somewhere.

He turned to look at the foyer again, and he caught a glimpse of a woman descending the stairway. She wore a beautiful green gown, hugging her curves and accentuating her figure. Her auburn curls were piled high on her head, and her emerald jewels sparkled under the light. As she drew closer, he looked at her lips—and he knew it was Emma.

She looked exquisite—but more than that, he knew the woman under the mask was kind and brave and full of a capacity to love unlike anyone he'd ever met before. She had been born into a home of pain and loneliness—yet, if he could have one wish granted, it would be to allow her to know true love and happiness for the rest of her days.

But was he capable of giving it to her?

He maneuvered around the crowd and waited at the base of the stairs. Her eyes scanned the room below, but when she reached the bottom she stopped and looked at Cade. A slow smile formed on her full mouth. "Hello."

He didn't speak, but offered her his arm.

She smelled of sweet floral perfume and her brown eyes sparkled under the light of the chandeliers. She wrapped her hand around his elbow, and he led her to the dance floor.

The *Waters of Venice* waltz had just begun, and Cade put one hand on her waist and the other he entwined with her fingers. Her hand went up to his shoulder and the sensation sent tingles down his back, reminding him how exquisite her touch felt.

They began to waltz, swaying with the rhythm of the music. It was a lively tune, and she smiled as they danced around the room. Her curls bounced and her dress swished as their feet shuffled on the parquet floor. The room spun with them, and everyone else became a blur.

And still they did not speak.

She was an elegant dancer, allowing him to guide her around the room. He imagined how striking they must look, both wearing formal clothes out of the last century.

He danced her through the front parlor and into the back where people had gathered to watch the dancers. In one seamless move, they stopped dancing and he took her hand and walked her into a long hallway. He didn't know where it led, but he needed to be alone with her—to tell her what he had come to tell her.

She went with him willingly, clutching his hand with hers.

The hallway was shadowed, with wall sconces interspersed between doors. To the left, the hallway opened into the foyer, and to the right, it ended at a door about fifty feet away. He stopped, unsure which way to go. She pulled him further down the hall and opened one of the doors, guiding him over the threshold and into a beautiful library.

His heart beat strong and sure, and desire flared within his chest. The memory of their kiss had stayed with him all week. She had so enraptured him, he could think of nothing else but this moment.

Emma closed the door, and the sound of the music became muted. A lamp glowed from the corner of the room, and the fireplace crackled, sending smoke spiraling up the chimney.

She turned to him, her brown eyes searching his face. "How—?"

"Sam."

Her smile almost undid his self-control. He took a step toward her and slipped his fingers through the hair at the base of her neck and lowered his lips to hers. The kiss was even more magnificent than the first, and she met his passion with her own. Her hands encircled his neck, and she pulled him closer until they were pressed up against the door.

He wanted to tell her he loved her—but he also wanted to kiss her and revel in the way she made him feel. He had kissed other women before—too many to number—but none of them had been like Emma Merrick. His feelings for her ran so deep and so powerful, he knew he would never kiss another woman.

He finally pulled away, though it was the hardest thing he'd ever done. He smiled down at her, and she looked up at him with a desire that matched his.

"You've captured my heart, Emmie—and I fear I will never be the same man. You make me want to be good, and brave, and honorable—things I never thought I could be before I met you."

She opened her mouth to speak, but the clock struck midnight, and a great cheer arose from the front of the house.

Her face softened and she whispered, "Happy New Year, Cade."

"Happy New Year, Emmie."

Voices filled the hall, and Emma turned her ear toward the door. "It sounds like Thomas."

"Are you sure they went down this hallway?" Thomas's muted voice drifted into the room.

"Yes—but I'm not sure which door they went into," said a second male voice.

"You look on the right, and I'll look on the left."

Emma glanced back at Cade, concern in her gaze. "He can't find us here."

"Why not?"

"He'll be angry."

"I don't care if he's raving mad."

She put her hand on his chest. "Cade, please. I don't want him to make a scene."

He frowned at her. "Are you planning to continue seeing him?"

She hesitated and his heart felt as if it dropped to his stomach.

"I don't know what I'm going to do," she said.

Thomas's voice came closer and confusion clouded Cade's mind. "But—I thought—"

"Please, Cade. I need time to think." She clutched her hands, looking around the room.

Anger and hurt knotted together in his chest. "What is there to think about?"

She put her hands to her temples and spoke quietly. "Why must I make a sudden decision? Both you and Thomas have asked it of me tonight." She took a step away from him and toward a door leading to a connecting room. "As soon as he's done looking through the family parlor, I'll sneak through this door. You can tell him you came in here alone."

She put her ear to the door as Cade stared at her. Was she really contemplating Thomas Overton as a husband? And, if she was, had he been a fool to open his heart to her?

They heard a door close in the hallway and Emma opened the connecting door into the other room. She looked at Cade, an apology in her eyes. "I'm sorry," she mouthed, and then slipped through the door and closed it behind her.

The door leading to the hallway opened and Cade stared at Overton. He wore a ridiculous outfit with puffed sleeves and tight pants.

Overton's eyes scanned the room and landed on Cade. "Where is she?"

Cade clenched his jaw until pain radiated into his ears. "Who?"

"You know who." Overton stepped into the room and looked behind the door. "Emma."

"She's not here."

"But she was."

Cade lifted his arm and made a sweep over the room. "Go ahead and look."

Overton took a step closer to Cade, his breath heavy with the smell of wine. "I warned you, Bailey."

"What are you going to do?" Cade taunted him. "I have nothing you can destroy."

Overton's blue eyes turned ice cold. "You have a family, don't you?"

Repulsion slithered through Cade, and he clenched his fist. "What are you saying?"

Overton straightened his spine. "I'm saying you have something that could be destroyed."

Cade pulled his head back, loathing the sight of this man.

"If you continue to see Emma, I will personally destroy everything that's dear to you."

"You're bluffing."

Overton's eyes became deadly. "Try me. I stand to lose everything if she doesn't marry me."

Cade couldn't believe Emma would even consider this man—but clearly she did.

He straightened his spine, his face becoming hard. Maybe, if she had made her choice clear, he would have stayed and fought, but he wasn't about to sit around and wait for her to choose between them. He would never stoop to begging.

"Fine." Cade's throat constricted with the word. He pushed past Overton, knocking his shoulder in his quest to leave the room.

Cade walked down the hall toward the back of the house, willing his feet to take flight.

Chapter Twenty-Two

ST. PAUL,
MINNESOTA
APRIL 25, 1864

Matthew

"Please bring this file to the governor. I need his signature before the end of the day." Matthew handed the file to his clerk and didn't bother to look up from the document he was reading. His voice held an edge of irritation he was so accustomed to hearing these days, he didn't bother to adjust his tone. "Also, tell him I just received a letter from the US Senate regarding the Headwater Treaty signed in October and I'll need to see him as soon as he's available."

"Yes, sir."

"Mr. Abbott." Matthew finally glanced at his clerk. "I do not want to be bothered by anyone else today."

"Of course."

The door to Matthew's office opened and closed leaving him in silence—but not peace. Feelings of tranquility had eluded him since last fall.

He picked up the letter and let out a frustrated sigh. The Senate had not ratified the Headwater Treaty and had sent the document back with lengthy amendments that would need to be signed by the band members once again.

Would this chapter of his life never close? He had thought to leave the treaty—and Elizabeth—far behind, but almost daily they both returned to visit in his waking thoughts and disturbing dreams. Melancholy plagued him until he thought he might go mad from the hopelessness he felt deep in the pit of his soul.

He threw every ounce of his energy into his work and dreaded the hours he spent at home with Helen. He had told her about Elizabeth soon after they had returned to St. Paul, hoping she would call off their engagement and he could move on with his life. But Helen didn't love him anymore than he loved her, and the reason she was marrying him had not changed. He'd been promoted to the Chief Legal Counsel of the governor and being married to him would give her the social standing she desired. She made it clear, though, that once they were married, she would not tolerate unfaithfulness.

Matthew's home life was filled with incessant chatter and endless social obligations. When bedtime arrived, his exhausted body would lie down to sleep, but his mind would remain alert with the memories. Even if sleep arrived, it was not refreshing but filled with images and visions of Elizabeth and his unborn child.

He lived with Helen as husband and wife, but his heart and mind had not bonded with the woman he married. Helen never commented on it because she was too busy climbing the social ladder to worry about their relationship.

A knock brought him out of his reverie, and he snapped his head up to look at the door. "What?"

Mr. Abbott poked his head inside, his spectacles riding at the end of his nose. "Pardon me, sir, but there's a—" he hesitated and pushed his spectacles up. "A gentleman to see you."

"I said I didn't want to be disturbed."

"But this—a—gentleman has come a long way."

Matthew set down the Senate's letter. "Who is he?"

"Tuck, sir. Just Tuck."

Matthew rose from his seat, his senses alert in a way they hadn't been since the treaty was signed. "Send him in."

Mr. Abbott nodded and a moment later Tuck walked into Matthew's office.

He looked exactly as Matthew recalled with his buckskin clothes, long white beard, and piercing blue eyes. He still wore his backpack and walked with his tall stick, even here inside the capitol building.

"Come in, Tuck." Matthew rounded the desk and extended his hand to the old fur trader.

Tuck took Matthew's hand and squeezed it firmly. "It's good to see you again, Major."

"Won't you have a seat?"

Tuck sat in the wooden chair across from Matthew's desk, and Matthew returned to his own leather chair, questions racing through his mind. What had brought this man all the way to his office? Was it good tidings—or bad?

"I didn't think I'd ever see you again," Matthew said.

Tuck looked around Matthew's office, wonder on his bedraggled face.

The room was decorated with rich mahogany furniture, tall leaded windows, and dozens of potted ferns. Elaborate bookshelves lined the wall behind Matthew and maps of the State of Minnesota hung on the wall opposite. It was a comfortable room—one he spent most of his time in.

Tuck's attention returned to Matthew, and he studied his face. "Did you heed my words, Major?"

Matthew blinked at the unexpected question—and then wanted to play naïve—but he knew exactly what Tuck was referring to. He looked down at his desk and shook his head. "I'm afraid I didn't."

Tuck sighed and nodded. "I've come to tell you something most people don't like to hear, but whether you like it or not—it's true."

Matthew waited—unsure how to respond.

"The Lord has sent me with a message for you. It comes in two parts. The first is news—the second is an admonition."

"The Lord?" Matthew readjusted his position in his chair. His mother's Bible was buried at the bottom of the trunk he had brought back from Crow Wing—and promptly stored in the attic of his new home on Portland Avenue.

"The Lord God Almighty." Tuck's eyes softened and he chuckled. "He's been bothering me all year—won't let me forget about you—so here I am."

Matthew wasn't sure if he should be awed—or concerned. Had Tuck really heard from God—and if so, what did God possibly have to say to Matthew? Part of him wanted to ask Tuck to leave—but a greater part wanted to know what this man had to say.

"What have you come to tell me?"

Tuck's smile disappeared and he was silent for a few moments. "I don't know what happened in Crow Wing—so I won't pretend to tell you I understand what any of this means—but I heard news about your clerk, Jacob Bailey—and I feel obligated to tell you."

Matthew leaned forward. "Go ahead."

"Jacob Bailey's wife gave birth to a son a week ago—"

"A son." Matthew's chest suddenly felt heavy—joy and sorrow warring within his heart.

Tuck continued to study Matthew with those perceptive eyes. "Sadly, his wife died during childbirth."

The world felt as if it came to a sudden stop and every emotion seeped from Matthew's being as he stared at Tuck. "Died?"

"Shortly after the child's birth. They say she passed on while holding the baby in her arms. They tried to take him away from her—to tend to her—but she refused to give up the child."

Matthew turned his chair and stared out the tall window toward St. Paul and the world coming alive with the promise of spring. Tears stung the back of his eyes and his throat tightened.

Elizabeth was dead? He closed his eyes and buried his face in his hands. He saw her again at the creek where they had put their initials in the willow tree. It felt as if a lifetime had passed—had it only been eight months? She had been so alive and vibrant and full of love.

Yet, she had died bringing his child into the world. A child that now bore the name of Bailey.

He longed to weep—to mourn—to leave the capitol and go to Elizabeth's grave if only to be near her, but Tuck rose from his chair and put his hand on Matthew's shoulder.

"You were the child's father..." Tuck's voice held a sense of new understanding. "I had wondered why the Lord wanted me to come here with this news—now I see."

Matthew turned to him, anger and regret raging like a burning inferno in his soul, devouring anything good that had been there before. "Now you see what? That I am a sinner? I could have told you I was the day I met you on the Woods Trail. I never pretended to be anything else."

"But you did." Tuck's eyes were gentle—not rebuking like Matthew thought they would be. "We all do, Matthew."

"I took the wide and straight path—and it led directly to destruction." Matthew's words were bitter. "Why didn't your God stop me?"

"He tried."

"He could have prevented all of this."

"He never compromises our freewill. You had choices to make, and you made poor ones."

"So now He sent you to rub it in my face?" Matthew was disgusted. "I want no part of a God like that."

"He sent me to admonish you—to tell you the choices you made were not part of His plan—but if you would turn to Him and receive the forgiveness His Son offers, He will draw you close. He still longs for you, Matthew, now more than ever. He longs to comfort you in this time of sorrow."

Matthew shook his head and stood. "What you speak is repulsive to me. God has never cared about me. I was born fatherless—not by my choice. Your God made that decision for me. Why are some born into loving families and some into depravity and sin?"

"We are all born into the same sinful world—"

"Yet some are more fortunate than others."

"I cannot begin to understand the workings of God."

"Of course you can't." Matthew's jaw became hard. "Sooner or later every Christian gives that same answer."

Tuck gripped his walking stick, sorrow in his gaze. "I'm sorry I don't have all the answers. I seek after God every day, and every day He reveals a little more of Himself to me. It's a journey He and I will walk through Eternity. God's ways are not our ways, Matthew, and His thoughts are not our thoughts. He is so vast and so much bigger than our human understanding it will take an eternity to explore His existence. I don't know everything, but I trust the God who does."

Matthew hardened his heart to Tuck's words and turned his back, too raw and too wounded to try to comprehend.

Tuck walked into Matthew's line of sight, his eyes serious. "No one wants to hear the truth—but here it is: God's protection is limited when we walk outside His will. He drew the line and you crossed over it. You are now suffering the consequences of your sin."

"Are you quite through?"

"You will be given more opportunities to make choices—and if you continue to walk the wide road, you will continue to walk toward destruction. It's never too late to find the narrow path, Matthew—it's the only one that leads to life."

Matthew rounded his desk and opened his door.

Tuck's shoulders sagged as if under a great burden. He walked across the room and stopped before Matthew. "I will continue to pray for you, Matthew Merrick, and God will continue to pursue you—that I do know."

The old man passed by Matthew and walked through the front office and out into the bustling capitol building beyond.

Matthew closed the door and leaned against it, his body shaking. Never had he felt the searing pain of loss course through him as it did now. Elizabeth was gone from this life—and his son was in the arms of a man he despised.

Matthew jerked open the door and Mr. Abbott's head came up. "Cancel all my appointments for the next two weeks." His voice shook with emotion. "And purchase a ticket for me to take the stagecoach to Crow Wing. I will leave in the morning."

"But, what about the governor?"

"I will see him when I return. This matter cannot wait."

Matthew grabbed his hat and coat and left the office.

He would go to Jacob Bailey and demand his son.

Matthew reined in his horse and sat for a moment to look at the land.

Anger and jealousy boiled in his gut. This should be his land—his and Elizabeth's.

Just thinking about her brought another wave of grief.

He touched the horse's flank and galloped toward the cabin. The pathetic structure was made of rough-cut logs with a single window and door. It sat at the top of a hill, rising to the west from the banks of the Mississippi.

The land wasn't much to speak of. The majority was low-lying swamps near the river with woods to the north and a few acres of plowed fields to the west and south. Though it didn't look good for farming, it was in an excellent location and the access to the river was exactly as Matthew had imagined.

A log barn sat behind the cabin with a horse and a cow in the small corral.

This is where Elizabeth had lived for the last six months of her life? It wasn't fit for the animals, let alone a young woman carrying a child.

The air held a chill, though the sun shone brightly in the pale blue sky. Little green buds and blades of new grass sprang forth over the earth.

Matthew stopped his rented horse near the front door and secured its reins around a small tree.

The door opened and Jacob Bailey stood with his feet planted and his arms crossed over his broad chest. His red hair and beard needed a trim, and his face was lined with fatigue and grief. Hostility radiated off his body. "What are you doing here, Merrick?"

"I'm here for my son." Matthew started to push through the doorway, but Jacob shoved him back and Matthew stumbled to the ground.

"He is not your son."

Matthew stood, panting. "I want him."

"What would your wife think if you brought home another woman's child?"

"She already knows the truth. We'll tell everyone else that the child's mother died and you are unfit to raise him. We'll take him on as our ward."

Jacob snarled at Matthew. "I will never give you Elizabeth's child, and the law is on my side. He was born while she and I were legally married and that makes him mine."

"I'll pay you." Matthew had secured a loan before leaving St. Paul and he was prepared to pay Jacob as much as he wanted. "I'll also buy this land. You will be a free man. You can go on with your life and never concern yourself with any of this again." He swallowed, hating to humble himself before this man. "This is my burden to bear. I am the one responsible for all of this, and I should be the one to do what needs to be done."

Jacob took a step toward Matthew, his voice breaking. "I loved Elizabeth." He looked away, trying to regain control of his emotions. "I spent the past six months trying to make her happy, and I was there with her when she died. I dug her grave with my own hands." He swiped at his eye with his fist. "That baby is mine."

Matthew stepped back—surprise making him pause.

"He's all I have left of Elizabeth." Jacob looked at Matthew again, contempt in his gaze. "You don't deserve him—just as you didn't deserve her."

"Neither of us deserves him." Matthew's voice caught. "But he's mine."

The baby began to cry inside, and Matthew's heart pounded at hearing his son's voice. "I beg you, Jacob." Desperation clawed at his chest. "He'll have the best of everything."

Jacob appeared to consider his plea—but as the child's cries became louder, his eyes became harder. "I will never let you have Nathan."

"Nathan?" His son had a name.

"Elizabeth named him before she—" he choked on the words and then turned toward Nathan's cries.

"What will you do?" Matthew asked, grabbing his arm. "How will you raise him on your own?"

Jacob yanked his arm free. "My sister is coming to get him and bring him back east while I try to make something of this godforsaken land."

Some stranger would raise his child? "There's no need to send him away—I'll take him—and I'll take this land off your hands."

"No. This land was never rightfully yours. I wanted it before—and I want it now. I'll succeed here or die trying." Jacob stepped through the door and started to close it.

Matthew put his hand on the door. "Please, Jacob. He's my son."

"Get off my property, Merrick, before I get my shotgun."

"I'll pay you anything you want."

Jacob pushed the door closed.

Matthew pounded on the wood. "Please." Tears clogged his throat. How could he live knowing his son was in a stranger's home? Away from his protection and love? Would he grow up thinking Jacob Bailey was his father? Or would he know it was Matthew—and despise Matthew the way Matthew despised his own father?

"Let me at least see him," Matthew pleaded through the closed door. "I want to hold my son."

The door opened again, and the barrel of Jacob's shotgun pointed right at Matthew's chest. "Off my property. Now."

Nathan's cries continued as Matthew lowered his fists, knowing utter defeat.

The two people he loved most in the world were lost to him.

Chapter Twenty-Three

ST. PAUL,
MINNESOTA MAY
1891

MATTHEW

The day was gray, just as it should be. Rain pattered against the tent, sheltering those who stood beneath. Hundreds of mourners pressed in to hear the reverend's words, their black umbrellas protecting them from the dreary weather.

"Today, we lay to rest a beloved wife and friend," Reverend Addams spoke in his severe voice. "A woman of character, class, and distinction."

Matthew stood above Helen's closed casket, his eyes downcast, his body shrouded in black—wanting nothing more than to return home and be alone.

Friends had come from near and far, their love for Helen a comfort he didn't deserve—nor want. He had not been a good husband, though Helen had tried to hide the truth from her friends. She thrived on appearances, and he detested them, growing more disagreeable to live with as the years passed.

He had been a faithful husband, in body—if not in soul. The memory of his love for Elizabeth had overshadowed any affection he might have felt for Helen.

Now, at the age of fifty-one, he was alone in the world. There was no family left to mourn his wife's death. Her parents had passed on one after the other over a decade ago. She had no siblings, no aunts and uncles, and no cousins. Though Matthew's mother and sister were still alive, his mother was too old to travel. He provided for them just as he had promised, but they did not like who he had become, either.

There had been no children—not even a single pregnancy. It had only been Helen and Matthew—and now it was just Matthew.

A just punishment for his many sins.

The reverend droned on as cold, wet air seeped into Matthew's bones.

Helen's illness had been long and painful. At the end, she had wanted relief, and he was thankful her suffering was over—but he did not mourn her loss, not like he should. Though they had lived together as husband and wife for twenty-seven years, theirs had never been a love match. He felt numb—as if losing a roommate, one he hardly knew.

That was the greatest tragedy of her passing. But, like so many things in Matthew's life, he didn't realize his mistake until it was too late.

"Let us now bow our heads in a final prayer," Reverend Addams said.

All around him people lowered their faces—yet Matthew raised his. He looked at the group assembled. There was not a pauper among them. Though his wife had been charitable with their fortune she had never dirtied her hands, never looked into the eyes of those in need. She had surrounded herself with beautiful people—people just like her.

Matthew's gaze stopped when he came upon the dazzling brown eyes of an attractive young lady watching him from across the tent. While everyone else kept their heads bowed, she looked straight at him, regarding him with undisguised interest. She couldn't be more than nineteen or twenty—at the very most. Her flawless skin was pink with health and little wisps of auburn-colored curls peeked out from beneath her black bonnet.

She didn't look embarrassed to be caught staring at him—if anything, his own interest was piqued by her confidence. Who was she? Had he seen her before?

"Amen," the reverend said. "Go in peace."

Matthew sucked in a deep breath, as if he had been punched.

It was done.

Helen's funeral was over.

People began to approach Matthew to offer their condolences. A line formed and one after the other they came forward.

He groaned inwardly, wishing to escape this chore. Why wouldn't they just let him be? How many of them truly cared about him, anyway? They had loved Helen—sweet, sociable Helen. He was the ogre they had come to tolerate. Even now, they looked as if this was more of a chore for them than it was for him.

The young lady stepped into line, slowly moving forward with each departing mourner.

Matthew glanced at her from time to time. Why did she stand out to him in a sea of faceless acquaintances?

Finally, she stood before him. Helen's friend Mrs. Crandall stood at her side.

"I'm very sorry for your loss, Major Merrick." Mrs. Crandall lifted a lace kerchief to her eyes. "I don't know what we'll do without Helen."

"Thank yo—"

"Have you met my daughter?" Mrs. Crandall pushed her daughter forward, her tears forgotten.

He looked at the young lady and found her assessing him with those direct brown eyes. He wasn't a young man, but he was still lean and muscular, and his dark hair only showed a hint of silver. Women still smiled at him with interest from time to time. "I don't believe I have."

"This is Edith." Mrs. Crandall's pride was evident—and so was her intention. "She's a debutante this year."

Matthew's skin crawled with the inappropriateness of the subtle hint—and the poor timing.

"Edith, this is Major Matthew Merrick," Mrs. Crandall continued. "Helen's widower."

"It's a pleasure to meet you, Major Merrick." Edith extended her hand and offered a little curtsy, her voice melodic. "I'm sorry for your loss."

Matthew took her hand and bowed over it. "Thank you."

"It won't be the same around your home without dear Helen's companionship." Mrs. Crandall's grief returned, and she dabbed at her eye, once again. "Should you get lonesome, you know where to find us."

Matthew nodded and the ladies turned away—though Miss Edith looked over her shoulder at Matthew and offered a smile.

An hour later Matthew was in his carriage driving down the muddy street to his home on Summit Avenue. The imposing stone mansion was still one of the grandest on the street, though many fine brick and sandstone homes had been built in the years since the Civil War.

Matthew recalled the night of his engagement party almost three decades before and how he had longed to one day own a home as fine as this. He had been a man of great dreams and aspirations—and he had achieved everything he had set out to achieve.

Though one thing still eluded him—the one thing he wanted more than anything else.

His son...

Matthew couldn't shake the chill from the funeral as the driver turned down the cobbled drive and pulled to a stop under the grand portico. Mr. Stearns, the butler, was at the carriage door in a moment. "Welcome home, sir. I hate to bother you, but there's an urgent telegram that's just been delivered."

Matthew stepped past him and entered the foyer, his joints stiff from the cool, rainy weather. He removed his gloves and hat and handed them to Mr. Stearns. "Can this not wait, man? I've just buried my wife."

Mr. Stearns dipped his balding head. "I beg your pardon—but the delivery boy said it is most urgent. I left the telegram on your desk."

Matthew strode down the long hallway toward his office, his heels clicking on the marble floor.

Mr. Stearns followed close behind. "I've laid a fire in the hearth, sir, and there's brandy waiting for you—just as you requested."

Matthew entered his office—the one room in the house that had been truly his. He took up his brandy and moved to the fireplace, staring into the flames.

He should have been thinking of Helen—yet it was Elizabeth that occupied his mind as she had so often over the years. Though they had only spent a few short months together, those stolen moments had impacted him forever.

The village of Crow Wing had all but disappeared off the map when the railroad had bypassed it for Brainerd in 1880. In a few short years, all the buildings had been hauled away and the town was now an empty valley along the shores of the Mississippi where a young man had fallen in love with a young woman.

He stood straight next to the hearth and sighed. He was no longer that same young man and it did him no good to relive the past.

The telegram caught his eye, and he crossed the room to his large, walnut desk.

He set down his brandy and picked up the envelope. As always, the words became scrambled on the paper, and he had to force himself to concentrate and read slowly.

"NATHAN BAILEY HAS RETURNED FROM NEW YORK CITY WITH HIS WIFE STOP HE IS FARMING WITH HIS FATHER ON THE OLD LAND STOP."

Matthew sank into his chair and stared at the telegram.

After twenty-seven years, his son had returned to Minnesota.

He had followed Nathan's life through his solicitor in New York City. He knew the name of Jacob Bailey's sister, Christine, who had raised Nathan. He knew of the primary school they had sent Nathan to as a young boy and the preparatory school he had attended before he went to university. He had graduated with a degree in husbandry, though he did not return to Minnesota immediately, but took work in New York at the Stock Exchange. He had met Miss Victoria Kincade and promptly wed her two years ago.

Matthew knew all there was to know—yet he had never laid eyes on his son. Did he look like Matthew? Or did he favor Elizabeth's native ancestry?

Matthew leaned back in his chair and surveyed his study. He had achieved everything he'd set out to do in life, even meeting his father as a grown man on a trip to Washington, DC several years before with

Helen. They'd been invited to a ball at the White House and he'd been introduced to the man who had fathered him, now a retired congressman living on his past glories. Matthew hadn't told him who he was right away but spent the entire evening impressing the man with his accomplishments. And when the ball came to an end, Matthew finally told him the truth. But his father's shock and apology did not change anything inside Matthew.

It had only made Matthew feel more hollow and unhappy.

Now, as he sat in his cold mansion on Summit Avenue, his life looked bleaker than ever. He was tired of chasing after wealth and accolades. With the news of Nathan's return, Matthew was ready to do something he had wanted to do for years.

He pulled a fresh piece of stationary from his desk and picked up a fountain pen.

It was time to write to his solicitor and put his plan in motion.

"Dear Mr. Silverman,

As per our discussion of last fall, I am in position to purchase the Elk City property and all the holdings from Mr. Randall. Please draw up the necessary paperwork. I would also like for you to contact the architect and have him begin designs for the home I will build on the little rise overlooking the Mississippi and the town site. This shall be a grand home, unlike any other in the area. I want no expenses spared."

Elk City was a small manufacturing and milling town of about fifty people on the banks of the Mississippi. It sat nestled just above Little Falls—only twenty miles south of Jacob Bailey's land. The businesses were doing poorly, and Mr. Randall was ready to sell. Matthew was confident he could make Elk City prosper—just as he had made everything he touched succeed.

He put his pen to the paper and finished the letter.

"Please be advised that I will bring a bride with me when I come to Elk City next year—and have the architect plan accordingly."

Matthew lowered his pen.

His marriage to Helen had not produced an heir—but that did not mean there couldn't be one in his next marriage.

Elk City, Minnesota

June 11, 1892

Edith Crandall was a blushing bride as she sat next to Matthew at the long banquet table in Elk Manor's lavish dining room. Over fifty guests were seated around the table, their champagne glasses lifted to toast the bride and groom.

Matthew sipped his champagne, feeling the warm effects of the bubbling liquid as it slid down his throat. He felt like an eager groom with his prize beside him and could hardly wait until the celebration ended when he and Edith could explore the mansion together. He was excited to show her the bedroom adjoining his where they would spend their first night together.

Just twenty-years-old, Edith was young and vivacious and full of life—exactly what Matthew needed. He was a new man, no longer the ogre people had come to fear. Together, he and Edith would create a thriving family and build Elk City, giving Matthew a second chance at life.

Cheerful conversation filled the room while silverware clinked against fine china. The serving staff moved in and out among the revelry, their quiet presence almost imperceptible.

Edith leaned toward Matthew, her attractive body pressed close to his. "My mother is in tears," she said quietly, for Matthew's ears alone. "I do wish she would pull herself together."

Matthew smiled at his young wife. "She's only happy, my dear—just as I am."

Edith looked at him, her auburn curls outlining her pretty face. "She's overjoyed I'm married and she doesn't need to worry about me anymore." Edith took a sip of her champagne and smiled ruefully. "It's a great deal of work to marry one's daughter off well."

"I'm the one who married well." He gently placed a chaste kiss upon her cheek.

Edith froze, her champagne glass suspended on its way back to the table. She did not look at him as she spoke through her teeth. "Do not kiss me in public, Matthew. It's vulgar."

Heat gathered under Matthew's evening coat at the rebuke, and he pulled back. Not once had she chastised him for physical attention when they had been courting.

In fact, she had encouraged it.

Perhaps the strain of the wedding had put her in a poor mood.

Edith set her glass down and turned to him with a smile. "The house is lovely. I'm pleased with the décor—of course there are things I will change, but wherever did you find all this beautiful wood?"

Her sudden change in subject made Matthew pause, but he didn't speak of the kiss. "I had much of it imported. The dining room and parlors are of solid mahogany from central America, the library and my office are English Cherry, and our bedrooms upstairs," he offered her an intimate smile, anticipating the moment he would show her to her room, "are Birdseye maple and African wood."

"We'll be the envy of everyone in Minnesota." Edith lifted her fork and took a dainty bite of wedding cake. "I've heard our home is the largest in the northwest." She set down her fork. "Imagine me, mistress of such a place. Mother fears I will be too removed from society here, but I'm determined that I will take society with me."

The home was a magnificent Queen Anne Victorian, with eight large fireplaces, a grand central foyer and staircase, a large, modern kitchen, indoor plumbing, and electrical lighting throughout. The outside had been finished in stone and clapboard, with a large turret, a wraparound porch, and a balcony protruding from the front of the second floor.

Matthew touched her hand, enjoying the pleasure his wife took in the fortune he had amassed over the past twenty-eight years. "You'll have all your heart desires, Edith. Everything and more."

She pulled her hand away and set it in her lap. Her mother leaned over to speak, and Edith turned away from Matthew.

His bride was young and would have much to learn about life and marriage, but she had been eager to wed and move to central Minnesota with him. Once she began to have children she would mature even more.

Matthew smiled, thinking of the children that would one day fill this grand home.

The celebration lasted much longer than Matthew intended, with Edith's mother sobbing as she finally took her leave. The wedding party would proceed on the evening train back to St. Paul.

Matthew and Edith stood under the front portico and waved as their guests drove down the road in a number of carriages Matthew had hired for the day. The sun sat low on the western horizon, brandishing Elk Manor's thousand acres with a golden glow. The property spread out toward the Mississippi in gently rolling hills, with Elk City to the north.

As the last carriage disappeared around the bend, Matthew turned to his bride, suddenly as nervous as a school boy. "Did you enjoy yourself today?"

"I'm so relieved my mother has gone." Edith picked up the long train of her silk gown and turned toward the front door, as if she didn't hear him. "I think I'll retire for the night. Please don't allow the servants to wake me in the morning." She smiled, though she didn't quite look him in the eyes. "Now that I'm mistress of my own home, I shall sleep in as long as I like and do as I please—without my mother's constant nagging."

She swept through the front door and called for her lady's maid to attend to her in her bedchambers.

Matthew stood for a moment, unprepared for her sudden departure. He had hoped to sit for a moment in the back parlor and talk over the day's activities and then retire together, just as he and Helen had done on their wedding day.

Perhaps she was preparing herself for him to visit her later.

He moved inside the house and closed the front door. Mr. Stearns appeared, his graying hair combed over his bald spot. "Would you like for me to send for your valet, sir?"

How much time would Edith need? "Perhaps I'll have some brandy in my office first."

"Very good, sir." Stearns bowed as Matthew walked past.

He entered his office, marveling at the magnificent room. One long wall was filled with windows, looking out on his newly acquired kingdom and another was covered with bookshelves from floor to ceiling. A massive brick fireplace took up a third wall, and his large desk sat in the center of it all.

He lifted his glass of brandy and stood at the large window. For as far as he could see, there was not another home or building to mar the scene. He took a deep, cleansing breath, thankful for the solitude of the country.

His eyes wandered to his bookshelves and a strange sight caught his eye.

There, sitting in a prominent location, was his mother's old Bible. He knew it was hers because it was the only Bible he owned. He hadn't laid eyes on it since the day Elizabeth had married Jacob.

He set down his brandy and walked to the shelf where he lifted the Bible. Someone had probably come across it in the move and assumed he wanted it here in his office.

The Bible fell open to the Book of Matthew and one of the scriptures Tuck had quoted to him so long ago jumped out from the sixth chapter. For the first time, the words were not jumbled and he read it with surprising ease. "*Lay not up for yourselves treasures upon earth, where moth and rust doth corrupt, and where thieves break through and steal: But lay up for yourselves treasures in heaven, where neither moth nor rust doth corrupt, and where thieves do not break through nor steal: For where your treasure is, there will your heart be also.*"

Matthew swallowed the discomfort in his throat. He had laid up a great store of earthly treasures—and hoped to gain more. Was this scripture suggesting he be a pauper? As always, the unusual words of the Bible confused him with their impracticality.

His mind wandered to the old fur trader. He had apparently heeded the scripture and had probably died a pauper. Matthew suddenly pictured him sitting with Jesus at a banquet table in a mansion much grander than Matthew's, talking to Jesus like He was an old friend.

The vision disturbed Matthew—not because he was uncomfortable thinking of Christ or the afterlife, but because he was uncomfortable thinking he might not sit at that same table someday. Could it be possible that Tuck had been poor on earth, yet wealthy for eternity? Could it also be possible that Matthew would be a pauper for eternity?

Chapter seven caught Matthew's attention and he sat down on the chair, almost hearing the old fur trader's voice. "*Enter ye in at the strait gate: for wide is the gate, and broad is the way, that leadeth to destruction, and many there be which go in thereat: Because strait is the gate, and narrow is the way, which leadeth unto life, and few there be that find it.*"

Matthew slammed the book closed, his hands shaking and sweat gathering under his jacket.

He strode from his office, calling for his valet to meet him in his bedchambers.

Within thirty minutes, he stood outside the door connecting his dressing room to Edith's. He wore his nightclothes under a robe and slippers on his feet.

Should he knock on her door or simply walk in?

He was her husband, after all, and she should be expecting him.

Matthew opened the door and found Edith sitting up in bed, a book in hand, wearing a shimmering silk nightgown. She was a picture of exquisite beauty and his desire for her increased.

He took a step into her room, and she looked up in surprise, quickly pulling the bedclothes over her body. "What are you doing in here?"

He untied his robe, appreciating her modesty. "It's our wedding night, darling."

Her eyes became enormous, and she shook her head. "Get out of here."

Matthew stopped his advance toward her bed. "Don't be alarmed, Edith. This is a natural part of marriage." He smiled, trying to reassure her. "I will be kind."

"No." She pulled the blankets up to her chin. "You will never enter this bed."

He hesitated and then indicated his bedchamber. "Would you care to join me in my room?"

She shook her head once again. "I will never share any bed with you."

"Edith." He walked closer to her bed, irritation replacing his good humor. "We're married now. I expect you to welcome me whenever I ask. I assumed you understood."

She reached over and lifted an expensive vase from her nightstand. "You will never touch me. Do you understand?"

"You've got to be jesting with me." She had not once hinted that this would be a marriage in name only. She'd flirted, teased and been suggestive to the point of improper on some occasions, leading him to believe that she would welcome him to her bed.

Had it all been a ploy?

She gripped the vase until her knuckles turned white. "If you touch me, I'll kill you."

Alarm raced through Matthew's body, turning him cold. "Maybe, in time…"

"Never." She looked him up and down, revulsion on her face. "You're older than my father for heaven's sake."

"But surely you understood the expectations of our marriage."

"I will be the mistress of this home and fulfill my social obligations for your career but that is all." She had gained a bit of confidence as she looked down her nose at him. "I can't abide the idea of your touch."

Matthew backed away, more than his pride injured. Anger and disillusionment welled up within him. "Why did you agree to marry me?"

"Is it not obvious?" She looked truly stunned. "I married you for wealth and status—and to get away from my mother. Surely you knew." She blinked, as if she was confused. "Why else would a leading debutante, with an endless choice of suitors, choose you?"

Her words stung his pride like nothing ever had. But weren't those the very reasons he and Helen had married?

"What of children?" he asked her.

She stared at him.

"Don't you want to be a mother?"

She snorted, her expression truly aghast. "I have no desire to birth a child, nor raise one."

What a fool he had been. He had never assumed she loved him—but he had assumed she was marrying him out of common respect and the hope for a family.

He took a deep breath and cinched his robe belt. He would never beg, nor would he force himself upon his wife. If they were to share a bed, it would be a mutual decision.

"I will leave you."

He strode across the carpet and passed into the dressing room, slamming the door behind him. A mirror slid from the dressing room wall and crashed to the floor, breaking into hundreds of shards. Edith shrieked but he continued to his room, yanking off his robe and tossing it to the floor.

Edith Merrick had indeed become the mistress of Elk Manor, but she would never be the mistress of his heart.

Matthew sat on the edge of his bed and buried his head in his hands, accepting a fate he had thought he could outwit.

An heir was still out of his reach, and he was more alone than ever before.

Chapter Twenty-Four

Matthew

Matthew woke early the next morning and dressed before the sun rose. He left the stone mansion and walked to the two-story carriage house attached to the stable where he held his prize geldings. The dark sky sparkled with the early morning stars, while a low rim of color edged the eastern horizon.

Lantern light glowed from inside the carriage house. The groom, Samuel Turner, met him by the door, a wide smile on his face.

"Good morning to you, Major Merrick." Mr. Turner was a young Irishman, not more than twenty-two or twenty-three, straight from his home land. His dark brown hair curled out from under his tweed flat cap and his black eyes danced with merriment. He had come to Matthew highly recommended and had been knowledgeable and confident with the horses. "What can I do for you, sir?"

"I'd like a saddled horse, please."

"Would you be needing a carriage today?"

"Only a horse, thank you."

Mr. Turner nodded. "Right away, sir." He whistled as he walked down the center of the barn and stopped at Prince's stall. "Prince, me fine one, it's you the major will be needing today, I think." He led the beautiful bay horse from the stall and rubbed his nose.

He spoke in low, cheerful tones as he quickly saddled the horse and brought him to Matthew. "I forgot to congratulate you on the occasion of your marriage." Sam grinned. "We had us a wee bit of cake last night in the kitchen to celebrate."

"Thank you," Matthew said, taking the reins from Mr. Turner. He would rather not think about his wedding—or the sore encounter he had with his wife afterward.

Matthew led Prince out into the early morning. The sky had turned to a dusky shade of purple and only a few stars dotted the expanse.

"Have a grand time." Mr. Turner leaned his tall frame against the door. "And be sure to make Prince work for his oats."

Matthew mounted the horse and rode north over the bridge spanning Elk Creek and past the flour mill at Elk City. He touched the horse's sides with his heels and let him have his lead, relishing the fresh air and freedom.

He stayed on the Mississippi road, following it for fifteen miles until he came to the remains of old Fort Ripley. It had been occupied until 1877, when the government felt the Indian threat had passed, and so it had.

He stopped his horse where the fort gates had once stood, remembering the day he had brought Elizabeth to the dance. Little was left of the fort, but some rundown buildings and a few pickets from the stockade. It was hard to imagine this place had been alive with a fiddler's music and dozens of stomping feet.

Matthew leaned down and pet Prince's neck. "I brought a beautiful young woman here once. So long ago, it almost feels like a dream."

The horse lifted his head and blew through his nose.

Matthew directed Prince into the river and forded over a shallow stretch. He continued north on the old Woods Trail and pushed him for another seven miles until they came to the place where Crow Wing village had once thrived.

Matthew plodded along the trail near the old boardwalk where broken pieces of wood were still in the ground. Crumbled cellars stood out like decaying teeth and the few ramshackle buildings that remained were weatherworn and falling apart. Uncle Clem's trading post, which had stood like a beacon at the top of the hill, had been removed and the hotel across the way had burned.

He rode up the hill and then down into the valley where Elizabeth's cabin once stood. Weeds grew up where the children had played.

Wind blew across the valley and Matthew turned to look over his shoulder, half expecting to see the village alive again.

A haunted silence hung over the land.

He dismounted and tied Prince to a tree, then he climbed the hill and went into the woods.

The old trail he and Elizabeth had used was now grown over, but he still knew the way.

It was almost as if she walked beside him, smiling at him with that confident tilt of her head, questioning him with those big brown eyes, and challenging him to be a better man than he was capable of.

The creek bubbled along, and Matthew found the rock where they had first kissed. He laid his hand upon it for only a moment as he passed and continued across the creek. He didn't bother to take off his socks and shoes, or roll up his pants, but splashed through until he came to the ancient willow tree.

He climbed the steep creek bank, not as limber as he once was, and rounded the tree.

There, engraved in the bark, dimmed with time, was the heart with the initials M & E. Tears stung the backs of his eyes and his throat ached as he laid his hand over the letters.

"*Here is where our heart shall always remain,*" he had said to her so long ago. "*Not two separate hearts, but one.*"

Matthew slid to his knees at the base of the trunk and wept.

"Elizabeth." Her name left his lips on an anguished sob. "I'm so sorry."

If only he could go back and do things differently.

He sat by the tree for over an hour reliving the memories of their time together. Twenty-eight years had passed, but for this one moment in time, Matthew was young again with Elizabeth beside him and his whole life before him.

He finally stood, stiff from being on the ground, and touched the heart one last time.

"Our heart will remain here forever, Elizabeth, no matter where we go."

He descended the hill to his waiting horse, anxious to make his next stop before returning to Elk Manor and the work that awaited him.

He mounted Prince once again and forded the Mississippi just south of Crow Wing. A trail hugged the western shore of the river, and he followed it for three miles until he came to Jacob's land.

A new house stood at the top of the hill where the old cabin once resided. It was two stories tall with white clapboard siding and sparkling windows. A large red barn sat to the north of the house, and a line of mature Norway pine edged the western side. A woman stood at the clothes line pinning sheets to the wires as a baby lay in a basket nearby.

A strange sensation tugged at Matthew's heart, filling his insides with a warmth he'd never experienced before.

This must be Nathan's wife and child—Matthew's grandchild.

The woman turned and put one hand up to shade her eyes and Matthew urged his horse forward, unsure what he would say but needing to see this family who didn't know him.

The woman picked up the baby as Matthew turned in at their drive. He took a deep breath as she walked toward him, a smile on her pretty face.

"Hello," she called.

Matthew was close enough to see the child's face. Big green eyes stared back at him—eyes exactly the color of Matthew's.

Matthew dismounted his horse and couldn't take his eyes from the beautiful child.

"Can I offer you something cool to drink?" She smiled at him, and her gentle countenance drew him in. She was a lovely woman with blonde hair wrapped in a loose bun and tendrils framing her face.

"No, thank you. I'm just passing through and thought I would introduce myself." His voice filled with a tinge of bitterness he couldn't stop. "I used to work with your father-in-law many years ago."

The woman's smile fell for a moment, and something shifted in her eyes, but she quickly regained her composure. "I'm sorry, but my father-in-law is in Brainerd today, seeing to some personal matters—my husband is around here somewhere—"

"Right here, as a matter of fact." A man's voice interrupted their conversation and Matthew turned to find a smiling face. "I'm Nathan Bailey," he said, extending his hand. "Jacob's son."

Jacob's son.

Matthew's heart pounded as he stared at *his* son. His black hair and dark brown eyes were so much like Elizabeth's, he ached for her presence. He was as tall as Matthew and built similar, but he looked like his mother. Everything in Matthew cried out to tell him the truth—proclaim him as his son—but it wouldn't be fair to Nathan.

Nathan lowered his hand, uncertainty in his eyes as he looked at his wife.

Matthew finally gained control of his senses and lifted his hand. "I'm pleased to meet you. I'm Matthew Merrick."

Nathan shook his hand and lifted his brows. "Major Merrick?"

"Yes."

He grinned. "We've heard all about your new house at Elk City—and your recent marriage. Congratulations."

"Thank you."

"This is my wife Victoria and our son Cade."

"Cade?" Matthew looked at the boy.

"His full name is Jacob Kincade Bailey." Victoria nuzzled her nose against the boy's cheek. "But we call him Cade."

"He's a lovely child," Matthew said, though it rankled him that he was named after Jacob.

Nathan laid his hand on the boy's downy hair and smiled with pride, then he looked at Matthew. "I'm surprised my father didn't mention knowing you."

"He was my clerk at the Crow Wing Agency, but we only worked together for a few months."

"Then you knew my mother." Nathan's face lit with interest and expectation.

Matthew glanced between the couple, emotions and memories clogging his throat. "I did know your mother."

"She died when Nathan was born," Victoria said. "But Nathan's father won't speak of her."

Matthew offered them a sad smile. "Perhaps one day I'll tell you all about her."

Nathan frowned but didn't ask for more.

Matthew looked over the farm. Though the house and barn had been added, there was little change from thirty years ago. "I once asked to buy this land from your father."

"And I'm sure he ran you off the property with a shotgun."

Matthew's gaze jerked back to Nathan. "How do you know?"

"You're not the only person who's asked to buy this land." Nathan shook his head. "He won't even entertain any offers."

"He won't admit it, but I think it's because your mother is buried here," Victoria said, a soft smile on her lips.

A rider approached the farm from the north.

"There he is now," Nathan said.

Matthew watched Jacob advance, wondering what he would say when he saw Matthew.

He had aged a great deal in twenty-eight years, no longer the strapping young man he had once been.

Matthew knew the moment Jacob recognized him. He became stiff in his saddle and gripped his reins. "Get off my land, Merrick!"

Nathan and Victoria shared a concerned glance.

"Father, Mr. Merrick stopped by to introduce—"

"I don't care why he's here." Jacob dismounted and took a step toward Matthew, fear on his face. "Get out of here. Now."

Matthew studied him for a long time. "I didn't come to make trouble." He nodded at Nathan. "Just wanted to introduce myself."

"I know what you want." Jacob's fists shook by his side. "You're not welcome here."

"Father." Nathan took a step forward.

But Jacob raised his hand "This man is no good, Nathan."

"I should go." Matthew moved toward his horse.

Nathan followed Matthew. "I'm sorry, Major Merrick."

"Don't trouble yourself. If you're ever near Elk Manor, please stop in and see me." Matthew mounted Prince. "Good luck."

"God Bless you." Nathan reached up and shook his hand once more, kindness in his brown eyes.

Matthew paused and stared at his son. Was he a believer?

"Go!" Jacob stepped over and slapped Prince's hind end.

Matthew looked back at Nathan's family one last time as he rode away.

He used to dream of telling Nathan the truth...but he wasn't sure he ever could.

Chapter Twenty-Five

MARCH 19, 1918

Cade

Cade stood at the edge of the barren field, his hands in his pockets, kicking a clod of dirt. Spring had come early to central Minnesota, thawing the land and breaking apart the frozen river. Water rushed along the swollen banks, pushing and pulling on its blind quest to flow south.

The early spring might be a blessing to some farmers, but to Cade, it meant more toil, and for what? There was no way they would raise two-hundred and fifty dollars by June first. With nothing of significance to harvest until fall, it would be impossible. He had taken odd jobs, but with the war marching into a second year, people were holding tight to their money.

They had to borrow a bank note to purchase their seed—another debt that needed to be repaid. Cade felt buried beneath the weight of the responsibilities.

Emma had come to the farm a week after the New Year's party to get her Ford, but Cade had been short with her, and she had left upset.

She hadn't come back.

Two and a half months later, he was as hurt as before, but his longing for her had only increased. He closed his eyes, trying to think of something other than Emma.

He walked toward the barn and sighed. There was so much work to do, and he had no drive to do it. His airplane sat next to the barn, waiting to be flown, but even that had little appeal to him. Where would he go?

Dad was about the same, his health forcing him to spend most of his days in bed. His spirits had stayed bright, as Cade knew they would. Cade had done everything in his power to avoid having a heart to heart conversation, though his father had tried numerous times. He didn't know why, but he dreaded the idea of having that final talk. His father would try to apologize, and Cade would tell him it wasn't his fault, then Dad would give him some sage advice about God and Cade's eternal future, and Cade would listen, but he'd harden his heart and not change his ways.

What was the point? God felt a million miles away and Cade was convinced He couldn't hear a single prayer Cade had uttered.

A Ford appeared on the road, at the edge of the woods, and Cade's heart jumped. It did every time he saw a black Model T.

But this time, the automobile didn't continue down the road—this time it turned into the Bailey's drive.

Cade stopped near the barn, hope and dread warring within his chest.

Emma pulled the Ford up to the barn and stalled the motor.

He felt like he did the first time she had come—both irritated and enthralled by her presence.

She opened her door and stepped out of the car. She wore a brown day dress, with a matching brown hat. It looked pretty with her auburn hair and deep brown eyes. He stopped himself from letting his eyes wander over her appearance, and prepared himself for whatever she had come to say.

"Hello, Cade."

He nodded hello, not trusting his voice to work properly. It was good to see her after so many months apart. She looked fresh and bright after a bleak winter.

Emma closed the door and walked over to him, her shoes crunching the gravel. She stopped a few feet away, but he could still smell the floral perfume she wore. It made him think of the dance and the kisses and the moments when they had been close.

Moments he'd tried to forget as he pushed thoughts of her from his mind.

"Why are you here?"

"The weather has been so nice. I've come for my next flying lesson."

Flying lesson? He couldn't be expected to teach her. Not after what had happened. "I'm not offering lessons any longer."

She took a step closer. "Cade, I'm sorry for the night in the library—"

He turned and walked into the barn. He didn't want to hear her apology.

She followed him. "I was wrong to run away from you that night, but you have to understand why I did it."

"I don't have to understand—and don't bother trying to explain. You've made your choice."

"But I haven't."

Pain pulsed in his chest. "You did."

She dropped her gaze and looked at her hands. When she glanced up, there was pleading in her eyes. "I know you need the money, and I want to learn how to fly. Please teach me. I want to go to St. Paul and take my test as soon as you think I'm ready."

"No."

"Cade, you promised to teach me."

He took a garden rake from the wall. The handle was splintered and he'd wanted to fix it all winter. He put it on a workbench and rummaged around for a screwdriver. "Things have changed."

She put her hand on his arm and he stilled his work, but wouldn't look at her.

"Nothing has changed," she whispered close to him. "I know I hurt you, and I'm sorry, but I need time."

"I hate when you say that." He pulled his arm away and grabbed the screwdriver. "If you don't know by now, what will it take?"

"It's complicated."

He turned, desperation making his voice tight. "Why?"

She took a seat on a stool near the bench, her shoulders slumped. "It will sound horrible."

"Nothing will be as horrible as the night you left me in the library."

She looked at him with so much regret, he wanted to comfort her—but he held himself back.

"My father has threatened to disown me if I don't marry Thomas."

"So this is about money?" Revulsion rolled through his stomach. He had not felt this small and insignificant since his grandfather had been alive. He knew his face revealed the disgust he felt. "You will marry Overton and be miserable just to hold on to your fortune?"

"No." She shook her head and stood, her brows dipped low. "This is not about my father's money. This is about being rejected, once and for all, from a man who has never loved me or treated me like his daughter." Tears gathered in her eyes. "It will be proof that I do not matter—that I *was* a mistake—and I don't know if I can live with myself if I truly believe that."

The wall of ice surrounding his heart slowly began to melt. "Emmie..."

"I know it's foolish—I know I could make the biggest mistake of my life—but I can't force myself to walk away from Father. If I do, he will not think of me again, and—" Tears trailed down her cheeks. "It will be the greatest heartbreak of my life."

Cade pulled her into his arms and held her as she cried, knowing something of heartbreak. He had never liked Matthew Merrick for what he had done to Grandfather—and ultimately to their entire family. But now he despised Matthew for what he had done to Emma. No one deserved to be treated the way he had treated her, no matter what the circumstances. But to treat his own daughter this way was unforgivable.

She pulled back and placed her hands on Cade's chest. "Please, give me time. I care for you, very much, and I know it's not right for me to ask, but I keep hoping Father will change his mind. I had thought maybe, after his heart attack, he would be a different man—but I haven't seen any proof. I keep praying, hoping God will soften his heart."

Just as Cade's parents had prayed for his grandfather.

"I will give you all the time you need." He wouldn't pressure her, or make it harder for her. He would keep his distance and allow her the space she needed.

He moved away from her embrace and leaned against the workbench.

She wiped her cheeks and looked at him with her weary eyes. "I want to fly again, Cade. I feel such freedom when I'm in the air—I've missed it."

He wanted to teach her—to share his passion for the air—but he didn't trust Overton and what he might do to the people Cade cared about. "If I teach you, no one must know."

She nodded. "I won't tell anyone. I don't want them to try and stop me."

"I need to tune up the plane and make sure it's in working order. Can you come back tomorrow?"

"I will be here in the morning."

A ray of sunshine broke through the gray clouds as Emma returned to his life.

Emma

Emma's cheeks hurt from grinning. She held the control stick in her hands, flying above the Mississippi River toward the old village of Crow Wing. She turned and looked at Cade. He lifted his arms in the air to show her she was the one controlling the aircraft.

His smile warmed her heart.

He had asked where she wanted to go, and she said she wanted to see the place her father and his grandfather had met over fifty years ago. A field lay just east of the town site and Cade had said she could bring the airplane down—with him helping from the dual controls in the back cockpit.

The wind pushed against her face, and the sound of the engine roared in her ears—but she felt as light and carefree as a bird.

Just up ahead, the Crow Wing River converged with the Mississippi and Emma located the field Cade had told her about. She took a deep breath and began to descend toward the earth, her heart racing and her mind focusing on the landing.

She lowered the plane until they were a few feet off the ground and then she eased up on the throttle. She held her breath and stiffened her body as the first tire hit the hard ground. It bounced several times before the second one hit and then they were both on the ground, riding over the bumpy field.

She had landed.

They stopped the engine and Emma tore her goggles and cap off her head. "I did it!"

Cade jumped out of the back cockpit and helped her down. "Congratulations."

They inspected the airplane, and he told her what each part did, before they turned their attention to Crow Wing.

"The old town site is on the other side of that grouping of trees," Cade said. "Would you like to see it?"

Emma nodded and they set off across the field. "Have you ever been here?"

"Years ago. My father brought me here to show me where Grandfather had worked and where he met my grandmother."

"You don't talk much about her."

"I never knew her—neither did my father—and my grandfather never spoke about her."

"What do you know?"

"Her name was Elizabeth, and she was the daughter of a Chippewa Chief."

"I've always thought your father looked like he could be an Indian warrior."

Cade smiled as he held a branch up to allow her to pass into the woods.

They soon came to a delightful little creek. The spring thaw had made it gurgle over stones as it raced downhill. A large rock sat next to the water's edge—perfect to sit on.

They followed the creek until they came to an opening. A gentle valley dipped the land and looked out over the Mississippi and Crow Wing Rivers. Deep depressions indicated where cellars and buildings had once stood—but there was nothing else left. They walked down into the valley and then up a hill and stopped at the top.

Emma shaded her eyes and looked out over the land—trying to imagine what her father had thought when he saw this town for the first time.

"Has your father ever told you about his work at the agency?" Cade asked, drawing her attention.

"My father has never told me anything. Everything I know, I've learned from other people."

"Can you picture him here?"

She closed her eyes and listened to the wind rustling the trees and the flow of the river—but could not see her father.

Opening her eyes, she sighed. "I wish I knew who he was—and is. I wish I knew what he had done here, who he talked to." She studied Cade. "It's remarkable to think he knew your grandparents. Just imagine, our destinies first crossed paths here in this place over fifty years ago."

"I know what my grandfather thought of Matthew Merrick—but I wonder what my grandmother thought of him."

There would be no way to ever know.

"Shall we go back?" he asked.

She nodded, resigned to the fact that she still didn't understand her father or his past.

They took the path back into the woods and came across the large rock again.

"Cade, I'd like to talk to you about something."

He turned his curious gaze on her. "Should we sit here for a while?"

They sat on the rock, and it felt warm from the spring sunshine. She was silent for a moment, hoping she presented her idea in a way he would accept.

He sat close to her—so close, his leg brushed hers. She recalled their kisses and the passion she had felt from his touch. He had been a gentleman all day—but now, sitting alone together, part of her hoped he would kiss her again—while the other part knew they needed time and space.

His voice was low as he spoke. "What would you like to discuss?"

"I've been thinking a lot about your farm and how important it's become to you. I know you're struggling to earn enough money for the mortgage payment, but there's a way you can earn the money—and then some." She turned and studied his side profile, committing every nuance of his features to memory. "You need to overcome your fears and perform an aerial show."

"Emmie—"

"I know you can do it—you were made to fly."

"I can't."

"You can."

He looked across the creek, his gaze far away. "I've hurt so many people—I can't abide the thought of being the cause of more pain."

"It was an accident—"

"It's not just about the woman at the airfield." He turned his attention to her. "My grandfather suffered from apoplexy when I was ten. He became angry at me and I didn't respond to his call. The doctor said it was caused by over-exertion and my grandfather blamed me for his paralysis the rest of his life."

"Cade—"

"That same night, I ran away from home, and I was caught in a winter storm. My father came looking for me, and he carried me all the way back. When we reached the house, he collapsed and then became very ill. His heart was never the same after that night—and he's lying in his bed right now because of me."

His green eyes were filled with so much sorrow, Emma's chest ached.

"The woman at the airfield died because I didn't listen to my manager. I did a stunt he told me not to do. The same is true for my grandfather and my father—I did things I was told I shouldn't do, and other people suffered because of it."

She placed her hand on his arm. "It sounds to me like you've suffered, too."

"My suffering is nothing compared to theirs."

"You can't carry the guilt for these mistakes all your life. We weren't meant to bear such heavy burdens."

"If I don't carry the burden, then it's almost as if I don't care what happened to them."

"Jesus said in the Book of Matthew to come to Him with our heavy burdens and He would give us rest. He tells us to take His yoke upon our shoulders, for Jis load is light. Cade, Jesus will take the load, if you ask Him."

"And that's it?"

Emma smiled. "That's it. He took our sins upon Him at the cross so we don't have to bear them any longer. If you continue to carry them, it's your own doing—and not His."

He was silent for a long time—and then he reached over and took her hand in his.

She leaned her head on his shoulder—hoping he would at least consider her idea. "An airshow is the only thing that will save your family's farm."

He caressed her hand with his thumb. "I'll think about it."

Excitement raced up her spine. "You'll need to plan it in May to wait for the weather to become more predictable. That will give us time to advertise—"

"I said I'd *think* about it."

She went on, as if he hadn't spoken. "I have one more thing to ask you—don't answer me right away, but hear me out."

"I can't make any promises."

"I've been reading about an army pilot named Ormer Locklear who has been doing wing walking stunts—"

"No."

"Cade—"

"Don't even think about it, Emma. I will never allow you to attempt something like that."

"But I'm strong and I have excellent balance. I took ballet lessons all my life—and I'm not afraid of heights. Just think of the publicity we'll get if we advertise wing walking. People will come from all over the state to see me."

"You have no idea what you're talking about—you've only been in an airplane four times—you hardly have your bearings, yet you want to climb onto the wings?"

"We'd have over two months to practice—I could do anything in two months."

He let go of her hand. "I won't even discuss it."

She took a deep breath and tried a different tactic. "You're one of the best pilots in the country—if anyone can help me, it's you."

"There will be enough of a draw with me flying—we don't need to add a wing walker to the show."

"I know I can do it. Put me to the test. I can walk the ridgepole of a house, I can balance on one foot for an indefinite amount of time, I can do a cartwheel on a balance beam—I know I can stand on the top of the airplane if you're flying straight and steady. I'll hold on to ropes—it will be simple." She laid her hand over his. "Just think about it."

He stood and offered her his hand. "We should get back."

Emma took his hand, and he helped her off the rock. She would not give up her idea—she knew it would be good for the show and Cade did, too.

She glanced around one last time, remembering the rock, and the creek, and the ancient willow tree hanging over the banks, its branches just beginning to bud with new life.

Chapter Twenty-Six

MAY 20, 1918

CADE

Cade ran the cloth over the fuselage of his bi-plane. The shiny red paint glistened in the warm sunshine and promised to impress the spectators who would come at the end of the week to see the show.

Emma had been true to her word, and she had advertised the show extensively. No matter where Cade went, it was all people wanted to talk about. There had been nothing like the aerial show in central Minnesota, and everyone he spoke to was planning to come.

With the war heavy on people's minds, and more boys being drafted, it was something for people to look forward to. There was no way of charging admission, as anyone could watch from the roads surrounding the farm, so he had decided to make his money giving rides at the end of the show. He would charge ten dollars a ride, and if he had at least twenty-five passengers, he would make the money he needed. With the potential of two or three thousand on-lookers, he was confident he could get twenty-five who would want to go up in the air.

He stopped his polishing and took a step back to admire the plane. Emma had advertised it as the plane from *Flying High*, which was another draw. The Milo Theater in Little Falls was rerunning the movie this week, in anticipation of the event, and Cade had been invited to the opening night. Hundreds of people had come out to meet him, and for a few hours he wasn't the farm boy trying to provide for his family. He had wanted Emma to come, but they had not appeared in public together.

He climbed onto the lower wing and then pulled himself up to the top wing. It was hot to the touch, but not too hot to make his inspections. He had fastened a rope with two large eye hooks and had checked them—and re-checked them—at least a dozen times in the past two days. He was probably crazy to allow her to try it—but he had agreed to let her wing walk during the show to prove to others that flying was safe and they should pay for a ride. But he had only agreed to let her after checking her strength and balance—and she had been right. She was a beautiful athlete and had amazed him with her skills. For weeks, they had practiced on the ground and then two days ago he had taken her up and she made the climb. His heart had been in his throat the entire time, but she had been graceful and competent.

If all went as planned, she would be the first public aerial wing walker in Minnesota.

Mama and Gracie had been a big help, preparing the farm for the show and the expected crowds. Dad said he could see the field from his window and enjoyed watching Cade and Emma practice.

Cade would wait until after the show to plant the wheat crop in the north field. He had sowed the cornfield and the potato field, and had even helped his mother plant her garden. He had never worked so hard in his life—but he did it for his family and for Emma. If she would have him, he needed an income, and the farm was his only source.

They had spent the past two months getting to know one another—but he also knew Thomas Overton was often at her home, spending evenings with her. She had made Cade no promises and was honest with him about the situation, so he had no right to demand she stop seeing Overton—as much as he wished she would. She continued to pray for her father, but saw no improvement in his health or his plans.

Cade walked into the quiet farmhouse to get a drink of water from the sink and to check on his father. Mother had taken Gracie into town to purchase some odds and ends they would need for the show.

He walked through the parlor and quietly pushed open the bedroom door, not wanting to disturb his father if he was asleep.

Dad sat in his bed, his gaze focused out the window, a serious look on his thin face. When he heard Cade, he turned and offered him a smile.

"I'm checking to see if you need something." Cade didn't step into the room.

"I do need something, son. I need to talk to you."

Cade's insides tightened and he glanced out at the field. "I have a lot of work to do today—"

"I've allowed you to put off this conversation long enough. I sensed it wasn't the right time—but now I fear there will never be a right time for you."

"Dad, I don't—"

"I know you don't, but I do." His voice held more force than Cade had ever heard. "Grant a dying man a last wish and sit here and talk to me."

Cade took a deep breath and then walked into the room. He grabbed a chair from near the wall and placed it next to the bed. He hated to see his father like this. A man who had once braved a blizzard and carried him back to safety, was now reduced to practically nothing. It made Cade aware of his own mortality in a way nothing else ever had.

"Look at me, son."

Cade lifted his gaze and looked into his father's brown eyes. He could see a glimpse of his Grandmother Elizabeth in his father, though he'd never met her. Something kind and gentle lived within him—something he had not inherited from Grandfather Jacob.

"When you left, I allowed guilt and regret to eat me alive. I knew I had been the one at fault for your unhappiness—"

"Dad, I don't want to hear this."

"I don't care, Cade. I need to tell you." Dad readjusted his position and studied Cade with an intensity that left Cade squirming in his chair. "I sacrificed your happiness, and your childhood, to try to save my father. I didn't know him growing up. I was raised in New York City by my aunt. It was a good home—a happy home—where I was taught about God and I was loved unconditionally. My aunt told me my father was angry and bitter, and it was my greatest dream to come back here and show him the love of Jesus.

"Your mother and I saw this as our missionary work—but we put up with far too much in our quest to save him. For some reason, he chose you, out of all of us, to focus his rage. We hoped and prayed he'd see the Light—and we talked to him all the time about his behavior toward you—but nothing seemed to help. After his apoplexy, it was especially hard, because we couldn't leave him on his own. When you left—" Emotion caught in Dad's throat. "I was almost relieved."

"Relieved?" Cade frowned. "You were relieved I left?"

"I knew you were finally free—and I thanked God you no longer had to put up with my father. I prayed fervently, every day, that you were safe and happy—but more importantly, that you were seeking God." Dad's face became gentle. "When I knew I wasn't long for this earth, I began to pray you would come home, so I could tell you the most important part of this story."

He reached over and took his Bible from the little table by his bed. He opened the front cover and removed a sealed envelope. "I've been waiting to give this to you for five years—it's a letter from my father."

Cade took the envelope, but he couldn't bring himself to open it. The words on the page were probably more blame and anger and disappointment—and he didn't want to see it—never wanted to hear another word his grandfather had to say.

"When your grandfather became very ill at the end," Dad said. "I spent hours with him sharing my faith. At first, he was angry and didn't want to listen—but slowly, his heart began to soften, and I told him about the love and forgiveness of Jesus Christ. I will never know if my father accepted Christ as his savior, but I do know there was a gentleness about him in his final days, and he no longer forbid me to speak of my faith. I hope he made his peace with God—but that's between them." Dad rested on his pillows, as if it took too much energy to talk.

Cade turned the envelope around, looking at the seal. "I don't know if I can open this."

"He gave it to me the day before he died and told me to give it to you. Open it when you're ready."

Cade held the envelope loosely in his hands.

"Cade, please forgive me for putting you through so much pain and torment. If I had to do it over again, I would have made a different choice."

"I never blamed you—I blamed myself."

Dad frowned. "Why?"

Cade's chest hurt from the memories. "I could never manage to obey you—if I had, Grandfather wouldn't have treated me the way he did."

"No." Dad sat up and grasped Cade's hand. "An adult must always forgive a child's disobedience and never lash out in anger. He must guide and direct him through love and discipline. You are not at fault for the decisions my father made."

Cade put his free hand over his fathers. "And neither are you."

Dad offered a weak smile.

They sat together for a long time—and it felt good.

Emma

May 25, 1918

The moment Emma's eyes opened, she sensed there was something exciting about to happen. In the next moment, she remembered what it was.

The air show was today!

She pushed aside her covers and stretched her arms toward the ceiling. Just out her window, a faint light peeked over the eastern horizon above the Mississippi. She had promised Cade she would arrive at the farm as early as possible to go over last-minute details.

She stepped out of bed and quickly dressed in her morning gown. She had packed a bag with her flying clothes and hid it at the back of her closet. She had ordered a pair of small men's trousers from a catalogue and they had arrived last week. They were surprisingly comfortable and easy to wear—perfect for flying and walking on wings.

Anna, her lady's maid, arrived in time to help Emma with her hair. She styled it up in a pile of curls with a wide headband secured around her head.

Emma took her bag and quietly left her room, hoping she would not disturb her mother or father whose rooms were just across the hall.

Mother had an elaborate party planned for later in the evening, and she would be far too busy to worry about where Emma was all day. Father had gained enough strength to be out and about doing light work, but spent most of his days in his home office. He wouldn't notice her absence, either.

Already, Emma could hear the staff on the main level preparing the house for Mother's party.

She tiptoed down the hall, toward the servant's quarters. Her father's bedroom door opened and he stood in his morning suit. His eyes landed on Emma and she froze.

"I'd like a word with you," he said, and then proceeded to walk toward the front staircase. "In my office."

Trepidation filled Emma's chest as she followed her father. Twice now he had spoken to her—and neither time had been good. She was only six days away from the first of June. No doubt he wanted to know her thoughts on Thomas.

She began to pray fervently that he was going to tell her he had changed his mind, that he would not disown her if she didn't cooperate.

They walked down the stairs and Father turned in the foyer to enter the long hall that led to his office.

Emma clutched her bag, not knowing what to do with it. Hopefully he didn't inquire about what was inside.

He opened his office door and they passed over the threshold.

"Close the door," he said.

Emma obediently closed the door and then walked across the room to stand in front of his desk.

Father took a seat and stared at her. "I imagine you're off to work."

She didn't correct him.

"I fully intend for you to be at your mother's party this evening."

Emma frowned. When had he become concerned with Mother's parties? "I don't think I'll attend the party."

"There is no discussion here. You will be at the party."

She planned to spend the day with the Bailey's. Cade would offer rides after the airshow, and she wanted to stay until the very end to help clean up and—just be with the family. "I'm sorry—"

"We will announce your engagement to Thomas tonight."

Emma's heart felt heavy as she dropped into the chair across from Father's desk. "My engagement?"

"Yes. Your time to get to know him is now expired and I expect your cooperation. I will make the official announcement tonight."

"Does Thomas know you intend to do this?"

"Of course—it was his idea."

"You said until the first of June—that's almost a week away."

"What might change in a week? You've had plenty of time to get to know the man."

What might change? She had hoped Father would—but now she could see he had no intention of changing. She wanted to tell him how she felt—but she couldn't bring herself to speak up. More than anything, she wanted his love and acceptance—but was she willing to marry a man she didn't love to earn it?

Emma stood. "I'm leaving now—and I will make no promises as to whether or not I will be at the party tonight."

Father stood, his face turning crimson. "You know I am not well—yet you would deny me this last request?"

"Deny you?" She stared at him. "You don't know what you're asking. I do not love Thomas."

He slammed his fist on the desk and Emma jumped. "I married two women I did not love—don't tell me I don't know what I'm asking."

Emma stared at him.

She had always known he didn't love her mother—but she didn't know he hadn't loved his first wife. "Why would you marry them?"

"Because they were a means to an end," he said in a weary tone.

A means to an end...just as Thomas was for her—a means to her father's heart. It seemed preposterous now that she thought of it. Emma did not want to be anything like her father. He was miserable, lonely, and cold.

She suddenly saw the truth in startling clarity. She could never marry Thomas, because if she did, she would turn out exactly like her father. "Did you never have true love?"

He froze, and the guard fell from his face. "I did have true love—a long time ago—and it brought nothing but heartache to all involved."

"But how could you marry someone you didn't love when there was someone you did?"

It was strange to watch him as his thoughts seemed to reach back in time. He looked older than before, and yet, a spark of his youth shone from his eyes. Slowly, his gaze dimmed, and he said, "It's complicated."

She had never spoken so freely with her father. If she didn't tell him this now, she would never say it. "I love someone else."

His gaze lifted to her face, and he came fully back to the present.

"I love him very much." She choked on the words, tears coming to her eyes. "And I've made him wait far too long to hear me say the words. I cannot marry Thomas—even if it means you will disown me and turn your back on me. True love doesn't come along every day—but when it does, we must seize it and revel in it for as long as the Lord allows."

He studied her for a long moment and then his shoulders fell as he walked around his desk to face her. For the first time in her life, he looked at her as if he saw her—as if her feelings mattered. "I'm sorry, Emma. Life rarely gives us what we want. It's far more important that we reach for what we need. I won't be here forever. Even if you don't realize it, I do have your best interest in mind."

Emma stared at him for several seconds, hoping he would continue and tell her something she wanted to hear. But when he didn't, she turned and walked out of his office.

She suddenly saw her home for what it was—a prison for her mother and father. They were both miserable—and for what? For wealth? Was that truly what they needed?

Mr. and Mrs. Bailey had a love that was beautiful and honorable. They might be poor, but they had joy and laughter. Would her parents consider giving everything up if they could have a love like the Bailey's? Would Emma?

She walked down the hall and entered the kitchen, wiping her tears away. Sam sat at the table in his chauffer's cap, drinking a cup of tea and reading the *Little Falls Daily Transcript*.

He looked up and smiled—but then his face filled with concern. "What's the matter, lass?"

Martha stopped her work at the counter and came to Emma, wiping her hands on her towel.

"I'm leaving," Emma said.

"You'll be going to Cade's airshow?" Sam asked.

They knew about the airshow—everyone in Minnesota knew—but she hadn't told them she would be wing walking.

"Yes." More tears came. If she had to leave this house, then she would also have to leave Sam and Martha. She could still see them—but it wouldn't be the same. She wiped her cheeks and then put her arms around Martha. "Good bye."

Martha hugged her back and then Emma went into Sam's arms. "Good bye, Sam."

"What's this about?" Sam asked, pulling away. "You act like you're leaving us for good."

A handful of kitchen staff worked in the room, tossing curious glances at Emma. She could not tell Sam and Martha what her father planned to do.

She walked to the door and offered them both a wobbly smile and then stepped outside.

Sam was right behind her, his brown eyes filled with concern. He put his hand on her shoulder and stopped her on the cobblestone drive. "Tell me what's going on."

It felt as if her heart was breaking into a thousand little pieces. "Oh, Sam." She threw her arms around him. "He doesn't love me."

"Who, lass?" He patted her back. "Who doesn't love you?"

"My father." The word came out on a sob.

"There, there, Emmie." Sam held her close and allowed her to cry. "He loves you, in his own way."

"No. He's willing to disown me if I don't marry Thomas." She pulled back and looked Sam in the eyes. "A real father—a loving father—would want me to marry the man I love."

"And that's Cade, isn't it?" Sam asked.

Emma nodded. "He's been so kind and patient with me—and I've been selfish to ask him to wait."

Sam laid his hand on Emma's cheek. "If I know anything about a man in love, I know he'll wait for you—as long as it takes—and he'll love you all the more when you're finally in his arms."

A seed of hope was planted in Emma's heart. "Do you think so?"

"I know so."

He put his arm around her shoulders and led her to the carriage house. "How about I get the Ford and you go to Cade and you tell him how you feel."

Emma nodded, wiping the final tears from her face.

"If your da disowns you, it won't be the end of the world." Sam squeezed her shoulders. "You still have me and Martha—and you'll have Cade and his family. I know that none of us can replace the love of a father—but we do love you, very much."

Emma reached around and hugged him tight. "You have been like a father to me, Sam, and I'm so thankful."

He hugged her back and then walked to the Ford and pulled it out of the carriage house for her.

Soon she was driving down the road toward Cade and a bright future away from Elk Manor.

Chapter Twenty-Seven

ELK CITY,
MINNESOTA
MARCH 29, 1896

MATTHEW

Edith's cries pierced the night while Matthew paced in his bedchamber. Rain pattered against the window as he ran his hands through his hair. He took another sip of his brandy, hoping to ease the strain in his temples.

For eight hours, he had listened to her moan and wail in agony, half wishing he could ease her pain—while taking some measure of satisfaction in her suffering.

The child she would bear this night was not his.

He had been furious when she told him about her pregnancy but after almost four years of marriage, he was not naïve to his wife's dalliances. She entertained incessantly, hosting elaborate parties and balls. Visitors came from all over the state and beyond—and many of them were gentlemen. She attempted to be discreet, but Matthew was no fool.

He had considered divorcing her but had not wanted to deal with the scandal while he was building Elk City. The town flourished under his management, doubling in size. His lumber business continued to grow, as well, and he had acquired thousands of additional acres of woodlands to the north.

Another scream filled the air and set Matthew's hair on end. Had this been what it was like for Elizabeth while she gave birth to his son? He had never imagined the depth of suffering a woman went through to bring forth a human life.

A baby's cry met Matthew's ears, and he almost sank in relief that the ordeal was over.

Finally, an heir—though not of his making.

The child Edith bore would carry his name and be entitled to his fortune but would not have his blood coursing through its veins. While his true heir would never carry his name, nor be entitled to anything he owned.

The irony had not escaped him.

He longed for a son to perpetuate the Merrick name and carry on his business. It would be a small comfort in his old age.

If he could not have his rightful heir, then Edith's child would have to suffice. She had refused to name the father, and he suspected he would never know. The man had probably come and gone and didn't even know he had a child.

Matthew began to pace again and waited for a summons. The world believed the baby to be his, so he would act the part of the dutiful father.

Wind rattled the windows, and the electrical lighting flickered. The fire in his hearth had dwindled down to embers and he hadn't bothered to stir them.

Finally, a knock at the dressing room door drew his attention. He opened it to find a maid on the other side. She offered a quick curtsey. "The doctor said you may come in now."

Matthew followed her through the dressing rooms and into Edith's dimly lit bedchamber.

"Your wife is already asleep." Dr. Roberts lifted an amber bottle. "I gave her a little something to comfort her. She's been through quite an ordeal."

"Where is the child?" Matthew asked.

The doctor nodded to a nurse standing near the blazing fireplace. In her arms was a tiny infant wrapped in a soft blanket.

Matthew's stomach knotted with nerves as he approached the nurse. She had a gentle smile and warm eyes. "Would you like to hold the baby?"

He had never held a baby in his life—but this was to be his son. He swallowed the anxiety creeping up his throat and reached for the small bundle.

He held the baby in his arms, amazed at how light he felt. His little pink face was wrinkled, and his eyes were swollen. Dark, glossy hair covered his head. He was a homely baby, though Matthew had few children to compare him to.

The nurse stood close and smiled. "Your wife named her Emma."

Matthew looked up. "Emma?"

"She said it was her grandmother's name."

"This is a girl?"

The nurse nodded, appreciation glowing in her eyes. "And a fine girl she is. I think she has your coloring."

Matthew thrust the child back into the nurse's arms and took a step away.

"Don't you want to hold her for a bit longer?" The nurse chuckled. "She won't always be this sweet—not when she's hungry or needs her diaper changed."

"The governess will see to her needs." Matthew extended his hand to the doctor. "Thank you for your service."

Matthew strode from the room without a glance back.

A female heir was useless to him.

November 14, 1903

Matthew sat in the back of his finest carriage and looked out the window to the Mississippi as they traveled toward Jacob Bailey's farm. The cold afternoon air seeped into the vehicle, chilling Matthew's aging bones. He patted his gloved hands together to bring warmth back into his fingers and then glanced at his watch, wishing Samuel Turner would drive faster.

It had been years since Matthew had stopped to meet Nathan and Victoria—but whenever he was in public, he searched the faces of the men who walked past him, hoping to catch another glimpse of his son.

Familiar land spread out on either side of the carriage, now in shades of brown and gray on winter's eve. A flock of late season geese flew overhead in a v pattern, headed south to warmer weather.

Nervous energy skittered through Matthew's body as he thought of the upcoming encounter. With Elk City prospering, and the expansion of logging in Minnesota, Matthew was now turning his complete attention to his lumber business. Over the years, he had worked hard to purchase all the land surrounding Jacob's farm—but it wasn't enough. He needed the natural landing near the river and the easy access from the woods to get his logs to the Mississippi. If his information was correct, the Bailey's farm was not doing well, and they might be ready to sell.

The farm came within sight and Matthew rubbed his palms against his pant legs. It looked much as it had nine years ago when he had stopped, though the red barn paint was now peeling and the house roof needed to be replaced.

Movement near the edge of the river brought Matthew's head up.

There, cutting wood from a fallen tree, stood Jacob Bailey and a young boy of about ten or eleven.

Matthew pounded on the roof of the carriage with his walking stick and Mr. Turner slowed the vehicle to a stop. The carriage shifted as Mr. Turner climbed down from the top and walked around to open the door for Matthew. "It's a wee bit cold to be traipsing about, don't you think?"

"I'll be fine." Matthew nodded to the two people at work. "I need to speak to that man."

Mr. Turner glanced over his shoulder and then back at Matthew. "Just be careful."

Matthew wanted to roll his eyes. He might be sixty years old, but he was still hearty and in good health.

He exited the carriage and started toward Jacob who watched his approach. The boy stood next to him in a red and black checkered coat and a black cap, his arms loaded with wood. A small cart sat nearby, wood stacked inside.

Jacob hadn't aged well. His once tall, muscular frame was slightly bent, and his middle had spread with weight. His head was covered in gray hair, and his long gray beard was snarled and shaggy. He glared at Matthew, his mouth set in a scowl.

"Hello, Jacob," Matthew said.

"What do you want?"

Matthew looked at the boy and recognized the bright green eyes. He smiled. "Are you Cade?"

The boy nodded, though his face was wary.

"Leave him be." Jacob's harsh voice made the boy jump. "Why'd you come here?"

"Can we go inside your home, out of the cold?"

"You're not welcome in my home."

Matthew let out a frustrated sigh. "I'm here to make you a generous offer for your farm."

"I'm not selling." Jacob bent over and picked up two more sticks of wood and put them on the boy's arms.

"I've heard the farm is not doing well—has not been doing well for some ti—"

"The farm is fine," Jacob barked.

"This is not farming land. It was never meant to be a farm. Let me buy it—"

"No." He put two more pieces of wood on Cade's pile.

The boy swayed and lost his footing. The whole pile of wood fell from his arms.

Jacob took a step toward the boy and slapped him over the head. The boy's cap went flying. "See what you did, you clumsy fool? Pick up all that wood and stack it in the cart."

Matthew sprang forward to help the boy, but Jacob stepped into his path. "Leave him be."

Tears hugged the rim of Cade's eyes, but he swallowed and blinked them away. He glanced at Matthew and then quickly picked up the spilled wood.

Matthew helplessly watched as the boy worked.

"You're wasting your time." Jacob picked up his ax and set a log on end. He swung the ax into the wood, and it split down the center. His face was red from the effort and anger burned in his eyes. "I told you over thirty years ago I wouldn't sell."

Matthew's frustration grew until he felt warm under his coat. "Why? Because you're too stubborn? Because you think you're hurting me by keeping this land from me?"

"Because you don't deserve it!" Jacob growled at Matthew. "You don't deserve anything you have."

The boy shied away when their voices rose.

"I've worked hard for everything I have." Matthew tried to control his voice, but it shook with his anger. "I had nothing as a young man, and I paid the price for the wealth I've accumulated."

"You're not the only one who paid the price." Jacob lifted his ax and then thrust it down with a wide swing. The ax stuck in the log and Jacob yanked on it, but it wouldn't come lose. He suddenly turned to Matthew and stepped close to him. "She died of a broken heart—and nothing I did would save her."

Matthew stared at him. "What?"

"Elizabeth."

"I thought she bled to death."

Jacob shook his head. "The bleeding stopped—but she wept through the night, holding Nathan in her arms—and no amount of love or comfort I could offer would ease her broken heart. I've never heard such suffering." He wiped at his wrinkled cheeks. "I found her the next morning dead."

Matthew took a step back. Could someone truly die from a broken heart? And, if she did, had it been Matthew who killed her?

"I wish I could make you pay, Merrick—but I can't. I've cursed God every time I've heard of your success." Jacob stepped close to Matthew, the sweat from his body assailing Matthew's senses. "The only thing I can do is keep you away from this land—and I'll do whatever it takes to succeed."

Matthew suddenly remembered Cade, but the boy was nowhere to be seen. Had he run off while they argued?

"For the last time, Merrick, get off my land."

Matthew stared at Jacob. He was more adamant today than he was thirty years ago.

He would not sell.

Matthew turned toward his carriage where Samuel Turner stood watching. He was far enough away he couldn't have heard their argument—but his face revealed his concern, nonetheless.

"The lad walked toward the river," Mr. Turner said as he opened the carriage door. "I hope he's okay."

Matthew turned and looked toward the river, still flowing strong toward the south. He caught a glimpse of red in a willow tree along the banks, and his heart beat strong for the little boy who had been hurt by the man he thought was his grandfather.

"He'll be fine." Matthew stepped into the carriage and Mr. Turner stood by the door.

"Was it a successful meeting?"

Matthew shook his head. "Not what I had hoped."

"I'm sorry to hear that."

Mr. Turner stepped up onto the driver's seat and turned the carriage around to go home.

Matthew moved to the other side of the carriage and looked toward the willow tree hoping his grandson would one day know the truth—but doubting it would ever come to be.

Chapter Twenty-Eight

Emma

Emma parked the Ford beside the barn, scanning the farm for a glimpse of Cade.

He was out in the north field sectioning off the airfield with rope. Grace was with him, holding the rope as he pounded the stakes into the ground.

"Emma! There you are." Mrs. Bailey stepped out of the house with her own coil of rope. "Would you please stake this rope around my garden? I would be so disappointed if anything was trampled."

Emma longed to talk to Cade, but she took the rope and stakes and went to work.

The morning sun beat down, promising to be a hot day.

After she was done with the garden, Mrs. Bailey put her to work in the kitchen helping make lemonade. They would sell the cool beverage for five cents a glass, and with the warm weather, they were sure to sell out quickly.

Mrs. Bailey sliced the lemons and Emma squeezed them into a large Red Wing stone crock. They would add sugar to the lemon juice and then haul the crock outside before they added the water and ice from the ice house.

The morning sped by and Emma could not get Cade alone. Just after lunch, people began to arrive, pulling into the drive one after the other. They parked their wagons, buggies, and automobiles in the large yard and then began to line the two country roads that intersected near the Bailey farm.

The show was to begin precisely at two o'clock. At one, Cade went out to talk to the spectators. Emma watched him from the lemonade stand, smiling at the way the people revered him.

This was Cade in his truest form. He was gracious and humble, answering questions about flying, about being in the movies, and about his airplane.

She had never seen him look so happy. His face shined.

People continued to pour into the farm. Thousands were waiting to watch Daredevil Kincade and the mysterious wing walker.

Butterflies filled Emma's stomach at the thought of performing in front of all these people. It had been one thing to be alone with Cade in the sky—but an entirely different thing to have all these eyes upon her.

At half past one, she went into Gracie's bedroom and changed into her trousers. She put sensible boots on her feet and laced them up tight. After that, she put the leather flying cap over her curls. She tucked them up inside to hide them from view, and looked in the mirror, a bit shocked at her own appearance. If her mother saw her now, she would be mortified.

Emma didn't want her identity known. It would not be good if her parents—or even Martha and Sam—learned about her wing walking.

"Emma, are you ready?" Mrs. Bailey called up the stairs.

Emma took a deep breath. "Coming."

She had wanted desperately to speak to Cade privately before they went up in the airplane. There was so much to tell him.

"Cade is waiting outside."

The stairs creaked as Emma walked down the steps. The house was unusually quiet. Cade had moved Mr. Bailey to a chair just outside the door where he could watch the airshow. He sat near the lemonade stand to be close to Mrs. Bailey, in case he needed help.

Emma passed through the parlor and then went into the kitchen. She put her goggles on her face, hoping no one would recognize her, and then she slipped out the door.

Cade stood near Mr. Bailey, his hand on his father's shoulder. Mr. Bailey had his face raised to Cade, pride and admiration glowing from his eyes.

Cade glanced at Emma, his gaze sweeping her appearance. Surprise, and then pleasure, evident on his face.

He met her near the corner of the house. He wore the golden wings she'd given him at Christmas on the collar of his leather jacket. "Are you ready?"

"Not quite." Before they went up in the air, she wanted to tell him she loved him—that she had chosen to say no to her father.

Concern filled his gaze. "Are you having second thoughts? You don't have to go through with the stunt."

"I'm not having second thoughts about wing walking—are you?"

"I've had second thoughts about it since the moment I said yes."

"Cade, it's already five minutes past two," Mrs. Bailey said, pointing to her watch. "The crowd has been waiting."

Cade turned back to Emma. "Shall we?"

Their conversation would have to wait—but maybe that was better. She wanted his full attention, and right now he needed to think about the show.

Together they walked through the crowd and onto the temporary airfield.

Thousands of spectators had gathered, and the moment they saw Cade, a great cheer arose.

Emma grinned at him. "They love you."

Cade waved at the crowds, his face beaming, and then his beautiful green eyes turned to her. "In a moment, they're going to love you, too."

Emma's cheeks warmed and she took a deep breath. She would go up in the airplane with him and sit in the front cockpit as he performed his stunts. He had not practiced with her, so it would be a new experience to fly upside down, and around in loops. He had warned her about the death dive. The thought sent chills through her body, but he assured her it would be safe.

They arrived at the airplane and Emma climbed into the front cockpit. She secured her safety belt tightly around her body, her palms sweating.

Cade did one final inspection, and even climbed onto the top wing to examine the ropes she would use for her wing walking one more time.

When he climbed down, he went to the front of the airplane and spun the propeller while Emma started the engine. The airplane whirred to life and Cade came around and climbed into the back cockpit. The plane began to roll into motion, and soon they were picking up speed as they crossed the north field. The moment the wheels left the ground, Emma's stomach dropped and she was thrilled by the sense of weightlessness.

She would never tire of the feeling.

Cade

A rush of adrenaline coursed through Cade's body as he took his plane in all the old familiar tricks. It had been over six months since the last airshow—but it felt as if he had never stopped. He rolled the airplane, looped the loop, flew upside down, dipped the airplane, and then sent it straight up into the air.

The whole time, Emma sat in front of him, gripping the edges of the cockpit. He cared more about her pleasure than he did the thousands of spectators. He could recall the first time he rode in an airplane and experienced the thrill of stunt flying. He knew her heart would be racing, and her stomach would be turning, and she would be grinning.

The engine zoomed and roared as he took the plane through his routine. Finally, he came to the death dive, his sweating palms gripped the control stick, the memory of the last time he had done this stunt still fresh in his mind. He pulled the control stick back and the airplane climbed into the brilliant blue sky. Higher and higher it climbed.

Emma turned and gave him a smile—and it was all he needed.

They leveled out at five thousand feet and he said a quick prayer. With Emma in the airplane, there was much more at stake. He pushed the control stick down and the airplane dove straight toward the earth. Wind pushed against his face as the ground rushed up to meet them. His pulse pounded in his veins and he held his breath.

At the last moment, he pulled up on the stick and the airplane leveled out. Below them, the crowd went crazy waving their hats and jumping up and down. Emma turned once again, and he could see the awe and terror on her face—but she smiled and he grinned at her.

It was now time for her stunt. His prayers went heavenward and he wondered why he had ever agreed to let her do this thing.

He pulled back on the stick and the airplane climbed a few hundred feet before he leveled it out. Emma unlatched her safety belt and slowly stood on her seat. She climbed out the front, under the top wing and walked onto the left, lower wing, holding onto the wires. She waved at the crowd and Cade slowly turned the aircraft to come back around. When he was level again, she climbed back to the center and stepped onto the fuselage, then she pulled herself up on top of the wings and slid across on her belly until she came to the ropes. She grabbed them in tight hands and then slowly stood, finding her balance as she rose.

Cade let out his breath and allowed himself to admire her standing there, waving to the crowd. She had become the first wing walker in Minnesota—though no one would ever know her name.

After a moment, she lay back down and started scooting backward to get into the front cockpit. First her right leg came over the edge and then her left leg. She put her right foot onto the edge of the cockpit—and it slipped.

Cade's heart leapt into his throat as she frantically grabbed for something to hold on to. She lost her footing and slid down the wing.

Cade screamed her name as she grabbed for the cockpit, but missed the edge and fell to the bottom wing, grasping a wire as she slid.

She hung by one hand, suspended above the air.

Blood pumped hard through Cade's veins as he began to lower the airplane, one eye on her and the other on the ground. "Emma!" He screamed. "Hold on!"

Emma turned her wild eyes to Cade, pleading him to do something.

"Hold on!" he screamed again as he lowered the plane closer and closer to the earth.

Her legs dangled and she tried desperately to grasp the wire with her other hand.

The ground drew closer and closer, but how long could she hang on? And when he landed, would her legs be crushed? He tried to focus, to use all the skills he possessed.

Emma's knuckles were white where they grasped the wire, and he knew she couldn't hold on much longer.

They were just coming in for the landing, about ten feet from the ground, when her hand gave way and she fell from the aircraft.

Cade screamed as he watched her hit the ground hard, her body rolling over the field.

He landed the plane and jumped out of the cockpit before it stopped moving. He ran on unsteady legs to get to her, just as his mother and a handful of other people rushed across the field.

He was the first to arrive at Emma and his stomach turned at the gruesome sight. Her leg was twisted and broken, and she was unconscious—her face filling with bruises and swelling.

"Emma." He dropped to his knees, but didn't want to touch her, for fear of hurting her more. "Emmie!"

Her breathing was shallow and she didn't respond to his call.

He looked up and saw Mama—and Thomas Overton. What was he doing here? Had he heard Emma was in the show?

"My God, man!" Thomas screamed. "What were you thinking?"

"Is there a doctor?" Cade yelled. "We need to get her to a doctor."

A man emerged and Cade recognized him as Dr. McCall, the man who had helped Mrs. Girvan and Gracie. "I'm a doctor," he said.

He knelt at Emma's side and checked her pulse and then listened to her heart and her lungs. He palpated her stomach and ran his hands down all her limbs. "Her leg is broken, and she's been knocked unconscious, but it's hard to tell if there's internal damage. We need to get her to the hospital immediately."

"I can bring her in the airplane," Cade said.

"Are you insane?" Overton asked. "She will never ride in that thing again." He turned to the doctor. "I'll take her in my automobile."

Cade stood. "But I can get her there faster in my airplane."

"It doesn't matter, unless you can get me there, too," Dr. McCall said. "And I don't think there's room for both of us in the airplane." Dr. McCall looked up at Overton. "Who are you?"

"I'm her fiancé."

Cade wanted to deny the claim, but it didn't matter. They just needed to get Emma to the hospital.

"I'll get my automobile," Overton called, racing off the field.

"When will she become conscious again?" Cade asked the doctor.

"It's hard to tell with a head injury." Dr. McCall gently took Emma's cap and goggles off, examining her head. "There could be a great deal of damage and memory loss. For all we know, there could be internal bleeding and swelling. Only time will tell."

Internal bleeding and swelling on her brain? Cade dropped to his knees next to Emma. Dear God, why had he let her do this? It was his fault. He should have never agreed to her idea.

"I'll need help lifting her into the auto," Dr. McCall said. "We'll need to be careful. I don't think her neck was injured, but we don't want to take any risks."

Cade wanted to weep. Why had this happened again? He hadn't wanted to do another air show. He should have listened to his gut.

Overton raced onto the field with his automobile and came to a stop a few feet away from Emma.

Cade bent down to help lift her, but Overton pushed him aside. "Don't touch her! You've done enough. I told you to stay away from her."

He had, and Cade hadn't listened.

Cade watched helplessly as the doctor and Overton lifted Emma's limp body into the back of the car. He wanted to hold her and tell her he loved her, but he just stood watching.

Dr. McCall entered the back with her, and held her on the seat. Overton jumped into the front seat and they sped away.

"Cade." Mama put her arms around him. "I'm so sorry."

"I have to go to the hospital," Cade said.

"But what about the airshow? And the rides?"

He had planned to raise their mortgage money from the rides—but he could not follow through, not when Emma was lying in a hospital.

"I can't." He took off across the field toward Emma's Model T. He didn't care if he was unwanted at the hospital. He had to be there with Emma.

Chapter Twenty-Nine

Cade

Cade ran inside the front doors of St. Gabriel's Hospital, sweat dripping from his brow. His legs were shaking as he stopped the first nurse he could find. "Where is Emma Merrick?"

The nurse jumped at his sudden appearance. She wore a white uniform, with a matching hat. "She's in the operating room with Dr. McCall."

"Where is that?"

"You can't go in there."

"Why is she in the operating room?"

"I believe he's working on her leg."

"When can I see her?"

The nurse shook her head. "It's hard to say. It may be a few hours."

"Was she conscious when you saw her?"

She lifted her palms. "I'm sorry, I didn't see her."

"Stop badgering the nurse," Overton said from behind Cade.

Cade spun and found Thomas Overton just rising from a chair in the waiting room. He wore a well-tailored suit coat, and his hair was perfectly combed. He looked calm and collected—though his gaze was furious.

"What were you thinking?" he asked. "You could have killed her."

Cade had asked himself that same question all the way into town—and he had no answer.

"I told you to stay away from her," Overton said.

A handful of people sat in the waiting room, their curious gazes lifted to Cade and Overton. Two nurses stood near the front desk, concern on their faces.

Cade walked toward the doors, needing fresh air and space.

Overton followed.

Sunshine streamed down from a clear blue sky. Tender new leaves unfurled from the trees around the hospital and orphanage next door. Cade walked away from the building, toward the open field just beyond.

"I warned you, Bailey."

Cade turned, his hands balled into fists at his side. "Who are you to tell me who I can and cannot see?"

"I am Emma's fiancé."

Cade took a step toward the man. "You're not her fiancé."

"We were going to announce the engagement tonight. Her mother is throwing a party in our honor."

"I don't believe you."

"It's true. She talked to her father this morning and agreed to make the announcement this evening."

Was it true? He couldn't believe Emma wouldn't have told him—but then, why would she tell him if she was planning to announce her marriage to another man?

Cade felt overwhelmed with a flood of emotions—none of them good. "How did you know to come to the airshow?"

"Her father inquired with the staff—and they told him."

Cade wished he had a chair to sit. Nothing had gone as planned—and he had been the cause of yet more pain. Flashbacks visited him from the Bay Meadow's airfield and the night his father collapsed after rescuing him from the storm. Was he destined to wreak havoc and death everywhere he went?

"Am I correct to assume you won't come up with enough money to pay your mortgage in a week?"

The farm. Cade closed his eyes. His grandfather and father had been able to hold on to it for fifty years—and within six months it had slipped through his fingers. Where would his parents and sister live?

"I'm still willing to offer top dollar if you sell it to me now," Overton said. "If you wait a week, you'll lose it to the bank and not earn a penny from it." He watched Cade carefully. "You could buy a nice place for your family with the money I'm prepared to give you."

What choice did Cade have?

"There's only one condition," Overton said. "You must leave. Immediately. I'll see to the sale, and I'll help your parents find a new home."

"Leave?"

"I don't want you anywhere near Emma. Soon she'll be my wife, and I'll be able to give her everything her heart desires. Her father has chosen me—and now she has chosen me."

It would be so much easier to run away—to start over—to leave the painful memories attached to his family and now Emma.

"You're going to lose the farm either way, and you have nothing to offer her." Overton looked at Cade as if he felt sorry for him. "You know it's true. Get away from here and start over—go back to flying. It was something you were actually good at. You're not a farmer. Sell me the land and walk away from Emma—and we'll all get what we want."

A sleek automobile approached the hospital, its cream-colored paint gleaming in the sunshine.

"There are the Merricks now." Overton pinned Cade with his stare. "What will it be, Bailey? Sell the land now and have somewhere for your family to live—or wait out the week and walk away with nothing?"

Either way, he would walk away with nothing. If he stayed, he would lose the farm and have nothing to offer Emma. Or, he could sell the land, giving his parents and sister a place to live, but he'd have to leave Emma behind.

"If she really wanted you—don't you think she would have made that decision by now?" Overton asked, almost as if he could read Cade's thoughts.

The man was right. Emma had plenty of time to make up her mind about him.

Overton stuck out his hand. "Do we have a deal?"

Cade's chest felt heavy as he reached out and shook Overton's hand. "You have a deal."

Sam stepped out of the automobile. He glanced at the hospital, his face filled with fear, and then stepped to the back and opened the doors for Major and Mrs. Merrick to exit the car. They moved toward the hospital until Major Merrick caught a glimpse of Overton.

"How is she?" Major Merrick called to Overton.

Overton turned away from Cade and approached Major Merrick. "The doctor is working on her leg right now. I haven't heard if she's conscious."

"Who's responsible for this travesty?" Mrs. Merrick asked.

Overton pointed at Cade. "Mr. Bailey is the one who took her up in his airplane and allowed her to walk on the wings."

"You did what?" Mrs. Merrick asked, her eyes ablaze with anger.

"Mr. Bailey?" Major Merrick looked at Cade for the first time.

It had been years since Cade had seen the major on the fateful day his grandfather had suffered from apoplexy. He had aged a great deal, but he still carried himself with the same air of confidence and determination.

"How long has Emma been flying with you?" Major Merrick asked.

Cade glanced at Sam and then back at Merrick. "Since last fall."

"Last fall!" Mrs. Merrick put her hand to her throat. She resembled Emma so strongly, it hurt to look at her.

Merrick took a step closer to Cade, his eyes desperately searching Cade's face. What was he looking for?

"You're the one she—" Merrick paused and his face turned an ash grey.

"We must get inside and speak to the doctor." Mrs. Merrick turned and entered the hospital, not bothering to wait for the others to follow.

Sam stood by the automobile, uncertainty on his face.

Overton stood near Major Merrick. "I know this is not an opportune time to tell you, but Mr. Bailey has agreed to sell us the property."

Merrick did not take his eyes off Cade. "Do you remember me?"

"I remember how much my grandfather hated you."

His words hit their mark, and Merrick looked struck with pain. "Is that all you know about me?"

Anger rose in Cade like a ferocious bear. "I know you caused Emma heartache, and I also know you caused my grandfather to be bitter and hateful. That's all I know about you, but that's enough." He didn't care what Merrick thought of him. "Your daughter is lying in that hospital bed, broken and bruised in body and spirit. I caused half of her misery—but you caused the other half." He looked at Overton. "My father is the owner of the farm. You can have him sign the deed over to Merrick Lumber. His heart is weak, and he's been bedridden for almost a year now. He's in no position to fight you."

"Nathan is bedridden?" Merrick stared at Cade.

Cade frowned at the old man. "He'll cooperate—but don't you dare hurt him."

"Why would I hurt him?"

"You've hurt everyone else in your path."

Cade walked away from Merrick and Overton. He had no vehicle and no way to get back to the farm—but what did it matter? He would walk to the draft board office and enlist in the air service. The government was eager for more instructors. They would probably have him on a train within a couple hours.

He stopped by Sam, his voice desperate. "Tell Emma I've gone to enlist. Now she's free to marry Overton."

"Cade—"

Cade didn't wait for Sam to continue. He turned away and began to run.

Emma

The first thing Emma felt was pain. It radiated from her leg and shot up into her hip. Her head hurt and she couldn't turn it right or left. She groaned as she tried to open her eyes, but it took too much energy.

Where was she and what had happened?

"Emmie, me darlin.'" Sam's voice sounded far away. "Are you awake?"

Emma groaned again. It hurt to move her jaw.

"Thank the Lord." She could hear tears in Sam's voice.

"Where—?"

"You're in the hospital. You had an accident today."

An accident? Why couldn't she remember?

Her throat felt dry and she tried to swallow, but it hurt too much. "Cade?"

There was a pause, and then Sam said, "He's fine."

Emma worked hard to open her eyes. At first, the light hurt, but then she was able to make out Sam's face. He stood near her, tears in his gentle eyes. He smiled. "I'm so happy you're still with us."

She licked her swollen lip and pain shot through her jaw. "What happened?"

"You fell from an airplane."

The airshow! It all came back to Emma in that instant. She had been in the air with Cade, looping and barreling and soaring past the crowds. She had tried to get off the wing, but her foot slipped and she had fallen. But had she fallen all that way? She couldn't recall the last moments after her foot slipped.

"Where's Cade?"

Sam laid his hand over Emma's. His touch was tender, though it hurt. "Why don't you rest? Thomas just left with your parents, but he said he'd be back later to see you."

"But the airshow. Did Cade take passengers? Did he make the money he needs to save the farm?"

"Emmie—let's talk later."

"No." She wanted to know now. "What happened?"

Sam looked down, his countenance heavy. "He didn't take passengers. He came to the hospital to see you."

"Where is he?" Oh, why had he come to see her? He needed to take on passengers to make money. She must tell him to go back to the airshow.

"He's gone."

Emma almost sighed in relief. "He went back to give rides?"

Sam shook his head. "He didn't go back to the airshow."

"Where did he go?"

"Would you like something to drink?" Sam asked. "You've been unconscious for over twenty-four hours."

Twenty-four hours? Emma looked to the window, but pain shot through her whole body. It was bright as day—was it already Sunday? The airshow was yesterday? Her head pounded and she felt sick to her stomach. How extensive were her injuries? She tried to look down at her body, but her neck was stiff and it hurt too much to move.

Panic took root and she looked at Sam. "Please—tell me what's going on, Sam."

"You broke your leg. The doctor had to perform surgery to fix it—but he said you're lucky. You're pretty banged up, but you could have been paralyzed. He didn't know the extent of internal injuries, but you're talking and moving, and that's what he hoped you would do when you woke up."

They had been waiting for over twenty-four hours to see if she would be permanently damaged. Sam and Martha and Cade must have been sick with worry.

"Where is Cade?" she asked again. "I want to see him—tell him I'm sorry about the farm. I'll help him find a way to save it."

"Emmie—" Sam's mouth turned down and he shook his head. "I'm sorry, lass, but Cade is gone—for good."

"Gone?" What did he mean? "Where did he go?"

"He's enlisted in the air service. Yesterday, after you came out of surgery I went to the draft office and asked about Cade. They said he had left on the six o'clock train."

Emma didn't understand. She closed her eyes to the pain and confusion. "Why?" Why would he suddenly leave?

"He lost the farm, Emmie. Your father bought it."

"He lost the farm?" Tears gathered in her eyes. "Because of me?"

"He decided to sell it."

It was because of her. It had been a mistake to try the wing walking. She had failed him—but why would he leave? Was he that upset with her?

Thomas suddenly appeared at the door—and she could tell by the expression on his face that she looked horrible.

"I'm sorry, lass." Sam stood. "I'll give you and Thomas a moment together."

Emma didn't want Sam to leave. He was her only form of strength right now, but she didn't have the physical or emotional energy to beg him to stay.

Sam slipped out of the room and Thomas took his seat next to her bed.

"Hello, Emma. I'm happy to see you're awake." He set his hat on the table next to her bed. "Are you in much pain?"

A tear slipped down her cheek, but she didn't bother to lift her hand to wipe it away. "Why did Cade leave?"

Thomas's eyes filled with anger—but she didn't care. She needed to know why he left her.

"I don't know."

"Please, if you know, tell me."

"You've just returned from the brink of death, and your fiancé walks into the room and all you can think about is another man? The man that did this to you?"

"He didn't do this to me."

"He did—and he left you for dead."

"No."

"Do you see him? If he was concerned about you, don't you think he would have stuck around to see if you had survived?"

Emma turned her head away from him, but the pain made her cry out and more tears gathered in her eyes. Why had Cade left her? She had never felt more retched in her life—and the man she loved had walked away when she needed him most.

Thomas sighed. "I didn't come in here to talk about Cade. He left—and you won't ever have to worry about seeing him again."

She looked back at him, fear building inside her chest. "What did you do?"

"It's not what I did. It's what he did. I told him I would buy his farm and save his family from humiliation if he left you and never returned."

He had forsaken her, just for money?

"Emma, your relationship with Bailey was a mistake—it should have never happened."

A mistake. It seemed Emma was a mistake to everyone—to her mother, to her father, and now to Cade.

"Leave me."

"Emma—"

"Go."

He stood. "I will go, but I'll be back. What would people think if I left my fiancée alone in the hospital for too long?"

"I'm not your fiancée."

He bent down and kissed her cheek, sending a stabbing pain through her jaw. "You don't have a choice, Emma. You either marry me, or you'll be disowned and forgotten by your family."

She despised his touch—despised his greed and selfishness and the truth he spoke.

He walked out of the room leaving Emma alone and dejected.

Chapter Thirty

Matthew

Matthew stood at Emma's bedroom door, watching as two nurses helped her settle into her pillows. The bruises on her face had begun to fade, changing to a yellowish-green color. The swelling had gone down, and the cuts and scrapes had started to heal, but she still looked miserable.

"The doctor wants you to keep your leg elevated at all times," one of the nurses said. "If you need to get up for any reason, please ring your bell and someone will come to help you. Sister Agatha or I will be here once a day to check on you and make sure you're healing properly."

"Thank you, Jaqueline." Emma leaned back into her pillows, closing her eyes.

"It's taken a great deal of energy to move you from the hospital, so you just rest," the nurse named Jaqueline said, patting Emma on the shoulder. "We'll tell the staff not to disturb you, unless you call for them."

Emma nodded, but didn't respond.

"Be well, Emma," Jaqueline said. "We'll see you tomorrow."

The nurses left the room, passing by Matthew, nodding a greeting.

Matthew stood where he was, unable to take his eyes off Emma.

It had been two weeks since the accident, but he hadn't been able to bring himself to visit her at the hospital after that first day. Every time he thought of her, he also thought of Cade and the horrible accusations he had made before leaving.

Matthew still couldn't believe Emma and Cade had found each other—and fallen in love. When he had seen Cade's face, he had understood the depths of his pain and misery. It was like Matthew was looking at himself fifty-four years ago. All the repressed memories had resurfaced, and it felt as if he had lost Elizabeth just yesterday.

He recalled the conversation he'd had with Emma the morning of the accident when she had said she was in love with someone other than Thomas—that she loved him very much.

Matthew had no idea it was his very own grandson.

It wasn't until he saw Cade standing with Thomas, and recognized the agony in his eyes, that he knew he was the man Emma loved—and in that moment, Matthew's life had come full circle.

He stepped into the room and Emma opened her eyes. Tears slipped from her eyelids, trailing down her cheeks—and for the first time in his life, he did not see Edith when he looked at her. He saw Emma—just Emma—and his heart broke for all the pain he had caused this young woman.

She had not asked to be born the way she had—just as Matthew had not asked to be born from an illegitimate relationship.

He looked into her gaze and realized he and Emma had much more in common than he'd ever realized. Instead of push her away, he should have drawn her close and comforted her.

She studied him through her watery eyes—yet she didn't say a word.

"May I sit with you for a moment?" he asked.

She looked as if she would deny him—and he couldn't blame her—but then she nodded.

He took a chair from her vanity and pulled it close to the bed.

He recalled that first month after he had married Helen and Elizabeth had married Jacob. He had covered his anguish and buried his pain in his work, knowing there was nothing he could do about the course of events he had put into motion. As he gazed upon Emma, he recognized the same agony, though she exhibited it in a way he had never allowed himself.

Was this how Elizabeth had looked—how she had felt before she died of a broken heart?

"Emma." He stopped and swallowed, unsure how he could begin to make this better—but wanting to try. "I'm sorry—for everything."

She closed her eyes and took one deep breath after the other.

Matthew remembered how it felt to focus on breathing—not knowing how to deal with the grief, but forcing himself to breathe, as if his body had forgotten.

"After the accident, when I went to the hospital, I saw Cade."

She opened her eyes and watched him.

"I spoke to him—and I realized he was the one you love."

Her face crumpled and tears began to stream down her cheeks, one after the other.

He reached out—and then hesitated. Would she allow him to hold her hand? He took a breath and placed his hand over hers.

She looked at him, surprised.

"I know he's the one you love," he said again. "And I know he loves you."

"Then why did he leave?"

He knew why—but didn't want to admit it to her. Thomas had made a deal with him—one so similar to the deal Jacob had made with Matthew, it felt like a stab in his heart all over again. Thomas would get the land and the girl, just as Jacob had. "Thomas promised that Merrick Lumber would purchase the land and Thomas would see to Cade's parents, if Cade agreed to leave and never return." He scooted to the edge of the chair, hoping she would understand why Cade would agree to leave—and why Matthew had made his choices all those years ago. "It was the only way he could provide for his family. Selling to Merrick Lumber was the only way he could offer them some protection."

Emma closed her eyes, as if she didn't want to hear more.

"You have to see it from his perspective," Matthew said. "I know he loves you—but he had to take care of his family. Do you understand?"

She pressed her lips together and swallowed—but then she nodded. "I understand why Cade made the decision he did." She turned and looked at Matthew, betrayal in her eyes. "What I don't understand is why you allowed Thomas to do such a horrible thing."

Guilt washed over Matthew and he felt as if he was drowning under the weight of it. "I'm sorry, Emma. I didn't know about the agreement at first—and then when I discovered the truth, Cade was already gone."

"And that's supposed to make everything better?" she asked. "A simple apology?"

He shook his head. "What more can I do? Nathan Bailey isn't able to take care of the farm, and with both of his boys gone to fight, I felt it best to purchase the land and see that they have a better place to live. Closer to town." He would go to the ends of the earth to make this right for her—for all of them.

"You can't do anything." She removed her hand from under his, bitterness taking root in her countenance. "I expect you to do nothing, just as you've always done where it concerns me."

"Emma—"

"Please leave."

"Emma." He took her hand in his and would not let it go when she tried to pull away. "I realize the great mistake I've made in pushing you away—and I wish to God I could undo the past twenty-two years." He hoped his face conveyed his sorrow. "I have many regrets—far too many to number—but one thing I regret above the others is hurting you."

"Why are you telling me this?" she asked, tears dripping from her chin.

"Because I've finally realized my mistakes and I don't have long to make them right." He squeezed her hand. "I will not make you marry Thomas Overton. It was never right of me to give you the ultimatum. I want you to marry for love and love only." He wished he could go back and marry for love. His opportunity had come and gone—but Emma's hadn't. There was still time for her.

She dropped her chin as more tears appeared. "What if Cade doesn't come back?"

Matthew moved from the seat to the edge of Emma's bed and surprised them both by putting his arms around her. He couldn't recall the last time he'd given a hug or been this close to another human being. Something warm and tender entered his heart, and he couldn't let her go—even if he had tried. "We will pray, Emma. We will pray and trust that God will keep Cade safe."

And he meant it.

Chapter Thirty-One

OCTOBER 1918

Emma

Emma stood at the entrance to the children's ward, her heart heavy at the sound of crying babies. The mask over her face, a constant companion these two weeks, itched and irritated her skin.

"You're not to touch the children unless absolutely necessary," Sister Agatha said readjusting her own mask. "You must keep your mask on at all times and wear an apron and gloves when you change their diapers. When you feed them—if you can get them to eat—do not pick them up."

"But, they're babies," Emma said. "They need love and affection."

"They need a nurse who is healthy." Sister Agatha shook her head, her shoulders sagging with grief and exhaustion. "The death toll has reached over five hundred in Minnesota since the outbreak began just three weeks ago—we must take all precautions. Nurses are in great demand." She touched Emma's shoulder. "You'll be relieved in the morning." She turned to leave, but then looked back at Emma. "Be careful and don't let your heart get in the way of your head."

Emma watched Sister Agatha walk down the long hallway and then she turned her attention to the large room filled with two dozen babies under the age of two years old. The Influenza pandemic had reached Minnesota, and almost every community across the state had been closed-down by local governments. No one was allowed to go out to work or conduct business, except for those who were necessary to the health and well-being of the community.

Emma had worked every day for three weeks, sometimes taking double shifts to cover the great need. She had been ordered to work at the hospital and not attend to her Town and Country job, because it would be almost impossible to see to everyone's needs in the county.

She missed her daily drives and missed seeing familiar patients like Mr. Bailey. He and Mrs. Bailey had found a home on the outskirts of town, near Green Prairie Lake. Emma visited them often, trying to bring comfort as they daily waited for news from their sons.

She walked into the babies' room, wishing the stark white walls were painted a softer color. The cribs lined the room on both sides, and many of the children lay listlessly inside—though some sat up, crying for their mamas. These were children of people who were too sick to care for them—and some had been orphaned. The healthy children were at the orphanage, but those with symptoms were transferred to the hospital.

Emma stood near the first crib and looked at the baby lying within. He lifted his arms to her, his cheeks bright red and his curls slick with sweat. What must he think, looking at her with the mask on her face? The children were terrified to be without their parents—and even more terrified to be with strangers in white masks. She couldn't help herself. She reached in and picked the little boy up.

He couldn't be more than nine or ten months old and he weighed next to nothing. Emma held him against her shoulder and bounced and cooed until his tears subsided. Other babies around the room watched her and a few lifted their arms to her. The baby she held soon fell asleep and she laid him back in his crib, placing a blanket over his little body.

She had been exposed to the Influenza virus every day for the past three weeks—surely, if she was going to get it, she would have become sick by now.

Slowly, she untied the top of her mask and let it hang from her neck. She walked to the next crib, this one filled with a little girl about eighteen months old. She lifted her hands to Emma, great big tears streaming down her cheeks. Emma smiled and reached in to lift the girl from her bed. She walked her over to the rocking chair near the window and took a seat, then cradled the girl in her arms, rocking back and forth, singing a song her nanny used to sing to her.

Her mind wandered to Cade, as it did whenever she had a moment of respite from the hard work. She had come back to work in September after taking the summer off to heal from her injuries. Work was a good diversion from the melancholy she had suffered through the long months of recuperation.

She waited for a letter, but he had never written.

As soon as she was able, she began to visit the Bailey's hoping for news. They eagerly shared Cade's letters, though there had only been a few. He was stationed at Camp Hancock in Austin, Georgia as a flight instructor. She had been thankful he wasn't flying combat missions, but his last letter had been sobering. His flying skills were so highly valued, he had been told he could expect orders to go overseas any day—and that had been a month ago. Even now, as she rocked the baby in her arms, Cade could be shooting down enemy planes—or worse.

A *Little Falls Daily Transcript* lay next to the rocking chair, but Emma didn't bother to pick it up. The news from the frontlines continued to grow more horrific every day. As the Allies pushed German forces back through the Argonne Forest, the U.S. Army was now leading the fight and suffering in ways Emma couldn't begin to fathom. Trench warfare and disease were taking their toll, and already Morrison County had lost three dozen young soldiers—some Emma had known for years.

The little girl had fallen asleep. Emma placed her back in her bed and then picked up the next crying baby.

All night long she did this—never wearing her mask, and soothing each baby until exhaustion overtook them.

As the sun rose on a new day, Emma stood in the quiet room, watching the eastern horizon from the window. Her body had healed from the day of the airshow, but her heart was still broken. She knew Cade had left because he thought it was best for all of them, but oh how she wished she could take him in her arms and tell him he had been wrong.

Thomas Overton still worked for her father, but he no longer pursued Emma—and was no longer in line to inherit the Merrick fortune. The last she had heard, he was courting someone else and she was happy for them.

Father had told Emma she would one day inherit everything—and though she was thankful he had finally acknowledged her, and accepted her for who she was, she could not grasp the idea of being in charge of such a vast fortune.

Footsteps sounded in the hallway just outside the door and Emma quickly tied her mask around her face.

"Nurse Merrick?"

Emma turned from the window, finishing the knot just as Sister Agatha stepped into the room. The nun looked about the room, her eyes huge above her mask. "Are they all asleep?"

Emma nodded, recalling all the feverish bodies as she had rocked them to sleep, praying for each baby.

Sister Agatha crossed the room, her gentle eyes filled with concern. "You've been called home, Emma. It's your mother."

"My mother?" Emma had just seen her yesterday, before she had left for her overnight shift.

"She began exhibiting symptoms just before bed, and her temperature has now escalated to a point where they are very concerned—I'm sorry."

"I need to go to her."

Sister Agatha nodded. "I have someone coming in to relieve you, and I'll stay until she can get here. Hurry home."

Emma didn't wait another moment. She rushed through the hall, down the stairs, and grabbed her coat before she raced out the front door to her waiting Ford. The morning was cool and crisp, but she hardly took notice.

She and her mother had never been close, but the idea of losing her made Emma's chest tighten with fear.

Martha met Emma at the kitchen door, her apron twisted in her hands. "Oh, thank the Lord you're here. She's been asking for you."

Emma didn't bother to stop and ask Martha what she knew. She raced up the servant's stairs to the back of the house and then passed through to the main hall and went straight to her mother's room. She took off her coat and draped it over a floral brocade chair near Mother's fireplace.

One of the maids was with Mother, wiping her brow with a damp cloth. When she saw Emma, she backed away and curtsied. "She's been asking for you, Miss Emma."

"Thank you," Emma said, taking the cloth. "I'll see to her now."

Mother lay on her pillows wearing an intricate nightgown, her auburn curls splayed out around her head in snarls. Her cheeks were bright red and sweat glistened on her brow, but it was her glazed eyes that Emma noticed. She looked about the room in a sort of delirium, not resting on one object, but roaming as if she were looking for something.

When she saw Emma, her eyes focused and she let out a soft cry. "You came—I didn't know if you would."

"Of course I'd come." Emma dipped the cloth in the lukewarm water and turned to the maid who was opening the drapes. "Please, keep those closed and change this water. I'd like it to be cooler. I'd also like some broth sent up and some drinking water. I have cinnamon oil in my emergency kit. Put ten drops into the drinking water. We must keep as much liquid in her as possible."

"Yes, Miss Emma." The maid left the room, and it was just Emma and her mother.

Emma sat on the bed and put the cloth to her mother's brow.

"I'm so afraid, Emma."

"Don't be afraid—just rest and allow your body to fight this disease." The disease had been deadliest for people between the ages of twenty and forty, killing the healthiest among them. Mother was healthy and strong, which would have served her well if this had been the average case of influenza—but there was no way to know if she would survive and the thought paralyzed Emma for a moment.

Mother grabbed Emma's wrist and held with surprising strength. "I need to talk to you. I asked for you all night, but they said I must wait. I was scared I wouldn't survive long enough to tell you."

"Shh." Emma extracted her arm. She had heard numerous patients talking this way. It was the fever that made them frantic. "Rest, Mother."

Her eyes became desperate. "I want to tell you something."

Emma smiled, trying to ease her mother's distress. "Tell me."

"It's about your father."

Emma wasn't sure if it was the fever talking or if her mother was in her right mind, but she nodded. "What about my father?"

"I've been a wretched woman, Emma. I've done things I'm ashamed of—things too terrible to mention."

Emma recalled the night she had discovered her mother with another man. There was little she needed to confess to Emma. She had known for years that her mother wasn't faithful to her marriage.

"You don't need to say anything."

"But I do." Her mother began to weep. "I never consummated my marriage."

Emma's hand froze on her mother's forehead, and she lowered the wet cloth. "What?"

"I've never loved Matthew. I only married him to get away from my mother and to have money and status. He wanted an heir, but I refused him."

"What are you saying?"

"I'm saying you are not Matthew Merrick's daughter."

Emma pulled back as if she'd been slapped. She stood from the bed and stared at the pitiful woman under the covers. "What do you mean?"

Mother swallowed and looked at Emma with misery in her eyes. "I have dallied with countless men, but only loved one."

"No." Emma put up her hand. "I don't want to know."

"But you must."

Emma felt lightheaded. What was her mother saying? If Matthew Merrick was not her father, then who was? "Do you even know who my father is?"

Mother nodded, her face contorted and tears racing down her cheeks. "He was the first man I—after I married your father." She stopped and shook her head. "After I became pregnant, he ended our relationship—he became religious and told me what we had done was wrong."

Emma put her hands over her ears, wishing she did not have to listen.

"I know he loved me—but we could no longer continue our relationship."

"But that didn't stop you from dallying with other men."

Mother closed her eyes. "I was heartbroken after you were born. I began to seek love with other men to spite him—but nothing I did made him change his mind."

Emma lowered herself to a chair near Mother's bed, feeling sick to her stomach. She wanted to know who he was—but she didn't think she could bear to know.

"Emma—he loves you, has always loved you."

She looked up at her mother. "What?"

Mother's face was filled with so much anguish, Emma felt sorry for her.

"I wanted him to leave, but he refused to go—and I eventually accepted that he wanted to stay and be near you. It has difficult to see him every day—but he has brought you so much joy, I could never bear to tear you apart."

Emma rose on shaking legs, tears stinging the back of her eyes. "Sam?"

Mother nodded. "I'm sorry, Emma."

The maid returned to the room as Emma turned, blindly walking out of the room.

"Miss Emma?" the maid asked.

"Please see to her needs—I must—" She couldn't finish.

She exited her mother's bedroom and leaned against the wall, her lungs burning from lack of breath.

Sam? Her father?

So many things came into focus. Sam had always been there for her—always. He had been her father in every sense of the word—and the whole time, he knew. He knew he *was* her father, yet he had watched her pine after Matthew Merrick's love and acceptance.

She buried her face in her hands and wept. She needed to see him, to demand he explain himself. He had been her moral compass as a child and then as a young adult. She trusted him implicitly—believed him to be above reproach. Yet—he had fathered a child with a married woman.

Emma's entire world had been turned on its side in a matter of moments. Everything she believed to be true about herself was now a lie.

She walked down the front stairs, not wanting to face Martha—or anyone else in the kitchen—and left the house.

A cloud had gathered, marring the brilliant October sky, threatening a storm. Emma raced across the cobblestone drive, anger and disillusionment choking her spirit. She pushed open the door to the stables, but Sam was not downstairs.

She exited the stables and took the stairs to his apartment, climbing them as fast as her weary legs would take her. Exhaustion was her companion, making her sluggish—yet her emotions pushed her past her limited strength.

Tears clouded her vision and she wiped them away in frustration. She hated that she was crying—hated that it hurt so much to learn the man she had trusted had lied to her.

She didn't knock on his door, but pushed it open and stepped into his apartment.

He sat in his favorite chair, near the back window, a mug of steaming tea in one hand and a book in the other. His books and plants were scattered about as usual—but none of these things brought her comfort—not like they usually did.

He looked up in surprise at her sudden appearance. "Emmie, me darlin.'"

"How could you lie to me?" Pain surged out of her with each word. "How could you do something so horrible?"

He set his book and mug aside and rose. His brows creased as he walked across the room. "What are you talking about?"

"Me." She sobbed. "I'm talking about me."

"Emmie—" The confusion on his face suddenly cleared. "She told you."

Emma nodded and swallowed the choking pain in her throat. "She told me everything."

Sam's shoulders drooped. "I'm sorry, lass. I'm so very, very sorry."

"Why?" She could hardly look at him. "Why would you do such a thing?"

"There's no good explanation," he said. "We were young and foolish. I saw your father as an old man, and she led me to believe he mistreated her." He tossed his hand in frustration. "I have no cause to justify my actions. It doesn't matter what she led me to believe—but I thought I could save her from a loveless marriage—and in the end, I realized I had been wrong."

"How could you teach me about morality—about right and wrong—when you had made such an unforgiveable mistake?"

"That's the thing, Emmie. When I met Jesus, I realized it wasn't unforgivable. I was filled with guilt, and I carried the shame of it—until I learned I could be forgiven—and then I was. I taught you right from wrong, because I had lived a wrong life, and I knew what I wanted you to avoid." He reached out to touch her arm, but she pulled away, and he dropped his hand. "I'm not perfect—but I've been saved by grace—and it was with that grace that I taught you."

Emma closed her eyes. "My whole life I felt I was a mistake—but until today, I didn't realize how much of a mistake I am."

"No." Sam took a step closer and put his hands on her shoulders. "You, Emma Merrick, are not a mistake. What we did was a mistake, but you are perfection. God knew you before He formed you. He took an ugly sin and made something truly beautiful as only He can."

Tears gathered in Emma's eyes once again, but this time she did not wipe them away.

"Oh, lass." He drew her into his arms and held her tenderly. This time she didn't pull away. She needed his love—had always needed it. "I remember the first time I laid me eyes on you—and I knew, in that moment, that no matter what else I accomplished in life, it would never compare to you. I begged God to let me stay close to you—and He answered me prayer. Though it was hard to watch you grow up in a house without love, I tried to be enough love for you." He pulled back and looked her in the eyes. "God redeemed me soul, Emma—but He also redeemed me sin, by blessing me with you."

She buried her face in his chest and allowed the tears to continue to fall. His love was unconditional—had always been unconditional.

Didn't she owe him the same love in return? "What about my father—Matthew. Does he know?"

"Aye." Sam took a long breath. "It took me many years to work up the courage to tell him—it was a battle I fought with God—the telling of it. My greatest fear was that the major would make me leave you. But he didn't. I think he was numb to your mother's ways by then." He pulled back and looked Emma in the eyes. "He said I could stay—but only if I kept a close eye on you." Tears glistened in his eyes. "Matthew Merrick forgave me—could you find it in your heart to forgive me, too?"

"Oh, Sam." She returned to his embrace. "I forgave you, even before you asked."

"That's me girl." His voice sounded thick with emotion. "I love you, Emmie."

"I love you, too."

"Somehow we'll get through this."

She didn't know how she would come to terms with the truth she had just learned—but what she did know was that Sam had been a father to her, even when it had been difficult for him.

She stayed in his embrace, not wanting to think about how complicated things had become. Was this only the beginning of more life-changing events?

Chapter Thirty-Two

DECEMBER 1918

MATTHEW

Matthew walked across the yard of the old Bailey farm. The white house and red barn were silent, and the dry grass rose above his knees. The winter winds had yet to blow, leaving the earth brown and desolate.

Sam waited in the car, near the empty house, as Matthew made his pilgrimage to the little graveyard just beyond the tree line to the south. His land inspector had told him where he could find the gravestones under a big oak tree, near a small lake.

Matthew was still weak from the heart attack, and he tired easily, but he found the strength to keep walking when he would have rather sat and caught his breath.

He pushed through the tree branches and came to the little lake. The land was covered in brown and gray, and the sky was a pale blue. Geese honked overhead, and little woodland creatures scurried under the fallen leaves at his approach.

Two gravestones stuck out of the dead earth, side by side, with a peeling picket fence surrounding them.

Matthew opened the gate, its rusty hinges squeaking in protest.

His breath caught to see Elizabeth's grave. Her name was displayed at the top in elegant letters. *Elizabeth Bailey.* Under her name the years 1846-1864 were etched in the same font, and beneath that was the inscription: *Here lies a wife and mother, loved in life and now in death.*

Matthew's legs became weak, and he gripped the picket fence as he dropped to his knees, the weight of his grief a heavy burden.

"Elizabeth," he whispered. She had laid here in the ground for fifty-four years, and not one day had passed that he had not thought of her. "I've made a mess of my life—a horrible mess."

The decisions he had made continued to haunt his descendants—though they didn't realize it. He had studied his Bible, from front to back, and he had read in the passage about the Ten Commandments that the sins of the father would be visited to the third and fourth generation. It was true—so very true. Not because God despised him—but because Matthew had made poor choices and there were consequences for those choices.

But there was hope—there was always hope. It also said God showed love to thousands of generations of those that loved God and kept His commandments.

After his talk with Emma, when she had come home from the hospital, Matthew had sought counsel from a pastor at a small church Sam had recommended, and Matthew had finally found the answers he longed to know.

"I met a man named Tuck once," Matthew said to Elizabeth's grave, knowing she couldn't hear him, but needing to share his news with someone. "I hope you've met him in Heaven. He once told me about the treasure I could lay up for myself in eternity. If you see him, please tell him I finally understand what he meant. I've given my heart to Christ now. Someday soon I'll leave my earthly wealth to rust and decay, and I'll arrive at the Heavenly feast, and dine with the King of Kings in the mansion He's prepared in advance for me. The mansion that will be eternal."

Matthew's gaze moved to Jacob's grave. *Jacob Bailey, 1838-1912. Here lies a husband and father, loved in life and now in death.*

"Jacob." Matthew's voice broke. "I never asked for your forgiveness—nor offered mine. We made each other miserable, and I'm sorry. I pray we will meet again in Glory, and that we will see each other as we truly are—sinners saved by grace." He did hope he would see Jacob again. He hoped his old nemesis had found the love of Christ.

"I hope you two don't mind." Matthew slowly rose, his joints stiff. "But I need to go see our son. I want to make peace with him before I join you. I think all three of us would agree he was the victim, and he deserves an explanation."

Matthew wasn't under the belief that he would set a lifetime of wrong to right, but he knew he needed to tell his son the truth before one of them joined Jacob and Elizabeth.

His gaze lingered on Elizabeth's grave. "Once, a long time ago, I told you my heart would forever remain with yours at the creek near Crow Wing—but I'm here to tell you my heart is now in Christ, where it should have always been."

He turned and slowly walked back toward the car. Sam was there to greet him, concern and care on his aging face.

"Did you do what you came to do?" Sam asked, helping him into the car.

Matthew nodded and sighed as he took his seat. "I did. But the job is half done. Take me to see Nathan Bailey."

Sam nodded and closed the door.

Matthew leaned his head against the seat back and took several deep breaths, hoping he would be welcome at his son's home.

The drive back to town took less than an hour. Matthew nodded off several times, only to be awakened with a start and a reminder of the task ahead of him.

They finally arrived at the cottage he had bought for Nathan and Victoria. It sat on a beautiful lake and had a wraparound porch off the front. He had told Thomas to spare no expense in finding them a home, but it needed to be something they could easily maintain. He was thankful his general manager had done as he'd requested.

Trees shaded the little house, and a small barn stood off to the east. Chickens scurried about the neat yard, and a horse nibbled on grass in the corral.

Victoria appeared at the door as the car pulled into the yard. She stood wiping her hands on her apron. She was still a beautiful woman, though time and heartache had aged her faster than it should have.

Sam opened the back door and Matthew stepped out of the car. He approached the house, and Victoria cracked open the door, but she did not smile at him.

"Hello, Mrs. Bailey," he said.

"Hello, Major Merrick."

He had never grown used to the title. It reminded him of Crow Wing and the course of events that had shaped his life.

"Is Nathan up for a visitor?" Matthew asked.

Victoria studied him for a moment, as if weighing the wisdom of letting him enter. Finally, she nodded. "He's in the front parlor." She opened the door wider, and he crossed over the threshold into a small foyer. Pretty floral wallpaper graced the entrance, and a mirror reflected Matthew's advanced appearance.

He followed her into a hall with an open staircase. She motioned for him to go left, into the front parlor.

Nathan sat in a rocking chair, a blanket over his lap, and a Bible in his hands. He looked up at Matthew, a gentle smile on his face.

Matthew was reminded how much he looked like Elizabeth.

"Hello, Major."

Matthew nodded and removed his hat. "May I have a word with you?"

"Of course." Nathan closed his Bible and indicated the rocking chair beside him. "Have a seat."

Victoria took Matthew's hat and overcoat and stepped out of the room.

Matthew sat and studied his son. At the age of fifty-four, his hair was beginning to gray and wrinkles had lined his face, but he was still a striking man. His illness had taken a toll, but Matthew was surprised to see how healthy he looked today.

"Have you been feeling better?" Matthew asked.

Nathan nodded. "Since we moved into this house, I've been regaining a bit more strength every day. The doctor has been by to visit, and he can't give an account for my increased health—but I know Who I owe thanks and praise to."

It warmed Matthew's heart to hear his son speak of God.

"And how are you?" Nathan asked. "I had heard you were ill."

"A heart attack, last winter." Matthew wasn't here to talk about their health—he needed to speak to Nathan plainly, as hard as it might be.

"What can I do for you?" Nathan asked. "I hope you've been able to use the farm as you'd hoped."

Matthew had planned to have his crews harvest his property around the farm this winter, and in the spring he would send his logs downriver, but guilt had started to rob him of his peace. "That's part of the reason I wanted to see you. I feel terrible about how I acquired the land."

"You shouldn't." Nathan smiled. "It was a blessing in disguise. If we hadn't moved, I don't think I'd feel as hearty as I do today."

Matthew hadn't expected Nathan to be glad, and he felt flummoxed for a moment.

"Is that the only reason you came?" Nathan asked.

"No." Matthew readjusted his position. "I also came—"

Victoria entered the room with a tray of coffee and cookies. "Would you care for a refreshment?" she asked.

"No thank you." Matthew needed to say what he had come to say before he lost the courage. "Mrs. Bailey, please take a seat. I have something I need to tell both of you—and it may come as a shock."

Mrs. Bailey looked at her husband and then sat on the sofa. "Is this about Emma?"

"No—it's not about Emma."

She looked relieved—but how long would that last? "It's about me—and Jacob—and Elizabeth." He looked at Nathan. "And about you."

Nathan watched him carefully. "Go ahead."

"I met your mother when I became an Indian Agent. Her father, Chief White Thunder, asked me to teach her proper etiquette to attend a dance at Fort Ripley. I despised the idea—and apparently she did, too, because she wasn't happy to see me when I arrived." He recalled the day like it had happened yesterday, remembering the weather and the village and the cabin. He swallowed—pushing through the grief to continue. "I fell in love with Elizabeth, but I was engaged to another woman and Elizabeth was promised to an Indian chief. I also met Jacob Bailey that summer. He was my clerk—and he fell in love with your mother, as well." Matthew looked down at his hands. "When your mother learned she was promised to another man she was upset, and she came to me. Two months later, she told me she was pregnant with my child."

Victoria inhaled a breath, and Matthew looked up, knowing he had shocked them. "I had also taken annuity money to buy the land you just sold to me. When Jacob learned about Elizabeth's pregnancy—and the land—he threatened to tell the authorities, unless I gave up your mother and the property." Matthew felt all the emotions rolling through him once again. "Your mother didn't give me a choice—she married Jacob and left me to my own future. Seven months later, after I had married my fiancée, you were born—and your mother died."

Nathan's clear brown eyes filled with an emotion Matthew couldn't identify. He took a deep breath and clasped his hands on his lap. "Jacob Bailey was not my biological father?"

Matthew shook his head and said the words he had longed to say for fifty-four years. "I fathered you."

"Why didn't you tell me before now?"

"There were many reasons—but I've finally come to see how wrong I was—about everything." He paused, humbled by his admission. "I finally found redemption in Christ, and I've felt compelled to set my life in order."

A glimmer of joy lit in his son's eyes. "You've become a believer?"

"Yes."

A smile filled Nathan's face. "Then there is good that has come of this."

Good? "But there has also been much suffering and pain."

"What the enemy of our soul intends for evil, the Lord will use for good," Nathan said. "I confess, this comes as a shock—" his face turned ashen and he looked at Victoria. "Cade and Emma."

Matthew put up his hand. "No—no. They're not blood relations." He hated to admit the rest of the truth, but he knew his son deserved it, so he told him the whole story.

He spent the rest of the afternoon visiting with Nathan and Victoria—thanking God for redemption and his son's forgiveness.

Cade

The Armistice had been signed, and Cade had been mustered out of the army. He sat in the back of the hired cab and watched the unfamiliar land pass before him as he made his way to his parents' new home on Green Prairie Lake.

He should have felt relief that the war was over—but it only meant the next chapter of his life would begin—though he had no idea what he would do with himself. Some of his friends from Camp Hancock were banding together to buy army surplus planes to start a flying show and they had asked Cade to come and be their ace flyer—but he had told them he would have to think about it.

When he left Little Falls to join the war, he had run away for the last time. He had met far too many men who left Camp Hancock to fight overseas who would never return home. Cade had been one of the lucky ones to have a choice, and he was choosing to return and face his past.

First, he would apologize to his parents for not saving the farm and then he would somehow find the courage to apologize to Emma and wish her well on her marriage to Thomas Overton. He had taken the coward's way out one too many times, but today was a day of new beginnings.

"How much longer to the Bailey home?" Cade asked the cabby.

"About ten minutes."

Cade leaned back and the envelope in his breast pocket crinkled. Dad had mailed Grandfather's letter to Cade while he was in Georgia, but Cade had not been able to open the envelope. He took it out of his pocket now, knowing his father would be disappointed if he didn't read it before coming home.

He slowly opened the sealed flap and then lifted the yellowed paper from its resting place. Whether he liked it or not, this letter was part of the past he needed to face.

With a deep breath, he unfolded the letter and let his eyes fall on his grandfather's slanted script.

"Dear Cade,

I write this letter today knowing I have little time on this earth. I don't intend to use this space to tell you I was wrong—"

Cade stopped reading, feeling his pulse increase. He almost balled the paper in his hands—but he forced himself to read the rest of the letter.

"—but to ask for your forgiveness. I was heartless and cruel to you—not because you deserved it, but because I was bitter. I've made my share of mistakes, and I've asked God to forgive me. I hope now you and your family can forgive me, too."

Cade read his grandfather's confession, his heart finding hope in his grandfather's redemption, but he was numb from everything he'd endured.

He had mourned the loss of Emma for seven months, thinking of her when he laid his head down to sleep and when he put his feet on the ground in the morning. He had longed to know what had become of her—but he never asked his parents, and they never offered him information.

Now, as he faced the end of the war and the beginning of the rest of his life, he had to face the loss in a whole new way. He could no longer depend on the war to keep him preoccupied.

"We're here," the cabby said.

Cade fumbled with his wallet to pay the cab driver. He took his bag and stepped out of the cab.

Matthew Merrick's vehicle sat in the yard. Cade stopped, feeling as if the world was spinning in a new direction, and he couldn't catch his bearings.

He walked up the porch steps and through the front door into the strange house. He could hear a low mummer of conversation to the left, so he turned into the room and found his parents sitting with Matthew Merrick and Sam Turner.

"Cade!" Mama jumped up from the sofa and ran across the room. She threw her arms around him, and he dropped his bag to hug her, the whole time keeping his eyes on Merrick.

Mama pulled away, wiping tears from her eyes, but her smile fell. "What's wrong?"

Matthew rose from his chair and stared him in the eyes.

"Sit down, son." Dad motioned to the sofa. "Major Merrick has something to tell you."

Cade finally noticed his father—looking healthier than when he had left. He went him, his emotions choking his throat as he grasped his father's hand.

Father smiled and nodded, and then indicated the sofa. Cade took a seat, wondering what had brought all these people together in one room.

Matthew also sat. His countenance was heavy, but there was something in his gaze that spoke of relief. Peace.

"This story may come as a surprise," Matthew began. "It starts over fifty years ago—but I'm not sure how it ends."

As he recounted his days at the Crow Wing Agency, meeting Elizabeth and Jacob, Cade listened intently. But when he learned that Matthew was his grandfather, he stood quickly, sick to his stomach. "Emma is my...aunt?"

"No," Matthew said, shaking his head.

"No?" Cade looked up and glanced at the faces of all those present.

Matthew sighed. "Emma is not my daughter."

Cade's mouth cracked open. "Then she's—"

"She's not related to you, Cade." Mama laid her hand on Cade's leg. "She has a different father."

Cade slowly sat down again, relief washing over him—but what did it matter now? Emma was married to another man.

"I'm sorry, Cade," Matthew said. "I know this is all a lot to deal with."

"Especially since you just got home," Mama added.

Cade stood and grabbed his bag. "I read the letter from Grandfather Bailey." He found it and handed it to his father.

Everyone sat in silence as Dad read the letter out loud. When he came to the end, tears filled his voice and he had to stop to clear his throat. "He finally found redemption," Dad said.

"Good came from his story, too," Mama added.

Cade looked between his parents. At one point, their faith had turned him away—but now he saw it for what it was—love, pure and simple.

Their steadfast faith had led Jacob Bailey to redemption. If it had been left to Cade, he would have given up on him at the very beginning.

If God could bring good from Matthew and Jacob's lives, then surely God could bring good from his life, too.

"I think I need a bit of fresh air," Cade said. "Will you all excuse me?"

"Take your time, son." Dad reached up and grasped Cade's hand. "We'll be here when you come back."

Cade walked out of the house and turned the corner.

The lake beckoned him.

He needed to find a place to make peace with God, the One who would never give up on him, either.

Chapter Thirty-Three

Emma

Emma turned her Ford into the Bailey's drive. She had her emergency kit on the seat next to her, but she didn't think Mr. Bailey would need medical attention today. His miraculous recovery had been good for her soul. In a world of dead and dying, she enjoyed the afternoons she spent with the Bailey's.

She eased up on the gas pedal when she saw her father's car parked in the Bailey's yard. Why would he be here?

Stepping out of the car, a cool wind blew from the northwest, and she wrapped her scarf tighter about her neck before she started up the porch steps.

Out of the corner of her eye, she saw a man standing near the lake. Her feet paused on the steps, and she looked closer.

Her heart began to beat wildly as his form took shape before her eyes.

Cade.

She backed down the steps and rounded the corner of the house. She longed to run to him and throw her arms around him. But it had been seven months since he had left. Much could change in seven months.

Even though she didn't know how he would receive her, she thanked God for bringing him home safely.

As she drew closer, a deep longing swept through her and tears gathered in her eyes. She had missed him with all her heart. Her love had not dimmed with time, but only grew brighter until it almost overwhelmed her with its brilliance.

He looked up—and in that moment, she saw the love and longing in his own gaze. He took a step toward her, but then paused, as if he was unsure he would be welcomed.

It was the only invitation Emma needed. She began to run, opening her arms wide.

He grabbed her in his embrace and held her with an intensity that took her breath away.

"Cade," she cried, kissing his cheeks and forehead and nose and finally his mouth.

He set her on her feet and pulled away, his expression stunned. "Emma!"

She almost toppled over without his support, a crushing pain stabbing her in the chest. Didn't he want her?

"What about Thomas?"

"Thomas?" She stared at him, confused for a moment—and then realization dawned and she smiled, feeling almost shy. "There is no Thomas."

Shock turned to joy and then he smiled, too, his voice gentle. "No Thomas?"

She shook her head. "Only you."

He grabbed her in his arms and spun her off her feet. She laughed and wrapped her arms around him. They held one another for a long time, neither caring about the cold air that nipped at their noses and chilled their ears.

"Emma—I'm so sorry," Cade said into her hair. "I should have never left the way I did."

She hugged him tighter. "It doesn't matter how you left. What matters is that you came home."

He held her for a long time. "I have so much to tell you. So much about my father and grandfather—and—" he stopped. "But all of that can wait."

She clung to him, not ready to let him go. "I have much to tell you, too—about my father." She would tell him about Sam.

"I'm so thankful you didn't marry Overton."

She pulled back and smiled. "How could I when I loved you?"

"I have nothing to offer," he said.

"Your love is all I'll ever need."

He rested his hands on either side of her face and captured her lips in a kiss he had been dreaming of for the past seven months. It did not disappoint and was sweeter than he'd ever imagined.

Epilogue

JUNE 1920

MATTHEW

Matthew Merrick could hardly believe his good fortune—or better yet, his blessings.

He sat under the lawn tent behind his home, watching his son-in-law—his grandson—Cade as he soared above Elk Manor. A level field in the back of the property had proven to be a good airfield, and Cade had built an airplane hangar to house his growing fleet of army surplus biplanes. The flying school he and Emma had started was drawing students from all over the country, putting Cade, and his school, in high demand.

"Would you like more lemonade?" Victoria asked Matthew. She stood in a white lawn dress, her cheeks flushed from the heat and excitement.

Matthew shook his head and smiled at his son's wife. "Sit down and enjoy the show—or, at the very least, enjoy that grandson of yours."

Emma glanced up at Matthew from where she sat next to him, a smile on her face as she bounced her little boy, Matthew Samuel Bailey. The baby was now seven months old and all rolls and giggles. He looked at Matthew and reached out his chubby hands.

Matthew took Mattie on his lap and smiled down into his green eyes. The baby reached for Matthew's pocket watch—knowing right where to find it—and promptly put it into his mouth.

"He's going to be a handsome boy," Matthew said to anyone who would care to listen. "I can already see the Merrick in him."

He had said it the day little Mattie was born, and he'd continue to say it every day until the Good Lord saw fit to call him home.

Henry Bailey stood at the edge of the tent, his hand lifted to shade his eyes as he watched Cade in the air. "I think he's trying a new trick."

"He is." Emma rose to stand near her brother-in-law. "He's planning to introduce it at the State Fair in September."

"I don't know about the rest of you," Nathan said, standing from his chair and stretching his long, lean body. "But I'm tired of sitting around. I feel like a game of croquet."

Gracie jumped up from the green grass near the lemonade and raced to the yard where the croquet course was set.

"How about it, Matthew?" Nathan asked.

"I think I'll sit here and enjoy my great-grandson a bit longer."

Nathan smiled and left the tent with Victoria on his arm.

"Do you mind holding Mattie for a while?" Emma asked. "I think I'll go out to the airfield and walk back with Cade."

"Go ahead," Matthew said. "I'm content to sit here all day."

Emma leaned down to place a kiss on the top of Matthew's head and one on her son's, and then left the tent to join her husband.

Henry came to Matthew's side and sat in the wicker chair Emma had vacated. "I have a few ideas I'd like to discuss with you about improvements on the mills at Elk City."

"Oh?" Matthew bounced Mattie on his knee. "Must we talk business on a Sunday?"

Henry leaned back and put his hands behind his head. "I suppose it can wait."

"Good." Matthew grinned at the baby on his lap. "There are more important things than business."

"Henry, come join us," Gracie called, jumping up and down with a croquet mallet in hand.

Henry stood and strode out of the tent. "I don't know why you ask me to play, when you know I'm going to win."

Gracie giggled and Henry put his hand on her head to ruffle her hair.

In the distance, Cade landed his airplane.

"Your daddy will be joining us in a few minutes, Mattie, and then we'll enjoy a nice Sunday luncheon here on the lawn—but I don't think your Grandma Edith will come outside. She doesn't like these family gatherings. She'd prefer to miss all the fun."

Mattie reached up and grabbed Matthew's goatee, tugging with gusto, a wet grin on his little face.

Matthew pulled the baby up to his chest and laughed. "I can't wait to watch you grow. I already have a pony for you—did you know that? I always wanted a pony when I was a little boy, but my mother worked hard to put food on the table for me and Margaret. Have I told you about my twin sister, Margaret? She would have loved you—but she's in Heaven now. Someday we'll see her again."

Sam appeared at the carriage house door, leaning against the frame, watching the family.

Matthew stood and walked across the drive. "Why don't you join us, Sam?"

Sam shook his head, his eyes on Mattie. "I think I'll watch from here."

Matthew looked down at his great-grandson and winked. He handed him over to Sam and smiled. "Enjoy him while he's young—he'll grow up much too fast."

Sam took the boy in his arms, love radiating from his face, and tossed him into the air. Mattie giggled, his chubby little arms flapping like a baby bird. "I do believe we have us another flyer on our hands."

Matthew watched Sam and Mattie for a moment, thanking God for redeeming their many mistakes.

Long ago Matthew had chosen the wrong path. But God, in His love and grace, had found him and set him on the right path—redemption's path—the one leading to his eternal home.

The blessings that followed would fill Matthew's remaining days with more than he deserved.

Historical Note

The first two books in the Ladies of the Wilderness Series explore an earlier time of European involvement in North American history, when Europeans and Native Americans worked side-by-side in the fur trade. *The Aviator's Lady* looks at a time in history when the land in Minnesota was ceded over to the United States government, ushering in a new age of settlement and change, when the Native Americans were removed to reservations and the two people groups ended centuries of co-habitation. The Mississippi Headwaters Treaty of 1863 was a pivotal moment in United States history, signed in the midst of the American Civil War. It is a complex and multi-faceted event that changed the course of history for people on both sides of the agreement, with many implications, both good and bad. I only scratched the surface of the political and social ramifications in this book and did not have the space to properly represent either side. Any mistakes or misunderstandings on my part were unintentional.

While the village of Crow Wing was a real place, and the treaty was really signed, the story I told in *The Aviator's Lady* was fictional and only loosely inspired by real people and events. Chief White Thunder's character was influenced by Chief Hole-in-the-Day II (Bagone-gi-izhig). He was a fascinating man, and his historical shadow still stretches over the lakes and rivers of central Minnesota. Among other things, Hole-in-the-Day II had several wives (between five and eight), many children, and was a well-known and powerful chief of the Mississippi Band of Ojibwe. He was an accomplished orator and diplomat, and spent a great deal of time in Washington, DC, meeting with Abraham Lincoln on at least one occasion. He wanted to be considered the preeminent chief of all the Ojibwe in Minnesota, but not all the chiefs agreed on this, especially because Hole-in-the-Day II became a very wealthy man from all the land treaties. At the time of his death in 1868, he was considered the wealthiest man in Minnesota, worth over $2 million (roughly $45.5 million in 2025). He was eventually assassinated by his people near the Crow Wing Indian Agency, but because it was an Indian crime on Indian land, the United States Department of Justice had no authority to prosecute the offenders. Everyone knew the assassins' identities, but there were many who theorized that they had been hired to do the killing. Eventually, in 1911, it was revealed that it had been a contract killing, instigated by several Métis businessmen (mixed-raced people of European and indigenous ancestry), fur traders, and illegal whiskey peddlers who saw Hole-in-the-Day II as an obstacle to their political and financial goals. *The Assassination of Hole in the Day*, by Anton Treuer, is a wonderful book about this complex individual.

The other man that loosely inspired Matthew's character was Major Ashley C. Morrill, an Indian Agent who arrived in Crow Wing in 1861, first as a clerk, and then as the agent not long after in 1862. He eventually moved to Minneapolis where he was married and worked in the lumber industry, while serving a term as a state senator. After his first wife passed away, he married the widow of an old friend from his time at Crow

Wing and brought his second wife back to central Minnesota where he purchased the Little Elk mills (south of Crown Wing) and built a lavish mansion near the small town. When he passed away, he had no children.

Fictional stories are so much fun to create, because they are an amalgamation of inspiration from real people, places, and events. The second half of *The Aviator's Lady* was inspired by a story I was told by an older gentleman who rented his century farm to my husband and me soon after we were married. His name was Dale Anderson, and he had grown up on the farm that his father had been born and raised on in central Minnesota. When he was showing us the house, he told me that the wealthy Weyerhaeuser family had a cabin on the lake nearby (this I already knew, because I was raised in the carriage house on the Weyerhaeuser property as a child and knew quite a bit about the family history). Whenever the Weyerhaeuser's would pass by the Anderson farm, they would stop to get fresh milk and eggs for their time at the cabin. Dale's father was apparently a pretty handsome young man, and in the mid-1920s, he caught the eye of the Weyerhaeuser's daughter, Sarah Maud. On one of these stops at the farm, Sarah Maud asked Dale's father if he wanted to go to a local dance with her. The story goes that his father was so awestruck by her, that he was too shy to say yes and missed his opportunity. Dale's mother loved to tease him that he could have been a wealthy man if he'd just had the courage to say yes.

It was the Anderson family lore that first gave me the idea to create Emma and Cade's story over 23 years ago. I didn't pull it together until many years later, and combined it with the history of Crow Wing, the Mississippi Headwaters Treaty of 1863, Chief Hole-in-the-Day, and Major Ashley C. Morrill. *The Aviator's Lady* is the story that was born. I'm so happy to finally publish this story and see it take on new life.

If you've enjoyed *The Aviator's Lady*, be sure to look for *The Fur Trader's Lady* and *The Lady of Red River Valley*, the first two books in the Ladies of the Wilderness Series.

Also by Gabrielle Meyer

If you've enjoyed *The Aviator's Lady*, be sure to look for these other books by Gabrielle Meyer

The Ladies of the Wilderness Series

Timeless Series

American Brides Series

GabrielleMeyer.com/books

About the author

Gabrielle Meyer is a Christy-Award winning, bestselling author of over 45 books, including her popular Timeless Series. For over a decade, she worked for the Minnesota Historical Society, where she became passionate about sharing real history through the art of storytelling. She continues to write fictional stories inspired by real people, places, and events. Gabrielle currently lives in central Minnesota on the banks of the upper Mississippi River with her husband and four children. You can learn more about Gabrielle and her books at www.gabriellemeyer.com.

Connect with Gabrielle on Facebook, Instagram, and Goodreads!

www.ingramcontent.com/pod-product-compliance
Ingram Content Group UK Ltd.
Pitfield, Milton Keynes, MK11 3LW, UK
UKHW042202290825
7649UKWH00002B/204

9 798999 232311